DYNEWAVE

BOOK 3

THE RORSCHACH EXPLORER MISSIONS

A NOVEL BY

K. PATRICK DONOGHUE

Published by Leaping Leopard Enterprises, LLC

DYNEWAVE
eISBN: 978-1-7378972-0-0
Paperback ISBN: 978-1-7378972-1-7
Hardcover ISBN: 978-1-7378972-2-4

Published by Leaping Leopard Enterprises, LLC
www.leapingleopard.com

First edition: October 2021
Cover design by K. Patrick Donoghue and Keith Draws
Cover illustration created by and licensed from Keith Draws
09282021

DEDICATION

To the memory of Lewis & Mary Patton,
who warmly welcomed me into the Patton family as their son-in-law

CONTENTS

ACKNOWLEDGMENTS

The creation of *Dynewave* included the contributions of several special individuals I would like to acknowledge.

First off, I would like to thank developmental editor Dustin Porta for his help in pinpointing opportunities to improve *Dynewave*'s complex story line.

I would also like to thank my copyeditor, Jade Hemming, whose keen editorial instincts helped enhance *Dynewave*'s readability and story flow.

Similar thanks are due to the trio of readers who reviewed the pre-release draft of *Dynewave*, including Lisa Weinberg, Paulette Jones and Terry Grindstaff. Their suggestions and proofreading edits helped me put the finishing touches on the story.

Lastly, I'd like to thank artist Keith Draws for his eye-catching design of the *Dynewave* cover, and for his additional artistry in refreshing the covers of all of the books in the Rorschach Explorer Missions series.

A NOTE TO READERS

Greetings, friends, fans and new readers! Thank you in advance for choosing to read *Dynewave*, book 3 in the Rorschach Explorer Missions series. As you prepare to begin reading, I would like to draw your attention to an important aspect of the story.

Dynewave is a continuation of the core storyline told in the preceding books in the series, but the main events in *Dynewave* occur in two distinctly different timeframes. The bulk of the story occurs four years after the events detailed in book 2 of the series, *Magwave*. However, a portion of *Dynewave* is a flashback to events that occurred earlier in the post-*Magwave* period. As such, *Dynewave* is organized in three different sections.

Chapters 1-5 take place in the present-day of the story and serve three functions. These chapters reacquaint readers with some of the main characters from *Magwave* and provide an overview of important events that have transpired since the end of *Magwave*. These chapters also set the stage for the action that follows in the rest of the book.

Dynewave then transitions to the flashback chapters (Chapters 6-13) where readers are provided insight into the activities of other main characters whose actions influence the present-day portion of the story.

With the flashback section completed, *Dynewave* then returns to the present-day in Chapter 14 and continues in the present-day for the duration of the book.

Why did I structure the story this way? Because the events that occur in the flashback chapters are largely unknown to the characters in the present-day — yet those events provide readers important context for the overall story.

Separately, given it has been two years since I published *Magwave*, I wanted to make sure readers who haven't read the series in a while could reacquaint themselves with the main characters and storyline before I dove into the core action of *Dynewave*. In so doing, I hoped to also make *Dynewave* accessible for those who have not read the previous books in the series.

Also, per the recommendation of a series' fan, I have added a "Glossary of Characters" at the end of the book that you may find useful if you haven't read the previous books in the series lately or at all.

Whether you use the glossary or not, I hope the above background information is helpful and I hope you enjoy the sci-fi adventure told in the pages of *Dynewave*.

And, as always, thank you for your interest in my stories!

CHAPTER 1

In the faint pre-dawn glow reflecting off Lake Tahoe, Dr. Anlon Cully could see the outline of the dock ahead and the silhouette of Pebbles McCarver. Seated on the left side of the pier, head bowed and feet dangling, she looked as if she might tip forward at any moment and slip into the frigid water.

Clasping the blanket draped around him, Anlon walked toward her, wondering how long she had already been up. She had not been in bed when their alarm clock began beeping at 3:30 a.m., and when he trundled through the kitchen to find her, he noted her half-empty coffee cup was lukewarm to the touch.

As he neared the end of the stand of pine trees between the house and dock, Pebbles looked in his direction, evidently alerted to his approach by the swish of his slippers on the bed of pine needles beneath the trees.

"Good morning," she said. Though she spoke softly, her voice carried far in the still air.

"Morning. Am I too late?" he asked in reply, looking toward the eastern sky.

"Not if you move your butt."

Spurred by her prodding, Anlon hoisted the blanket higher around his shoulders and picked up his pace, his slippers slapping against the wood planks of the dock. Once again, he looked up, training his eyes at the horizon above the mountain slope to his left. High in the sky to the northeast, he saw Pebbles' favorite constellation, Cassiopeia. Tracking his head to the right, Anlon spied the glitter of the waning Saturn.

"Watch where you're going, A.C.!"

The sharpness of Pebbles' tone caused Anlon to look down just in time to avoid walking off the side of the dock. Adjusting his direction and gait, he closed the final distance to Pebbles and sat next to her. She had a blanket layered over her torso too, but she immediately snaked her shoulders beneath his. Shivering from the shock of the chill from her blanket against his chest, he said, "Brr…"

"Shh. Pay attention. It's almost time."

Anlon huddled against her and looked up in the direction of her gaze. Shortly after, Jupiter, the object of Pebbles' vigil, sparkled into view. Pebbles clapped her hands and said, "Yay! There you are. Good morning, Jupiter!"

Glancing briefly at his smartwatch, Anlon marked Jupiter's rise over the tree tops at 4:01, though that wasn't the official time of Jupiter's appearance in the eastern sky over the lake. According to his star tracking app, the official rise had occurred at 3:36. But Anlon's Incline Village home was nestled so close to the lake's eastern mountains that they could not have seen the official rise. Anlon considered that a blessing, as it meant he had been able to sleep a little later.

Pebbles nudged him. "Aren't you going to say good morning to Jupiter?"

Participating in her ritual often seemed silly to Anlon, but he knew it made her happy. Looking skyward, he said, "Good morning, you big lug. Glad to see you're safe and sound."

"Amen," she said. "And stay that way."

Over the past three and a half years, they had similarly greeted Jupiter's rise hundreds of times. But until the last month, it had been a sporadic ritual, occurring most often when Jupiter rose between sunset and bedtime. Then, news had come within the last few weeks of new gamma-ray bursts near Jupiter. Since then, Pebbles' vigil had turned devout. So long as the planet's rise was visible, Pebbles greeted the occasion.

The ritual had begun shortly after the crew of the *Rorschach Explorer* had returned to Earth aboard an alien spacecraft, heralding news both exhilarating and ominous. By a twist of fate, Anlon, Pebbles and their friend Jennifer Stevens had been the first to greet the bedraggled *Rorschach* astronauts after they disembarked on tiny Late Island in the South Pacific.

There, they had learned the crew's mixed news in person from *Rorschach*'s commander, Colonel Paul "Skywalker" Morgan, the same information Morgan shared with the rest of the world later in a televised news conference.

On their way to investigate the wreckage of the *U.S.S. Cetus Prime*, marooned in a crater on Callisto, a moon of Jupiter, and an ancient, abandoned alien spaceport located in the same hollow, the *Rorschach Explorer* had been intercepted by a massive spaceship piloted by a race of quasi-humanoid aliens who called themselves the *Suhkai*.

Shocking and unexpected on its own, *Rorschach*'s five crewmembers had soon received another surprise. The alien ship was carrying four humans. One of them was Captain Nick Reed, the flight engineer of *Cetus Prime*, who had been presumed dead twenty-two years prior. The others were the children of Reed and his also-presumed dead *Cetus Prime* shipmates, Mission Specialist Christine Baker and Lieutenant Colonel Avery Lockett.

In his news conference, Morgan told the world Reed and the children had journeyed to Earth from their new home on a planet they called Tula, located eleven-light-years away. The ship Reed and the children had arrived in, Morgan said, was an ark built by the Suhkai to carry 210 willing humans back to Tula to help seed the nascent Lockett-Baker-Reed settlement there.

Had Morgan's press conference ended there, Anlon supposed Pebbles would never have begun her Jupiter vigil. But that had not been all the man known to most by his Skywalker nickname had said. There was a specific reason the Suhkai had helped the *Cetus Prime* trio find a new planet to call home, Morgan had stated, the same reason they had built the ark and traveled at nearly light speed back to Earth.

Jupiter, the Suhkai claimed, was at risk of destruction. There was a dormant but unstable type of star known as a magnetar located two light-years away from Earth's solar system. If the magnetar awakened, the Suhkai believed it would begin shooting out bursts of lethal gamma rays that would cut through a slice of Jupiter's orbit. If the rays were intense enough, Jupiter would explode, destroying the rest of the solar system, including Earth.

Morgan had tempered this sobering disclosure by saying the Suhkai had told him the magnetar might not awaken for thousands of years into the future and that the Suhkai believed they could stabilize it before it awoke. But, out of an abundance of caution, the aliens had built the ark to help ensure humanity's survival in the event the star erupted before the Suhkai could quell its instability.

Skywalker finished the televised conference by saying he had garnered commitments from the Suhkai to help build more arks and said that he, himself, would put together an international coalition of astronauts to accompany a squad of the aliens to attempt to stabilize the star and keep it dormant.

As Anlon recalled it, the reaction to Morgan's "good news, bad news" press conference had varied considerably. Some focused on the wonderous news of contact with an intelligent humanoid species and were delighted to learn another human-habitable planet existed. Others were frightened by the threat posed by the magnetar and bemoaned the implications for Earth. Most were caught somewhere in the middle, not really sure what to make of the contact with the Suhkai, nor how to gauge the degree of threat the magnetar posed.

Fast forward almost four years and those uncertainties had abated for most. A vocal contingent of scientists repeatedly assured the world the Suhkai were wrong. The dormant magnetar was too far away for its rays to destroy Jupiter. The scientists claimed its gamma bursts would be too dispersed when they reached Jupiter to disrupt the planet's atmosphere materially.

Spirits were further bolstered recently by reports from Morgan that he and his joint human-Suhkai fleet of six ships, three crewed by humans, three by Suhkai, were closing in on the magnetar, though Anlon didn't give Morgan's updates much credence. They had been transmitted over a year and a half prior. No one knew what had happened since.

Had the fleet arrived at the magnetar? Had they been successful in stabilizing it? Were they on their way home now? Given the two-light-year distance between Earth and the magnetar, these questions would remain a mystery for at least another six months.

From Anlon's point of view, the communications time delay was difficult for most people to keep in mind. A message sent from 1.5 light-years away took 1.5 years to travel through space, as radio signals moved at the speed of light. So every new update received by Morgan now had actually been broadcast 1.5 years ago…and the further the fleet moved away from Earth, the longer it would take to receive their radio signals.

In truth, the people of Earth were blind to the real-time status of the fleet and the real-time status of the magnetar. Still, Morgan's reports gave many people hope the risk posed by the magnetar would soon be extinguished…*or better said*, thought Anlon, *had been extinguished sometime in the last two years.*

Then there was a small group of people like Pebbles…and Anlon to a lesser degree. People who could not reconcile why the astronauts of *Cetus Prime* and the Suhkai would have gone to such lengths to warn Earthlings of their peril if the magnetar was not a grave risk. Why would they have searched for a new planet? Why would they have built an ark and returned to Earth? The Suhkai had hundreds of thousands of years' experience traveling throughout the galaxy. Who on Earth was in a position to question their claims?

But question the claims, they did. And, for reasons not entirely clear to Anlon, Pebbles and many others, the handful of Suhkai who did not accompany Morgan's fleet and stayed behind in the solar system as the aliens' ambassadors, offered no tangible rebuttal to Earth's scientific skeptics challenging their claims. Earthlings were better served, the Suhkai said, by preparing as if the risk was high and imminent. That advice, repeated over and over again, had now become a running joke on Earth. The skeptics declared the Suhkai were like Chicken Little.

Emerging from his thoughts, Anlon hugged Pebbles and prayed the skeptics were right. She hugged him back and said, "I feel like the ancients must have felt thousands of years ago, watching the stars for signs of doom."

Anlon's eyes drifted up toward the W-shaped constellation Cassiopeia. "That's a cheery thought."

"Well, it's true, don't you think?"

"I guess. But at least we won't have to wait as long as the ancients did for their doom to arrive. If Jupiter explodes, we'll see the flash within forty minutes, and most of us will be fried within hours."

Pebbles elbowed him sharply in the ribs. "Now, who's being cheery?"

Thankfully, the blanket wrapped around her softened the blow, so the jab didn't hurt much. Anlon begged forgiveness and said, "Just trying for a little comic relief."

"Talking about frying is *not* comic relief, Anlon. It's morbid."

"Hey, you're the one who introduced doom into the conversation."

Pebbles sighed and lowered her head. "I can't help it. Thinking about what might happen makes me gloomy."

He wanted to say, *"well, then don't think about what might happen,"* but knew such a response would only anger her. So, instead, he said, "Then trust Paul Morgan was able to stop it from happening."

She turned and stared at him. "I want to, Anlon. *So bad.* But I can't help but feel the fleet got there too late. The gamma bursts have already started and the last we heard from Skywalker, he was still like 500 billion kilometers from the magnetar."

When Anlon responded, he invoked the shorthand name the world had adopted when referring to the magnetar — R5. If he recalled correctly, the magnetar's full name was SGR-RE5. The SGR was an acronym for soft gamma repeater, the term used by scientists to codify a class of magnetars, and RE5 was an acronym identifying the specific magnetar in question. The latter acronym paid homage to the five crew members of the *Rorschach Explorer*, who first reported the magnetar's coordinates as shared by the Suhkai.

"True," Anlon said, "but Jupiter won't make its first pass through R5's gamma cone for at least another three to four months. Right? And all the media reports thus far indicate the bursts are way too weak to cause Jupiter issues, so they might not mean R5 had fully awoken. The fleet might have gotten there in time."

Pebbles looked away at the lake, seemingly unconvinced. Anlon tried another tack. "Even if he was too late, for all we know, the gammas will stay as weak as they are right now. Jupiter will sail through the cone, and we won't have to worry about R5 for another twelve years. That's plenty of time to come up with a plan B before Jupiter's next pass through the cone."

Anlon's comments attempted to remind Pebbles of a point often misunderstood by many on Earth. A gamma burst from a magnetar originated as a highly focused explosion, a powerful ejection known as a *collimated beam*. The radiation particles in this type of beam traveled in parallel rays that did not significantly disperse as the beam flew through space.

This feature of R5's gamma bursts was both a blessing and a curse for Jupiter. On the one hand, by the time R5's future rays made their way to Earth's solar system, the diameter of the beam-cone would still be narrow. This meant the bursts would only cut across a tiny slice of Jupiter's twelve-year loop through the solar system, limiting the planet's exposure to R5's radiation for a short period every twelve years. But on the other hand, the energy packed into the tight beam might prove lethal if future bursts strengthened.

Judging by Pebbles' response, she obviously was focused on the curse part of the equation. She turned and rapped him on the top of his head. "Hello in there...remember what Augie said the Suhkai told him? If the magnetar awakes, Jupiter's demise is a certainty. Whether it happens on Jupiter's first pass through the cone or later doesn't matter. Jupiter's toast. We're toast."

She was twisting what Augustus Amato had actually said, but Anlon saw no value in pointing out the aerospace magnate had not been so definitive. "Well, we're not toast yet. And as long as Jupiter keeps twinkling, I'll keep hoping the Suhkai are wrong."

"I guess that's the only thing we can do. *Hope*," said Pebbles.

Anlon nodded and looked down at the reflection of stars on the lake. For what seemed like several minutes, neither of them spoke. He closed his eyes, the sounds of wind whistling through the pine trees and water lapping up against the dock posts lulled Anlon toward sleep.

Hovering at the edge of consciousness, Pebbles uttered a deep sigh, stirring Anlon back awake. He opened his eyes and looked at her. Head bowed, shoulders slumped, she was massaging her wrists. Anlon reached out and smoothed his hand on her back.

"It'll be okay, Pebbles."

She nodded and wiped her eyes. Then, turning to Anlon, she said, "Come on, let's go back to bed. I'm tired of thinking about R5."

He kissed her on the cheek and, together, they headed back to the house. Just before they disappeared into the trees, Pebbles stopped, turned around and looked up at the eastern sky.

"See you tomorrow, Jupiter," she whispered. "Keep on twinkling, please."

DOCTOR KIERA WALSH'S RESIDENCE
PUMPKIN KEY, FLORIDA

On days like this, Kiera Walsh rued many of her past decisions. And she was damned good at it. In fact, revisiting her gaffes had almost become a game at this point. She would start with the most recent of her regrettable moves and step backward in time touching upon the succession of her preceding flubs.

When she was *really* feeling sorry for herself, she could trace the roots of her misery all the way back to her choice of aerospace engineering as a major. But more often than not, she focused on joining the *Rorschach Explorer* crew as the catalyst for her downward spiral. As she emptied the last of her wine bottle into a glass, she mumbled, "Fucking Skywalker."

It felt good to curse Col. Morgan by his legendary nickname, even though, if she was honest with herself, he hadn't twisted her arm that much. Still, if he hadn't asked her to join the mission, all her troubles since wouldn't exist. Kiera could hear her therapist's voice push back on that conclusion. *"All decisions have unintended consequences, Kiera. Many times they are good."*

Turning from the counter, Kiera sipped from her glass and said, "Yeah, well, sometimes they're not."

The floor felt cold on her bare feet as she walked toward the patio door. Shivering, Kiera scampered outside into the thick heat of the south Florida afternoon, sloshing wine onto her coverup along the way. As she dipped her feet into the cool water, she looked down at the splotches soaking through the coverup and groused, "Oh, for fuck's sake. Can't you even walk right?"

In answer, Kiera teetered on the top step and sloshed more wine. However, this time, the wine missed her and splashed into the pool, adding more ripples to those extending out from her feet. Exasperated, Kiera staggered down the remaining steps. As more of her body submerged under the water, she closed her eyes and sighed. "Ah, now that's more like it."

Farther and farther she waded, until, at last, she began to float in the deep end of the pool. Opening her eyes, she doggy-paddled to the side and placed her glass on the flagstone ledge. Then, she reached down to gather the edges of her billowing coverup and whisked it off.

Naked and treading water, she held the soaked garment above the surface and squeezed it, trying to wring water from the thin material. It was still sopping wet when Kiera tossed it onto the patio, but she didn't care. The sun would eventually dry it out. She turned away from the ledge and glided toward the deep end.

Stretched out and bobbing on the surface, she looked up at the sky. *Whoop-dee-do,* she thought. *Another day in paradise. Wonder what shit storm is going to hit me today? More pervy photographers snapping me naked in the pool? You would think people would grow tired of seeing my boobs and butt, let alone my stretch marks and scars. But apparently not.*

Kiera's mother's past chiding invaded her thoughts. *"Well, if you're tired of it, then wear a bathing suit, for heaven's sake."*

"I should be able to wear what I want in private," Kiera most often said in rebuttal. *"It's not my fault they're trespassing."*

"But you're a celebrity now, dear," her Mom would remind her. *"You're famous and rich. People are curious about you."*

Kiera swirled the water with her fingers and murmured, "Why would anyone be curious about my stretch marks?"

Anyway, her mother was wrong. People weren't curious about her. They liked to make fun of her. They mocked her appearance, chided her addiction and scolded her for sending Jasmine to Nepal to live with Ajay's parents.

They didn't care that Kiera had done so to protect her daughter, to give her a chance of living a normal life. Hell, they didn't even believe her. To the prying minds invading her life, Kiera had been forced to surrender Jasmine due to her drinking. She wanted to scream back, *"You don't know shit!"* But Kiera knew anything she said would get twisted.

If she forgot to smile at the barista when she bought coffee, someone would post a picture and declare her a privileged snob. If she declined to sign an autograph or pose for the ten-thousandth picture, she was labeled a stuck-up bitch.

They made horrible insinuations about her love life, which Kiera found laughable given she had none. They criticized her clothes, hair and weight. Anything and everything they could opine on, they did. Whether it was true or not, or was hurtful, didn't matter.

Kiera slipped below the water and curled into a ball. Holding her breath, she slowly began to sink. *It's my fault,* she thought. *I should have never taken the money. I should never have put myself out there. I should have asked people to respect my privacy and just faded into the background like Julia Carillo did.*

Carillo had been wise to pass up on all the endorsement deals, appearances and speaking engagements. She had kept out of the limelight and, eventually, people left her alone. *Smart cookie,* thought Kiera as her lungs begged for a quick return to the surface. *Shit, I didn't need the money. None of us did. Mr. Amato took care of us. God bless him.*

The truth, as hard as Kiera found it to admit, was that she had enjoyed all the attention at first. She had been one of the Rorschach Five, the first humans to make contact with aliens, a feat the public seemed to equate with walking on water. Never mind the fact the Rorschach Five were *not* the first to contact cytons or the Suhkai. That honor belonged exclusively to the astronauts of *Cetus Prime*: Avery Lockett, Christine Baker and Nick Reed. But they weren't around to worship, so people glommed onto Kiera and her shipmates.

Kiera uncurled and pushed her body upward. Breaking through the surface, she took a deep breath and smoothed back her hair. She thought of the early days after their return to Earth. *Man, what a crazy time that was.* Not just for Kiera, for everyone. With the arrival of the Suhkai, the possibilities of exploring space shot up exponentially.

And, wow, people flipped out when Skywalker made the announcement about Tula, the ark he called *Venture* and the ship's four human passengers…actually, Kiera vividly recalled Skywalker calling the children Tulans, not humans. For a short time, the only people more famous than Kiera and her *Rorschach* shipmates were Sarah, John and Annie, the first Tulans, the progeny of the Lockett-Baker-Reed trio.

But then someone let the secret slip about the true story behind Kiera's pregnancy, and everything changed for her. In retrospect, the most frustrating part of the revelation was the bullshit she had agreed to peddle about it beforehand. *Yet another dumb-ass decision on my part.* Kiera turned and swam toward her wine.

As she downed the rest of the glass, she recalled the pleas Amato and Skywalker had made, begging her to leave out the part about the Suhkai mating her with Ajay without her knowledge or consent. Telling the truth about that icky detail would have spurred too many uncomfortable questions at a time when the two men were busy trying to sell the public on the Suhkai as valiant creatures.

The Suhkai had rescued the *Cetus Prime* crew and helped them establish a new home on Tula. Not only that, but they also volunteered to build an ark and return to Earth seeking willing colonists to join the Lockett-Baker-Reed family on their new home planet. That was the tale Skywalker and Amato had wanted people to believe about the aliens. They certainly didn't want the world to know the *real* reason the Suhkai had provided the ark.

They wanted people to focus on how these wonderous beings could help Earthlings. The Suhkai were willing to share their technology, help humans build colonies on Mars and construct more arks bound for Tula. The aliens wanted to share their knowledge of space, enabling humans to expand their footprint throughout the galaxy. Kiera raised her empty glass and toasted the sky. "What heroes! Bravo, Suhkai!"

Angry now, Kiera splashed her way to the steps and stomped out of the pool. Eschewing the pyramid of rolled towels stacked on the nearby chaise lounge, she headed inside for another bottle. "Fucking Suhkai. Filthy lizards."

Slipping and sliding her way across the kitchen floor, Kiera reached the refrigerator and extracted another bottle. As she carried it back to the pool, she twisted off its cap and returned her thoughts to the litany of lies she had been party to for the past four years…and what those lies had cost her. *That's what sucks most. I did the right thing and got shredded for it. I carried a child inside me I never intended to create. I birthed Jasmine and cared for her while Ajay hopped aboard* Venture *and flew off for Tula. I tried my best to shield her from all the vultures who wanted to treat her like a circus freak because of how she was conceived. And I lost my relationship with Dante on top of all that.*

An inner voice mocked her. "Oh, boo-hoo! Stop whining. Stop feeling sorry for yourself. Get over it and move on. Put the God-damned bottle down and start over, for Cripe's sake. It's not that complicated."

Kiera descended into the water and sighed. *You're wrong. It's not that easy.* And the longer she pondered starting over, the harder it seemed. *Anyway, what's the point? We're all going to be burnt to a crisp soon. It's just a matter of time now.*

CHAPTER 2

Jenna Toffy stood to the right of the shiny black stage with her hands clutching a rolled-up script. Behind her, there was a star-dotted backscreen with a large image of a slowly rotating Jupiter positioned on her left. Dressed in a gold blazer, white button-down shirt and black slacks, the blond World News Network anchor awaited her on-air cue.

There would be no intro sequence tonight. As soon as the director provided the cue and the camera light illuminated, she would dive right into her script. In the final seconds of her wait, she stared down at her black, patent leather pumps and wondered how the world would react to the coming interview with Augustus Amato.

He had once been a hero to most people but was now broadly viewed as a pariah. She wondered whether perceptions of him would flip back after the broadcast or whether the interview would only deepen viewers' animosity toward him.

"Lift your head, Jenna. Camera One going live in five, four, three…"

She inhaled deeply and complied with the director's instructions, turning her body slightly to create an angled view of her head for Camera One. When the light appeared, she said, "Good evening and welcome. I'm Jenna Toffy and tonight, WNN is proud to present an exclusive interview with the co-founder and chairman of Gateway Ventures, Augustus Arturo Amato."

Toffy paused and paced a few steps across the stage, shifting her gaze to Camera Two per the previously rehearsed introduction. Reading from the camera's teleprompter, she resumed. "Forty-four months ago, Mr. Amato and Col. Paul Morgan took to the world stage to announce contact between the astronauts of the *Rorschach Explorer* and two intelligent alien species, cytons and the Suhkai. Their announcement instantly and irrevocably changed life on Earth as we knew it. Initially, people greeted their news with a great deal of excitement but, in the time since, much of the euphoria has been replaced by skepticism, anger and now, with the recent disclosure of gamma bursts detected near Jupiter, fear.

"Tonight, in our wide-ranging interview, we examine the events that led to the drop in public support for Mr. Amato and his firm's galactic initiatives and provide him a platform to defend his record and quell the growing worldwide uneasiness about the future of Earth…"

MAJOR JULIA CARILLO'S RESIDENCE
CHARLOTTESVILLE, VIRGINIA

Three hundred fifty miles south of WNN's studio, Maj. Julia Carillo watched the image of Jenna Toffy fade to black on the family room television and reached out to hold hands with her physician husband, Sam. Seconds later, the sound of distant ocean waves echoed through the room's surround-sound speakers. Slowly, the screen faded back in on a sandy beach bordered by brilliant blue waters rippling their way onshore.

Toffy's voice penetrated through the peaceful scene. "The last few years have been hard on you, haven't they?"

Augustus Amato's gravelly voice replied, "Yes, they have."

The screen switched to a view of the two walking at the edge of the incoming surf. The eighty-three-year-old Amato, bald and rotund, waddled along with his head down. Dressed in Bermuda shorts and a floral Hawaiian shirt, he looked to Julia like a retired tourist on holiday rather than the world's richest man.

Beside Amato, the far younger and slimmer Toffy kept her eyes on him as her hair and white summer dress fluttered in the brisk wind.

"What's been the hardest?" she asked, scooping strands of hair away from her face.

Amato stopped and looked out to sea. "Constantly jumping from tightrope to tightrope."

"What do you mean by tightropes?"

Amato turned to Toffy with a laugh. "Take your pick. Managing nonstop demands for access to space and Suhkai technology, trying to build our Martian colony and new arks amid lawsuits and government interference, dealing with the ever-slippery Suhkai, fending off criticisms about *Venture*, worrying about Paul Morgan and, of course, the looming threat posed by R5."

Toffy picked up a seashell from the sand and smoothed it between her fingers. "Sounds overwhelming."

"At times, it can be."

"Some say you brought it upon yourself. Creating Gateway Ventures, controlling access to space and the Suhkai the way you have."

"I've heard that criticism often."

Amato resumed walking, hands clasped behind his back, eyes peering ahead. Toffy scooted up beside him, still turning over the sea shell in her hands.

"A lot of people believe you've never really responded to the criticism."

Amato laughed again. "Not true, not true. I've responded many times. People just don't like my answers. The Suhkai bestowed *Venture* and their other spacecraft, their facilities on Callisto and Dione, their technology and allegiance on one man, my co-founder, Paul Morgan. They did not bestow these things on all of humanity. And the Suhkai did this for a reason, one that appears very prescient now."

Julia winced upon hearing Amato's answer. Though she understood the point Amato was trying to make, the way he said it came across as elitist and combative. To her surprise, Toffy didn't call him on it. With an earnest, almost compassionate tone, the journalist said, "You mean their experience colonizing other worlds and interacting with other intelligent beings? I've heard you mention this reason in the past."

"Yes, that's right." Gesturing with his hands as he talked, Amato said, "The Suhkai know how disruptive the sudden access to space can be for a culture like ours. We are *not* one people. We are a collection of disparate societies with different customs, aspirations, capabilities and resources. Providing immediate, universal, unfettered access to the Suhkai and their technology would have been a recipe for disaster. They have seen such disasters firsthand in the past."

This answer from Amato was much better in Julia's view, especially the line about *we are not one people.* But it only partially addressed the concerns raised by many. The issue people struggled with was not why the Suhkai wanted a gatekeeper between them and Earthlings. Rather, people wanted to know why Amato was the gatekeeper.

The screen switched to a close-up of a nodding Toffy. When Amato finished speaking, she said, "Your critics say that's just an excuse to justify control. They point to bodies like the United Nations, the European Union and the like and say, why can't we form a similar international coalition for access to space, for interacting with the Suhkai? Col. Morgan selected such a coalition for the crew of his fleet. Why can't you do the same on Earth, Mars, Callisto and Dione?"

Returning to a wide shot of the two together, the camera captured a look of frustration on Amato's face as he responded. "There *will* be a day when such a coalition is possible, but it is not now."

"Why?"

"Because of the magnetar. We cannot allow bureaucratic red tape and nationalistic squabbles to delay our efforts to prepare for its possible awakening."

At that same moment in south Florida, Kiera Walsh opened her third wine bottle of the day in her kitchen. The deed completed, Kiera returned to her family room and saw Toffy and Amato were now seated on pastel-colored Adirondack chairs under cover of a porch awning. Hanging above them were two ceiling fans rotating with gusto.

"Let's talk more about magnetars," said Toffy. "It's a word that's become commonplace in our lexicon over the last few years, but still many don't know what a magnetar really is. How would you describe a magnetar to our viewers?"

"In the simplest terms," Amato said, "it's a type of star, or sun, with unusual characteristics."

"Unusual characteristics such as what?"

"Well, first of all, magnetars are very small. One would easily fit on this island. But despite their small size, magnetars are incredibly dense. In fact, most are more than ten times as dense as our sun. They are also incredibly magnetic, hence their name. So far as we know, they are the most magnetic objects in the universe."

Don't leave out how hard they are to detect, thought Kiera as she carried her wine bottle into the adjacent family room.

"I see," said Toffy. "So, they're like magnets floating in space."

The screen switched to a close-up of Amato. "You could look at them that way, I suppose. But they are more than just magnets. If you were to talk to a physicist about magnetars, he, or she, would tell you they are neutron stars, which are essentially the collapsed remains of suns like ours. Therefore, they retain star-like qualities too."

As she refilled her wine glass, Kiera mumbled, "Yeah, like the ability to kill planets."

With her pour accomplished, she sat down on the sofa and returned her attention to the television, mentally urging Amato and Toffy to move beyond the basics and talk about R5. *Quit wasting time. Is the damn thing going to blow up Jupiter or not? That's what everybody wants to know.*

"Okay, so they're like super-magnetic suns," Toffy said.

Kiera rolled her eyes and gulped down a mouthful of Chardonnay. *We get the picture, Jenna. Move on to R5.*

Another close-up of Amato was shown as he answered. "When they're active, yes. But the vast majority are dormant. Most are undetectable to us on Earth. You see, when they're dormant, magnetars do not emit detectable radiation..."

As Amato continued to speak, Kiera whispered, "There you go. Now we're getting to the important stuff."

"…Ironically, when they are active, they're still tough to detect because the radiation they emit is in the form of focused beams, so focused that you have to be directly in line with a magnetar's beams to detect it."

The camera view zoomed out to show both Toffy and Amato again, just as Toffy said, "That's a good segue to discuss R5 in particular. It's a dormant magnetar, correct?"

"It would probably be more appropriate to describe R5 as mostly dormant. As you know, it has recently begun emitting sporadic bursts of gamma rays."

Kiera laughed when Amato said *mostly dormant*. It reminded her of a scene from one of her favorite movies where a magician refers to a fallen swordsman as *mostly dead*, not all the way dead. She tuned back into the interview just as Toffy said, "You mean beams, not bursts."

"Well, technically, both terms are correct," said Amato. "Active magnetars emit beams of radiation, but, to us, they appear as bursts. This is because magnetars spin around very fast, typically once per second, giving their beams the appearance of intermittent bursts. A good analogy to help your audience visualize what I mean is a lighthouse. The light projected by a lighthouse lamp is a constant beam, but because the lamp spins around, the beam is not always visible, giving the beam the appearance of a blinking light."

"Got it," said Toffy. "So, right now, R5 is like a balky lighthouse lamp, sporadically blinking gamma rays. But there's a concern it will become more active, that the lamp of the lighthouse will turn on and stay on."

"That's right. If R5 were to fully activate, it would emit beams of gamma rays non-stop for ten thousand years."

"And that is a problem because?"

Kiera grew tired of Toffy's spoon-feeding, but she understood why the journalist was doing it. There had been a lot of public interest in magnetars when Kiera and her *Rorschach Explorer* crewmates had first returned to Earth after contacting the Suhkai. But over time, with R5 dormant, the public's "space" attention had turned elsewhere.

Who could blame them? Kiera thought. There were many more excit-
ing topics resulting from contact with the Suhkai. There was the planet
Tula, where the ark *Venture* was headed. People loved imagining what
life on Tula would be like, and a certain romanticism had developed about
Venture's journey there.

There was also a great deal of interest in Meridiani Planum, the Martian colony Gateway had built, and the new arks under construction there,
Vanguard and *Valor*. When finished, they would ferry several hundred
more settlers to Tula...*assuming Jupiter doesn't blow up before they launch*,
thought Kiera.

People were also fascinated by the Suhkai facilities on the Jupiter moon
Callisto and the Saturn moon Dione. Built thousands of years ago, they
had served as refineries for liquid metallic helium and hydrogen extracted
from Jupiter's and Saturn's atmospheres. While portions of the massive
facilities remained as the Suhkai had built them, Gateway had transformed some of their sections into science centers and tourist venues.

Space tourism also captivated people. Gateway had modified two of
the twenty-four "cruiser" spacecraft the Suhkai had gifted into tour shuttles. Powered by the aliens' propulsion system capable of near-lightspeed,
the shuttles launched from Mayaguana three days a week. Some flights
transported passengers for week-long stays at one of Gateway's three off-
world facilities, while others performed "flybys" of various planets, moons
and asteroids throughout the solar system. Tickets were awarded via a
monthly lottery run by Gateway. For a buck, you could buy a chance to
win an all-expense-paid trip of a lifetime.

Of course, people thirsted to learn more about the Suhkai and cytons,
and there was a lot to learn. For those not lucky enough to win a trip to
one of Gateway's off-world facilities and catch glimpses of the aliens in
person, Gateway had created a subscription streaming service with a variety of programming about the aliens, Tula and space. Kiera was not a
subscriber, but she knew it had become the most popular streaming service in the world. *Bet that really pisses Jenna off*, thought Kiera as she focused back on the interview.

Amato was just finishing telling Toffy why R5 awaking was a problem.
"The Suhkai believe R5's rays will disrupt Jupiter's atmosphere, causing

the planet to explode. If that were to happen, the fallout from the explosion would render Earth lifeless."

How lovely, can't wait, thought Kiera, downing the rest of the wine in her glass. Over the top of the glass, she watched Toffy ease back in her chair. She seemed relaxed, accepting of Amato's gloomy forecast. Then, as Kiera reached for the bottle for a refill, the camera zoomed in on Toffy's face. Her placid expression suddenly turned stern. "Does it bother you that so many people call you a huckster, a fearmonger?"

On Kiera's TV, a flurry of alternating close-ups marked the exchange that followed in the interview.

"I'm neither."

"Many scientists say you're stoking fear, *irrational fear,* about R5."

"Nonsense. The threat from R5 is real."

"Is it? I've been told R5 might not 'activate' for thousands of years, that the recent spate of gamma bursts might be nothing more than the result of isolated starquakes on its surface."

"That's certainly possible. I hope that to be the case."

"Isn't it also true that many experts dispute gamma rays from R5 are capable of destroying Jupiter?"

"Based on what?" challenged Amato as the camera finally zoomed out. "And don't say data from other magnetars. Of the millions in the galaxy, only twenty-three other magnetars have ever been detected from Earth, and all of those are thousands and thousands of light-years away. R5 is two light-years from us, Jenna. *Two.* Your so-called experts have no idea what gammas from a magnetar at such close range could do."

"I'll flip that back on you," Toffy said. "What data do *you* or the Suhkai have to prove the opposite, that R5 is capable of destroying Jupiter?"

"I have none."

"Then why should anyone believe you? Why should anyone trust the word of the Suhkai? You, yourself, called them slippery earlier in our conversation. And it's well known they've been dishonest about other things in the past. What they did to Kiera Walsh and Ajay Joshi on Dione, for example."

Anger spiked inside Kiera. She gripped her glass so tight, wine sloshed over its rim and splattered her hand, legs and the sofa. *Don't you drag me into this, Jenna! You're right. The Suhkai can't be trusted, but leave me out of it.*

On the television, Amato frowned at Toffy with apparent frustration and remained silent for several seconds. When he finally spoke, his voice was steady, his manner composed. "From the very first moment the Suhkai told us of R5, they've regarded it as an imminent threat. Their actions, both before and since, have done nothing to dispel that perception."

Growing more animated, Amato held up his hand and stretched out his fingers. Pointing to his index finger, he said, "Fact: the Suhkai traveled here from eleven-light-years away to warn us of the magnetar."

False, thought Kiera. *They traveled here to kidnap humans to help colonize Tula. They only fessed about the magnetar after Skywalker refused to allow them to snatch people.*

Waggling his middle finger, Amato continued. "Fact two: knowing what was likely to happen to Earth, they searched for and found us a new planet to colonize, Tula."

True, Kiera mused, *but only because they felt guilty for causing R5's instability in the first place. They were warned by cytons to stay away from R5, but they ignored the warning.*

Amato pointed at his ring finger. "Three: they built and brought us an ark to transport there."

Kiera swigged more wine. *True and false. They built an ark all right, but they had no intention of giving it to us. They were going to snatch people and fly away without ever saying a peep, forcing the unlucky snatchees to breed all the way to Tula.*

"Four." He wiggled his pinkie. "They sent a fleet with Col. Morgan, along with a colony of cytons, to attempt to stabilize R5 before it awakes, and they're helping us build more arks."

"Hah!" Kiera burst out with a laugh, inadvertently sloshing more wine on herself. Standing up, she railed at Amato's image on the TV. "Come on, Mr. Amato. Be honest with Jenna. The Suhkai are only so helpful now because cytons are making them help!"

Cytons, thought Kiera. *They're the real heroes, not the Suhkai.* Cytons looked like nothing more than tiny balls of light flitting around in space like fireflies on a midsummer night, but they were so much more than that. Cytons were sentient, electromagnetic aliens who fed on free-floating ions in outer space, most often living in colonies near planets and moons with strong magnetic fields, including Earth.

Like honeybee colonies on Earth, each cyton colony had its queen and her "subject-cytons" each had defined roles. Most Kiera had seen were white, golden or blue, but they came in other colors too and could even cloak themselves invisible. They also varied in size, with the smallest about the size of a golf ball and the largest as big as a basketball.

The Suhkai claimed cytons were the oldest of the thousands of species they had encountered in the galaxy, ancient aliens who had sparked life to begin with their zaps of electrical energy. Kiera didn't know if that was true, but she did know a colony of blue cytons had saved her life, helping her escape the Suhkai and a contingent of golden cytons holding her captive. Once again, she cursed the Suhkai as she recalled what they had done to her.

After she finished her profanity-laced tirade, Kiera returned her attention to the interview and realized she had missed some of Amato's comments. Curious to know what other garbage he was peddling, Kiera snagged the remote and rewound the video stream to the point where Amato had lauded the Suhkai for helping to build more arks. Clicking play, she listened to him say, "Tell me, why would the Suhkai act so aggressively, selflessly, and invest so much of their time and resources if the threat posed by R5 was not real?"

Oh, the threat's real, all right, Kiera thought, *but they ain't acting selflessly. They're all about easing their guilt.*

Returning to her place on the sofa, Kiera waited for Toffy's verbal reaction. From her facial expression, Kiera sensed the journalist remained skeptical. *Good for you! Make him squirm, make him tell the truth!*

"So, you seem to be saying the Suhkai should be absolved of proving their claims about R5 because they've gone out of their way to help us."

"No. I'm saying the Suhkai's actions *are* proof of their claims."

"Bullshit!" screamed Kiera, leaping from the sofa once again.

The scene cut on that note and, once again, the program returned to the live feed of Toffy in WNN's studio. "It was clear from this segment of our conversation that Mr. Amato strongly believes the threat posed by

R5 is significant. However, he produced no evidence beyond what you've just witnessed in support of his beliefs, and the scientific community at large remains unconvinced about his conclusions. When we return..."

Kiera muted the sound and headed outside onto the patio to clear her mind. Amato's shading of the truth and his portrayal of the Suhkai as altruistic heroes sickened her. She was also curious why Amato had refused to discuss the threat posed by R5. He had to know the skeptics would not accept his word or the word of the Suhkai. They wanted scientific facts, historical data and projection models, and Kiera was sure Amato and others at Gateway had pressed the Suhkai for this kind of information.

In her mind, Amato had shied away from getting into specifics for one of two reasons. Either the Suhkai had provided data that Amato deemed suspect, or the Suhkai had refused to produce any data. Of the two options, she leaned toward the latter. She didn't trust the Suhkai. Never had. Never would.

Back at the Carillo household, Julia was anxious for an update on her friend and fellow *Rorschach Explorer* shipmate Paul Morgan, as well as the other astronauts who had joined him for the trip to R5. The fact that Gateway had stopped sharing updates from Morgan about the same time the gamma bursts began was troubling. To her, the sudden silence seemed to imply Morgan's fleet had run into a problem or, worse, had failed in its attempt to stabilize the magnetar.

If that were true, Julia reasoned, Amato's reluctance to elaborate on the Suhkai's view of the R5 threat suggested he believed a risk assessment was moot at this point. This perception was bolstered by the content of the interview's final segment, in which the focus shifted to the ark *Venture*, already on its way to Tula, and the two new arks Amato was building on Mars, *Vanguard* and *Valor*.

After a fluff-filled minute or two, during which Amato provided an overview of *Vanguard*'s in-process construction, Toffy said, "So, let's step back a moment and revisit our earlier conversation about R5. You've said the reason you've held such a tight grip on access to the Suhkai and their technology is to focus efforts on building and launching these arks before R5 awakens."

Standing beside a table model of *Vanguard* in a conference room of Gateway's Mayaguana HQ, Amato said, "Yes, and I think it's important to clarify a point I don't think I emphasized adequately earlier. I have no idea whether R5 will erupt soon or not. I'm concerned it will, especially given the recent gamma burst activity, but I don't know that it will.

"Plan A in dealing with R5 has always rested on the fleet headed by Col. Morgan, his Suhkai counterpart, Haula and the colony of cytons who accompanied them. Their goal: try to stabilize the magnetar before it stirs awake. The trouble with relying on that plan as our only course of action was the reality the magnetar could awake at any time, and the trip to reach it, even with Suhkai lightspeed technology, would take Morgan and the others two years.

"As it stands now, three years since they left, if they did reach and stabilize it a year ago as planned, we won't hear about it from them for another year from now. Four years was too long to sit back and wait for confirmation of success from the fleet. We had to concurrently pursue a Plan B, and we had to be aggressive about it."

Julia nodded as she listened. She turned to her husband and said, "Augie did a good job explaining the time lag dilemma. I'm glad Jenna didn't cut him off."

Meanwhile, on the television, Toffy placed her hand on the *Vanguard* model. "The arks are your Plan B."

"Precisely. As you know, *Venture*, the ark the Suhkai brought to us, left for Tula a few months after Morgan's fleet departed for R5. As you also know, it will take *Venture* another eight years to reach Tula. We were concerned about the risks associated with their journey, so we approached the Suhkai to assist us in replicating *Venture*. With more arks, we could start a cyclical convoy between the two planets. This is where time became such a crucial factor.

"We had to do what we could to build the new arks as fast as possible so that one or both might be ready before Jupiter first crossed into R5's gamma cone. That meant avoiding red tape, which meant setting aside a coalition. One voice, one focus was critical to achieving our Plan B objectives. I raised the necessary money by forming Gateway Ventures, and we've spearheaded the construction efforts with the help of many sub-contractors from many nations. As it is, we will likely not complete both arks before Jupiter begins its first pass, but I believe with all my heart, nei-ther would have gone beyond the drawing board stage by now if we had pursued a coalition.

"That said, if Jupiter makes its first pass through R5's cone without in-cident, we will have eleven-plus years to reassess Gateway's role in man-aging access to the Suhkai and their technology."

Looking up at the den clock, Julia noted the time. Unless the program ran over its scheduled length, the interview was nearing its end. "Doesn't seem like we're going to get an update on Paul and the fleet."

"Unfortunately, I think you're right," Sam said.

Julia's stomach churned. "That concerns me, Sam. It really does."

As a pilot for Gateway, Julia had enough access to staff at the Maya-guana facility to know the R5 mission control center was still receiving periodic updates from Morgan and raw data transmissions from the ships in the fleet. But Amato had clamped down on access to the information received from Morgan as soon as R5's bursts began, and no one Julia knew in mission control would divulge what was going on.

Stirred by the sound of waves, Julia focused back on the TV where Toffy and Amato were walking on the beach again. In the background loomed Gateway's Mayaguana spaceport. On one of the launch aprons sat a Suhkai cruiser. Next to it on another apron was the much smaller *Rorschach Explorer II*, the ship Julia captained for Gateway's space tour-ism division.

The modified version of the original *Rorschach Explorer* was on screen for only a few seconds before the TV picture switched to a close-up of Toffy. "A little over a month ago, Gateway stopped releasing updates from Col. Morgan's fleet. Why?"

"Finally," said Julia under her breath.

With the camera still trained on Toffy, Amato's voice could be heard replying to the question. To Julia, he sounded very defensive, almost dis-missive. "We explained why in our statement weeks ago."

Toffy frowned. "Many people considered your statement unsatisfactory. It's led to a belief Gateway is hiding something from the public."

The TV picture switched to a closeup of Amato. His face twitched as he answered. "Yes, I know. And the media is doing its best to fan speculation."

The picture then zoomed out to include them both on-screen as Toffy pressed on. "Has something happened to the fleet?"

"No, of course not."

"So, you're still receiving transmissions from Col. Morgan?"

"Periodically, yes."

Julia's stomach-churning kicked up a notch. She had never known Amato to lie, but his facial reactions and curt answers sure came across like those of someone not telling the truth.

Once again, the camera zoomed in on Toffy. A sudden gust of wind swirled her hair into snakelike tendrils that twisted in the air around her head. "He's told you R5 has awoken, hasn't he, Mr. Amato? That's the reason you've cut off the updates."

Amato's voice boomed. "Nonsense!"

When the TV picture switched to show his face, he looked furious. "That kind of speculation is reckless. You could send the whole world into a panic unnecessarily."

Toffy seemed unfazed by the criticism. "It's not *my* speculation, Mr. Amato. It's the speculation of millions of people around the world. People are fed up with Gateway's secrecy, with your vague, innocuous statements. They want to be told the truth. *The whole truth.*"

"We *have* told the truth," Amato said. "And we will continue to do so. But what we won't do is succumb to public pressure and release incomplete, unclear information. As of right now, we have no definitive proof R5 has activated. Nor does anyone else. End of story."

Julia cringed as she listened to Amato. Whether he was telling the truth or not, she doubted his defiant answer would be received well in most quarters. She personally found his *no definitive proof* line discomforting and imagined many other people would feel the same way. It seemed to imply Amato had access to something more than circumstantial proof.

Without a word to Sam, she rose from her seat and left the room just as Toffy fired back with another question. Julia didn't want to hear any more. She didn't want to believe Paul Morgan had failed. But after Amato's weaselly definitive proof answer, she couldn't help but think that was precisely what had happened.

CHAPTER 3

Three weeks after the WNN interview, Anlon Cully received an odd invitation from Augustus Amato. The Gateway chairman requested he and Pebbles join him the following weekend for an excursion aboard his boat. Under the circumstances when they received the invitation, Anlon and Pebbles had been surprised by the seemingly bizarre overture.

To begin with, R5's gamma bursts had not abated. In fact, according to information released by NASA, they had increased in intensity and frequency toward the latter part of June. While NASA had declined to declare R5 had awoken when discussing the new data, their release was widely taken as bad news.

This negative perception was further solidified by Gateway's continued silence regarding R5 and Morgan's fleet, particularly after Amato's interview with Jenna Toffy. A broad majority believed Amato knew more about R5 and the fleet than what he had stated during the broadcast.

If that wasn't bad enough, Amato had become the subject of fresh attacks of vocal scientific skeptics on the opposite side of the public opinion spectrum who claimed the R5 threat was a farce. Even if the magnetar had awoken, they said, it was lunacy to believe its gamma rays could blow up Jupiter. These skeptics were joined in their renewed castigation of Amato by influential leaders across the globe who supported the contention the threat was a farce. They said Amato continued to fuel fear to line his pockets and hoard control over Suhkai assets.

In sum, by the time Anlon and Pebbles received Amato's lighthearted invitation, the man was under siege on all fronts.

Aside from Amato's circumstances, there was another aspect of the invitation Anlon found odd. While he considered Amato a friend, they didn't exactly rub elbows socially.

Amato was thirty-plus years older than Anlon, the richest person in the world and a businessman who had devoted his life to the exploration of space. By contrast, Anlon was an animal biomechanics expert whose professional experience was entirely terrestrial. Yes, he had parlayed that experience into a lucrative technology patent that made him wealthy and allowed him to retire at a young age, but he was hardly a contemporary of Amato's in any way.

But their paths had crossed several years ago when Amato's space probes encountered cytons for the first time. Amato reached out to Anlon through a mutual friend to query Anlon about some odd behaviors the cytons had exhibited.

Anlon noticed certain similarities between cyton behaviors and traits of Earth wildlife, which Amato found compelling. And since then, Amato reached out from time to time to chat about the latest Gateway learnings about the aliens. These conversations typically included friendly preambles about recent events in each other's lives, but that was the extent of their social interactions. So Amato's sudden spend-the-weekend-with-me invitation seemed out of place.

On this point, Pebbles disagreed. She had been a participant in many of Anlon's conversations with Amato, and she believed the aerospace magnate viewed Anlon as more than a source of information, especially after the Rorschach Explorer returned to Earth.

"He likes you, Anlon," Pebbles had said when Anlon expressed his puzzlement over the invitation. *"He respects who you are as a person. You've been there to help him when he's asked. You've given him good advice. You've never asked for anything in return."*

Pebbles then paused a moment and said, *"But don't kid yourself, A.C. He's not looking to lounge around with us on his yacht. He's got something else in mind."*

"Like what?" Anlon asked in return.

"Hello? R5's bursts have worsened. I think he's gonna tell us Earth is a goner and to party like it's 1999 while there's still time."

The possibility of hearing such news proved too much for Pebbles, and she declined to go. But Anlon decided to make the trip without her, believing there had to be a different motivation for Amato's out-of-the-blue invitation and he was curious to discover what it was.

GATEWAY VENTURES' HEADQUARTERS
MAYAGUANA ISLAND, THE BAHAMAS
JULY 7, 2023

From the earliest moments following Anlon's arrival at Gateway's Mayaguana headquarters, Amato had been quiet and reflective, but not overly pessimistic. He seemed to want nothing more than to talk to someone about his burdens, someone outside of his inner circle. So, Anlon played the role of a listener and walked quietly beside Amato as they kicked off the visit with a stroll along the Mayaguana shoreline.

At one point, Amato stopped short of the incoming surf and stared out at the Caribbean Sea. "You know, Anlon, there's a damnable truth about going after *Cetus Prime* I wish I had properly considered before we set out to find her."

Digging his toes into the wet sand, Anlon followed the path of Amato's gaze out to sea. "Oh? What truth is that, Augie?"

Amato turned to him and smiled. "I suppose it's a lesson all explorers have learned at one time or another." He paused and wagged a finger in the air. "Unintended consequences accompany every discovery."

"I suppose that's true, Augie." Anlon nodded and patted his friend's shoulder. "But, come on, what choice did you really have? Letting sleeping dogs lie would have been worse, don't you think?"

Lowering his head, Amato mumbled, "Sometimes I'm not so sure."

As the older man turned and resumed walking along the surf line, Anlon lingered for a moment. Frowning, he slid his hands into the pockets of his shorts and pondered whether to rebut Amato's comment. Thinking better of it, he marched off to catch up with Amato just as the latter came to another stop and pointed out to sea. "Behold one of my unintended consequences."

Anlon turned his head toward the water as he walked up to Amato. About a quarter-mile off shore, a small boat slowly motored parallel to the coast. While it was too far away for Anlon to discern much detail about the craft, he could tell the people aboard it were looking toward the beach.

"They like to pretend they're tourists or fishermen, but they're not," Amato said. "I'd guess CIA, but it might be the Chinese or Russians. They all surveil Mayaguana in every way imaginable, satellites, drones, patrol boats, even submarines on occasion. You would think the Bahamians would raise a fuss about nuclear subs in their waters but, apparently, they are too timid to protest. I don't blame them, though. They've taken a lot of heat for selling me the island."

Anlon turned around to look back at the Gateway spaceport complex a few hundred yards inland from the beach. There, on one of the launch pads, was the likely target of the boat's surveillance, a sleek-bodied Suhkai spaceship. "I guess *the-powers-that-be* don't trust you, Augie."

"You're right." Amato turned to face him. "And it's a shame. I've spent the better part of the last four years trying to build bridges with them. But no matter what I do, it's never good enough. You know the worst part? They pay the least attention to the matters of most importance."

Amato looked skyward and pointed. Anlon followed the direction of his aim and saw a star glimmering in the fading light of the eastern sky. It wasn't Jupiter, but it might as well have been.

"They needle me endlessly about their pet issues," Amato said. "They seem to only care about profits and achieving an advantage over each other."

It was easy for Anlon to understand Amato's frustration. As a distant observer, Anlon had witnessed his attempts to parcel out nuggets of the Suhkai largesse through subcontracts with Gateway Ventures.

But people didn't want dribs and drabs passed down by Amato. They wanted unobstructed access to everything the Suhkai had to offer. Amato had rebuffed these demands and quickly became the subject of hatred and the target of suspicion. Some called him a self-anointed dictator, while others labeled him as a hoarding profiteer. They did not see Amato like Anlon did, as a man desperately trying to do the right thing on behalf of his fellow Earthlings.

"Don't let them drag you down, Augie. You're on the high road of the situation."

"You are one of the few who seems to think so." Amato laughed. "Come, let's head inside. We have much to discuss, and I prefer not to have prying ears listening in."

Shortly afterward, Anlon was surprised and thrilled to learn their destination was not the complex of buildings making up Gateway's Mayaguana compound. Instead, Amato had guided him to a portable ramp leading up to the airlock of the Suhkai spacecraft.

He had seen many pictures of the Suhkai's ships before, but this trip to Mayaguana was his first time seeing one in person. From a distance, even in the faint light of dusk, the ship's hull seemed to gleam like silverish metal. But, now, from his vantage point on the jetway, the ship's shell looked more like glass.

Anlon was tempted to ask Amato about the materials making up the unusual-looking surface but knew it was a closely guarded secret. Well, one component of the composite was a closely guarded secret. The rest of the materials had already been disclosed through leaks. As Anlon recalled it, the mystery component was "not of this world" and appeared to provide the ship with a combination of radiation protection and internal gravity stability. He stopped halfway up the ramp and turned to Amato, who trailed behind. "It gives me shivers just looking at it."

"I felt exactly the same the first time one landed here, Anlon. Trust me, the more you learn about the cruisers, the more you shiver." Amato stopped and swept his arm from the nose to the tail of the jumbo-jet-length ship. "Twenty-six-years-ago, a ship just like this carried Avery Lockett, Christine Baker and Nick Reed from Callisto to Tula."

Shape-wise, Anlon found it tempting to compare the cruiser's tubular main body to an airplane, but its flattened, elongated snout reminded Anlon more of a platypus bill. In fact, dimensionally, the whole main body reminded him of a platypus. The body's core was somewhat wider than it was tall, and it terminated in an elongated, flattened tail that contained the Suhkai's propulsion apparatus.

Unlike a platypus, however, the Suhkai cruiser had eight feet instead of four. From videos of liftoffs from Mayaguana, Anlon knew these feet were landing struts with liftoff thrusters that retracted inside the main body before flying into space.

As they resumed walking, Anlon asked, "Remind me. How many of these ships do you have, Augie?"

"All told, twenty-four."

Amato went on to say that the Suhkai had actually gifted Paul Morgan all thirty-four cruisers that had been mothballed in their abandoned refineries on Callisto and Dione, but that Morgan had taken three of those for his fleet and left the rest at the disposal of the Suhkai who remained in the solar system as ambassadors and technical advisors.

The latter comment reminded Anlon of how few of the Suhkai were still in the solar system. Most of the aliens who had arrived on the ark carrying Nick Reed and in the escort cruisers accompanying the ark had departed not long after their arrival. As Anlon recalled, some of the Suhkai and escort cruisers had been assigned to Morgan's fleet while the rest remained with the ark now on its way to Tula.

Shaking his head as he resumed walking up the boarding ramp, Anlon said, "It's crazy that so many Suhkai arrived here four years ago, and so few are around now."

"Well, they never intended to stay at all," said Amato, following behind, "so I guess we should be glad that Paul convinced Haula to leave some of his comrades behind."

Anlon nodded. It was a point people on Earth often forgot about the Suhkai. They hadn't traveled to Earth to make contact and establish relations. Instead, they had come at the behest of Avery Lockett, Christine Baker and Nick Reed to collect colonists for Tula and deliver a warning about the risk R5 posed. If not for the agreement Paul Morgan struck with Haula, all of the Suhkai would have departed four years ago.

When Anlon reached the cruiser's open airlock entrance amidships, he paused and asked Amato if it was permissible to touch the glass-like material coating the fuselage.

"Of course. I'm curious to know what you think of it."

Anlon slid his fingers along a small section. Though it was slick to the touch, it didn't feel like glass. It felt more like a smoothed rock. He craned his neck to look down the length of the body toward the tail of the windowless spacecraft. Turning back to Amato, now standing beside him. "Amazing. It looks like it was cast in a mold. I don't see any evidence of panels or welds."

"Looks are deceiving," Amato said. "What you see is one property of *Suhkonium*. That's the name NASA's scientists have decided to attach to the so-called mystery element incorporated by the Suhkai. Come on, let's board and I'll tell you more about it."

Anlon's heart raced as they entered the ship. Looking around, he whistled long and low. *Holy crap! If Pebbles could see me now!*

"It looked a lot more alien when we first took possession, but like the other Suhkai cruisers we have, we've humanized it," said Amato. "We had to. The Suhkai primarily used these ships to mine and transport liquid metallic helium and hydrogen, not ferry human passengers. The internal configurations were built to suit the Suhkai and their mining operations."

Pictures Anlon had seen did not do justice to the dimensions of the main cabin. The rounded ceiling was at least fifteen feet high, which made sense to Anlon given the Suhkai averaged ten feet in height. The compartment was also twice as wide as it was tall, presumably constructed initially to accommodate the elephant-like girth of Suhkai bodies. Into this space, Amato had transformed the interior to look like that of a luxury airliner, only more generously spaced and outfitted with far more technology.

"Where you're standing now used to be a Suhkai cargo bay of sorts," said Amato. "Now, we use this ship as a shuttle to ferry people and cargo between Earth and our Martian colony. From liftoff to touchdown, we could make that trip in under an hour if we chose, even when the two planets are at their farthest from each other. But we've not pushed it that hard yet. Most of our flights to Mars average six hours."

"Incredible, Augie. Absolutely incredible. What you and your team have done with the shuttles, the colony on Mars and the new arks you're building boggles the mind. In many ways, to do so much in four years puts the sum of human space exploration to shame."

Amato waved his hand dismissively. "Without the Suhkai, without their technology, their knowledge, their help, we'd be nowhere."

"Oh, come now, Augie. That's not true, and you know it. We walked right past *Rorschach Explorer II* on our way out of the hangar. You've had your own breakthroughs. Significant ones."

"Here and there, yes, but what we accomplished with the *Rorschach* program is a gnat on the toenail of an elephant compared to what the Suhkai brought to us. In fact, we've replaced much of the core tech we originally built into *RE-II* with Suhkai tech...the propulsion system, thruster controls, gravity environment, and so on. I would do even more to revamp *RE-II* if I could but, right now, it's more important to finish the two new arks and the Martian colony. Time grows short. Very short. To be candid, my concern about time is the primary reason I asked you to come to Mayaguana."

Anlon's stomach gurgled as Pebbles' *"Earth is a goner"* comment replayed in his mind. "You'll forgive me, Augie, but I don't understand the connection between your concern about time and me."

Jesus, please don't say it's time to party like it's 1999, thought Anlon.

"You will understand, my friend," Amato said. "Eventually, you will. And when you do, I will have hard questions to ask you. But for now, please choose a seat. Make yourself comfortable. We will have plenty of time to talk things over on Mars."

Blinking several times, Anlon stood staring at him with his mouth agape. When the initial shock wore off, he said, "Uh...say what?"

Amato began to walk toward the front of the cabin. "I'll be back in a moment. I need to let the flight crew know we're almost ready to go."

"You're serious? We're going to Mars?"

Amato stopped his march and turned around to look at him. "Yes. You don't mind, do you? I asked you to visit for the weekend. Does it matter where we visit?"

Scratching the back of his head, Anlon looked down at his sandy feet, shorts and T-shirt. "No offense, Augie, but it is kind of sudden. I mean, look at me. I thought you said we were going to take a little cruise on your bo—"

Anlon darted his head up. "Oh, I see...*this* is the boat you meant in your message."

"My apologies for the trickery, Anlon," said Amato with a laugh. "Not to worry. We shall take good care of you. You will want for nothing during our flight and stay." His demeanor suddenly turned solemn. "Please, Anlon. Do me this favor. You will not regret it."

Looking at the earnest expression on Amato's face, Anlon thought, *how can I say no to this man?* This query was followed shortly by another thought, *are you kidding me? Why should I say no to this man?*

But before he agreed to the trip, Anlon pressed Amato to explain why he wanted him to accompany him to Mars. "I'm not a physicist. I have no special knowledge of magnetars or the Suhkai."

"I understand that. I've not invited you here to consult you about either."

"Cytons, then? Something new has surfaced about them?"

"Well, we learn new things about them every day, it seems, but my interest in meeting with you and in taking you to Mars has nothing to do with cytons."

"Then, I'm at a loss, Augie. What is it you want from me?"

"I don't want anything from you, Anlon, other than to talk and listen to your opinions."

"My opinions about what?"

Amato sighed. "I'd just like to pick your brain about some of the challenges that lie ahead, hear what you think. Can we leave it at that, for now?"

There was a pleading quality in Amato's voice that Anlon found hard to ignore. Combined with his weary expression, it reaffirmed Anlon's earlier perception that Amato primarily desired a sounding board rather than a technical consultation. Given the weighty matters the man faced, it was completely understandable. And so, even though he was frustrated by Amato's evasiveness, Anlon agreed to go. In so doing, however, he said, "I don't have a crystal ball, Augie. I'm not sure you should weigh my opinions too heavily. I'm just one voice."

"Yes, I know," said Amato, "but I value your voice more than most I know."

Before liftoff, Anlon was afforded the opportunity to change into a Gateway visitor's uniform, a white flight suit piped across the shoulders and down the legs by strips of silver. This was accompanied by a footed, long-john type undergarment and a pair of silver boots. He was surprised at the fit of all the attire and mentioned this to Amato, seated next to him.

As they were strapped into safety harnesses by male and female flight attendants, Amato said, "We scanned your dimensions when you first arrived at the spaceport." He craned his head to look at a young man across the aisle, two rows back. He was the only other passenger aboard. "My assistant, Mark Myers, took care of the rest."

Anlon noted Amato and Myers had changed into similarly styled uniforms, although theirs were black with yellow piping. Amato explained the different colored attire identified them as residents of Gateway's Martian colony, Meridiani Planum.

"We allow off-duty personnel to dress as they please," Amato said, "but when on duty, the uniforms reinforce to our people that we're all part of the same team with the same mission. I thought the younger colonists would rebel against it; you know how casual they tend to dress these days. But, to my surprise, they took to the uniforms quite happily. They seem to think it makes them astronauts, which I suppose they are."

Just as Amato finished speaking, Anlon noticed a stewardess standing in front of him. Having caught his attention, she handed Anlon a pair of heavy-duty headphones, complete with a microphone bar. "You'll need to wear this until the lighted sign indicates it's safe to remove them."

Anlon looked in the direction of her gaze. On both sides of the flight deck door were lighted signs. One was familiar, indicating seat belts were required. The other showed an image of headphones.

"The ascent into space is noisy," Amato said, accepting another pair of headphones from the steward. He layered them on his bald pate and waited for Anlon to do the same. As soon as Anlon's were affixed, Amato spoke to him through his microphone. "There will be g-forces during the ascent, but nothing like you see in the movies. The shuttle arcs into space quite gracefully thanks to the Suhkai gravity tech, but the engines do produce deafening decibels."

Anlon nodded and gave Amato a thumbs up. Inside, however, he was nauseous and about as nervous as he ever recalled. Through his headphones, the pilot indicated liftoff would take place in five minutes. Above the door to the flight deck, a countdown clock began ticking. He turned to Amato and nudged the microphone bar closer to his lips. "Suddenly, this doesn't feel like such a great idea."

Amato bellowed with laughter, his prodigious belly jiggling against his safety straps. It was the first time Anlon had seen anything close to joy from his host. "There's no shame in closing your eyes, Anlon. Just pretend the ascent's a roller coaster ride. Once we're in space, it'll all be different. We'll glide along so peacefully, you'd never guess we're traveling at millions of kilometers per hour."

Despite Amato's attempt to quell his uneasiness, Anlon's body began to shake. Then, when the countdown clock hit one minute, he closed his eyes and started cycling silent Hail Mary's interspersed with renditions of the Lord's Prayer.

Later, when they were in space, Anlon reflected on the launch experience. It had been turbulent but no worse than takeoffs from Reno on a windy day, and the pressure of the g-forces, while breathtaking at first, had abated quickly.

He wished he had been able to watch the ship's penetration into space, but the cabin had no windows. The only cue to indicate they were beyond Earth occurred when Anlon felt a brief sensation of weightlessness in his arms. Fascinated by the feeling, he released his grip on the arm rests and let his arms drift up. But they soon began to drift back down. Amato had evidently been observing him and told him the Suhkai gravity system was kicking in. Within another minute, Anlon felt no different than he did on Earth. Then the headphone sign turned off, and the flight stewards unbuckled and began to move about the cabin. Turning to Amato, he removed his headset and said, "What a surreal experience." Inside, he thought, *wow, Pebbles will be royally pissed when she finds out she missed a trip to Mars!*

Amato smiled and unbuckled his harness. As he rose from his seat, he said, "'Tis only the beginning, my friend. Wait until we get to Mars."

Following Amato's lead, Anlon unbuckled and stood, shifting his balance from leg to leg. "Amazing. I feel completely normal. How does the ship's gravity system work?"

"It's quite remarkable. You know the Suhkonium I mentioned earlier? The mystery element in the ship's fuselage everyone wonders about? Well, in its resting state, it's a solid. There's a coating of it underneath the top layer of the fuselage shell. When stimulated by sensors lining the underlying inner hull, Suhkonium turns into a liquid that can be manipulated." Amato looked up and arced his finger across the cabin. "Right now, that liquid is whipping around between the inner hull and the outer shell of the fuselage. As it spins, Suhkonium generates gravitational pressure."

"Where does the element come from?" asked Anlon, returning to his seat. "Where did the Suhkai get it?"

Amato sat back down as well. "Ah, now, *that* is truly amazing. You've heard of dark matter?"

"Yeah. It's the glue that holds galaxies together. Right?"

"*Theoretical glue*," corrected Amato with a wag of his finger. "No one on Earth has ever detected dark matter. We only suspect it exists because there is not enough observable mass in galaxies to prevent solar systems from drifting through space. But, as it turns out, the theory is partially accurate."

"Meaning what? Suhkonium is dark matter?"

"Yes…and no," said Amato. "In our typical human arrogance, we've labeled something we don't understand with a moniker that implies this theoretical glue is a solitary substance. But, surprise, surprise, the Suhkai tell us dark matter is a slurry made up of many components, including Suhkonium."

"I see. So, the Suhkai extract Suhkonium from the slurry?"

"Again, yes…and no. These slurries are evidently not homogenous mixtures, and they are in constant flux in response to the different forces around them. They are like swirling pools that expand and contract like rubber bands. As the slurries change shape and size, they shed and attract components. The Suhkai collect free-floating Suhkonium sloughed off from the slurries."

"That's fascinating."

"Indeed. We have so much to learn from the Suhkai, Anlon. So much." Amato turned his head and stared off into the distance. "I just wish they were more forthcoming about all they know."

The old man then turned back to face Anlon, cocking one eye into a squint. "They're cagey. They tell you only as much as they deem necessary. What I've just described to you took us nearly *two years* to pull out of them. It's an ongoing problem...particularly regarding R5."

"Ah, yes, the infamous R5."

"Infamous is an apt description," Amato said, "but I prefer bedeviling."

Believing discussion of the magnetar was fair game now that Amato had raised the subject, Anlon said, "Earlier, you said you were concerned about time. I take it the situation with R5 has worsened."

Amato sighed and stared blankly at the wall in front of him. "The truth is...I don't know. The most recent gamma data we've collected near Jupiter is concerning. There's no question about that. And the lead Suhkai scientist who remains in our solar system, a female Suhkai named Hexla, is adamant the data confirms R5 has awoken and is just as confident its rays will destroy Jupiter." Amato paused and turned to face Anlon. "But our computer models do not square with Hexla's conclusion. And when we question her, when we ask her why she is so sure of the outcome, when we press her for proof, when we show her our data, she clams up. And none of the other Suhkai will dispute her. It's maddening.

"Meanwhile, I'm caught in no man's land trying to urgently finish building the new arks in case R5 has awoken, while at the same time trying to avoid stirring a global panic over something that may prove benign if the Suhkai are wrong."

"Why do you think they clam up, Augie?"

Amato shook his head. "I have pondered that question for a very long time. If they were consistently evasive across all matters, I would say it's just part of their nature. But they are selectively cagey, Anlon. Part of me fears the reason they have been sly about R5 is that they know more about the characteristics of magnetars and/or gamma bursts than they have been willing to share with us."

He paused and leaned closer. "Keep this in mind, our scientists have only observed magnetars from a very great distance — tens of thousands, hundreds of thousands of light-years away — so we inherently know very little about how magnetars behave in general. And no one on Earth has ever witnessed a magnetar come to life before. Oh, some will claim they have discovered new magnetars, but there's a big difference between noticing one that hadn't been detected before and truly discovering a newly awoken one. Perhaps there is a cataclysmic flashpoint the star experiences when it awakes. Perhaps in its early life, a magnetar's beams are far more powerful than any our scientists have previously observed. I just don't know, and the Suhkai won't say anything."

The more Amato talked, the more frustration built within Anlon. "I take it Paul Morgan hasn't been successful prying any information out of the Suhkai in his fleet?"

With a snort, Amato said, "Oh, he's had it worse. Haula, the Suhkai commander accompanying the fleet, has been beating the drum to abandon the attempt to stabilize R5 since the early days of the mission. And Haula has been just as tight-lipped as Hexla, according to Paul. I'm sure he kept trying, but at this point, given the communications time lag, I fear if Paul did pry something more from Haula, the information will arrive too late to matter."

Sensing the line of discussion was upsetting them both, Anlon changed subjects to ask him more about the Martian colony. But Amato seemed disinterested. In fact, he abruptly stood and excused himself, indicating he needed to discuss some matters with his assistant Myers.

"We'll talk more later," he said as he walked aft. "And in a few hours, you'll see the colony in all its glory with your own eyes."

Thus, Anlon was left alone to ponder all they had talked about, and the two subjects still left unaddressed — *Why are we going to Mars? And what is it Augie wants to discuss with me?*

CHAPTER 4

Jenna Toffy began the recorded interview with a zinger. "Does it bother you when your critics say *Venture*'s mission is nothing more than an eleven-year orgy?"

While Dr. Dennis Pritchard considered the journalist's description crass, he could not deny its underlying accuracy. The settlers chosen to make the eleven-year trip to Tula were expected to aggressively reproduce during and after their journey to the distant planet.

"I'm sure it's titillating to some to portray it that way, Jenna, but, obviously, we at Gateway view *Venture*'s mission as far more meaningful."

The blond-haired Toffy leaned forward as she asked her next question. "Many people believe the mission will fail. They say the culture of rampant sex will ultimately lead to a breakdown of order aboard the ship."

She was only two questions into the interview, and Pritchard already regretted agreeing to the sit-down with Toffy. "You know, Jenna, I think that characterization is unfair to the brave women and men aboard *Venture*. They've given up their lives on Earth to colonize another planet. Reducing them to sex-crazed maniacs trivializes the sacrifices they've made to extend humanity's reach. Further—"

"You can't deny there have already been problems, Doctor."

Toffy's allusion was not unexpected. Pritchard had suspected a leak the moment the journalist requested the interview. In fact, his suspicion of a leak was the only reason he agreed to grant the interview. Given all the negativity about Gateway already circulating on Earth, the last thing the company and Augustus Amato needed was a scandal. And *this* scandal, if made public, would crater what little support Gateway had at the moment.

The last few transmissions received from *Venture* had included write-ups about an escalating series of incidents during the first year-and-a-half of the ship's journey to Tula. While most of the reports detailed garden variety disciplinary actions, two of them involved allegations of sex crimes. Another described a murder committed during a brawl over mating rotations. Combined, the reports painted a picture of growing unrest among the settlers.

And given the line of Toffy's initial questions, it appeared someone at Gateway had passed her copies of the reports or had relayed descriptions of them.

"Please turn off the cameras, Jenna."

"Why? Afraid of some sunlight on the dirty details of your little pleasure cruise?"

Pritchard stood. "I'm serious, Jenna. Cameras off, now, or the interview is over."

She held up a thick stack of paper. "These reports demand answers to some serious questions, Dr. Pritchard, especially given Gateway's intention to launch two more arks for Tula in the not-too-distant-future. I'm sorry if that makes you uncomfortable."

"Look, there are sensitive matters involved here. I'll answer your questions off the record, but not on camera."

"No deal, Doctor. Gateway's been way too secretive about *Venture*, just like you all have been about everything else. People should know the real deal, not your fairy tale about brave men and women. You're out recruiting for more colonists for future arks. They ought to know what they're in for."

"The situation is more complicated than you're making it out to be, Jenna. It's a mistake to jump to conclusions about what's happening on *Venture*. It's an even bigger mistake to share those reports with the world."

Toffy appeared unsympathetic and twisted her knife deeper.

"Jump to conclusions? You've had a murder and two rapes, and these reports were sent a year-and-a-half into their trip! *Venture's* now, what, three years in? God knows what kind of mayhem's taken place over the last year-and-a-half. And what else might go down during the rest of the trip? The truth, Dr. Pritchard, is you won't know before you launch *Vanguard* and *Valor*. Every day *Venture* flies further away, the longer it takes for you to receive their reports."

Toffy's brutal assessment was spot on. She wasn't spinning lies or sensationalizing the situation. How could Pritchard tell her they had expected troubles like the ones detailed in the reports? All one had to do was look at the incidents that happen on extended aircraft carrier missions to know that bottling up young men and women, under constant stress, in close quarters, for extended periods was a recipe for potential interpersonal conflicts of all kinds.

What made *Venture's* problems appear more sinister was the outright acknowledgment that sex between the passengers was not only encouraged, it was expected. This was the crux of Toffy's gibes. She, like many others on Earth, questioned why natural procreation was necessary. *"Why not primarily seed a colony on Tula through artificial insemination?"* these critics asked.

The answer, Pritchard had replied on many past occasions, was rooted in the experience of the Suhkai. In colonizing other worlds, they had discovered natural procreation more often produced successful, sustainable populations when compared to artificially seeded populations.

It had nothing to do with the children themselves but rather the behavioral changes that occurred among adult colonists during long space flights. Without a profound motivation to procreate, the Suhkai had found the desire to produce offspring diminished dramatically over time. So much so that, by the time adult colonists arrived at their new worlds, it was extremely difficult to rekindle interest in mating for the purpose of creating offspring. And such an outcome would be catastrophic in *Venture's* case.

With a trip of *Venture's* duration, eleven years, children born through artificial insemination during the trip would be too young to procreate, meaning the adult colonists would be needed to continue to build the population for a period of time. If their will to procreate had been lost during the trip, then the colony's chances of survival would be severely diminished.

But the way Pritchard saw it, even if procreation wasn't encouraged or expected, even if artificial insemination had been chosen to seed Tula's population, sexual relationship issues were bound to happen during the eleven-year flight. As they would when *Vanguard* and *Valor* eventually took off. As they would after the settlers from all three ships reached Tula. As they did every day on Earth.

"Look, Jenna, it's regrettable that some bad things have happened. I wish they hadn't, but *Venture* is its own little planet right now. They have to learn how to confront and overcome problems like these, and I believe they will. Remember, they were mostly strangers to each other when they left. And despite all the efforts we made to pick people with personalities we thought would mesh well together, you can't predict how people—"

Toffy started to interrupt him again, but Pritchard cut her off. "Let me finish."

She closed her mouth and sat back.

"As I was saying, you can't predict how they'll react to stress. And this kind of stress is unprecedented. If you go and make a big splash about these reports, and it turns out later that they worked through these incidents, you'll have poisoned the well for *Vanguard* and *Valor*."

Toffy looked off into the distance as if pondering Pritchard's points. *Is it an act for the cameras*, he wondered, *or did I get through to her?* Hoping for the latter, he risked adding further perspective.

"They were never going to stay a happy family, Jenna. No matter how much structure we provided, no matter what rules we set, sooner or later, they were going to realize they were on their own. And when that soaked in, they were bound to push back on the rules, they were bound to revert to tribalism."

Though her blank stare continued, Pritchard noticed a slight nod from Toffy. A moment later, she turned to look at her crew. "Stop recording." The wave of relief that swept through Pritchard must have been apparent to Toffy because she quickly said, "Don't relax yet, Doctor. We're not done here." She then asked her crew to step out of the room. "I'll come find you when we're ready to roll again."

While Pritchard and Toffy waited for the party of five to leave, they gazed at each other as if appraising adversaries. When the last of the WNN crew shut the door, Pritchard thanked Toffy.

She put her stack of paper aside and removed the microphone from the lapel of her blazer. The formality gone from her voice, she eased back in her chair and said, "Don't thank me yet, Dennis, I still have *lots* of questions."

Pritchard liked this side of Toffy. When the cameras were off, her manner was typically very different than her on-air persona. While he realized the change in her demeanor was intentional, an effort to put him at ease, he preferred the atmosphere of diminished antagonism.

"I'd expect nothing less, Jenna." Pritchard removed his own microphone and settled back in his chair as well. "Fire away."

"You guys really shit the bed, didn't you?"

Salty language was another aspect of her off-camera personality.

"What do you mean?" Pritchard asked.

"You rushed to launch *Venture*. If you had taken more time, been more thorough, selecting and training the settlers like you have been with *Valor* and *Vanguard*, the situation on *Venture* wouldn't be, as you put it, reverting to tribalism."

"Not true," said Pritchard.

"Oh, please, Dennis. I'm not a dope. I do my research. The approach you took with *Venture* is so different than what you're doing now with the other two ships, it begs the question, *why*?"

He started to answer, but Toffy talked over him. "And don't tell me it's different because *Vanguard* and *Valor* are still under construction, that you have the luxury of time. That's not an excuse for rushing *Venture*. Just because you had a ready-made ark at your disposal didn't justify slapping together 210 fertile, horny twenty-somethings and shooting them off into space with barely any training. It's not like you weren't warned of what might happen."

The arch of her eyebrow as she said warned gave Pritchard a pretty good idea where the leak about the incidents had originated…Doctor Albert Lyman. Warned was a frequent word used by Lyman…as in *I warned you this would happen.* As a member of the settler selection committee, the sociologist Lyman had fought against the composition of *Venture*'s passenger manifest. He also had warned against the twelve-week training program the passengers received. He had argued for a *twelve-month* program.

It wasn't as if Pritchard had ignored Lyman, but there simply hadn't been time to incorporate Lyman's ideas into the *Venture* process. Not so with *Vanguard* and *Valor.* Many of Lyman's recommendations were baked into the settler selection process and the training programs for both missions. And in Pritchard's estimation, Lyman's suggestions were paying off, leaving him puzzled why Lyman would have chosen this moment to air his grievances about *Venture* with Toffy.

Turning his attention back to her, Pritchard said, "We're learning as we go, Jenna. It's as simple as that."

"Bullshit." Toffy stuck out her hand and spread out her fingers. Wiggling her index finger, she said, "Let's start with the makeup of the passengers. You were advised to primarily select committed couples, but you chose singles instead." Her middle finger began to twitch. "You were urged to have the settlers live together on Earth for a while so that a bond developed in the community…and so troublemakers could be weeded out before launch. You didn't do that."

Jiggling her ring finger, Toffy continued, "You ignored the advice to let them self-select their own leaders and laws. Instead, you appointed a high council and gave them a rule book." Leaning forward again, she waggled her pinky. "Should I go on?"

"No, I think you've sufficiently made your point. We've done all of these things for *Vanguard* and *Valor,* but we didn't for *Venture.*"

His acknowledgment seemed to satisfy her. She smiled and lowered her hand to her lap. Then, her smile disappeared. "Why, Dennis?"

"There's no silver bullet answer, Jenna. Each of the examples you ticked off has different explanations."

"Fair enough. Let's go through each one separately. Start with the decision to exclude committed couples and send a frat-sorority mixer of singles instead."

"We're off the record, right?"

Toffy held up her hand as if taking an oath. "We're off the record."

"All right…*Venture*'s mission was and is a numbers game. Pure and simple. We chose singles because we wanted to create the maximum number of babies possible as quickly as possible. Specifically, babies with the broadest array of genetic diversity possible.

"You see, we know very little about what human characteristics are necessary for long-term survival on Tula, so a population with a broader genetic make-up improves the odds of quickly learning attributes that translate well to Tula's environment and those that don't.

"Going with a committed couples model failed on both criteria. *Venture* launched with 70 men and 140 women, giving us higher odds of producing more babies each pregnancy cycle as opposed to the yield possible from 105 committed couples. And the rotation of different mating pairs will yield greater genetic diversity than we would have achieved through committed couples."

At various points in his explanation, Toffy nodded as if she was in agreement. But when he finished speaking, she said, "You're discounting the value of creating bonded families. Some suggest survival on Tula will rely on family dynamics more than genetic diversity. Deeper familial bonds lead to greater cooperation. Greater cooperation leads to a stronger sense of community."

She was speaking right from the pages of Lyman's hymnbook. It was a debate that had raged for weeks during the selection process. Ultimately, however, the committee opted for a village model to build community, whereby children would be raised by groups of adults rather than exclusively by their biological parents.

This method was chosen to minimize the social stigmas bound to arise as the children reached reproductive maturity. In a small colony trying to establish a sustainable foothold in a new, potentially harsh environment, everyone had to be committed to procreation, even if it meant the rotation of mating pairs sometimes included biological parents mating with their offspring.

"We considered that point of view, Jenna, but decided on a different approach for *Venture*. I don't know what else to tell you."

"Do you think the public really gets that your different approach advocates incest?"

Pritchard rolled his eyes. This topic had been widely discussed and debated long before *Venture* launched. Toffy knew that. "The approach advocates survival by whatever means are necessary."

"In other words, you and your Gateway pals are pro-incest."

So much for the diminished antagonistic atmosphere, thought Pritchard. "No. We're pro-survival."

Pritchard then reminded Toffy the average age of the females aboard *Venture* was roughly twenty-four when the ship departed. By the time they reached Tula, they would average thirty-five. "Within fifteen years after that, many of them will reach the end of their child-bearing years. Accounting for the likelihoods that some will die before then, and others will lose the motivation to mate at some point, the burden of childbirth will shift to girls who were born during and after the trip to Tula."

As to the males, Pritchard pointed out the starting complement of seventy was a pretty thin number. "There's no guarantee their reproductive capabilities will outlast *Venture*'s women, and the men are just as at risk of premature death. Who knows what kinds of diseases and predators exist on Tula?

"There's also no way to know upfront how many boys and girls will be born, how many will be fertile and how many will survive long enough to reach reproductive maturity. With all these uncertainties, it would be foolish to declare certain mating pairs off-limits. Intra-family mating is a survival insurance policy to offset unexpected population losses and add to the colony's growth. That's how it should be viewed."

Pritchard had made the same arguments ad nauseam over the last four years. Judging from Toffy's yawns and fingernail-gazing, she had heard them all before. As soon as he finished speaking, she ceased admiring her nail polish and looked back at him. "Sorry, you can whitewash it any way you want. It's gross. A lot of people agree with me."

Pritchard desperately wanted to say, *survival ain't pretty, toots. Just ask Adam and Eve,* but he resisted the urge. "Well, the opinions of us Earthlings are moot at this point. Whether it happens or not will be up to the men and women on *Venture.*"

"Great, you left the pervy decision up to a ship full of sex addicts. Wonder how well that will turn out?"

Tired of Toffy's jabs about *Venture*'s passengers, Pritchard said, "I'd appreciate it if you stopped portraying *Venture* as Sodom and Gomorrah. Yes, we did prioritize selecting people with high-octane libidos, but that doesn't mean we didn't weigh their morals. You shouldn't minimize who they are as people."

He reminded her the applicant pool for *Venture*'s mission topped 20 million people, and that the average IQ of the 210 selected for the trip was north of 130. He pointed out that among them were astronauts, doctors, nurses, engineers and teachers, as well as artists, musicians, farmers and tradespeople. They had been picked from countries all over the globe, he told her, and represented many races and differing beliefs. "They're not irresponsible or immature. And they all understood what they were volunteering for and what was being asked of them. I trust them to make good decisions. You should too."

Toffy uttered a sarcastic laugh and lifted the stack of incident reports.

Pritchard removed his eyeglasses and rubbed the bridge of his nose. "They're not perfect, Jenna. No one is. We all have flaws, some hidden better than others. The fact that some of those flaws have shown themselves shouldn't surprise anyone. And don't kid yourself. Similar issues will arise on *Vanguard*, *Valor* and on *Tula*. Just like they do every day on Earth. Even among our best and brightest."

"That'll be your defense when news of these reports gets out? Shit happens?"

"Off the record, yes. On the record, no comment."

"Oh, that'll do wonders for Gateway's stock price."

Pritchard redonned his glasses and stood. "Anything else, Jenna? I've got a lot on my plate today."

Toffy remained seated, legs crossed, the stack of reports in her lap. "Why did you rush *Venture*'s launch?"

"A host of reasons. None of which make a hill of beans difference now." Pritchard motioned for her to leave. "Now, if you'll excuse me…"

She rose, buttoned her blazer and walked up to Pritchard. In her high heels, the WNN personality was a little taller than he was. She was close enough that Pritchard could see some of her wrinkles cracking through the thick makeup coating her face and neck. "Are you booting me off Mars, or do I still get a tour of *Vanguard* tomorrow?"

"Depends. Are you going to run a negative story on *Venture*?"

Toffy looked down and picked off a stray strand of hair from her blazer. As she let it drift toward the floor, she shrugged. "Not sure. Haven't made up my mind yet." Darting her eyes back at him, she winked. "The tour might help me come up with a different story idea."

Nothing like bribery, thought Pritchard. As much he liked the mental image of giving Toffy a swift kick onto a shuttle bound for Earth, making an enemy of her was not advisable. "So long as you sit on the *Venture* reports, the tour's still on."

Patting him on the shoulder, she said, "No promises, Dennis, but I'll think about it overnight. See you tomorrow."

Moments after she left, Toffy's crew scurried in to collect the rest of their gear. As they packed up, Pritchard returned to his desk and opened his email app. Perusing the headers of his unopened messages to rid his mind of the interview, he saw one had been sent by Col. Paul Morgan. The subject read: URGENT. OPEN IMMEDIATELY. YOUR EYES ONLY.

As soon as Dennis Pritchard finished viewing Morgan's video message, he stepped outside of his office and spoke to his assistant, Hal Barnes. "Do me a favor, Hal. Shoot Augie a note and tell him I'd like to speak with him as soon as he lands."

"Okay, no problem," said Barnes. "He'll want to know why. What should I tell him?"

"Just tell him to read his email. He'll understand." Pritchard began to close the door but then paused for a moment. "And no more visitors until Augie arrives, please. I'm working on something."

"All right. Got it."

With the door shut, Pritchard retraced his steps to his desk and sat down. He turned on his computer monitor and sighed as he stared at the frozen image of Paul Morgan on the screen. Still reeling from his earlier viewing of the message, Pritchard tapped out a command on his computer keyboard and turned away from the monitor. He couldn't bear to look at Morgan this time through the video message.

"Hello, Augie. Hello, Dennis," Morgan began, *"I'm afraid I have bad news to share."*

Pritchard closed his eyes. He could visualize the astronaut bowing his head and rubbing the back of his neck as he said, *"We're not going to make it in time."*

There was another pause as Morgan inhaled deeply and blew out a long puff of air. In his earlier viewing of this moment in the message, Pritchard had seen Morgan massage his forehead while he gathered his emotions. His voice quivered as he said, *"I'm so sorry."*

"Me, too, Skywalker," Pritchard mumbled.

"The bursts from R5 are now repeating," Morgan continued. *"Haula is convinced they indicate a full-scale eruption has already happened…which means you won't have much advance warning. By the time you receive this message, I suspect the bursts we reported weeks ago will have already spiked exponentially. If you haven't done so already, launch* Vanguard *and* Valor *as soon as you receive this."*

"Way ahead of you, my friend," Pritchard said.

He had already given the order to begin prepping the two arks for a "training mission" that was really a precautionary launch to move the ships and their scheduled passengers out of the solar system before Jupiter transited into R5's cone sixty-two days from now.

As Morgan continued to speak, Pritchard envisioned the once-dormant neutron star revolving once per second, ejecting lethal bursts of radiation from fissures on its surface. His vision shifted to an image of Jupiter arcing along its orbital path.

Of all the times for R5 to wake up, this is the worst. Pritchard buried his head in his hands. *If only the damned thing had waited just another six months to erupt, we might have had a fighting chance. Paul and Haula might have been able to stabilize it by then. Even if they hadn't been able to stabilize it, we still would have had twelve more years in front of us to come up with another solution and evacuate more people to Tula. But now, who knows?*

As it was, Jupiter was a scant sixty-two days from entering the leading edge of R5's gamma cone. And once inside, it was estimated Jupiter would be subject to twelve-days' worth of gamma bursts. Arriving once per second, this meant over a million bursts would hit Jupiter while in the cross-hairs of the cone.

If Jupiter somehow survived the first pass, it would transit the cone again in twelve years when it completed its next orbit. And so the cycle would repeat for the next *ten thousand years.* In total, Pritchard had estimated Jupiter would transit through R5's gamma cone over eight hundred times before the magnetar fell dormant again.

Can Jupiter possibly withstand such an onslaught? Pritchard wondered. If the Suhkai were to be believed, the answer was no. The cumulative effects of the photon barrage would eventually strip away Jupiter's atmosphere in an epic explosion, spewing deadly radiation and debris throughout the solar system.

Opening his eyes, he lifted his head and paused Morgan's message. He turned to look at the picture of his wife and daughter and thought of how long it had been since he had seen them. Reaching out, he touched their faces and said, "We'll just have to hope Jupiter is stronger than the Suhkai think."

CHAPTER 5

A shadow loomed over Doctor Dante Fulton as he knelt down to inspect the interface between *Valor*'s propulsion system and the flight deck's engine control station. Exasperated by the sudden darkness, the black aerospace engineer and former mission director of the *Rorschach Explorer* journey to Callisto called over his shoulder, "Zylun, you're blocking my light again."

Behind him, Dante heard a snort, and the shadow moved away. Turning his head, he thanked the tunic-clad Suhkai. "No one's blaming you. Okay? I'm sure it's a glitch with our electronics. But I can't sort it out with you constantly hovering over me."

Zylun's crest tubes vibrated, producing another snort, this one resonating longer and at a higher pitch. Dante turned back to continue his inspection, hiding his smile the best he could. It took time to learn the nuances of Suhkai snorts, but Dante was learning quickly. Zylun's high-pitched woof meant he was offended.

A small golden cyton glided into Dante's line of sight and began to flicker. Concurrently, Dante received a telepathic thought from Zylun. *"I can remedy the problem faster than you. Let me conduct the inspection."*

Dante shook his head and stared at the glowing ball of light. Among the many fascinating qualities of cytons was the ability to communicate telepathically with other beings possessing electromagnetic consciousnesses. They could project thoughts of their own, and they could also act as translators, as this one was doing for Zylun now. Focusing his mind, Dante conjured a reply to Zylun. *"If you do it, I learn nothing."*

Once again, the cyton began to flicker. Zylun snorted again and, in short order, Dante received his retort. *"I will store the solution in* Valor's *databank. Now, move aside."*

Dante stood and turned to face Zylun. At ten feet tall, with legs and arms as thick as elephant limbs and hands so large they could swallow Dante's head, Zylun was a prototypical Suhkai. He had the same gray-green scaly skin and a head that looked like a prehistoric dinosaur known as a Parasaur.

However, some people likened Suhkai heads to that of horses, and Dante could see that. They had a similar protruding snout set ahead of their big black eyes. But that's where the horse comparison ended for Dante. Horses didn't have scaly skin and alligator-like teeth. Horses also lacked the most prominent feature of Suhkai heads, the one that drew the Parasaur comparison, a crest that extended behind their skulls with tubes on each side.

These tubes served as speaking orifices for Suhkai, although Dante considered it more accurate to call the chambers radio transmitters. By vibrating the tubes, Suhkai projected radio waves of different frequencies rather than form speech patterns like humans.

Dante had been told that, with practice, Suhkai could emit human-like speech from the tubes, but he had not met any who had mastered the skill. Most were like Zylun, who grunted and snorted to convey short-hand messages when cytons were not available to translate their thoughts. Ironically, Zylun understood most of what Dante verbally said to him. Suhkai brains were apparently adept at interpreting audible sounds as well as radio waves.

He often wondered if that capability stemmed from their unique auditory system. Suhkai had no ears. At least, not on their heads. Instead, they had a sizeable mound in the center of their chests and rectangular pads on their forearms and thighs. These were sonar receptors that captured radio waves emitted by their crest tubes as well as sounds.

Aside from their alien-lizard-man appearance and unique characteristics, Suhkai were strikingly human in their movements, mannerisms, thought patterns, and emotions. As a result, Dante sometimes thought they were human. Especially Zylun.

In fact, Zylun often reminded Dante of Kiera Walsh. Just like her, Zylun could be stubborn, arrogant and impatient. Also, like Kiera, he was bold, protective and occasionally funny. And Zylun was just as mentally tireless as Kiera or as tireless as she had been at one time. So, Dante often resorted to interacting with Zylun as he had with Kiera.

Pointing down at the open panel beneath the engine control station, he said, "Look, Zylun, if you want to help, have your cyton give me some light by the circuit boards. Then you can hover behind me all you want."

Zylun shook his head, and the cyton drifted down into the open panel. Before Dante could react, a telepathic vision formed in his head. It was a 3D image of a section of the circuit board at exceptionally close range. Quickly, the view shifted to another part of the board and then a third.

Dante glared at Zylun. The blasted alien had ignored him and was using the cyton to search for the faulty connection while transmitting the images of his inspection. The breech of decorum was made all the more irritating by the shit-eating grin on Zylun's face. Once again, Dante was reminded of Kiera.

Just as he began to tell off Zylun, the alien interrupted. *"Time is of the essence, is it not?"*

As frustrating as Dante found it to agree with Zylun, he conceded his point. Two days prior, *Valor* and its sister ship, *Vanguard*, had been ordered to prep for a so-called "training exercise" in sixty-two Earth days. Neither ark would be fully outfitted by then, but they would launch anyway, warts and all. However, Dante, Zylun and their team of engineers and technicians continued to work around the clock. They wanted to shrink the number of warts as much as possible before launching.

"All right, Zylun, you win. Just make sure you catalog your repairs in the databank."

"It will be done."

"I'm going to check on Habitat B. I'll see you later."

Zylun saluted and turned back to the engine control console. The gesture of respect would have been more meaningful to Dante if the alien still hadn't been grinning as he saluted.

On the walk from the flight deck to the forward elevator bank, Dante ran through a mental punch list of open items that had to be completed before the launch of the training mission. Most of them were related to the build-out of the living spaces for *Valor*'s ultimate mission — the journey to Tula.

The ship's superstructure and core systems had been built and tested months ago, but the construction of the passenger habitats and support facilities had lagged behind. A good part of the delay had been caused by the need to re-engineer many of the components the Suhkai had originally built into *Venture*, the ark already on its way to Tula. The rest of the delay was due to logistical priorities. The buildout of the Meridiani Planum colony had taken precedence over constructing the living quarters aboard *Valor* and *Vanguard*.

Dante was still amazed at how much Gateway and its contractors had accomplished in four years. The effort to build the two arks and the Meridiani Planum colony was analogous to building two aircraft carriers and a domed football stadium…on Mars…simultaneously.

Pausing his thoughts at the elevator bank, Dante spoke to the touchpad mounted on the wall. "Deck 6." Moments later, one of the doors slid open and he stepped inside the elevator's tubular glass car. Just like the hallways and rooms on many decks of the ship, the car was huge. It had to be to accommodate both humans and the much larger Suhkai.

During the descent, Dante returned to thoughts of the massive undertaking made possible by the convergence of money, might and minds. The money, hundreds of billions of dollars, had been raised by Augustus Amato, the co-founder and controlling shareholder of Gateway Ventures.

The might had been partially provided by human sub-contractors from all over the globe, firms eager to participate in Gateway's ambitious endeavors in space. The rest had come from the Suhkai in the form of their spacecraft. For four years, humans trained by Zylun had been shuttling workers and material between Earth and Mars in their cruisers. As Dante recalled it, during the peak of construction, the Suhkai had flown nearly fifty round-trip shuttle flights daily. That was in addition to other Suhkai cruisers ferrying Earthlings to Callisto and Dione.

Suhkai brainpower had also been a significant component of their contribution. Zylun and his cohorts had freely collaborated with Gateway's project teams, providing access to their technology and their vast reservoir of knowledge and experience building deep-space vehicles and creating otherworld colonies.

An intercom announced the elevator's arrival at Deck 6, stirring Dante from his reflections. As the door opened, he removed his eyeglasses and slid them into the open chest pocket of his black-and-gold flight suit. The glasses would steam up as soon as he entered Habitat B, rendering them useless until they adjusted to the climate.

Outside of the habitats, the temperature on *Valor* was kept at a dry and chilly sixty-four degrees to accommodate the Suhkai aboard the ship. It took some getting used to, but Dante had adapted. Inside the habitats, however, the atmosphere was kept at a balmy and humid eighty-five… the average temperature colonists could expect in the area where Avery Lockett and Christine Baker had settled on Tula.

Dante approached the entrance to Habitat B and said, "Open airlock." Once inside the sealed chamber, Dante closed his eyes and said, "Enter habitat." As soon as the door on the far side of the airlock opened, a blast of humid air invaded the chamber, coating Dante's face with a fine mist.

Accompanying the air blast was an immediate chorus of construction sounds. Dante could hear the engines of trucks, cranes and tractors, plus the pounding of hammers and shrill sizzle of circular saws.

He opened his eyes and strode into the cavernous space. Though the entry to Habitat B was on Deck 6, it was actually two decks in height, its ceiling sixty feet from the floor. At three hundred feet wide and nine hundred feet long, the habitat was over six acres in size.

Right now, it looked like a half-finished cul-de-sac. It would look like a tropical paradise when it was completed, with sixteen 3,000 square foot houses set around the perimeter and two park-like open spaces. Separated by dense, rainforest-like vegetation, each home would initially house only three people, a mating trio comprised of two women and one man. However, the homes could accommodate up to eight people comfortably. They would need that extra space as *Vanguard*'s population grew during the flight to Tula.

In total, there would be three habitats when construction was complete. However, for the training mission, only Habitat A and B would be available. There was not enough time to build out Habitat C.

To many spacecraft designers on Earth, the habitats seemed an inefficient use of space. But the Suhkai considered them essential to maintaining mental and emotional stability during long-haul space travel. Dante agreed with them. Eleven years in outer space equated to a little over 4,000 days. He could not imagine spending that time confined in 10x10 cabins.

As Dante walked down the dirt path in the center of the cul-de-sac, he retrieved his glasses and put them on. Ahead, Habitat B's foreman, Charlie Zimmer, exited one of the half-built homes. Zimmer waved to him and yelled something, but Dante couldn't hear him over the construction sounds. His glasses began to fog as they walked toward each other. He pulled them off and wiped the lenses on the sleeve of his uniform. When Zimmer was within a few feet, Dante slid the glasses back on and said, "How's it going, Charlie?"

With a scowl on his face, Zimmer said, "Where's your hard hat, man?"

Dante cringed as he came to a halt. "Gah, sorry about that."

"Don't apologize to me. It's your noggin at risk, not mine."

The retort was one Dante had heard many times before. He routinely forgot his hard hat, and Zimmer routinely made him pay for it. Pointing to a rack of hard hats by the airlock entrance, he said, "Come on, let's get you a spare. Can't have the ship's captain setting a bad example for the rest of the fellas."

As Zimmer marched alongside him, several of the workers grinned at him, but it didn't bother him. He smiled back at the workers and waved. The burly foreman beside Dante must have noticed the interaction with his crew. He leaned closer to Dante and said, "It does my people good to see brass treated just like them."

Dante nodded and switched subjects. "How did they take the news about the pushed-up deadline?"

Zimmer shrugged. "Some of them bitched and moaned, they're homesick, but most were okay. I told them they'll never see overtime premiums like this again, so gobble it up while you can." He swept his arm toward the beehive of activity. "Most of these guys and gals will make more in the next sixty-two days than they'll earn in two years on Earth."

As Dante picked out a hard hat, he thought, *let's hope they live long enough to enjoy it.* Then, after wedging the helmet onto his head, he turned to Zimmer. "Feeling good about hitting the new deadline?"

"So long as there are no supply foul-ups, we'll make it. Might not look as pretty as A, but we can put the spit and polish on B when you get back."

"Music to my ears, Charlie." Dante patted him on the shoulder. "Let me know if you need me to lean on Gateway logistics about supplies."

"Thanks, we're good right now, but you'll be the first to know if we hit a snag."

Dante didn't doubt it. Zimmer was not shy about raising red flags. Hell, he wasn't shy about anything, which reminded Dante of the second reason for his visit. "We have a VIP tour tomorrow. I'd like to show her A and B, and I'd like you to join us."

The man's jowls fell. "Oh, for Christ's sakes, Dante. Not another dog and pony show. I've got too much shit to do."

"You don't have to lead the tour. Just be there to answer any questions I can't handle."

Dante paused as Zimmer looked away and grumbled inaudibly. Knowing it was better to just get all the pain out at once, Dante said, "Although, she may want to interview you…on camera."

Zimmer's head snapped around. "On camera? Who is this VIP?"

"Jenna Toffy from WNN."

In the span of a second, Zimmer's facial expression changed from one of suspicion to one of disgust. "Nuh-uh. No way. I wouldn't talk to that bitch even if she had my balls in a vise."

Visualizing Toffy tightening a vise on the burly New Yorker's crotch caused Dante to laugh, which angered Zimmer even more. "I'm not kidding, Dante. She's all about gotchas, and I ain't gonna be made a fool of."

Dante didn't think Toffy was that bad, but he understood Zimmer's reaction. She did have a reputation for trapping her interview subjects but, most of the time, they deserved it. "Okay, okay. No interviews, but I still want you there."

As Zimmer began to protest further, Dante cut him off. "It's an order, Charlie, not a request." While on *Valor*, Zimmer and everyone else were part of Dante's crew and subject to his authority. "Be at A's airlock at 0900 tomorrow. I'll make sure she keeps her hands off your balls."

Zimmer's glare immediately softened as Dante delivered his quip. Bellowing with laughter, he said, "All right, Captain. I don't like it one bit, but I'll be there."

Clapping him on the shoulder, Dante said, "Good man, Charlie. See you tomorrow." He removed the spare hard hat and tapped it. "Bring a bag of these with you. I don't know how big her entourage will be, but I'm guessing five or six. I'll remember to bring my own. Promise."

The pledge seemed to amuse Zimmer. When he replied, his voice was thick with sarcasm, "Uh-huh…I'll throw in an extra one just in case. Now, get out of here and let me get back to work."

Abruptly, he turned and marched away. Dante waved goodbye at his retreating back and replaced the hard hat on the shelf. As he entered the airlock, he thought of Zimmer's gruff departure. *Why does everyone remind me of Kiera?*

EINSTEIN GAMMA OBSERVATORY CONTROL CENTER
NASA'S JET PROPULSION LABORATORY
PASADENA, CALIFORNIA, USA

Project manager Ed Chen had a bad feeling about the data in front of him. "Have you ever seen gamma readings like this?"

He turned to look at the hunched over Sergei Kolov sitting next to him. The seven-foot-tall analyst was squinting at Chen's computer screen. In a thick Russian accent, Kolov said, "Never. Repeaters are consistent. They pulse in rhythm."

Chen agreed. While he did not have as much experience observing magnetars as Kolov, he was very familiar with X-ray pulsars. Both were neutron stars that ejected bursts of radiation at relatively precise intervals. The primary difference between the two was the dominant form of ejected radiation. Magnetars primarily ejected gamma rays instead of X-rays.

"It's got to be interference, don't you think?" Chen said. "Something messing with our scopes?"

Kolov sat back and ran his fingers through his mop of curly hair. "That's the only explanation that makes sense, but I have never seen interference like this before."

"Me neither. You think Gateway might be jamming our feed?"

"Possibly. But it could also be Roscosmos or CSNA."

Chen disagreed with Kolov. He couldn't see any motivation for the Russians or Chinese to interfere with NASA's Einstein Gamma Observatory. Gateway Ventures, on the other hand, had plenty of reason. At the moment, they held a monopoly on anything to do with space, and they had never warmed to NASA's launching of EGO nor the gamma observatories deployed by Roscosmos and CSNA.

In fact, as Chen recalled it, Gateway's co-founder, Augustus Amato, had seemed downright offended by the launches. Gateway had its own gamma observatory, Amato had said, and he pledged to share the observatory's data. No one at NASA had been comfortable with that arrangement given the stakes involved, nor had any other space agencies.

Thus far, Gateway had been faithful to Amato's pledge, but the data they shared lagged several days behind the "live" readings captured by EGO.

Pushing back from his desk, Chen turned to Kolov. "We should contact Helen Brock. Ask her if she's noticed the same anomalies."

Doctor Helen Brock had been a long-time NASA employee, finishing her career there as chief administrator. But she had since gone over to the "dark side" as far as Chen was concerned. She was now Gateway's chief science officer and was stationed on Mars.

"Ha! She won't tell us shit," Kolov said.

"I don't know about that, Sergei. I think she might. Helen's not as butt tight as most of Gateway's people."

Hands behind his head, Kolov stretched out his long legs and smirked. "She is when it pertains to R5."

Chen had to admit Kolov was right about Brock and R5. Since joining Gateway, she had rarely commented or entertained questions about R5. But as Chen saw it, until a month ago when the gamma bursts started, she hadn't had much reason to say more than, "we have no update on R5. The magnetar remains dormant. We continue to scan for signs of activity."

Given that it appeared the magnetar was no longer dormant, Chen knew Brock would have to discuss it sooner rather than later. Four years ago, Gateway had told the world the magnetar might pose a mortal threat to the solar system if and when it "awoke." While most scientists still considered such a catastrophe impossible, Gateway didn't. As such, Chen didn't see any way Brock could remain silent now that NASA was aware of the activity from R5. He said as much to Kolov, who begrudgingly agreed.

"I guess you are right," Kolov said, "but I would not get my hopes up. I doubt you will get more than a few words from her."

"Well, a few words is better than nothing. Washington's waiting on us for an explanation, and the only one we have is interference. And you know they'll press us for alternative explanations, and the best we'll be able to say is…we have no fricking idea."

That was the crux of Chen's bad feeling. If interference was not the source of the anomalous data, then R5 was exhibiting unusual behavior compared to other magnetars, and he could not explain why.

Instead of strobing like a typical magnetar, pulsing out gamma rays once per second, the rays from R5 were intermittently scattering. The troubling part about the bizarre behavior was what happened after each round of scattering. Inexplicably, the photons in the rays would concentrate for a while, suddenly disperse, and then just as suddenly reconcentrate. This was counter to how gamma bursts traveled through space. Unless some other force intervened, there was no way a dispersed beam could reconcentrate.

But that was what the data seemed to suggest was happening sporadically with R5's photons. It was as if there were an aperture controlling the breadth of the gamma cone, flexing in and out at random. Chen knew of no force that could exert such an effect on photons. *If anyone does, it's someone at Gateway or their Suhkai buddies.* Turning to compose a message to Brock, Chen finished his thought. *That's another good reason to ping Helen.*

HELEN BROCK'S OFFICE
MERIDIANI PLANUM COLONY, MARS

It was times like these that angered Helen Brock the most. When a crisis arose, the first few hours were nothing but an unorganized melee of messages flowing back and forth between people on Mars, Earth, Callisto and Dione.

On the current date, transmitted radio messages between Mars and Earth took nineteen minutes to travel through space. Whereas, between Mars and Callisto, the transmission time was fifty-three minutes. And between Mars and Dione, the time lag spanned ninety-four minutes.

And people in those various locations were not just communicating with Brock on Mars. Message traffic was flowing in every conceivable direction between the four bodies, as well as between multiple parties located on the same planet or moon. The sheer amount of crosstalk was overwhelming.

Such was the situation Brock found herself in now. Gateway's telescope array positioned near Jupiter had detected three significant changes in R5's gamma burst behavior that commenced in quick succession.

The first of the changes was a dramatic increase in the photon concentration in the bursts. While this had been somewhat expected if the magnetar had truly awoken, the spike in photons was far more significant than predicted by any of Gateway's computer models.

Not long after the spike, the bursts settled into a consistent repeating pattern, passing across the telescope array's field of vision every 0.87 seconds. Up until this change, they had been arriving at inconsistent, albeit increasingly narrowing, intervals. The establishment of a consistent repeating pattern combined with the spike in photon concentration were clear signs R5 was now officially an active magnetar.

Alone, these two developments were significant enough to raise alarms, but then came the last of the new behaviors. The size of R5's gamma cone began to expand and shrink in anomalous surges, a seemingly impossible action.

Even more baffling than the flexing in and out of R5's gamma cone were further spikes in photon concentration that accompanied each surge. When the cone shrank, the photons surged. When the cone expanded, the gamma radiation concentration dropped.

If Brock's telescope team on Callisto had been the only ones to notice the changes, she might have considered it a malfunction of the array. But soon after, Brock was besieged by messages from various parties on Earth inquiring if Gateway had detected R5's changed behaviors.

One of those messages had come from Ed Chen at NASA. In it, he also vaguely questioned whether Gateway was interfering with the signals from the space agency's EGO telescope array. Similar messages followed from Roscosmos and CSNA.

Before long, she started receiving copies of messages going back and forth between astronomers at various institutions with access to NASA's EGO data. The astronomers were already postulating theories about the new R5 data.

Seeking to quell as much of the madness as possible, as quickly as possible, Brock began replying to the space agency messages with a largely boilerplate response, such as the one she had just finished typing to Ed Chen at NASA.

"Ed, I can assure you Gateway is NOT jamming nor otherwise interfering with EGO nor any other NASA asset. As to your question about R5's recent burst data, we are currently analyzing data from our observatory and will have no further comment until our analysis is complete. Regards, Helen."

As soon as she sent off similar messages to the other space agencies, Brock leaned toward her open office door and called for her assistant, Mary Evans. "Mary, have you tracked down Hexla yet?"

Seconds later, the frazzled Evans appeared in the doorway. Just like Helen, she was clad in one of Gateway's black-and-gold uniforms.

"Not yet," Evans said. "She's on Dione, I know that much, but she hasn't responded to my messages yet."

"Dione? What the hell is she doing on Dione?"

"I don't know."

Hexla's lab was intentionally stationed on Callisto on a floor above the offices of the R5 telescope team. Her absence at a time like this was vexing, especially given the communications time lag between Dione and Mars was double the lag between Callisto and Mars. Brock needed Hexla to help analyze and interpret the telescope data.

"Okay," Brock said, "Book me a shuttle to Dione, then send Hexla another message. Tell her to stay put until I arrive, and tell her to review the latest R5 telescope data as soon as she gets it." Brock stood and began to shove items into her backpack-styled briefcase. "I'll be back in thirty minutes. I need to touch base with Dennis and pack." Evans nodded and offered to pack an overnight bag for her, but Brock declined. "The walk will give me a chance to clear my head."

Evans stepped aside and waited for Brock to exit the office first. "Roger that. I'll shoot you a text when the shuttle's ready."

DENNIS PRITCHARD'S OFFICE
MERIDIANI PLANUM COLONY, MARS

Sighing deeply, Augustus Amato looked at his friend and colleague Dennis Pritchard. The two were seated in armchairs in Pritchard's office and had just finished another replay of Paul Morgan's video message.

"I had sincerely hoped and prayed this moment would never come," Amato said. "But, now that it has, our path ahead is clear."

The trim, bookish-looking Pritchard nodded and said, "Augie, before we announce anything, I think we should consider activating the first steps of the *Sanctuary Plan*. I've already moved up the date for the arks' training mission to early September, but I think we should go farther than that. At a minimum, we should start evacuating Callisto."

The suggestion caused a spike of anxiety inside Amato, but Pritchard was right. Waiting until the last second to evacuate people, ships and critical equipment from Callisto was not advisable. "I suppose that's the prudent thing to do, but I worry news of the pull-out will trigger a panic on Earth."

"I think we can manage it so long as we stage the evacuation over a couple of weeks," Pritchard said. "The more orderly it appears, the less likely anyone will freak out." He paused then continued, "I also think we ought to immediately suspend departures of all tourist shuttles from Mayaguana until Jupiter safely passes through R5's cone. I realize that will be more controversial, given the media will make a big deal about it. Still, I think the average person will understand we don't want to risk endangering civilians."

Amato only half-heard Pritchard's answer. His mind at the moment was 15 trillion kilometers away, thinking of Paul Morgan and his crew of thirty-five. *What must they be thinking now?* Amato wondered. But that was the wrong question, he realized. Morgan's message had been transmitted a year-and-a-half ago. Whatever thoughts and emotions Morgan and his crew had felt at the moment they realized their mission had failed were long in the past.

What became of them? Amato wondered. *Where are they now?* These questions, and others, raced through his mind. Suddenly, he became melancholy thinking of Morgan and how uncharacteristically distraught he had seemed in his video message and how adamant he had been about launching the arks. *He must have known more than he shared.*

Shaking from his thoughts, Amato interrupted Pritchard as the latter was discussing what to do with the tourists now on Mars, Callisto and Dione. "Enact Sanctuary, Dennis. *All of it.* Do it *now*. Before it's too late."

Before the stunned Pritchard could react to Amato's outburst, a loud knock caused both men to turn toward Pritchard's office door just as it opened. The moment Amato saw the look on Helen Brock's face, he knew it was already too late.

CHAPTER 6

CONSULTATION CHAMBER ABOARD THE SUHKAI
SPACECRAFT *FLASH*, FLAGSHIP OF COMMANDER HAULA
POSITION: 1.5 LIGHT-YEARS FROM EARTH,
0.5 LIGHT-YEARS FROM MAGNETAR SGR-RE5
DECEMBER 3, 2021
(1.5 YEARS BEFORE THE EVENTS IN CHAPTERS 1-5)

In the center of the darkened chamber, the Suhkai alien named Haula knelt before the cyton queen and projected a telepathic greeting. *"Hail, seeder, what news do your scouts bring?"*

The cyton queen, a pulsing blue ball of electromagnetic energy, floated closer to Haula's dinosaur-like head and transmitted her telepathic reply. *"It has begun."*

"Are you certain?" Haula asked.

Light flickered inside the hovering queen as she answered. *"Yes. The star has awoken."*

Haula snorted through the tubes lining the long crest atop his head and conveyed two new thoughts. *"Then we have failed. We are too far away to stabilize it."*

"Yes. Too far."

"Do the humans know?"

The queen began to flicker again. *"They do not."*

"I am not surprised. The humans use the wrong sensors." The ten-foot-tall Haula stood and spread out his two arms. They were as thick as tree trunks and were capped by enormous six-fingered hands. *"Rise, seeder, and hear my plea."*

The cyton floated up and glided closer to Haula's face, her blue light reflecting off the black orbs of the Suhkai commander's eyes. *"No plea is necessary, Haula. I know your thoughts already."*

"Then, what say you? Are we released from our service to the humans?"

Glowing brighter, the queen replied without delay. *"No."*

Haula lowered his arms and stepped back. *"But, seeder, we have done all we can do for them. There is no stopping what will come. We are too few. The distance to cover is too great."*

"Still, you must try."

"Why? There is no hope now. You know this."

"You forget I know your mind, Haula. Hope remains if you will accept the cost."

Haula glared at the queen and swept his arm as if to swat the cyton away. *"Leave my mind at once."*

The blue ball throbbed with light and withdrew several feet away. After that, there was a several-minute stretch of silence between the two aliens. Haula, eyes closed, stood motionless, seemingly deep in thought. The cyton queen, bobbing up and down in the air, pulsed every so often as if patiently marking the time of her wait.

At last, Haula opened his eyes and reengaged the queen. *"I will inform Skywalker the star has awoken. I will encourage him to divert his ships to Tula. If he agrees, we will escort him and his companions there."*

Amid a flurry of blue flickers, the queen responded. *"And if he disagrees? What then?"*

Haula turned to leave the chamber and imparted a final thought. *"If you know my mind, seeder, then you already know the answer."*

CHAPTER 7

Bleary-eyed, Col. Paul "Skywalker" Morgan sipped coffee and willed caffeine to chase away the fog clouding his mind. Exchanging glances with the two women standing before him, Morgan said, "Okay, let's hear it. What's happened?"

His gaze locked on Doctor Reshma Desai, the NASA physicist on loan to Gateway for the R5 mission. It had been Desai who had earlier entered his cabin to wake him. Dressed in her black and gold Gateway uniform, Desai did not answer him. Instead, she looked toward her superior, Doctor Mey Wan, *Resolute*'s chief science officer and one of China's most decorated astronauts. Like Desai, the uniformed Wan displayed a pensive expression.

"Christ, is it that bad, Mey?" Morgan asked.

After a pause, Wan said, "I'm not sure."

Morgan grabbed his pounding forehead and looked down at his rumpled T-shirt and shorts. They had summoned him so urgently, he hadn't bothered changing out of his sleeping clothes. "Well, if you're not sure, why the hell was I woken?"

"You have a visitor." Wan turned her head in the direction of the closed laboratory hatch. "Haula is here. He is in the ready room."

Puzzled, Morgan rubbed his head and sipped more coffee. Visits by Haula to *Resolute* were infrequent but not unheard of, so he was surprised to see Wan and Desai so rattled. Something more had to be afoot. Ceasing his head massage, Morgan looked at Wan. "Level with me, Mey. What else has happened?"

The astrophysicist uttered a long sigh and said, "The Suhkai have slowed their ships, Paul. They've instructed our ships to do the same."

Morgan frowned. "Did they say why?"

Wan shook her head, then addressed Desai. "Tell him the rest, Reshma."

The junior officer turned to Morgan. "We've detected new radiation bursts from R5, Colonel."

"The bursts are faint and sporadic," Desai continued, "but appear to be growing in intensity and frequency."

"Yeah, so?" groused Morgan. "R5's been burping and farting radiation off and on for weeks."

Wan interjected. "The bursts have begun to repeat, Paul."

"What? Are you sure?"

"Yes, the interval is erratic, but there's no mistaking a repeating pattern in the data."

As Wan finished speaking, Morgan set down his coffee cup on the counter of the computer console beside him. Lowering his head, he whispered, "Damn."

The news of *repeating* gamma bursts, combined with Haula's order to slow the fleet and the alien's unannounced visit to *Resolute*, meant Haula believed R5 had finally awoken. Morgan closed his eyes and envisioned the dark neutron star beginning to spin, shooting out beams of gamma rays from fissures on its surface. Caught in a momentary haze of despair, his vision shifted to the destruction of Jupiter and Earth. *We're too late.*

"I know it sounds bad," Wan said, "but we should not jump to conclusions. The repeats might just be foreshocks of a starquake."

Morgan stared at her, scowling with skepticism.

Wan crossed her arms and widened her stance. "Okay, fine. They're not foreshocks. But the repeats have not yet formed a consistent pattern. Until they do, we should not assume the magnetar has fully awoken. It may restabilize on its own and fall dormant again. If it does, we can still reach it in time."

"Uh-huh," said Morgan. "Then why have Haula's ships slowed? Why is he here?"

Both women looked away. Wan stared down at the floor while Desai stared blankly at the lab's wall of computer monitors.

"I'll tell you why," Morgan continued, "Haula's thrown in the towel. He's expecting us to do the same."

Peering up at him, the forty-six-year-old Wan scooped away strands of black and gray hair obscuring her right eye. "It's premature, Paul. I don't think we should give up yet. Not until we have a read on the photon concentration and model out gamma cone projections. The Suhkai might be wrong about the lethality of R5's bursts."

Morgan wanted to say, *you're grasping at straws*, but he didn't. Deep inside, he shared Wan's defiant attitude. They had come too far to give up now. As that sentiment began to overwhelm his pessimism, Morgan's anger began to build as well. *Who in the hell does Haula think he is? Ordering my ships to slow down. Without my consent, no less. Unacceptable. Completely unacceptable.*

Refocusing his attention on Wan, he said, "You're right, Mey. Let's launch a probe array ASAP. We need more definitive photon data before we make any decisions."

"Roger that. Consider it done."

"Good. As soon as you have enough data, I want to see cone scenarios." Morgan lifted his coffee cup and started walking toward the hatch. From behind, Wan asked, "What about Haula's order to slow the fleet?"

"I'm about to take care of that." Morgan stopped by the hatch and used the intercom to contact the flight deck. Lieutenant Lucas Bekker, *Resolute*'s communications officer, answered. "Bekker, Col. Morgan here. Belay Haula's order to slow down. Maintain *Resolute*'s course and speed toward R5. Pass the word onto *Ranger* and *Renown* to do the same."

After Bekker acknowledged his command, Morgan turned back to Wan and Desai. "Now, if you'll excuse me, I need to finish waking my ass up before I talk with Haula."

Major Eamon Douglas cursed and swiveled his pilot's seat to look at his co-pilot, Captain Jaime Silva. "Bloody hell! I told you he'd countermand Haula's order!"

"Take it easy, Eamon. I'm sure he'll come around as soon as Haula talks to him."

The relaxed tone of the Brazilian's reply annoyed Douglas. He glared at Silva and said, "Fat chance of that, mate. The old codger's as stubborn as they come."

Stirred by the sound of approaching footsteps, Douglas swiveled his seat further around and caught sight of Doctor Roksana Baronova passing through the flight deck hatchway. He called out to the Roscosmos physician. "You won't believe it, Roxy. Our daft leader has just ordered us to keep on course for R5 even though it's bloody evident it's a waste of time."

Baronova scowled at him and closed the hatch. "Lower your voice, Eamon, and calm down." Continuing on in her thick Russian accent, she said, "It is a delay, nothing more."

"Yeah, well, I'm tired of delays," Douglas groused. "We've wasted weeks waiting for him to see the light. It's enough to drive a bloke mad."

Baronova shrugged as she walked toward him. "He does not want to give up yet. Can you fault him for that?"

"You're damned right I can. Our mission is over. R5 is a full-fledged magnetar now, and there's nothing we can do about it. Believing otherwise is bonkers."

"Agreed," said Silva, "but Skywalker calls the shots, and he says fly on."

Douglas jutted out his chin. "I say it's high time for someone else to call the shots." He paused to assess Silva's and Baronova's reaction to his declaration and grew angry when both remained silent. "I know you agree with me, even if you won't say it."

Baronova crossed her arms below her chest and leaned her hip against the side of Silva's seat. "You are too rash, Eamon. The colonel may be stubborn, but he is not stupid. He will realize the futility of continuing on soon enough."

"I'm with Roxy," Silva said. "I think we should be patient. Another day or two of data from R5 should tip him in the right direction."

Douglas shook his head. "You're kidding yourselves. Even if he does finally abort the mission, he's still going to be a problem. He'll want to turn back for Earth in the hope that Haula's wrong about R5. He'll never agree to head for Tula."

"You don't know that," Baronova said.

Douglas' mouth dropped open. "How can you say that with a straight face? The old goat's never once considered Tula a viable option. Not once. Every single time we've brought it up, he's shut us down. He's done the same to Haula. Believe you me, the only way we have any chance of heading for Tula is if we get Morgan out of the way. And the sooner we do it, the better. We already know Haula will support us."

Baronova sighed and left Silva's side. Crouching down next to Douglas, she took hold of his hand and gently squeezed it. "Please, Eamon, be patient. Let us wait to see how events unfold over the next few days."

Pulling his hand away from hers, Douglas said, "Why? Why waste more bloody time, Roksana? You know he'll never see it our way. He's damn near seventy. And now he's hooked on *neefra*. Whether old age gets him or neefra does, he knows he won't survive the trip to Tula. Therefore, he's got no vested interest to try."

Speaking in a soothing tone, she retook his hand, "I understand. I do. Like you, I do not wish to waste more time, but a few more days is a small sacrifice. It is better for all of us if we allow Col. Morgan to come to his senses on his own rather than force the outcome we want."

Douglas sighed and lowered his head. "All right, but I'm telling you he won't come to his senses. He's a cowboy through and through. He'd rather go out with guns blazing than admit defeat."

ABOARD GATEWAY COALITION FLEET SPACECRAFT *RESOLUTE*

Morgan's first stop after leaving the science lab was *Resolute*'s crew bathroom. There, he splashed cold water on his face to help rid himself of the numbing effects of neefra, the Suhkai sleep potion he had taken only hours ago.

Peering at his reflection in the mirror above the sink, Morgan appraised the morass of gray-white hair on his head and the thick layer of stubble on his gaunt, wrinkled face. "Good God, man, you look like a strung-out junkie."

He ducked his head over the sink and splashed more handfuls of water onto his face and hair, all the while ruing his decision to keep using neefra. *You should know better than to touch that stuff,* he thought. *Look what it's doing to you.*

Lifting his head, Morgan slicked back his hair and once again stared at his reflection. "You better pull yourself together right quick," he mumbled. "We've got some serious shit to deal with. If R5 has awoken, difficult choices will need to be made."

As he toweled off, he pondered "what if" scenarios for what seemed like the thousandth time since the fleet departed from the solar system. Should they continue on to R5 and make the stabilization attempt anyway? Chances were that everyone in the fleet — human, Suhkai and cyton — would likely die in the process, but at least they would go out knowing they had given all to try and save Earth.

Or was it better to abandon their mission and return home, knowing they might arrive back in the solar system to find Earth already devoid of life? If so, the year-and-a-half return journey would prove to be a useless exercise, a waste of time that could have been better invested in a third option, turning the fleet toward Tula.

While Morgan suspected the Tula option would appeal to most of the crew, the planet was ten light-years from the fleet's current position. He seriously doubted they could survive such an arduous journey, especially if the Suhkai decided to part ways. And Morgan considered their departure a near certainty.

Haula had made it clear on many occasions that he and his crew had not joined Morgan's fleet willingly and that the Suhkai had done enough for humans already. They had searched for and found Tula, and they had built an ark to ferry a small contingent of Earthlings to seed a colony there.

Putting the towel aside, Morgan picked up an electric razor. As he began to shave, he thought, *thank God for Quant. If not for her and her colony, Haula would have boogied two years ago.* The cyton queen held sway over Haula, and four years ago, she had ordered the Suhkai commander to serve Morgan. And for the last two years, Haula had obeyed her.

But, if Haula now viewed stabilizing R5 as a lost cause, Morgan wondered how much longer the Suhkai commander would bow to the queen. *He probably thinks his obligation is over now. Why else would he have ordered the fleet to slow without my permission?*

Just as he finished that thought, a surge of blue light filled the bathroom, leading Morgan to put down the razor. He knew what the light signified. A cyton was decloaking in the room. Sure enough, he turned and saw Quant hovering a few feet away. The queen was easy to distinguish from the millions of cytons in her colony. They were golf ball-sized balls of light, whereas Quant was the size of a basketball. Frowning, Morgan verbally addressed her. "You're not supposed to cloak yourself on our ships, Quant. That's been the deal since day one."

Cytons could regulate the amount of light and the color they exuded, allowing them to become invisible if desired. Biologists back on Earth theorized the aliens had developed the invisibility feature to aid in hunting and to protect themselves from predators.

While Morgan was sure the biologists were right, he didn't like cytons cloaking on his ships. He considered it spying, given they could intercept every thought that passed through the minds of those in close proximity. The way Morgan looked at it, if cytons were going to read his mind, he at least wanted to see them when they did it.

The cyton queen flickered as she transmitted an apology. *"Forgive me, Skywalker. No harm was intended."*

"Uh-huh. How long have you been hiding in here, spying on me?"

"Long enough to know your mind."

Morgan shook his head. "Not cool, Quant." While he considered the queen an ally, he also knew she had a tight bond with Haula. "Have you shared my thoughts with Haula?"

"No."

"Good. My thoughts are off-limits to him. Understand?"

"Yes. I understand."

He wanted to believe her, but his suspicions remained. "If you understand, why did you want to read my thoughts?"

"To know if I should warn you."

"Warn me? About what? R5?"

"Yes."

"So, it's true then? The magnetar's awoken?"

"Yes."

Morgan nodded. Despite his irritation with her spying, he appreciated Quant's straightforward answers. "You're kind of stealing Haula's thunder, aren't you? Or did he get tired of waiting on me and send you in here to deliver the news for him?"

Quant floated closer to Morgan, rising up to eye-level with him. *"Be wary of treachery, Skywalker. It surrounds you."*

Frowning again, Morgan quizzed the cyton. "What's that supposed to mean?"

The glow from the alien ball of light throbbed brighter as Quant's reply passed through Morgan's consciousness. *"Much deceit has already transpired. I fear more may follow."*

The admission caught Morgan by surprise. "I don't understand. What kind of deceit?"

"Hidden information. Unnoticed whispers."

At the mention of hidden information, Morgan immediately thought of Haula. The Suhkai commander rarely parted with information that wasn't first solicited. And when responding to questions, Haula often provided clipped, minimal answers instead of robust explanations. Morgan probed for more from Quant. "Am I right? Is it Haula I should be wary of?"

"He is one. There are others. Suhkai and human."

A chill raced through Morgan's body, but the sensation was not sparked by his own thoughts. Instead, it had flowed through him in conjunction with the cyton's reply. He rubbed away goosebumps on the back of his neck and said, "Okay, Quant, you've got my full attention. What's going on? What is Haula up to?"

"You must discover that on your own."

"What? Why bother warning me if you won't tell me what's going on? If there's trouble brewing, I need to know about it in no uncertain terms. It's the only way I do anything about it."

"I cannot reveal harmful intentions, Skywalker. I can only warn you they exist."

Though Quant's hedged answer frustrated Morgan, he understood what she was communicating. Quant and the millions of cytons in her colony were privy to many of the thoughts and conversations of those in the fleet — Suhkai and human. Amid what the cytons had intercepted, Quant had apparently detected looming chicanery. But she would not reveal what she and her cytons knew, understanding that evil thoughts, in and of themselves, do not necessarily yield evil acts.

At the same time, however, Quant had indicated there had been past deceit. While she might feel compelled to protect the privacy of intercepted musings, Morgan saw no reason for her to withhold her knowledge of underhanded activity that had already taken place. As he started to make that point verbally, his mind filled with a vision of a snaking pink and white cloud.

The image depicted an alien life-form known as a zikzaw. Morgan and his former *Rorschach Explorer* shipmates had encountered one of the electromagnetic beasts in the asteroid belt two years prior. Morgan remembered the encounter vividly. Quant's colony had merged with another cyton colony to kill the zikzaw, using *Rorschach* as bait.

Knowing he had not conjured the image on his own, Morgan addressed Quant. "You're telling me zikzaws have something to do with whatever deception has already occurred?"

"Yes."

"In what way?"

"You must ask Haula. And do it quickly. Time grows short."

The cyton queen's blue glow began to dim, an indication she was returning to a cloaked state and preparing to leave. Morgan reached out his hand. "Whoa. Hold on, Quant. You can't drop a bomb like that and just disappear on me."

"I will say no more. You must learn the rest from Haula."

Seconds later, Quant vanished, leaving Morgan confused and exasperated.

Ten minutes later, Morgan entered *Resolute*'s ready room fully groomed and dressed in his Gateway uniform. Still unsettled by Quant's vague warning, he looked warily at Haula, who stood toward the back of the room with a small cyton hovering beside his head.

Haula was dressed in his standard uniform, a sleeveless, knee-length tunic with a tapestry of gold and purple designs on a background of olive. Morgan approached him. "Greetings, Haula, my apologies for keeping you waiting."

The small cyton began flickering. Shortly after, Haula's response entered Morgan's thoughts. *"Do not apologize, Skywalker. I realize how difficult it is to unexpectedly awake from neefra. Please know I would not have interrupted your sleep if it were not urgent that we meet."*

As Morgan neared him, the ten-foot-tall Haula lowered to sit on the floor, allowing for a face-to-face conversation with the still-standing, six-foot-three Morgan. However, before proceeding with that conversation, Morgan telepathically instructed the cyton to only convey his spoken words to Haula, not his private thoughts. In reply, the cyton glowed a brighter blue for a moment. Morgan then returned his attention to Haula.

With a pleasant lilt, Morgan said, "Not to worry. I'm not upset at being woken. I understand it was necessary." For a moment, he paused and weighed whether to continue on in a friendly manner or get right to the point. While the former approach was more in line with their past conversations, the latter seemed more appropriate under the circumstances. Edging closer to the alien, Morgan resumed speaking, only this time his voice had a harder edge. "I'll be honest with you, Haula, I'm not happy you ordered the fleet to slow without my consent. Regardless of what's going on with R5, you had no right."

The rebuke was met by a snort from the Suhkai's crest tubes, a gesture Morgan read as equivalent to a human scoff. It was evident Haula didn't like being called out, but Morgan didn't care. The fleet was under Morgan's command — including Haula's three ships — meaning Haula had issued a fleet-wide order without authority. It was a breach of protocol that needed to be addressed and an action Morgan wanted reversed.

"In the end, you would have made the same decision. Therefore, your displeasure is of no consequence," Haula replied through the cyton.

Morgan pushed back. "Bull crap. The whole reason we've come all this way is to save my planet, not yours. *You* should not be the one to decide when to call it quits."

Haula dismissively waved his massive hand, creating a gust of air that peppered Morgan's face as it whooshed by. *"Your ego blinds you, Skywalker. The star has awoken. Our mission is over. We have failed."*

Morgan crossed his arms over his chest and shook his head. "Sorry, I don't give up that easy. I want to see more data from R5 before I throw in the towel. In fact, I've already countermanded your slow-down order to my ships. Now I want you to do the same with yours."

The Suhkai snorted again. *"You doubt my word?"*

"You bet I do," snapped Morgan. "I'm not taking anyone's word that we've failed until I've judged the situation for myself. Now, give the order to your ships. Resume max velocity until I say otherwise."

Haula's tree-trunk-sized arms tensed. *"No. Continuing is foolish. We are too far from the star. We can do nothing for Earth now. If you desire to save your crew, you must divert the fleet to Tula immediately."*

Just as Morgan prepared to tell Haula to pound sand, the earlier image of the zikzaw projected by Quant reentered his consciousness. This time, it was shooting out tendrils of electricity. Clearly, the cloaked Quant was present in the room and had selected this moment to refocus his attention on the zikzaw. *But why?* Morgan wondered.

A portion of Haula's comments replayed in his mind. *"We can do nothing for Earth now."* Morgan perceived the replay as another message from the cyton queen. So he projected a thought back to her and prayed the small cyton hovering by Haula didn't pass it on to the Suhkai. *"Are you trying to tell me Haula's lying right now? That there is another way to save Earth? A way that has something to do with zikzaws?"*

As he awaited her answer, he took a chance and said to Haula, "I don't believe there's nothing else we can do. Even if the magnetar has awoken as you say, there must be other ways to prevent—"

Morgan stopped speaking, suddenly recalling a conversation with Haula's compatriot Zoor shortly after the *Rorschach Explorer*'s zikzaw encounter. She had said the zikzaw had been drawn to the asteroid belt by a burst of gamma radiation from R5, anticipating more bursts would follow. As he remembered it, Zoor had said zikzaws were drawn to cosmic disruptions. *Like Jupiter exploding,* thought Morgan, *or possibly a dormant star awaking. That's it! That's what Quant's trying to tell me! We can't stop R5 from awaking, but we can stop it from destroying Jupiter. Draw zikzaws close to R5, let them feed on the magnetar's bursts.*

He glared at Haula. "You lie. We can still save Earth!"

But just as the words left his mouth, a thought from Quant intervened. *"No! You have it wrong."*

At nearly the same time, Haula responded through the translating cyton. *"Neefra has affected your brain, Skywalker. I have never lied to you."*

Morgan flinched as a flash of blue lit up the room, followed by Quant's booming voice inside his head. *"You deceive, Haula!"*

Instinctively sensing an imminent confrontation, Morgan closed his eyes and turned away from Haula just as the Suhkai commander replied to Quant. *"Stay your outrage, cyton! What I have said is true. The Earthlings are powerless to stop their planet's annihilation. You cannot deny it."*

Static electricity popped and sizzled all around Morgan. Every inch of his body felt the bites of shocks. It seemed as if Quant was stoking all of her electrical power, readying to smite Haula in a redux of her attack on Zoor two years prior. Recalling that event now, Morgan fell to the floor and curled into a ball, praying her attack wouldn't kill him in the process.

"You are wrong, Haula! Humans are smaller than Suhkai and not as gifted, but they are not as meek as you presume."

Stabs from static electricity continued to rack Morgan's body, but he dared to open his eyes to watch the showdown between the two aliens. Haula now stood, his ten-foot shadow darkening the perimeter of the room. Quant hovered near Haula's chest, spinning intensely. Flares of her blue energy sliced through the air.

"Ha! You are swayed by Skywalker's empty bravado, seeder. He is old and frail. His crew knows it. Many of them say he is unfit to lead. Do not bind yourself, your colony, to the weakling who now cowers on the floor."

"Tell him of the zikzaws, Haula! While there is still time."

"Time to do what? Engage in ten thousand years of conflict against an enemy that never sleeps? Your blessing is your curse, seeder. You view all life as precious when that is not true. Sometimes it is better to save what you can rather than fight for all you want."

Alarmed by the rapid escalation of animosity between the aliens, Morgan pressed his body out of its curl and tried to raise up but every movement he made was met by a jolt of electricity from Quant. It was as if her shocks were telling him to stay out of the way. Teetering on his hands and knees, Morgan looked up and begged her to calm down. So intent were his pleas that he never saw Haula's gigantic hand swooping toward him. He only felt the blow that sent him slamming into the wall. Crumpled and gasping for air, Morgan turned back to see Quant zap Haula's legs.

The screeching behemoth crashed to the floor, crushing the ready room's conference table underneath him. As Haula writhed next to Morgan, Quant lowered in the air until she was within a foot of the fallen Suhkai. Fearing she was about to zap Haula again, Morgan raised his arms and shouted above Haula's wails of pain. "Stop, Quant! No more!"

Still wildly spinning and discharging arcs of electricity around the room, Quant responded, *"He defies me! He plots against you!"*

"I don't care, Quant. This is nuts." Morgan crawled closer to Haula and once again reached out his arms toward the queen. "Listen to me. Killing Haula isn't gonna help me. It's gonna hurt me."

"I know his mind, Skywalker. If I allow him to live, the Suhkai will not help you. They will abandon you."

"If you kill him, the rest of the Suhkai will abandon me anyway." Morgan placed his hands on Haula's arm. "Let me talk to him. If he won't help, so be it. He can go. But for Christ's sake, don't kill him. It'll just make things worse."

The screeches from Haula's crest tubes waned, and he rolled his head toward Morgan. *"I will talk...to the human."*

Morgan appealed to the swirling cyton queen. "Come on, Quant. Give him a chance."

Seemingly ignoring Morgan, Quant zapped Haula's crest with a bolt of lightning. *"You will tell Skywalker of the zikzaws."* Morgan recoiled away from Haula as the Suhkai wailed anew. Another zap followed, this one striking Haula's chest. *"Your plot against him will end at once."*

Clutching the spot on his chest where the last bolt had hit, Haula nodded toward Quant. *"Yes, seeder."*

Quant's spin abruptly halted, and she floated up and away from Haula. Seconds later, the room filled with a brilliant flash of light and Quant was gone.

Exhausted and in pain, Morgan wanted nothing more than to lie down on the floor, but he could see Haula needed medical attention. He touched the Suhkai's arm and said, "Hold on. I'll call for help."

Overhead, Morgan heard Mey Wan's voice echo from the room's intercom. "No need, Paul. Help is already on the way."

Collapsing next to Haula, Morgan closed his eyes and whispered, "Roger that."

CHAPTER 8

During the long wait to reconvene with Haula, Morgan devoted much thought to their earlier meeting, feeling primarily responsible for the unnecessary confrontation that had occurred.

Morgan had let his ego and anger get the better of him, spurring a contest of wills with the proud and also angry Haula. Perhaps if Quant had not intervened, Morgan reasoned, he and Haula might have simmered down after a few minutes of shouts and chest-thumping and worked out a compromise. But that hadn't happened.

However, he now realized that was what he should have sought from Haula in the first place. A compromise. Morgan should have slowed down *Resolute*, *Renown* and *Ranger* and hashed out the next steps with the Suhkai commander. A few hours delay in their race toward R5 would not have made that much of a difference in the long run.

After all, they had already stopped numerous times during the journey to resupply water and other needed resources from asteroids they had encountered. And each of those stops had lasted nearly a full Earth day, so what would have been the big deal about a few more hours' delay?

Instead, Morgan had engaged in brinksmanship that resulted in a delay anyway, and a fracture of his relationship with Haula, not to mention physical injuries to both of them. *Not exactly my finest demonstration of leadership.*

There were many reasons he could conjure for his reckless behavior: persistent insomnia, a little too much dependence on neefra, the grind of eighteen months in space, age, paranoia stoked by Quant's warning, the stress associated with trying to save Earth, and so on. He was sure all of these things had played a part in framing his interaction with Haula, but they were poor excuses for his conduct.

They were facing a seminal moment, one that might very well decide Earth's fate and the fate of everyone in the fleet. The moment cried out for calm, rational discourse and thoughtful conversation, not finger-pointing and brow-beating.

So, as Morgan entered Haula's quarters aboard the Suhkai commander's flagship, he was determined to reset the direction and tenor of their coming discussion. He would not focus on the unknown plot Quant had accused Haula of orchestrating or on Haula's apparent, purposeful omissions about zikzaws.

Instead, he would do as he should have from the get-go. Listen to what Haula had to say, discuss their alternatives and reach a consensus, if possible. As much as he distrusted Haula at the moment, it was an undeniable fact the alien and his comrades had given much of themselves to save the human race. Morgan owed Haula the opportunity to speak his mind.

Like other spaces on Suhkai ships, Haula's cabin was cold and cavernous. Morgan would have also called it spartan if not for the colorful murals adorning the walls and the shimmering orange glow that emanated from the arched ceiling.

The murals depicted various scenes of Suhkai on other planets. As Morgan understood it, they were historical in nature, recording some of the species' greatest exploration accomplishments. In each scene, Morgan noticed, the Suhkai were accompanied by sparkling cytons, a reminder of the importance of cytons in all Suhkai lore.

Aside from the colorful surroundings, the rest of the room was austere. The only furniture to speak of included a rounded, bed-like mat in the center of the room upon which Haula now rested, and a set of three metallic cubes lined up against one wall. From past visits, Morgan knew two of these cubes served as chairs, and the other was a table. All of the furniture was huge by human standards. Morgan would have needed a boost to sit on the chairs and, once seated, he would not have been able to see over the edge of the table without kneeling.

Thankfully, however, no such gymnastics were needed to speak with the reposed Haula. While the mat-bed came up to Morgan's waist, he was able to stand next to it and look Haula somewhat in the eye.

The Suhkai commander had seen Morgan enter the cabin but had yet to communicate with him. Morgan assumed that was due to the ongoing ministrations of the cytons tending to his wounds.

A thick salve coated Haula's legs and chest, which Morgan knew to be a Suhkai medicine known as *galfra*. It was a remarkable substance that healed burns and other skin trauma at an accelerated rate. The salve glistened under the pulsing light from clusters of cytons hovering above each of the injury sites. They were bombarding the wounds with the equivalent of ultrasound treatment to help speed the healing process. Morgan had never seen the cyton treatment in person before but recalled it had been used to heal the burns of Julia Carillo and Robert Shilling, two of his former *Rorschach Explorer* shipmates.

Shifting his attention from the wounds to look upon Haula's face, Morgan asked, "How are you feeling?"

A solitary cyton rose up from the cluster tending to the Suhkai's chest burn and began to flicker as it transmitted Haula's reply. *"There is pain, but it would have been worse if your medics had not applied galfra so quickly."*

Morgan nodded. "Galfra's amazing stuff. I'm glad we had a supply aboard *Resolute*. For your sake and mine." Under his fresh uniform, Morgan had bandages covering several minor burns that had been treated with the Suhkai salve. Reaching out, he touched Haula's arm. "I owe you an apology. Your injuries would not have happened had I not come in itching for a fight."

Haula grunted as the cyton passed along his response. *"Do not burden your mind with such thoughts, Skywalker. My injuries are the result of my own actions."*

"All the same, I feel responsible. A decision as important as the one we face shouldn't be made in haste or anger."

"Of that, I agree."

"Good," Morgan said, squeezing Haula's forearm. "I know we have a difference of opinion about R5 and what we should do now. I think it's important that we hear each other out and reach an accord we can both live with."

Haula snorted and pushed himself up into a sitting position. As he moved, the cyton clusters broke up and began drifting toward the open cabin door, leaving only the translator-cyton behind. Morgan stepped back as Haula swung his legs over the edge of the bed and let his feet touch the floor. Now facing Morgan, the seated Suhkai said, *"Very well. Where should we begin?"*

Morgan scratched his temple. "Well, I pretty much know your position. You believe R5 has awoken, that there's nothing we can do now to prevent it from destroying Jupiter, and you think we should turn the fleet toward Tula. And I think you understand my position. I'm not ready to give up yet. I want to keep on course for R5 for the time being and assess if there are options for us to still achieve our mission. I guess I'd like to better understand why you are so convinced my approach isn't worth pursuing."

"Because I know there are no options that will succeed."

Frowning, Morgan said, "See, that's my problem, Haula. You say that, but you don't back it up with anything. I need to know why you believe there are no options."

Haula turned to look at the cyton bobbing next to his head. As the ball of light began to flicker, a vision formed in Morgan's mind. It was a black orb against a backdrop of stars. Random ribbons of light rippled across the black surface. To Morgan, they looked like lightning bolts. Then millions of cytons formed a sphere around the orb.

"When the star was still more dormant than awake, our seeders could have assessed the star's magnetic field and told us whether it was possible to affect the magnetic stresses stirring the star..."

The vision shifted to show other cytons maneuvering nuclear warheads brought from Earth into the net-like cyton sphere surrounding R5's magnetosphere. When and where the cytons sensed an exploitable area of instability in the field, they propelled nukes into the area and detonated the warheads. Morgan nodded impatiently. He knew all of this. The hope was the energy and electromagnetic pulses from the nuclear detonations would disrupt the instability.

Scientists on Earth considered the plan impossible. They saw no way nuclear warheads could get close enough to a magnetar, dormant or otherwise, to affect its stability. Even though magnetars were tiny, no more than twenty kilometers in diameter, the scientists said the star's magnetic field was too big, too strong. The warheads would be destroyed before they could be detonated.

But Quant and Haula had been firm in their contentions that the feat was possible. So long as the star was dormant, so long as it was not emitting gamma rays, the electromagnetic cytons were capable of maneuvering and shielding the nukes through the star's magnetic field until they reached their desired positions. And the cytons, with their honed senses of magnetic fields, knew when and where to set the nukes off to counter the star's instability.

Morgan had believed them then, and he believed them now, but Haula was evading his question with a tutorial of their original mission. He interrupted Haula. "As far as I'm concerned, that option is still viab—"

A loud snort from Haula cut Morgan off as the cyton relayed another of the Suhkai's thoughts. *"Allow me to finish, Skywalker."*

Uttering a deep breath, Morgan suppressed his irritation, reminding himself to remain civil. "I'm sorry, Haula. Continue."

The vision altered once again, this time showing the star beginning to spin rapidly as fissures split its surface, coating the spinning black orb with bands of pulsing energy. *"This is an illustration of what has happened to the star. It now emits so much radiation, its magnetic field is so intense, we can no longer get close enough to affect it. We would die trying."*

As soon as Haula finished projecting his thoughts and vision, Morgan said, "I don't see how you know the activity level on R5 has already progressed so much. The data we've collected indicates the spin is erratic, and the bursts so far have been weak. Yeah, I know we're still six months from R5, meaning the data we have shows what happened on R5 six months ago, not what's happening right now, but that's my point. We can't be sure of what's going on right now unless we close the gap between us and R5. For all we know, it might stay in sort of a sputtering state for hundreds or thousands of years. We might still be able to get close enough to disrupt its field, cause it to wobble and point its gamma bursts away from Jupiter."

"Impossible."

Haula's obstinance triggered a fresh surge of frustration in Morgan. He edged closer to the Suhkai and raised his voice. "Prove to me it's impossible, God damn it! Show me your gamma data. Prove to me R5's magnetic field is too intense."

In a gesture that only angered Morgan more, Haula dismissively waved his hand. *"You look too far away for proof, and you seek the wrong kind of evidence."*

"What in the hell do you mean?"

"Proof of the star's awakening has been gathering much closer to us."

A new vision formed in Morgan's mind…snaking pink and white clouds, hundreds of them. Zikzaws again. For a brief moment, he wondered if Quant was cloaked and in the room, but then a new thought arrived from Haula, confirming the vision was created by the Suhkai. *"Zikzaws do not idly amass, Skywalker, nor do they collaborate unless they sense a great feast is imminent."*

The zikzaws in Haula's vision began to swirl together, forming a fast-spinning ring. Another ring formed behind the first one. Soon, more rings coalesced behind the second ring. In a flash, there were dozens of them all lined up in a row. *"If you want proof, scan for ultraviolent radiation in the path of R5's bursts…look ahead of the fleet and behind. You will see UV rays spiking exponentially in both directions, a clear indication zikzaws are gathering in large numbers."*

Morgan eyed the Suhkai suspiciously as he processed the implications of his vision. If Haula was right and zikzaws were flocking to feed on R5's bursts, that would be a good thing in Morgan's mind. They would feed on the radiation in the bursts, thereby diluting the rays before they reached Jupiter. Problem solved. Earth saved. But Haula obviously didn't see it that way. Otherwise, he would not have declared Earth's demise inescapable in their earlier confrontation in the ready room.

"I'm confused, Haula. If what you say is true and these zikzaw rings are forming, that would be welcome news. But you seem to view the zikzaws as omens of doom."

"Well said. Zikzaws not only forecast doom, but they will also cause it."

"Why? If they feed on R5's radiation, they'll dilute it."

Haula slashed his arm through the air as the cyton's flickers flared brighter. *"No! The opposite will occur. They will channel gamma rays through the rings, filtering out other radiation they prefer to consume. But the ignored gammas that exit each funnel will be more concentrated than they were before they entered. Imagine, then, many of these rings lined up between R5 and Jupiter, continually reconcentrating the energy of the gammas."*

Lowering his head, Morgan began to pace back and forth in front of Haula's gargantuan feet as he tried to visualize what the Suhkai was telling him. Ordinarily, a gamma burst would begin its journey in a tight beam but eventually disperse as it traveled deeper and deeper into space.

Haula seemed to be saying zikzaw rings reconcentrated gamma rays similar to how a magnifying glass refocused widely dispersed sunlight into an intensified beam. If Morgan's interpretation were correct, the net effect of a series of these "gamma-magnifiers" meant the gamma rays that would ultimately hit Jupiter would be far more potent than if the bursts had traveled through space naturally.

Morgan stopped pacing and glared at Haula. "You've known this all along and never said anything?"

Haula rose from the bed. His shadow swallowed the smaller Morgan. *"What would have been the purpose of sharing the information with you? You and your people could have done nothing with the knowledge."*

The alien's arrogance infuriated Morgan. "How do you know that? We might have made different choices."

"And you would have been a fool if you had. The two best courses of action were to stabilize the star before it awoke, which we attempted, and build more arks, a task your people have undertaken. Diverting resources to defend against the zikzaws would have precluded the pursuit of these more valuable objectives.

"And the diversion of resources would have been a waste. These rings will form, disperse and reform for as long as the star ejects radiation. It is impossible to predict when and where they will form or how long they will persist. The distances between rings in some cases will be vast, while in other cases, there will be multiple rings close together. We do not have enough ships, cytons or time to combat all the rings that will form. You must believe me, Skywalker. It is a hopeless battle. There is nothing that can be done to prevent Jupiter's annihilation now."

Stepping out from the blackness of Haula's shadow, Morgan continued to glare at the Suhkai. "Quant disagreed with you. Back on *Resolute*, she said there was still hope for Earth. What does she know that you aren't telling me?"

Once again, Haula snorted and waved his arm dismissively. *"Nothing. The seeder seeks to delay the inevitable. That is all."*

"Delay how?"

"She believes Jupiter can survive its first pass through the star's gamma cone, but what will that accomplish? There is no chance the planet will survive a second pass."

As Morgan pondered Haula's answer, he began to understand the gist of Quant's strategy. The sole reason the fleet launched so quickly after learning of the threat R5 posed was Jupiter's position relative to the gamma cone forecasted by the Suhkai. At that time, Jupiter had been four years away from venturing into the path of R5's projected cone. Now, Jupiter was only twenty months away.

Given we're a bit more than eighteen light-months from home, thought Morgan, *we have somewhere in the neighborhood of sixty days to disrupt zikzaw rings. If we can do it, we can buy Jupiter twelve more years before it orbits back into R5's cone.* Morgan looked up at Haula as he continued his thoughts. *That's twelve more years of life on Earth, twelve more years to build additional arks and twelve more years to figure out a plan for Jupiter's second pass.*

Morgan turned to the cyton floating next to Haula. "Send a message to Quant. Tell her I want to speak with her as soon as possible." As the cyton began to flicker, Morgan gazed back at Haula. "Delaying the inevitable may seem like a waste of time to you, but it isn't to me. But I'm not going to force you to fight a battle you think is a loser, so if you want to part ways here and now, it's your call. Me, I'm taking my ships and going after every zikzaw ring we can find."

Haula shook his head. *"You are foolish. From our position here, it will take you weeks to reach the closest ring. And once you find one, you will not be able to get close enough to disrupt it without entering the gamma cone. And entering the cone will result in death. The radiation inside will destroy your ships and everyone aboard. All the while, new rings will continue to form. You would better serve your species by adding your crew to the population of Tula instead of sentencing them to death in a battle you cannot possibly win."*

"We're going to have to agree to disagree on that, Haula. I don't think we'd stand a snowball's chance in hell of making it to Tula from here. It's ten-light-years away, for Christ's sake. We don't have arks with cryo chambers, habitats and the kind of supply stores necessary to succeed. Half my crew would probably die during the trip, and the rest would probably go insane before they arrived."

"Not all would indeed survive, but some would. And some is better than none."

Morgan briefly bowed and said, "I appreciate your counsel, Haula, but I can't turn my back on Earth to save my own skin. I'm just not built that way. Now, if you'll excuse me, I need to return to *Resolute*."

The walk from Haula's cabin on *Flash* back to *Resolute* took less than a minute, as the two spacecraft were docked together. As soon as Morgan passed through the airlock linking the ships, he walked straight to the flight deck and addressed the pilot on duty, Captain Jun Ikeda. "Jun, prepare to undock from *Flash*."

"Yes, sir."

Morgan then turned to Lt. Bekker, the communications officer. "Bekker, instruct *Renown* and *Ranger* to dock with us as soon as *Flash* is away. And then send another message to my senior officers. Tell them to join me in *Renown*'s ready room in one hour."

"Roger that," Bekker said.

Morgan turned to leave but stopped when hailed by Bekker. "Uh, Colonel?"

"Yeah?"

"I just received a transmission from Quant. She's requesting permission to come aboard."

"Permission granted. Tell her I'll be in my quarters."

On the way to his cabin, Morgan ducked in the science lab where Mey Wan and Reshma Desai were busy at instrument consoles, presumably analyzing gamma data from R5. He cleared his throat to gain their attention and said, "Put whatever you're doing on hold. I need you to coordinate a UV scan with *Renown* and *Ranger*. Pronto."

"A UV scan? Why?" asked Wan.

As he approached them, he said, "I'll fill you in later. Right now, let me show you where to scan." He picked up a pad and pen sitting on the countertop next to Desai and drew a long line bracketed by two circles. One circle he labeled Jupiter, the other R5. Pointing at the line in between, he said, "I want to know the range of all the detectable spikes in UV radiation along the line of R5's bursts, forward and aft. And while the scan's running, ping *Flash* for their UV data. They've evidently been collecting it for a while. Again, focus on quantifying the range of all the spikes in their data. I need a list of the coordinates ASAP. It's priority number one for our whole science team. Got it?"

"Yes, of course," said Wan. "But it would help to know why you want the data."

Morgan turned to leave. "Not to worry, you'll find out soon enough."

Returning to the main corridor, he proceeded aft toward the bisecting corridor housing the crew quarters, galley and bathrooms. As he neared the intersection, Morgan saw a surge of blue light appear from the hallway on the port side, signaling Quant had arrived.

Knowing she was close enough to communicate with him, Morgan projected a thought to her. *"I assume your translator gave you a download of my meeting with Haula?"*

"Yes," Quant answered.

"So, you know I gave him the green light to go his own way."

"Yes."

Morgan turned the corner and spied the hovering queen at the far end, just outside his cabin. *"I know it wasn't entirely my call to release him, but I didn't think he'd be much of an ally. His heart's just not up for the fight."*

"Do not be surprised if he chooses to remain, Skywalker. His standing among his kind will diminish if he abandons you."

Stopping just in front of her, Morgan said out loud, "Well, if he offers his help freely, I'll accept it. In the meantime, I'm not counting on the Suhkai joining us." He paused and knelt so he was at eye level with the queen. "However, I do need you and your colony to join us, Quant. I don't think we stand a chance without your help."

Quant briefly glowed brighter. *"We will join the fight."*

Morgan smiled. "You have no idea how good that makes me feel, Quant. Thank you."

If it had been physically possible to hug her while he said it, Morgan would have, but it proved unnecessary. The queen seemed to interpret the sincerity of his words, glowing even brighter as she projected her next thought. *"Let us discuss a plan. We must act quickly while the rays from the star are still weak."*

CHAPTER 9

A s Mey Wan approached the closed hatch to *Renown*'s ready room, she could hear raised voices coming from inside. Though the voices were muffled by the thick door, Wan had no trouble identifying the chief feuders as Majors Eamon Douglas and Shyla Thakur.

The respective commanders of *Ranger* and *Renown* had clashed from the moment they met. Both possessed alpha personalities and seemed locked in an unending battle for supremacy over one another. At least, that was the way Wan viewed their fractious relationship.

Of the two, Wan more often than not found herself allied with Thakur. The Indian fighter pilot was hot-tempered and biting at times, but she listened to counsel and weighed competing points of view. On the other hand, the Irishman Douglas was arrogant from head to toe, making it hard for Wan to cultivate an affinity for him, even when she agreed with his positions.

Ironically, however, Wan was in the minority among the crew. Most of the rank and file on all three ships adored Douglas. To them, he was charismatic, irreverent and bold. They loved to see him mix it up with Col. Morgan, and Morgan himself seemed to enjoy Douglas' challenges.

By contrast, Thakur was viewed by most as the quintessential bitch. She was considered overly demanding, humorless and brutal in her honesty. That said, Wan knew there was a softer side to Thakur, but most never saw beyond her perpetual scowl. Morgan did, however. Wan had seen him interact enough with Thakur to know he valued her blunt, all-business manner.

Early on in the fleet's mission, Wan had wondered what Morgan had been thinking when he chose the sugar and vinegar pair to command *Resolute*'s sister ships, but she had come to realize the answer over time. Douglas and Thakur exuded different halves of Morgan's personality traits. When they were together with him, they were like external balances for his thoughts and emotions. But when Morgan wasn't present, and there was no one to mitigate their extremes, they were like two rabid wolves fighting for control of the pack.

That imagery was forefront in Wan's mind as she entered the room and saw the two majors standing on opposite sides of the meeting table bellowing at one another.

"Bah! You wouldn't recognize a good idea if it bit you on your tight little arse!" Douglas said.

"How would *you* know?" Thakur shot back. "You've never had a good idea."

"Har bloody har. Smile all you please, luv. I'm right, and you know it." Douglas stopped and turned to Wan. "Well, well, look who's finally here. Where's the old man? Zonked out on neefra again?"

"Lay off, Eamon. Mey is not Skywalker's keeper."

The interjection came from Jun Ikeda, *Resolute*'s co-pilot. He was seated at the head of the table, arms and legs crossed, staring at the room's tall ceiling.

"He was supposed to be here an hour ago, mate," barked Douglas.

With his gaze still aimed at the ceiling, Ikeda said, "So, what? If he'd been on time, think about how much bitching and moaning you'd missed out on."

With a sweep of his arms, Douglas said, "Ladies and gentlemen, it appears we have another comedian in our midst."

Ikeda smiled and lowered his head to look at Douglas. "Start a clown show, and you get what you get, *mate*."

Wan bit her lip to suppress a smile. She liked the Japanese astronaut, despite his nationalistic distrust of her. He was even-keeled, polite and humble. Averting her eyes from him, she looked at the remaining three officers at the table: Jaime Silva, Douglas' co-pilot aboard *Ranger*, Captain Duncan Kassa, *Renown*'s co-pilot and last but not least, the fleet's chief medical officer, Roksana Baronova. She rotated between the three ships and was currently assigned to *Ranger*.

The Russian doctor must have noticed Wan's attempt to hide her smile because she looked straight at Wan and said, "It is not funny. We face a serious crisis. Eamon is right to speak up. Decisions must be made, and all options should be discussed."

"Nobody disagrees, Roksana," said Thakur. "But before Eamon or anyone else starts tossing out options, we ought to have the facts in front of us."

"Oh, for Almighty's sake, what more bleeding facts do you need, Shyla? R5 is awake. We gave it a go, but we came up short, and there's not a fly's fart we can do about it now." Douglas paused and glared at Wan. "Scanning for UV rays is bonkers. There's one course of action left open for us and one course only."

"And what might that be?" Wan asked.

"A four-letter word beginning with T."

Just as Douglas finished speaking, the hatch creaked open. Wan turned to see Morgan entering the room. Behind her, Wan heard Thakur beckon the officers to stand at attention. Wan stiffened her stance accordingly and watched Morgan wave off the formal greeting. "At ease and be seated."

He strode past Wan and took the empty seat on her left. On the other side of Morgan was Thakur, followed by an unoccupied seat between her and Ikeda at the head of the oblong table. To Wan's right sat Duncan Kassa. Next to him was Baronova at the foot of the table, with Silva on her right. Finally, Douglas sat directly across from Morgan with empty chairs on both sides of him.

As soon as everyone was settled, Morgan said, "My apologies for keeping you waiting. I was meeting with Quant. There was a lot to discuss, and I lost track of time." He turned to Wan. "Are the UV scans underway?"

"Yes."

"What about the Suhkai data?"

Wan nodded. "Reshma's analyzing the data right now."

"Good."

"Um, excuse me, Colonel?"

Wan turned to see Douglas raising his hand. When it was clear he had Morgan's attention, Douglas continued, "Do you mind explaining your sudden fascination with UV rays? To most of us, the shift in focus seems, well, a wee bit odd."

Out of the corner of her eye, Wan saw Morgan's hand drift up to smooth his walrus tusk-worthy mustache. "Yeah, I bet it does, Eamon. I'm sorry I didn't stop to explain to Mey. I was a little pressed for time, but it's not as odd a shift as it seems on the surface. In fact, had we known how the scans might help us, I would have made the shift a while ago."

By now, Wan had turned and was looking directly at Morgan as he panned his head to look at each of his officers, finishing with her. "See, those scans would have told us what was going on with R5 a whole lot sooner than our gamma spectrometers. I'll admit that having a good handle on the UVs around us wouldn't have made much of a difference for *our* mission, but it might have made all the difference for our loved ones back on Earth. As it is, *they* and we will be fighting an uphill battle from here on out."

Morgan paused again and ceased caressing the strands of his Fu Manchu mustache. Leaning against the back of his chair, he focused his eyes across the table. As Wan turned to follow his gaze, she heard Douglas blurt in exasperation, "What in bloody hell are you talking about?"

"Zikzaws," Morgan answered. "Ever see one, Eamon? No, I guess you haven't. About the time *Rorschach* ran into one in the belt, you were probably podcasting about your petrifying nine-minute ride from Baikonur to ISS."

Wan bit her lip again, but others were unsuccessful in hiding their reactions to Morgan's jab at Douglas' comparative inexperience. Thakur snorted, Baronova gasped and Ikeda said, "Zing."

Douglas laughed loud and long, breaking the tension. Everyone else joined in. Afterward, Douglas wiped his eyes and said, "Good one, Colonel. Now that you've put me in my place, why not enlighten us?"

"Why, I'd be glad to, Eamon."

For the next fifteen minutes, Morgan summarized the gist of what he had learned from Haula, including a detailed description of zikzaws that Morgan pulled from his memory of *Rorschach*'s encounter with one of the electromagnetic scavengers. But, of course, most of the zikzaw description Wan and the others knew already, as they had been thoroughly briefed on the beasts before the mission began, and all of them knew the tale of *Rorschach*'s zikzaw confrontation.

But the information about zikzaw rings and how they might hasten Jupiter's destruction was all new and profoundly sobering. By the end of Morgan's description, she found herself thinking they faced a hopeless situation. Jaime Silva shared her pessimism, as evidenced by his comment when Morgan finished speaking.

"So, essentially, what you're saying is…Jupiter is screwed."

Morgan tugged again at the strands of his Fu Manchu. "I suppose you could look at it that way, Jaime. Certainly, we have no chance of disrupting all the zikzaw rings between R5 and Jupiter…but every ring we do break up increases Jupiter's odds of making it through R5's gamma cone." He paused then added, "Of course, we can't do it alone. We'll need help from Quant and her colony, and the folks back on Earth will have to do their part too."

"And how do you propose we disrupt these rings?" Silva asked. "If we fly into the stream of R5's gamma bursts, we'll fry."

Wan had to agree with Silva. The radiation shielding of their Suhkai ships was nowhere near strong enough to withstand extreme gamma-ray exposure.

"We'll use our warheads," Morgan said.

Frowning, Wan piped up. "But, Paul, the gammas will fry the warheads too."

"True. That's why we'll detonate the nukes outside of the cone."

"Outside the cone? What in bloody hell good will that do?" Douglas asked.

The answer hit Wan immediately. Morgan intended to use the nukes as bait. She turned to Douglas and said, "The zikzaws will leave the ring to feed on the radiation released by the explosions."

"Exactly, Mey," said Morgan. "The only reason the zikzaws band together to form rings is they've learned it's an effective technique to extract X-rays mixed in with R5's gamma rays. But according to Quant, creating and maintaining the rings is hard work for the zikzaws, and the payoff isn't that great. On the other hand, X-rays will be more bountiful in a nuclear blast zone, and they won't have to work as hard to gobble 'em up."

Douglas was quick to pounce on Morgan's plan. "That's all well and fine so long as the radiation lasts, Colonel. But what happens when the zikzaws gobble it all up? Won't they turn right back around and form a new ring?"

Morgan nodded. "Those who don't get their fill will probably try, but Quant says many of the zikzaws will be sated, so if rings do reform, there will be fewer zikzaws in them, which Quant says will make the reformed rings weaker than they were before. And Quant believes it's just as likely still-hungry zikzaws will search out other rings to join rather than attempt to reform weak ones."

Wan was beginning to feel cautiously optimistic about the plan. If they split up the six ships in the fleet, they could theoretically disrupt up to forty-eight rings, as each vessel had been outfitted with eight warheads. But when she raised this point to the group, Morgan dropped a bombshell of his own.

"I'm afraid it doesn't look like the Suhkai will be joining us, and we don't have the storage capacity to safely add their warheads to ours. So, unless Haula has a sudden change of heart, we'll be going after the rings with three ships and twenty-four warheads."

"Whoa, back up, Colonel," said Ikeda. "Why aren't the Suhkai joining us?"

Douglas slammed his fist on the table, startling Wan. "I'll tell you why, Jun. Because they don't think Skywalker's plan will work. Isn't that right, Colonel?"

"Yeah, that's pretty much how Haula sees it," said Morgan, "but he doesn't have the vested interest we do to at least try to disrupt the zikzaws. It's not his planet, his species, on the line."

"Haula thinks we should go to Tula, doesn't he?" Douglas said, standing and leaning over the table.

Morgan's reply was as stern as it was firm. "He does...*but we're not...* not until we've exhausted every possible option to save Jupiter and Earth. Now, sit down, Major. That's an order."

Wan felt a surge of unease as Douglas remained standing. The sensation intensified when Thakur inserted herself into the confrontation, "You heard the colonel, Eamon. Sit your pasty ass down."

"Sod off, luv." Douglas turned his glare from Thakur back to Morgan. "Our mission was to stabilize R5. We've failed that—"

"Wrong," said Morgan with a roar. "Our mission was, *and remains*, to save the people of Earth *by any means necessary.*"

"You're batty," said the still-standing Douglas. "I want to hear from Haula directly. I want to know, *specifically*, why he won't join us."

"I'll save you the trouble, Eamon. He doesn't think we can disrupt enough rings to make a difference." Morgan paused and panned his head to look at each of his officers in turn. "You know what I say to that? I say there's only one way to find out."

The confidence in his voice was inspiring to Wan, but apparently not to Douglas.

"And I say your judgment is impaired." Douglas turned to look at his fellow officers. "His plan is insane. We should not accept it. We should appeal to Haula and ask him to escort us to Tula."

Wan fully expected Morgan to relieve Douglas of his post, but he said nothing in response to the Irishman's challenge. Instead, Wan watched him scan the faces of everyone in the room. Meanwhile, Shyla Thakur rose from her seat and faced Douglas. "I never figured you for a coward, Eamon, but you sure sound like one now." While Douglas sneered at her, Thakur turned toward Morgan and placed her hand on his shoulder. "I say we go for Skywalker's plan."

Thakur's gaze drifted to Wan, her eyes seemingly imploring Wan to echo her support for Morgan. Wan stood and looked at the colonel. "I will be honest. I have doubts the plan can succeed." In quick succession, she turned her gaze to Thakur then Douglas. "But I see no compelling reason why we should not attempt it."

"Nor do I," said Jun Ikeda.

Wan turned to see him rising from his seat just as Douglas blurted, "Of course you don't. You're a certified ass licker. All three of you are. No, sorry, all *four* of you are."

He was staring at Duncan Kassa as he uttered the last quip. At the periphery of her vision, Wan saw the Ethiopian seated on her right smile. "Insult me all you want, Eamon. I'm not the one running from a fight."

"The only thing I'm running from, mate, is that junkie's death wish."

"Not so," said Kassa, admonishing Douglas with a wag of his index finger. "You are running from your fears. If you were an honest man, you would admit that escaping to Tula has been on your mind for quite some time."

Wan darted a quick look at Douglas. His usually pale complexion was beet red. To her right, Kassa continued speaking. "As it has with *your* ass lickers, Jaime and Roksana."

Snapping her head toward Baronova, Wan saw the doctor tense just as Silva vaulted out of his seat. With his fists balled at his sides, the Brazilian said, "I lick no one's ass. My mind is my own."

"And what does your mind say?"

The question from Morgan was softly spoken. To Wan, his tone seemed more curious than antagonistic. Silva's eyes fluttered as he turned toward Morgan. Wan noticed him relax his hands as well.

"I do not mean to be disrespectful, Colonel," said Silva, "but in this matter, I trust Haula's judgment more than yours."

"I see." Morgan's voice remained soft, almost weary, as he said, "And what about you, Roksana?"

Baronova squirmed in her seat and looked toward Douglas and Silva. She seemed panicked to Wan, like she was caught in no man's land, exposed with no cover in sight. But then she inhaled deeply, clenched her jaw and turned to stare at Morgan.

"If we try your plan and fail, what then?" she asked.

"Oh, for Almighty's sake, luv, don't encourage him."

"I neither encourage nor discourage, Eamon. I ask a simple question."

Wan turned to Morgan. He looked around the table and said, "Before I answer Roksana's question, would you all please sit down." Douglas remained standing for a moment longer than Wan and the rest, but he eventually took his seat. Morgan thanked everyone then turned his attention back to Baronova.

"I assume your question is meant to determine whether I would agree to fly to Tula if our efforts are ineffective against the zikzaws."

The red-headed Russian physician nodded. Morgan bowed his head and sighed. For a moment, he stared at his clasped hands resting on the table before he looked up at Baronova and said, "The short answer is maybe. But not until we definitively determine whether Jupiter survived R5's first pass."

"Brilliant." Douglas huffed as he slapped his thighs. "Bloody brilliant. So, we spend months, maybe a year, searching out zikzaw rings, popping off all our nukes then turn around and spend another couple of years flying back to see if Jupiter's still there. Then, and only then, you'd *maybe* consider Tula."

Morgan shook his head. "Not exactly." He paused, then said, "We turn back for Earth immediately. We take on every ring in our path or until our nukes are gone, whichever comes first. If we don't run into too many delays, we should know whether Jupiter made it through the cone in less than two years."

While Wan listened to Morgan, she performed the rough calculations in her mind. At the speed of light, the gamma rays passing the fleet now would reach Earth's solar system in approximately 1.6 years, or nineteen months, roughly two months before Jupiter's orbit carried it into the cone of R5's rays. From her memory of the Suhkai's estimated cone dimensions, Jupiter would remain inside the cone for approximately two weeks. So, Jupiter's danger zone was between twenty-one to twenty-two months from now.

Presuming nothing went wrong, and the fleet traveled back at near lightspeed, factoring in a few months' additional time to take on zikzaw rings, and for resupply stops, Wan estimated it was possible to reach the solar system in twenty-three months. As she finished her calculation, Douglas replied to Morgan.

"Meaning that a decision to turn for Tula two years from now will make the journey at least two years longer than if we headed directly there now."

"That's right," Morgan said. He turned from Douglas to Baronova. "I don't know about you, but that seems like a small sacrifice to me. A two-year longer trip to Tula in exchange for a chance to save our planet and the eight billion lives on it."

"What if Jupiter and Earth survive?" Baronova asked.

"We return to Earth, just as we planned to do when we launched."

"But the zikzaw rings will continue to form, will they not?"

Morgan nodded in response to Baronova's follow-up question. "For as long as R5 is active, they'll feed on its bursts...which means a recurring battle with them every twelve years for the next ten millennia."

A shiver passed through Wan as she pondered a ten thousand-year struggle with the zikzaws. *What a bleak future,* she thought. In appraising the faces of the others around the table, it appeared many of them shared the same sentiment. Douglas, of course, was the first to vocally react.

"Now I see the *real* reason Haula won't take on the zikzaws. He knows they'll eventually win. Maybe not this pass, but somewhere down the line."

"You understand Haula well, Eamon," said Morgan. "That's exactly what he thinks. But, again, he doesn't have a compelling reason to take on the zikzaws. We do. It's our planet, our people, at stake. And every extra day we can help our people survive is another day they'll have to devise defenses against the rings *and* to build more arks."

As Douglas shook his head and opened his mouth to reply, Morgan held up a hand to silence him. "And remember, we are not alone in this fight, short term or long term. Quant and her colony are with us, and she has pledged to recruit other colonies. Also, Haula does not represent the thoughts of all Suhkai. He is the commander of a modest-sized squadron, that's all. According to Quant, there are *major* Suhkai bases and settlements in closer range to us than Tula. With Quant's help, Gateway can approach these other Suhkai outposts and appeal for the kind of assistance Haula is personally reluctant to provide.

"I realize there is no guarantee they will help, and even if they will, any assistance they could provide won't help us for the immediate crisis we face. But it sure as hell might help us deal with the longer-term battle against the rings."

Seemingly undeterred by Morgan's comments, Douglas said, "You make it sound so reasonable, but it's anything but. For Earth to survive, you have to string together so many *ifs* it boggles the mind. If we turn now, if we find rings, if the nukes work, if we can disrupt enough of them, if we make it back to Earth...on and on and on. Yet, there's a simpler, clearer path to helping our species survive. Go to Tula. Now."

"Oh, please!" said Thakur. "You don't give a shit about saving our species, Eamon. You just want to save yourself."

Douglas leaped from his seat. "Sod off."

Thakur rose just as quickly. "Kiss my ass!"

"Enough!" Morgan's voice boomed above theirs as he, too, stood. Glaring at Douglas, he said, "You seem to be laboring under the impression this is a democracy, Eamon. It ain't. I've allowed you to speak your mind, but I've made my decision. We're turning the fleet and taking on the zikzaws. So, fall in line and stow any further talk of Tula. Understood?"

Wan was stunned by Morgan asserting command but was pleased he had finally pushed back against Douglas. It was long overdue. But it didn't appear as if Douglas was prepared to back off. His face turned red again, and he tensed his whole body. Through gritted teeth, he said, "You'll get us all killed."

"Major, you are relieved of command. Return to your quarters and stay there until instructed otherwise." Morgan almost knocked into Wan as he spun around and looked past her to Duncan Kassa. "Capt. Kassa, you are now in charge of *Ranger* and her crew." Morgan focused his gaze on Wan. "Mey, we need that UV data ASAP."

"Roger that." Wan stood and turned to leave. As she began to walk, Douglas raged at Morgan. "You're a fool! Everyone knows it! The whole crew thinks you're a joke! Haula does too!"

"Eamon! Stop!" shouted Baronova.

Turning around, Wan saw Baronova and Silva restraining the snarling Douglas as he fought against their grips. Morgan brushed past her and walked to the intercom panel by the door. "Security to *Renown* ready room, on the double."

Wan scooted by Morgan and left the room. Behind her, she could hear Douglas continuing to rant. Picking up her pace, she headed for the airlock amidships and turned to reboard *Resolute* just as two security personnel dashed up *Renown*'s central corridor.

As she tried to refocus her thoughts on the UV scans, Wan felt a pang of nausea. She found the dark tone of Douglas' defiant barbs unsettling. But the sensation quickly faded as she willed her mind to concentrate on the tasks ahead of her. There was no time to dwell on anything else but finding the first zikzaw ring and putting it out of action.

CHAPTER 10

Several hours later, Morgan reconvened with Mey Wan in *Resolute*'s science lab to discuss the results of the UV scans. Shyla Thakur joined them as well. Earlier, Morgan had tasked her with developing the fleet's strategy for disrupting the zikzaw rings.

Wan led off the meeting with a review of the detected UV spikes. "The largest spikes are closer to R5, which may explain why its bursts have appeared weak and sporadic so far. The rings are probably influencing the flow of gamma rays." She paused and tapped a row of data on the computer screen. "The closest one is approximately a sixteen-day flight from our current position."

Sliding her finger further down the screen, she tapped another data row. "Looking back toward Earth, the spikes are much smaller, which makes sense given the concentration of radiation diminishes as the magnetar's gamma cone expands, so there's less radiation to attract zikzaws farther away from R5. However, even though the UV levels are lower in these spikes, they are rapidly rising compared to the UV rays closer to R5."

Morgan nodded. "In other words, the rings behind us are more likely still forming, whereas the ones closer to R5 are already fully formed."

"Exactly," Thakur said. "And that's good news for us, at least in the short term. The first rings we go after will have fewer zikzaws."

Nodding again, Morgan asked, "What's the distance between us and the closest ring behind us?"

"Just shy of thirty-seven days," Wan said.

As Morgan winced, Thakur said, "I know. It seems like a long way, especially given there's a ring much closer if we keep heading toward R5. We could split up and send one of the ships onward while the other two turn back."

Frowning, Morgan said, "I'm not in favor of splitting up until we know what it takes to knock out one of these rings."

"Then I think we should go for the closest ring, even though it delays our turn." Thakur quickly added the reasons for her recommendation. "We'll get a quicker read on the effectiveness of the warheads and potentially disrupt a more powerful ring."

"I agree with Shyla, Paul," said Wan. "Waiting thirty-seven days allows *all* the rings to grow stronger. We should take advantage of the quickest opportunity to weaken their influence on R5's bursts."

Flying farther from Earth did not appeal to Morgan, but it was hard to argue against the logic presented by Thakur and Wan. However, he did have two significant reservations. In his earlier meeting with Quant, the cyton queen had indicated it would be progressively more challenging to lure zikzaws from rings the closer the fleet flew toward R5. Nearer to the magnetar, the radiation in R5's bursts would be more plentiful, making the fleet's warheads a less appetizing alternative.

Second of all, there was a supply consideration. At the end of the meeting with his senior officers, Morgan had asked them to estimate how long they could stretch their current food, water and oxygen supplies. The answer he received back was approximately sixty days.

Therefore, turning back toward Earth now provided the fleet with a decent buffer, knowing they had resupplied in an asteroid cluster forty-two days prior. But proceeding onward meant draining an incremental thirty-two days of their supplies, well exceeding their eighteen-day buffer. That meant betting on finding icy, hydrocarbon-rich asteroids ahead of them before their supplies ran out.

Morgan relayed those concerns to his two officers, prompting Thakur to respond, "Admittedly, going forward is a bigger risk, but we have an idea that could substantially lower the risk."

She paused and exchanged a glance with Wan, who nodded and turned to Morgan. "It's not foolproof, Paul. It requires placing a lot of trust in Haula, but we think it's worth a conversation with him."

Thakur then outlined their idea: ask Haula to perform a final dual-purpose mission with his three ships. Objective A: disrupt the first ring behind the fleet. Objective B: extract supplies from the last asteroid cluster the fleet had encountered. Once the provisions were secured, turn back toward R5 and link up with Morgan's portion of the fleet on their return from disrupting the first ring ahead of them.

Morgan did the quick math in his head and concluded the plan wouldn't work. "Under the best of circumstances, our ships would run out of supplies two weeks before we could link up with Haula."

"Not if Haula's willing to part with some of his supplies before he goes," Wan said. "They likely have a bigger reserve than we do. Remember, Haula has fewer crewmembers to sustain, and Suhkai metabolisms are slower than ours. And, if need be, Haula's ships have cryo chambers. He can put some of his crew into deep sleep if his supplies run too low."

The points Wan raised were compelling, but Morgan still saw a problem with the plan. "All right, it might be possible to deal with the supply issues, but there's another big *if* that needs to be addressed. The ring we want to disrupt might not respond to a nuke given its close proximity to R5."

Thakur shrugged. "Then we set off two warheads, or three. Shit, set off four if necessary. When we link up with Haula later on, we can reload with some of the missiles on his ships. He won't need them. In fact, he'd probably like nothing better than to get our nukes off his ships."

The longer Morgan pondered Thakur's answer, the more he warmed to it. Turning his thoughts to whether Haula would agree to the plan, Morgan saw a good reason why it might appeal to the Suhkai commander. It would provide him a more honorable way to depart from the fleet.

On the flip side, however, there was an equally good reason why Haula might object. He clearly believed battling zikzaw rings was futile and dangerous. Morgan doubted if Haula would be willing to put any of his ships in harm's way.

Then again, Morgan thought he might be able to convince him to aid in the resupply operation even if Haula refused to take on zikzaws. Standing up, he looked at Wan and Thakur. "Okay, you've convinced me. I'll contact Haula and see if he's willing to cut a deal."

From the privacy of his quarters aboard *Resolute*, Morgan transmitted a message to Haula requesting a ship-to-ship conference to discuss Thakur's plan. As he awaited the Suhkai commander's reply, Morgan eased back in his chair and closed his eyes.

He felt very weary but knew that sleep would not overtake him if he stretched out on his bunk. Unfortunately, somewhere early in their mission, his body clock had been disrupted and never properly reset.

At first, it had been more of an embarrassment than anything else. Here Morgan was, the fabled astronaut *Skywalker*, the most seasoned space traveler among the crew, suffering from sleep deprivation. It was like he was a lifelong sea captain who suddenly developed incurable, ongoing sea sickness.

Every possible remedy had been tried, but all had failed to help Morgan reestablish a normal circadian rhythm. It was as if the farther they flew from Earth, the biological cues his body relied upon to discern when he should sleep had faded away. And no amount of simulated sunlight and darkness aboard the ships seemed to matter. Nor did sticking to regimented twenty-four-hour Earth cycles. Even neefra, the Suhkai potion that helped him sleep when all else failed, did nothing to reset his internal clock.

As a result, Morgan seemed to hover in a perpetual haze that could only be pushed away by caffeine, artificial stimulants, anger and rushes of adrenaline. But when these temporary energizers faded, like they were now, he descended back into the haze.

Forcing his eyes open, Morgan reached for a bottle of caffeine pills resting on the corner of his small computer station. *Wake your ass up, old man*, he thought. *This is not a good time to zone out.*

Just as he swallowed the pills, the reflection of a small blue ball of light zipped into view on the computer screen in front of him. Turning around, Morgan looked at the bobbing cyton and said, "Well, hello there. Haula's translator, I presume?"

The cyton pulsed brighter, and an image of a zikzaw arose in Morgan's mind. *"Danger! Go! Now!"*

At the same time, Morgan heard a click from the intercom on the wall, followed by the raised voice of his co-pilot Jun Ikeda. "Colonel, you're needed on the flight deck. Immediately."

Clearing his mind of the zikzaw image, Morgan leaped up and tapped the intercom call button. "Roger that. On my way."

Seconds later, he was dashing up *Resolute*'s central corridor with the cyton gliding through the air beside his head. As he neared amidships, Mey Wan ran into the passage from the portside airlock linking *Resolute* and *Renown*. She saw Morgan and halted. "There's a zikzaw heading toward us!"

"So I gather. Get to the lab and buckle in."

She nodded and ran forward. As Morgan closed on her, she ducked into the starboard side science lab. Passing by the open hatch, he heard Wan order whoever was in the lab to lock into their safety harness. Then Ikeda's voice echoed over the ship-wide intercom. "Now, hear this. Now, hear this. Initiating dock separation. All personnel move clear of airlocks immediately."

Next to Morgan, the cyton began to flicker. As he darted his eyes toward it, he received a thought from Haula. *"Move, Skywalker! Disperse!"*

Still a few steps from entering the flight deck, Morgan shouted to Ikeda at the co-pilot station. "Jun, take off as soon as we're clear of *Renown* and *Ranger*. Full power!" Running through the hatchway, Morgan directed a command to Lt. Bekker at the comms station. "Bekker, relay the same order to *Renown* and *Ranger*. Tell them to coordinate vectors with Jun and disperse."

Shortly after, a claxon began to sound, and the lights in the flight deck turned red. Morgan heard Ikeda broadcast another message over the intercom. "Now, hear this. Now, hear this. G-force acceleration commencing in ten seconds. Find a seat and strap in *now*. Ten, nine…"

Morgan flopped onto the seat of the closest open station and wrestled the safety harness over his head. The cyton zoomed in front of him, and another thought from Haula penetrated his consciousness. *"Beware. The beast will try to force you into the gamma cone."*

Snapping the harness buckle into place, Morgan called out above Ikeda's countdown, "Jun, keep clear of R5's cone. Bekker, pass that on to Shyla and Duncan."

The jolt from the engines firing on plastered Morgan to the seat. As sophisticated as the Suhkai gravity environment was, it could not adapt quickly enough to offset all of the g-forces caused by the sudden acceleration. For the next thirty seconds, the pressure against his body was as intense as any Morgan had ever experienced. He grimaced as he fought to breathe. To his right, Bekker groaned in pain.

Meanwhile, the cyton circled Morgan's head, flickering away as it transmitted images of what was transpiring outside the ship. For once, Morgan was glad Suhkai ships were windowless. Like the zikzaw the *Rorschach Explorer* had encountered four years ago, the one at the center of the cyton's vision moved through space like a thrashing snake, spewing clouds of pink and white plasma that absorbed free ions of radiation the clouds encountered. From beneath these clouds, the zikzaw's electromagnetic core shot out blinding tendrils of lightning that raked the vacuum of space like insect antennas feeling for radioactive prey.

While he had no way to measure the dimensions of the zikzaw in pursuit of the fleet, Morgan knew the aliens were miles long and wide. And they were as agile as they were fast, making their escape from one a daunting proposition. Morgan could not imagine confronting a more menacing foe, and it appeared to be trailing directly behind *Resolute*.

As he mulled evasive actions, Morgan noticed the g-forces beginning to abate. The Suhkai gravity environment was finally adapting to their acceleration. Looking ahead, he saw Ikeda intently examining the video and data monitors at his station, and a new thought from Haula entered Morgan's mind.

"Hard to port! Now!"

He was about to yell out the order to Ikeda when he saw him reach for the thruster controls. The cyton was evidently relaying Haula's commands to both of them now. Another jolt of g-forces pressed against Morgan as Ikeda executed the thruster maneuver.

Concentrating back on the vision projected by the cyton, Morgan saw a swarm of blue light slash across the zikzaw's path. Quant's colony had entered the fray. It appeared to be attempting to distract the zikzaw. The ploy worked. The beast began to veer toward the swarm. Then, a gigantic, spherical explosion ripped through the clouds surrounding the zikzaw's midsection. Then another explosion followed just behind where the first had occurred.

"Those are nuke blasts!" Ikeda said, his voice raised.

Morgan concurred. One of the ships in the fleet had detonated warheads close to the zikzaw. And if Morgan was interpreting the cyton's vision correctly, it appeared as if the explosions had cut the zikzaw in two. The clouds of the tail portion began to dim, and he noticed a gap appear at its leading edge. Meanwhile, the plasma of the forward half suddenly flared brighter, and spears of lightning stabbed the surrounding space. Two more explosions occurred. Separated by a good distance from the previous two, these bursts were less prominent, almost flashes. An angry shriek from Haula reverberated in Morgan's mind. *"No!"*

Oh, God, Morgan thought. *It got one of Haula's ships.*

The cyton pulsed and transmitted a fresh warning. *"More are coming. You must go."*

Layering on a headset, Morgan called to the lab. "Mey, we've got more zikzaws headed our way. Get a bead on them as fast as you can and feed the coordinates to Jun, *Renown* and *Ranger*."

Seconds later, Wan responded, "Copy that."

Morgan tossed off the headset, unstrapped from his seat and hustled forward to the empty pilot station. While he buckled in again, he donned another headset and darted his eyes at the station's three computer screens. The central monitor provided a video feed of the dissipating, stricken zikzaw. On the right-hand screen was a radar scope depicting the space around *Resolute*. Alarmingly, none of the triangle markers identified the fleet's other ships.

Tapping a quick command on the keyboard, he zoomed out the field of the radarscope's feed. Still, no markers. Zooming out even further, he breathed a sigh of relief. There, on the display, were the coded symbols identifying *Renown* and *Ranger*. While *Renown's* course was leading it away from *Resolute* at a widening angle, both ships were still headed in the same general direction toward R5. *Ranger*, however, had apparently reversed course when it dispersed and was traveling in nearly the direct opposite direction of *Resolute*.

Puzzled, Morgan frowned. He could not understand why Duncan Kassa had made such a drastic maneuver. *And why is he continuing to fly farther away? There's no zikzaw on his tail. At least, none that I can see.*

In search of an answer for *Ranger*'s wayward course, Morgan expanded the scope's display range again. While he did not spot any snake-like electromagnetic signatures, he did finally locate two of Haula's ships, *Flash* and *Fortune*, as well as Quant's swarm. They were arrayed in a V formation, with the cyton swarm at the point, flying at nearly a ninety-degree angle away from *Resolute*.

"Must be heading for the incoming zikzaws," mumbled Morgan. He turned to the ever-present cyton next to him. "Am I right? Is that where Quant's leading Haula?"

The cyton pulsed and answered, *"Yes."*

For a moment, Morgan considered turning *Resolute* to join Quant's attack, but then a plea from the cyton wedged into his thoughts. *"No. Flee. Save your ships."*

At almost the exact moment, Morgan heard the raised voice of Jaime Silva, *Ranger*'s co-pilot, in the earphones of his headset. "Mayday, mayday. *Resolute, Renown*, acknowledge. Requesting emergency assistance. Acknowledge."

Morgan exchanged stern glances with Ikeda as he replied, "Roger *Ranger*. *Resolute* acknowledging. State the nature of your emergency."

There was a long pause. Morgan flashed a look at the flight data screen to his left and realized why. *Ranger* was now more than 100 million kilometers from *Resolute*. At their respective velocities, the gap between them was growing dramatically with every second that passed.

Morgan turned to Ikeda. "Turn us around, Jun. Head for *Ranger*."

"But, sir, what about the other zikzaws?"

Glancing at the cyton beside him as he answered Ikeda, Morgan said, "We'll have to hope Quant and Haula can give 'em hell." Morgan swiveled his chair toward the comms station. "Bekker, what's the signal delay between *Ranger* and us right now?"

"Uh, 7.3 minutes, but expanding rapidly."

That implied there would be at least a fifteen-minute delay before any reply was received from Silva, more likely twenty or thirty given the growing distance between the ships. *That's plenty of time for* Renown *to link up with us,* thought Morgan. Speaking through his headset microphone again, he called to Thakur, "*Renown*, plot and execute an intercept with *Resolute* post haste."

"Roger that," Thakur said.

"Colonel, I've just received an email message from Capt. Silva," said Bekker. "Forwarding to your inbox now."

Morgan typed a command to pop up his comms panel on his central monitor. The message was addressed to the senior officers of all ships in the fleet and read, *"Mayday.* Ranger *hit by zikzaw electrical discharge. Multiple system failures. Multiple injuries. Engines out. Thrusters inoperative. Repeat. We have no navigational control. At current velocity, will intersect with R5 cone in 32.3 hours unless thrusters come back online or we come up with a workaround solution. Requesting immediate assistance and workaround recommendations."*

As soon as he finished reading, Morgan called to *Renown.* "Shyla, have you read Jamie's message?"

"Affirmative."

"All right. Scrub the link up with us. Head directly for *Ranger.* Fastest possible speed. Push your engines to the limit. We'll do the same."

"Roger that."

Morgan turned to Ikeda and filled him in on *Ranger's* situation. Then, he turned to Bekker and told him to summon *Resolute's* lead engineer to the flight deck. Next, he called Mey Wan in the science lab. "I need you on the flight deck." Lastly, he typed a quick reply to Silva, copying the response to all on the original message. *"Roger your mayday,* Ranger. Resolute *and* Renown *on our way to you now. Will engage engineers on workaround solutions immediately. Broadcast updates on your situation/progress every fifteen minutes until instructed otherwise."*

He pressed send just as Wan announced her arrival on the flight deck. Morgan turned as she slid into the seat of the science station directly behind him. "Keep tabs on those zikzaws, Mey. Let me know immediately if they get by Quant and Haula, or if you detect any others. I don't want to be caught by surprise again."

From behind, Morgan heard Bekker say, "Uh, Colonel?"

Swiveling to face him, Morgan said, "What is it, Bekker?"

"Maj. Thakur just asked to speak with you on a private channel. Said it was urgent."

"Okay, put her through." As soon as Morgan heard the beep indicating the switch in the channel, he said, "I'm here, Shyla. Talk to me."

"Paul, there's no way we can reach *Ranger* in time. We're too far behind her, and she's flying too fast. Unless her thrusters come back online, she's going to hit the cone eighteen hours before we can intercept."

Morgan fought off the urge to curse. "Then we're gonna have to pray they get them back online. But, in the meantime, keep your foot on the pedal. Understood?"

"Copy that."

"Oh, shit," exclaimed Ikeda.

Morgan whirled his head around. "What's the matter?"

"Another explosion...*Ranger* just dropped off the radar. It's gone."

Morgan darted a look at his radar scope. As Ikeda had indicated, the symbol marking *Ranger*'s position had disappeared. In the vicinity of where it had last appeared was the unmistakable, spherical radar signature of a powerful explosion. Nauseous from the implications, Morgan murmured, "My God."

CHAPTER 11

Diverting his gaze back to the radar, Morgan tried to make sense of what he saw on the display. The explosion signature surely looked to him like that of a detonated nuclear weapon. *But why would Ranger have fired a nuke?* Morgan wondered. The radar scope showed no evidence of zikzaws near *Ranger*'s last position. Turning to Bekker, Morgan said, "Ping *Ranger* on all channels."

As he swiveled back around, Morgan caught a glimpse of the somber look on Ikeda's face. "Don't assume the worst, Jun. *Ranger* might be okay. Her radar beacon just might have been knocked out by whatever caused the explosion."

Ikeda nodded, but the look on his face remained downcast. Behind him, Morgan heard Wan ask, "Do you think they detonated one of their warheads?"

Shaking his head, Morgan said, "I don't know. It sure looks like it, but I'll be damned if I know why."

"Maybe it wasn't a nuke," said Ikeda, his voice tinged with pessimism. "Maybe they tried an engine restart, and something went wrong."

It was certainly possible, Morgan conceded. The engines of Suhkai spacecraft were powered by superconducting, liquid metallic hydrogen fuel cells. If the cells had been damaged by the electrical jolt from the zikzaw, a restart attempt might have triggered a catastrophic explosion. But Morgan was not ready to give up on *Ranger* yet. Glaring at Ikeda, he said, "Enough gloom and doom, Jun. Until proven otherwise, we're going to assume *Ranger*'s still out there in one piece. Understood?"

Ikeda clenched his jaw at the rebuke, then said, "Aye, aye, Colonel."

"Good. Now, alter course for the coordinates of the explosion." As soon as Ikeda acknowledged the command, Morgan turned to Wan. "We should be in range of the site within thirty minutes, max. I want infrared scans of the area surrounding the blast zone. If we can't hail *Ranger*, we might be able to pick up her heat signature."

"Okay. I'll get Reshma on it right away."

Morgan then ordered Bekker to reestablish communications with Shyla Thakur aboard *Renown*. With the connection made, Morgan said, "I assume you've noticed *Ranger* is MIA."

"Roger that. The radiation surge where she went MIA is concerning."

"Agreed. *Resolute*'s heading to investigate. In the meantime, maintain *Renown*'s intercept course with *Ranger*'s last known heading. Whatever caused the radiation surge might have disabled her radar and comms, but she might still be flying."

"Copy that, *Resolute*. *Renown* out."

With the comms link with Thakur terminated, Morgan leaned back against the headrest of his seat and closed his eyes. At this point, there was nothing more he could do but wait. Unless *Ranger* suddenly reappeared on radar or pinged *Resolute* back, he would learn nothing of the ship's fate until they scanned the area of the explosion.

What a fiasco, he thought. A confrontation with a solitary zikzaw had cost the fleet two of its ships and divided the remainder. And for all Morgan knew, Quant and Haula might have since suffered further losses fending off the zikzaws drawn to the scene of the skirmish with the first of the beasts.

A couple of more confrontations like this, and we'll all be gone. This melancholy thought triggered Morgan to recall Haula's earlier warning. *"We do not have enough ships, cytons or time to combat all the rings that will form. You must believe me, Skywalker. It is a hopeless battle."*

Then, he thought of the crew aboard *Ranger*, and in particular Eamon Douglas, who had forcefully opposed Morgan's zikzaw plan. *"You'll get us all killed,"* Douglas had declared. And while Jaime Silva and Roksana Baronova had not gone as far as Douglas in expressing their disagreement with the plan, their opposition had been evident to Morgan. As Silva had said, *"In this matter, I trust Haula's judgment better than yours."*

Perhaps they were right, and I was wrong, thought Morgan. *Maybe I should have given stronger consideration to Tula.* As the situation stood now, if *Ranger* had been destroyed and Morgan had only *Resolute* and *Renown* left to confront the rings, how much could they really do to weaken the zikzaws' effects on R5's gamma rays? They were too few, with too little firepower at their disposal, to fight against such fearsome foes. Just as Haula had counseled. *Maybe it is time to throw in the towel,* Morgan mused.

He opened his eyes and looked around for the cyton who had earlier hovered beside his head. At present, it was hovering beside Mey Wan, flickering away as if engaged in a conversation with her. She, though, had her eyes glued to her bank of computer monitors, intensely concentrating on the screens in front of her. Then her head shot up, and she looked at Morgan.

"I've found *Ranger,* Paul! She's adrift, but she appears intact."

Morgan unbuckled from his seat and joined Wan at her station. Looking over her shoulder, he peered at the enlarged reflectometer image on her center screen. The infrared outline was blurry, but there was no mistaking the Platypus shape of a Suhkai cruiser. A surge of adrenalin coursed through Morgan's body. "Feed Jun and Lucas her coordinates. Quickly!"

As Wan typed, Morgan directed Ikeda to head for the stricken ship and ordered Bekker to hail *Ranger* on all channels and relay the adrift cruiser's coordinates to *Renown.* Turning his attention back to Wan, he said, "Let's hope they've still got life support."

She nodded, eased back in her seat and crossed her arms under her chest. Morgan noticed a frown form on her face. Without prompting, she said, "Why is she adrift, Paul?"

"Beats the hell out of me."

Wan did not appear to hear his reply. Staring blankly ahead, she continued on, seemingly speaking to herself. "Without thrusters, she wouldn't have been able to slow down."

From the co-pilot's station, Ikeda said, "Maybe *Ranger* used one of her instrument probes as a thruster." As Morgan looked in his direction, Ikeda swiveled his seat around and added, "It would have been crazy risky, but given the alternative of frying in R5's cone, maybe they thought it was worth the risk."

Ikeda appeared to be suggesting the crew aboard *Ranger* had extended her cargo armature with an instrument probe clamped in its grip and activated the probe's engine and/or thrusters, allowing *Ranger* to alter its velocity.

"If you're right, Jun, I can't imagine their cargo arm held on very long," Morgan said, "but I guess it didn't need to. All they needed was a few seconds of a push to angle away from R5's cone."

"But, Paul, a few seconds would not have slowed them down much at all," Wan said. "Something else had to have halted their momentum."

"Like what?" Ikeda said. "The warhead explosion?"

Wan shook her head. "No way."

"I guess there's only one way we're going to find out." Morgan stood back and turned to Bekker. "Lucas, any response from *Ranger*?"

"Negative, sir."

"Okay, keep trying." Morgan shifted his gaze to Ikeda. "Jun, you're on your own for the docking." Then he turned and tapped Wan on the shoulder. "Have Reshma take over your station. I need you to help me put together a boarding party."

ABOARD GATEWAY COALITION FLEET SPACECRAFT *RANGER*

Silhouetted by the dim glow of the flight deck's emergency lighting, Eamon Douglas prodded Jaime Silva for an update. "Well? How much time do we have?"

"Looks like *Resolute* will be in docking range in ten, fifteen minutes."

"What about *Renown*?"

"Easily an hour from now."

"And you're sure neither can access our systems?"

"Nope. I've disabled every possible comms link."

"Good." Douglas smiled. "We need to keep them blind and deaf until they come through the airlock."

"Roger that."

Winking at Silva as he turned to leave the flight deck, Douglas said, "I'll be back in a few, mate. Just need to check on our welcoming party before *Resolute* arrives."

He was met in the ship's main corridor by Roksana Baronova, who had just exited the medical bay. Immediately, Douglas' expression morphed into a devilish leer. "All hail the future queen of Tula."

Baronova maintained a stern expression as she advanced towards him. "Do not gloat, Eamon. There is still much that can go wrong."

When they met up a few steps later, he wrapped his arm around her. "Relax, Roxy. I've got everything under control." Leaning forward, he kissed her forehead. "Thanks to you."

Douglas was still amazed by Baronova's bold action. He had been imprisoned in his cabin when the order to strap into safety harnesses blared over the intercom, so he had been ignorant of the catalyst spurring all the turmoil that ensued. But he had known something was seriously wrong, especially when the ship went dark and quiet.

Replaying the scene in his mind, he recalled unbuckling from his harness when the g-forces had finally abated and loudly cursing Morgan while he felt his way in the dark to the locked cabin door. Douglas had cursed him even louder when no one answered his fist-pounding pleas for release from his confinement. But then, suddenly, the door had unlocked, and he had been greeted by the flashlight-toting Baronova.

"Come quickly," she had said. "We shall never have another opportunity like this."

Together, they had crept toward the flight deck while she divulged her spur-of-the-moment plan. Holding up a syringe at the periphery of the flashlight's beam, she had whispered. "I will take care of Duncan. You help Jaime get life support back online ASAP."

None of the five people in the emergency-light illuminated flight deck noticed them enter. They were all too busy trying to restore the ship's knocked-out systems. Baronova had played her next part beautifully, adopting a panicked voice as she made her way toward Duncan Kassa in the pilot's seat.

"What can I do to help?" she had asked as she halted beside Kassa.

Kassa had been so focused on rebooting the ship's main power, he never looked up at Baronova, making his neck an easy target for her syringe. Douglas had watched Kassa utter a sharp bleat and just as quickly slump over.

Amid the stunned stares of the others on the flight deck, Baronova removed the needle from Kassa's neck and calmly said, "Regrettably, Capt. Kassa has taken ill. Maj. Douglas is now in command. Any questions? No? Good." She paused and pointed at the three junior officers on the flight deck. "Now, you, you and you, help me carry Capt. Kassa to the med bay."

The three officers, all loyal to Douglas, had obeyed Baronova without question, leaving Douglas and Silva alone on the flight deck. Within thirty minutes, the two had restored power to all of *Ranger*'s systems. During that interval, Baronova had returned to the flight deck and, together with Douglas and Silva, they conceived a plan to secure their one-way ride to Tula.

Since then, all had gone according to that plan, evoking another devilish grin from Douglas as he once again kissed Baronova's forehead.

She seemed to soften for a moment before Douglas felt her tense and pull free from his arm. Glaring at him, she said, "Stay focused, Eamon. Stay hungry. We need to be ruthless to pull this off."

"All right, luv. All right. Don't you worry. I'll be one hundred percent wolfhound when it matters."

Baronova poked a finger into his chest. "You better be. This is an all or nothing move, Eamon."

Douglas backed away a step and held up his hands as if surrendering. "Easy, Roxy. You're getting yourself all wound up over nothing. I want Tula just as bad as you. Now, if you'll excuse me, I need to make sure everything is in order for *Resolute*'s arrival."

Without further exchange, they went their separate ways, Douglas heading for the main airlock amidships and Baronova proceeding in the direction of the flight deck.

As Douglas walked along, he wondered why Baronova was so tense. *It's gonna be a cakewalk*, he thought. *No one is going to want to follow that old fart anymore. Not now. And if any still want to, well, they'll get their chance to die alongside him.*

ABOARD GATEWAY COALITION FLEET SPACECRAFT *RESOLUTE*

Standing in the corridor outside of *Resolute*'s main airlock, Mey Wan and the other four boarding party members waited for Jun Ikeda to finish docking with *Ranger*. Each party wore a spacesuit over their flight suits, though they had yet to affix their helmets and gloves.

During the docking wait, Wan grew increasingly concerned. In her mind, *Ranger*'s circumstances just didn't add up. *The ship should not be adrift*, she thought. Unless the crew had restored thruster control, Wan saw no way *Ranger* could have decelerated to the space-flight equivalent of a slow crawl.

She did not buy Ikeda's earlier speculation about using the rocket engine of an instrument probe as a makeshift thruster. While the probe engine might have generated enough of a push to alter *Ranger*'s course, Wan did not believe it was powerful enough to almost completely arrest the ship's near-lightspeed forward momentum.

So, how did they decelerate? More importantly, why did they decelerate? If the crew restored thrusters, why didn't they attempt to link up with us? Or simply alter their course away from R5's cone, or just decelerate enough for us to catch up with her?

Earlier, Wan had posed these questions to Morgan as they put on their spacesuits but, to her frustration, he brushed them aside.

"Look," he had said, "our number one priority right now is to make sure the crew is all right. We'll sort out how and why they did what they did later on."

But Wan couldn't let go of her concerns, especially the mystery behind *Ranger*'s detonation of a warhead. The most logical explanation she could conceptualize was that the crew had restored thrusters, decelerated for some unknown reason then used the weapon as a distress signal to alert *Resolute* and *Renown* to her location.

However, as Wan recalled it, the ship had disappeared from radar at nearly the exact moment the warhead explosion occurred, meaning the decision to detonate occurred *before* their radar beacon had failed. And prior to *Ranger* dropping off radar, her last transmitted flight data had shown no change in velocity, indicating the ship's sudden deceleration took place *after* the detonation.

There was another mystery that vexed Wan, one that no one aboard *Resolute* or *Renown* had raised yet. Why hadn't Duncan Kassa been the one who broadcasted *Ranger*'s mayday? While Wan could understand Kassa delegating the responsibility to Jaime Silva amid the crisis the ship faced, it seemed strange that Kassa, *Ranger*'s newly installed commander, hadn't been an active participant in the communication loop at any point since.

No, *Ranger*'s circumstances just didn't add up. And the longer she pondered the oddities, the more uneasy Wan became. Fidgeting with her helmet, she looked up at Morgan ahead of her. He was engaged in a conversation with *Resolute*'s flight deck via an earpiece radio. She debated interrupting him to discuss her concerns again but decided to wait until he finished his talk. In the interim, she listened to both ends of the discussion in her earpiece.

Ikeda had just finished telling Morgan he would have to manually dock, as *Ranger*'s docking system was unresponsive to *Resolute*'s docking system's commands.

"Roger that," Morgan said. "Bekker, any success with comms?"

"Negative. Still no response from *Ranger* on any channel. No telemetry either."

"What about Haula's ships?"

"Nothing, sir. The only ship responding to my pings is *Renown*."

"Are Haula's ships and Quant's colony still on radar?"

Reshma Desai answered. "Yes, Colonel, but they appear to have their hands full with zikzaws. We've detected two more explosions near them, and they've changed course multiple times."

Wan watched Morgan lower his head and sigh. Meanwhile, Ikeda said, "Colonel, once we dock, I recommend we move farther away from *Ranger*'s radiation cloud."

With his head still bowed, Morgan replied, "Copy that, Jun. Go ahead and pick a rendezvous point for *Renown* and transmit it to Shyla."

After Ikeda acknowledged Morgan's commands, he said, "I'd also recommend we prep a warhead of our own and instruct *Renown* to do the same. If the cloud attracts more zikzaws, we may need a diversion."

Raising his head, Morgan turned and looked at Wan and the other members of the boarding party. She could sense reluctance in his eyes and body language as he said, "Affirmative, Jun. As soon as we lock onto *Ranger*, give the order."

Morgan then took a deep breath and addressed the boarding party. "Okay, folks. Here's the drill. We have no way of knowing what kind of shape *Ranger*'s in, but there's a strong possibility she's without power, which means she's also lost life support. Now, assuming the crew wasn't incapacitated during the nuke blast, they would have had plenty of time to put on and activate their spacesuits, so they're hopefully in okay shape.

"But we can't assume that. So, the first order of business is to hustle them aboard *Resolute* and suss out their conditions." He paused and looked at Doctor Bobby MacDowell, *Resolute*'s onboard physician. "Bobby, once we get 'em to the med bay, triage will be up to you."

After MacDowell acknowledged his task, Morgan turned his attention to the two flight engineers in the party. "Job number two is assessing *Ranger*'s systems and restoring power. Therefore, while Dr. Wan and I debrief the crew on the ship's status, I want you two to patch *Ranger* into our power supply and see if you can at least get life support back online and run diagnostics on her critical systems. Any questions?"

Wan's uneasiness bubbled up again. She cleared her throat and said, "Paul, before we board, I wonder if it might be a good idea to send our cyton ahead of us."

Morgan displayed a look of annoyance. "Why?"

"To give us...um...a preview of the situation on *Ranger*."

"Why do we need a preview?" Morgan quickly shot back. "We'll see for ourselves in a few minutes."

Wan briefly blushed and turned to the others in the boarding party. "Would you give us a minute alone? I'd like to speak with the colonel in private."

The request seemed to irk Morgan further, but he didn't countermand her request. As soon as the others moved out of earshot, Wan looked up at her irritated commander and whispered, "Send the cyton, Paul. Please. Ask it to cloak and make contact with Duncan."

Morgan studied her face, his eyes darting this way and that as if trying to glean her thoughts by observing her expression. "I don't understand, Mey. For what purpose?"

"To make sure he is all right, to make sure he is in control of the ship. And if he is not in control, to find out who is." As Morgan frowned, she said, "You may think I am paranoid, but I find *Ranger*'s situation... orchestrated."

The comment seemed to throw Morgan for a loop. His eyebrows arched, and he took a step back. "Orchestrated? Look, Mey, we've been over this already. Yeah, we don't know how they slowed down so fast or why they popped off a nuke, but that doesn't mean—"

He stopped speaking just as Wan heard Ikeda's voice through her earpiece. "Docking any second now. Hold onto something. Might be a little bumpy."

A few seconds later, Wan felt a slight vibration. Then, she heard the clamping mechanism of *Resolute*'s airlock, followed by another update from Ikeda. "Docking complete. Airlock secure."

She turned to look through the small window of the inner airlock door just as the chamber's light flickered on. Peering past the lights toward the airlock's outer door at the far end of the chamber, her heartrate quickened. "Please, Paul. Send the cyton before we open the airlock."

As Wan watched Morgan eye her with puzzlement, Bekker's voice sounded in her earpiece. "Colonel, *Ranger* just manually unlocked her airlock door."

"Roger that." Morgan looked past Wan to the other boarding party members and called out, "Gentlemen, it's go time," before turning back to Wan. "I trust Duncan, Mey. You should too. Now, let's get the crew aboard and get *Ranger* back in action."

CHAPTER 12

"Easy now," whispered Eamon Douglas as he, Roksana Baronova and two others prepared to pass from *Ranger*'s airlock into *Resolute*'s. "Smile and look relieved."

Leading them into the chamber, Douglas beamed when he saw Paul Morgan waiting to greet them. He had expected the old man would be perturbed to see him free of his cabin, but Morgan seemed quite happy.

"Thank God for small favors," Morgan said, stepping forward to shake hands with Douglas and the others. "It's good to see you all. We were very worried about you."

"We were worried about us too," said the still smiling Douglas, "but all is well now."

While Douglas and Morgan spoke, the other members of the respective boarding parties moved forward and greeted each other with a series of handshakes, hugs and salutations.

"You have life support, I see," Morgan said.

"Aye," said Douglas, patting the chest of his flight suit. "We have emergency power. Enough for a few lights and air to breathe."

"That's good news." Morgan turned to Baronova as she broke from an embrace with Mey Wan. "How are your people? Any injuries?"

"Only one," said Baronova. "Duncan Kassa. He received a bad shock when the zikzaw zapped us."

Douglas observed Morgan dart a look at Mey Wan as he asked, "What's his condition?"

Baronova provided a quick synopsis. "He is stable but unconscious at the moment. He was in pain from burns to his hands, so I sedated him while we applied galfra and bandaged them."

"I see," said Morgan. "Are the burns bad?"

Baronova gave a quick nod. "Yes, they are, but with a few more galfra treatments, he will recover fully."

Wan stepped forward. "I would like to see him."

"Of course," Baronova said. "I assume you would like to see him too, Bobby?"

MacDowell brushed by Douglas and stood alongside Wan. "Absolutely. And when we're finished, we can move him over to our med bay until your power is restored."

"Very well."

Baronova clasped her hands behind her back and began a return walk toward *Ranger's* airlock with Wan and MacDowell in tow. *Well done, Roxy,* thought Douglas. *Two down, ten to go!*

"Speaking of restoring power," Morgan said, "where do you stand with repairs?"

"Right, well…," Douglas paused and scratched the back of his neck before continuing on, "The zikzaw did quite a number on us, I'm afraid. We've got a wide assortment of fried fuses, damaged boards and other electrical issues. It's going to take a while to swap parts, reboot and test all of our systems. And that's after we get main power back online, but we need the engines for that. The problem is, every time we restart them, our fuel cells start acting dodgy, so we've had to keep shutting them down."

Just as he finished speaking, the linked ships lurched forward, causing Douglas and the others in the airlock to briefly stagger. He shot a look at Morgan and asked, "What's happening? Why are we moving?"

"Putting some distance between us and the radiation from your nuke. Don't want any more zikzaw encounters while we're fixing up *Ranger.*" Morgan paused, then said, "By the way, why *did* you deploy the warhead?"

"Had to get your attention somehow." Douglas shrugged. "Didn't want the clock running out on our emergency batteries while we tried to restore comms and get the engines back online."

Morgan nodded. Then, the colonel said, "Understood. Well, let's get you plugged into our power and start working the repairs."

"Roger that," said Douglas. "Why don't you come with me to the flight deck, and Jaime and I will give you the rundown on our damage assessment?"

"Sounds like a plan." Morgan turned to the other four men remaining in the airlock, two flight engineers from *Ranger* and two from *Resolute*. "Gentlemen, as soon as *Ranger* is tied into our power grid, concentrate on sorting out what's going on with the fuel cells. We need those engines back online pronto."

Douglas nodded to his two engineers as they turned to follow Morgan's men. They left together immediately, heading into *Resolute*, leaving Morgan and Douglas alone in the airlock. Douglas extended his arm toward *Ranger* and slightly bowed. "Colonel, after you."

Morgan held up his hand. "In a second. I forgot to tell the engineers something."

As the colonel bowed his head and tapped his earpiece radio, Douglas reached into the hip pocket of his flight suit and felt for the syringe Baronova had supplied him with earlier. For a brief moment, he considered attacking Morgan as soon as he finished talking to the engineers but decided against it because of the cameras in the airlock. While he doubted anyone on *Resolute* was surveilling the camera feed, Douglas was not about to take chances. It would be far easier to put Morgan down once they were aboard *Ranger.*

"Ellis? Dixon? Col. Morgan here. Have the cyton on the flight deck help you diagnose the fuel cells. I'm sure it's forgotten more about these Suhkai ships than we've ever learned."

Douglas tensed from head to toe. *Shit! There's a cyton aboard? Shit, shit, shit!* Sweat broke out on his forehead as Morgan turned and said, "Okay, Eamon. Lead the way."

"Uh, right. Follow me."

With his mind racing, Douglas began walking toward *Ranger*'s airlock. *What are we going to do? The cyton will learn what's going down any second.* He picked up his pace, hoping Morgan would follow suit, but the colonel lagged behind. *Come on, old man, hurry up. Just a few more feet 'til we're out of sight.*

"What's the matter, Eamon?" Morgan asked. "You look a little panicked."

Safely inside the darker confines of *Ranger*'s emergency-light illuminated airlock, Douglas turned and smiled. "I do? Guess I'm just anxious to get a start on things."

He stood aside and motioned for Morgan to pass by. "Right this way, Colonel."

When Morgan took the lead, Douglas seized the syringe from his pocket, stabbed Morgan in the neck, and plunged its contents into him. Morgan staggered, reached up to grab at his neck and wheeled around to glare at Douglas. "What the he—"

Douglas didn't let him finish speaking. He shoved Morgan to the ground and stood over him. "Stay down, Colonel. Go to sleep."

Morgan tried to roll onto his hands and knees, but, just as quickly, he collapsed face down. Douglas immediately raced into *Ranger*'s central corridor and shouted, "Everybody move! We have to take control of *Resolute* now! There's a cyton aboard. Move your asses before it's too late!"

Within seconds, six members of *Ranger*'s crew dashed into the corridor from rooms fore and aft of the airlock. As the first two approached him, Douglas urged them to hustle aboard *Resolute*. "Go, go, go! Flight deck is priority one!" To the next two, he said, "Head aft, search every room. Take out everyone you run into." When the last two turned into the airlock, Douglas prodded them to race forward with similar search and disable instructions.

Breathing heavily, Douglas bent over and grabbed Morgan's arms and began dragging him into the main corridor, stopping momentarily to wedge his earpiece radio into place. He clicked the device and began speaking as he resumed pulling Morgan. "Jaime? Roxy? We've got a problem. Morgan has a sodding cyton aboard."

In the distance, screams and shouts emanated from inside *Resolute*. At the same time, flashes of bright blue light reflected off the corridor wall opposing the airlock entrance. Before he could curse again, the cyton zoomed into view. Douglas let go of Morgan and turned to run, but before he took two steps, a searing jolt stabbed into his back, knocking him off his feet.

As he writhed on the floor, the cyton shot past him, heading toward the flight deck. Douglas closed his eyes and cursed. *So close*, he thought. *So close*. Behind him, he heard the sound of slow and steady footsteps. He opened his eyes and saw Baronova approaching. Inexplicably, she looked serene. Gritting in pain, Douglas said, "Run! Hide!"

Baronova ignored his plea and calmly walked past him. Douglas angled his head to follow her. With a syringe in one hand, she knelt next to the unconscious Morgan, pressed his neck against the floor with her free hand and injected him with the contents. Ahead of her, Douglas saw a blur of blue light zip back into view and shoot toward Baronova.

"Stop!" she shouted. "Shock me, and you will kill him."

The cyton halted inches from her face. Douglas curled his body around and watched Baronova clutch Morgan's neck with both hands while glaring at the pulsing alien.

"Read my mind, cyton, and you will see I speak the truth. He is old and weak, and I have given him a drug that makes his heart race. If you attack me, your shock will pass through my body into his and Skywalker's heart will fail."

For a moment, the two adversaries remained motionless, then to Douglas' astonishment, the alien flickered and backed away. Baronova edged her head forward and said, "You are wise, cyton. Now, go to *Renown*. Tell Shyla Thakur we are taking *Resolute* and *Ranger* to Tula. Tell her that if she attempts to interfere, we will kill Col. Morgan and all those aboard who oppose us."

The cyton flared brightly and zoomed out of Douglas' view. After it was gone, he stared at Baronova. "You're unbelievable, luv."

She turned to face him, her hands still gripping Morgan's neck. With a look of disgust on her face, she growled, "Get up and get us out of here, Eamon. Quickly!"

Seated on the edge of a bed in an unfamiliar cabin, Paul Morgan massaged his throbbing forehead and pondered his predicament. Eamon Douglas had started a mutiny, and Morgan was now his prisoner aboard *Ranger*. That much seemed apparent. And no doubt, the confrontation with the zikzaw was the catalyst that had driven Douglas to act.

Less apparent to Morgan was how many others had joined the mutiny and where things stood outside the cabin. Had the rebellion succeeded, or was it still in progress? Were *Ranger* and *Resolute* still docked? Had *Renown* docked as well? Had there been a resistance? Was Douglas holding other prisoners?

In the hours since he had awoken in the cabin, Morgan had asked himself these questions many times over. Though he had arrived at no firm answers, it seemed evident that Douglas was in control of *Ranger*. And as he looked around the locked, well-lit and warm cabin, it appeared clear that Douglas had restored more of *Ranger*'s systems.

Beyond these observations, however, Morgan was blind. He had tried several times to communicate with the cyton aboard *Resolute* by concentrating his thoughts, but the cyton had not responded, leading Morgan to conclude the alien was too far away to detect his thoughts. He had also tried to use the cabin intercom to hail Douglas and others, but the intercom panel was inoperable.

So, until he received a visitor or the intercom was reactivated, there was no way for him to acquire greater clarity on the situation. Sighing, he looked up at the ceiling and muttered, "What a God-damned fool I am. I should have listened to Mey and sent the damned cyton to scope things out."

Shaking his head, he said, "Jesus, man. What's the point of having senior officers if you don't listen to them?"

He wondered if she was a captive now, too. He suspected she was. Douglas had used a syringe to knock him out, which implied Roksana Baronova was party to the mutiny. And if that were true, Baronova had likely similarly knocked out Wan and Bobby MacDowell after luring them aboard.

Extending that line of thought, he speculated Duncan Kassa's "sedation" had nothing to do with getting shocked on the flight deck. More than likely, Kassa had been taken out as step one of the mutiny, which meant the entire distress sequence had been a ruse intended to lure *Resolute* and *Renown*.

"God, how blind am I?" Morgan said with another shake of his head.

The possibility of a mutiny had never crossed his mind, despite the clear warning of a hidden plot he had received from Quant. Nor had he contemplated the possibility when Douglas railed against the plan to disrupt zikzaw rings.

But now that the mutiny had happened or was in the process of happening, Morgan realized why Douglas had lured *Resolute* and *Renown* instead of just taking off for Tula with *Ranger* when the fleet dispersed.

One ship alone would likely not survive the journey. There were too many things that could go wrong along the way. Ample supplies and spare parts were needed, including backup vessels in the event *Ranger*'s systems failed.

As he pondered that likelihood, Morgan wondered why Douglas had not killed him instead of taking him prisoner. The Irishman had to know Morgan would oppose him every step of the way. He also had to know Morgan would not survive the trip. At his age and in his present condition, Morgan doubted he would last more than a year or two of the decade-plus odyssey.

Lying back on the bunk, Morgan closed his eyes and thought, *why the hell am I still alive?* Lolling on the edge of sleep, he whispered, "Wrong question, old man." *You should be thinking, how do I stay alive? How do I stop the mutiny? How do I convince Douglas to fight for Earth?*

CHAPTER 13

organ was dead asleep when he was grabbed and hauled off the bunk. Startled and glassy-eyed, he tried to struggle against the hands gripping both arms, but they were too strong for him. Then, through the haze of semi-consciousness, he heard a voice say, "Stop fighting, Colonel. We don't wish to hurt you."

He recognized the voice as belonging to Doctor Adam Hazan, an Israeli astronomer assigned to *Ranger*. Morgan turned his head in Hazan's direction as a second voice said, "Speak for yourself, Hazan. This maniac almost got us killed."

Morgan recognized this voice too. Lieutenant John Grimes, a.k.a. JP, *Ranger*'s chief logistics officer. As the burly man spoke, he firmly squeezed Morgan's arm. The painful gesture stirred Morgan's senses fully awake.

The two men were "escorting" him along the starboard wing of *Ranger*'s crew corridor, heading apparently for the ship's bisecting central corridor. Looking around, Morgan could see other closed cabin doors in the wing and wondered if they held other captives. Turning his head to Hazan as they turned into the main corridor, he said, "I'm sorry to see you mixed up in this, Adam."

The chiseled Hazan kept his eyes forward as he answered. "It was the lesser of evils."

"Since when did trying to save Earth become evil?" Morgan asked.

Hazan clenched his jaw while Grimes jabbed Morgan in the ribs and spat, "Shut up and keep walking, old man."

Wincing from the unexpected blow, Morgan looked ahead and saw a small congregation of people at the juncture between *Ranger*'s starboard and portside airlocks. One of them was the smirking Douglas. Next to him stood Baronova. She appeared stoic as she watched Morgan marched down the hall. The sight of the last person standing with them almost took his breath away. It was Reshma Desai. She was standing next to Douglas with a smile on her face.

As his escorts hustled him toward the trio, Grimes jabbed him again and said, "No funny business, now, or I'll mess you up."

"Enough with the rough stuff, JP," said Hazan.

"Oh, shut your yap. Skywalker's a big boy. He can take it."

Grimacing, Morgan tried to make sense of the scene in front of him. The group at the airlock was clearly there waiting for him to arrive. Morgan darted his eyes left and right. Both airlock doors were open, an indication *Resolute* and *Renown* were docked with *Ranger*.

When they closed within a few steps of Douglas and the others, a thought entered Morgan's mind. *"Say the word, Skywalker, and I will put an end to this treachery."*

Morgan flinched, and his eyes opened wide. Quant!

"Thank God you are here," Morgan telepathically replied.

At the same time, he heard Douglas laugh. "What's the matter, Colonel? You look like you've seen a ghost."

Desai edged a step away from Douglas and averted her eyes from Morgan. Hazan and Grimes halted and released Morgan's arms. Meanwhile, Baronova moved aside and pointed to a spot on the floor in front of the starboard airlock. "Stand here."

"What's going on, Quant?" Morgan queried as he looked through the linked airlocks. On the far side, he saw the steely glare of Shyla Thakur. She was bracketed by two of her crew. Lieutenant Paula Epps, a flight engineer, and Doctor Kyle Thurmont, *Renown*'s chief physician.

"They are exchanging you for the two with Maj. Thakur."

"Exchange?"

"Yes. There are provisions involved as well."

Before Morgan could respond to Quant again, Baronova stepped in front of him. "Farewell, Colonel. Whether you believe it or not, we have done you a kindness. Now, please, proceed through the airlock and join Maj. Thakur."

"Yeah, go to your balmy groupies," sneered Douglas, "and good riddance to the lot of you."

"I can stop them, Skywalker."

Morgan looked through the portside airlock and saw it was still linked with *Resolute*. He turned back to Douglas and Baronova. "You're taking *Resolute*?"

"Righto, mate. There's *twenty-eight* of us. That's too many for little old *Ranger* to transport on her own. "

The large number joining the mutiny staggered Morgan. *Twenty-eight of thirty-six?* Douglas grinned and twitched his fingers to imitate walking legs. "Now, move along. You don't want to miss your ride to hell."

Morgan ignored him and locked eyes on Baronova. "I presume you intend to go to Tula?"

"Not *intend*, chum," Douglas answered. "We changed course ten hours ago. Now, off you go. Me mates on the other side are anxious to come aboard."

"There are many cloaked cytons with me, Skywalker. I can restore your command of all vessels immediately."

"To what end, Quant? They will not follow me. They will try this again."

"My colony will ensure order is maintained."

Morgan turned and gazed at Desai. Two years ago, the former NASA program manager had forcefully lobbied him for a spot in the fleet. And in the time since, she had been among the steadiest of the crew. Not once had he noticed her express even the slightest misgiving about their mission. And yet, here she was, standing side by side with Douglas and Baronova. The gist of his thoughts must have registered with her at that moment. She blushed and briefly looked away.

"You're certain this is what you want, Reshma?" he asked.

Douglas shoved Morgan back and stood in between him and Desai. "Leave her alone and get moving."

Morgan held his ground. "What's the matter, Eamon? Afraid to let Reshma speak her mind?"

"She is like many of the followers, Skywalker. She feels regret for abandoning you, but not for choosing Tula."

Quant's observation matched with the conviction evident in Desai's expression and body language. As Douglas moved to shove him again, Desai said, "Don't, Eamon. Let me answer."

"Yes, Eamon," said Baronova. "Stand back. The colonel should hear what Reshma has to say."

Douglas shoved him anyway but then stood aside. In the gap between them, Desai stepped forward and looked up at Morgan. As she spoke, the tone of her voice was sincere. "The decision was not easy, Colonel, but I am content with it. Now that I have seen what zikzaws can do, it seems impossible to believe there is any hope of stopping them."

Morgan could have countered by saying it was just as impossible to believe *Resolute* and *Ranger* would make it to Tula, but he held his tongue. Reshma was smart enough to understand the challenge she and the others faced. And it was hard to argue against her conclusion. The odds of succeeding against the zikzaws did seem minuscule.

"Do not give up hope, Skywalker."

"I'm not, Quant. But I can't force them to share my hope."

He extended his hand to Desai. "I understand, Reshma. Thank you for explaining. Good luck to you."

Desai blushed again and mumbled something in return. Morgan turned and offered similar well-wishes to Hazan, who earlier had expressed similar "lesser of evil" sentiments. Finally, he returned his gaze to Douglas, Baronova and Grimes. "Any messages you'd like me to pass to your folks when we get back home?"

Douglas growled an obscenity and ordered Grimes to motivate Morgan through the airlock. Grimes seemed gleeful for the opportunity to manhandle him again. He grabbed Morgan roughly by the neck and pushed him forward.

As Morgan stumbled to regain his balance, the airlock filled with a flash of blue light and the sizzle of electricity. Behind him, Grimes wailed and thudded on the floor. When Morgan turned around, Quant was hovering over the twitching crewman. Looking past the queen, Morgan saw dozens of bright blue lights surrounding Douglas and the others.

Not surprisingly, the sudden appearance of the uncloaked cytons caused the mutineers to recoil in panic. All except Baronova. She remained composed. It was almost as if she had expected the intercession.

"No, Quant," Morgan shouted. "Let them be. They've made their choice. Let them live with it."

Shyla Thakur called out to him from *Renown*'s airlock hatchway. "Colonel, wait! They've left us with barely any food or water. And taken most of our med supplies and spare parts."

It took Thakur's plea a moment to register in Morgan's mind, and when it did, Baronova's earlier comment flowed through his mind. *"Believe it or not, we've done you a kindness."*

He glared at Baronova and shook his head. "A kindness?"

Expressionless, she said nothing in return. Morgan turned to Thakur. "Who are the six going with us on *Renown*?"

"Mey, Jun and Duncan. Plus Lucas Bekker, Bobby MacDowell and one of my flight engineers, Janie Gillespie."

"Okay. Form a team. Have them track down what was taken and recoup it."

Morgan motioned for Epps and Thurmont to proceed into the airlock toward *Ranger*. Pointing down at Grimes as they neared him, Morgan said, "Looks like JP could use some help getting back aboard *Ranger*."

With their eyes warily on the pulsing Quant, the two mutineers assisted Grimes to his feet, and together the three proceeded toward *Ranger*. Morgan looked past them to Douglas and Baronova. "Quant, do me a favor and make sure every scrap of *Renown*'s supplies are returned."

"It shall be done."

Thakur advanced toward him and said, "We should do more than that, Paul. We should take *Resolute* back."

Baronova quickly replied, "One ship cannot support twenty-eight people, Colonel. Not for an eleven-year journey. If you take *Resolute*, you are condemning us to death."

"Who cares?" said Thakur. "You didn't give a shit about leaving us with next to nothing to survive on. Why should we care about you?" She turned to Morgan. "We need *Resolute*'s warheads."

"Take them. You can have the bloody nukes," said Douglas. "Fat lot of good they did for Haula."

The mention of Haula caused Morgan to shift his gaze to Quant. *"What happened to Haula?"*

As Thakur fired back at Douglas, "You know we don't have the cargo space to safely store *Resolute*'s warheads in addition to ours," Quant answered Morgan. *"Haula and his ships perished fending off zikzaws."*

Morgan winced at the news. For all of Haula's reluctance to combat zikzaw rings, he and his crews had been valorous in defense of the fleet. As he took a moment to mourn the Suhkai commander's sacrifice, Thakur and Douglas continued to jawbone each other.

"Enough bickering!" shouted Baronova, silencing the debate and rousing Morgan from his thoughts.

He looked up and saw her strutting toward him. Stopping a few feet away, she said, "I suggest we negotiate a compromise, Colonel."

Morgan scratched his head and shifted his eyes to Quant. "Forgive me for saying so, Roksana, but it doesn't appear to me you have anything to negotiate with."

"It is true. With Quant and her colony to defend you, there is nothing we can do to stop you from taking *Resolute* back."

"Correction," interjected Thakur, "there's nothing you can do to stop us from taking all *three* ships back."

The jab did not appear to faze Baronova at all. She lazily turned toward Thakur and gave a slight shrug before returning her attention to Morgan. "We can modify our course to Tula to parallel your course to Earth for an agreed period. Say, two months. During that time, you will no doubt encounter zikzaws and expend your warheads. We can rendezvous and resupply you with additional warheads as necessary...from *Resolute* and, if needed, *Ranger*."

"What?" Douglas exclaimed. "Have you gone off the deep end, luv?"

Baronova's rebuke was swift and biting. "Be quiet, Eamon."

Morgan looked at Thakur. She quickly said, "I don't trust her, Paul."

"You do not have to trust me. The colonel will employ members of Quant's colony to ensure our compliance. If we break the agreement, they will seize control of our ships." Baronova paused and edged a little closer to them. "There are other advantages to this arrangement, Colonel. If you run short of supplies or parts during the sixty days, we can be summoned. If *Renown* becomes disabled, we can provide succor."

Quant, hovering directly beside Baronova, flickered as she transmitted a thought to Morgan. *"She is sincere, Skywalker...because she does not believe you will survive the next zikzaw engagement."*

"I'm right there with you, Quant. But I don't see a downside in accepting her proposal. Of course, I'll demand six months instead of two."

"She anticipates this already and has no qualms agreeing to a longer term, for she is convinced Renown *will be destroyed rather quickly. But she will counter with a request to retain some of the supplies you seek returned in exchange for the longer commitment."*

"Good to know. Thank you, Quant."

"Six months, Roksana," Morgan said. "Not two."

"But, Colonel, even two will be a challenge given our supplies, especially if you take back all we have transferred from *Renown*. Who knows when we will find suitable asteroids to resupply?"

Morgan turned to Thakur. "If I'm not mistaken, you said it was fortyish days to the asteroid cluster where we last resupplied."

"From where we were then, yes. Assuming max velocity and no stops, Mey and I calculated forty-two days to backtrack to the cluster."

"So, even if we account for the time spent during the run-in with the zikzaw, backtracking to *Ranger* and the change in course to Tula, we still should be able to reach the cluster within forty-five days, give or take a day or two."

Thakur nodded. "We can recalculate the exact time, but, yes, it shouldn't be more than that."

Morgan looked over at Baronova. From her flushed cheeks, he could tell she had realized he had outmaneuvered her. After mentally thanking Quant again for a glimpse into her thoughts, he said, "Sounds to me like resupply shouldn't be an issue if you aim for the same cluster."

Douglas, fists balled at his sides, turned beet red and stomped out of Morgan's view. Baronova stood firm, her arms crossed beneath her chest and a death-stare etched on her face.

"Do we have an agreement?" Morgan asked.

"Yes, we are agreed."

"Good." Morgan turned to Thakur. "Send your team to collect *Renown*'s supplies." As she left his side, Morgan looked back at Baronova. "I'd be much obliged if you had some of your folks lend a hand. The quicker the supplies are returned, the sooner you can undock."

He turned away and walked the rest of the way through *Renown*'s airlock. As he reached the ship's main corridor, he heard Baronova spew a flurry of words in Russian. Morgan doubted any of them meant *bon voyage*.

Morgan's reunion with Mey Wan and Bobby MacDowell was fleeting as both rushed by him in the corridor on their way to reclaim *Renown*'s supplies. But they stopped long enough to exchange handshakes and hugs before they continued.

Moments later, he also encountered Lieutenant Janie Gillespie, who was part of the supply retrieval team as well. Morgan didn't know Gillespie that well, having only interacted with her sporadically over the past two years, but they greeted each other like long-lost friends.

Similar receptions occurred on the flight deck where Morgan reunited with Jun Ikeda, Duncan Kassa and Lucas Bekker. Thakur was there too, and she and Morgan shared a long and hearty embrace. After which, she stood aside from the pilot's seat in deference to Morgan. He declined, declaring the ship was under her command.

After that, Morgan took a seat at the science station and typed a long message to Augustus Amato and Dennis Pritchard. He thought of summarizing all the events that had transpired over the past two days, but he ultimately decided to spare them the details for now.

The two men could do nothing with the details. Once transmitted, Morgan's message would take a year-and-a-half to reach them and, by then, both men would be consumed launching the arks and cobbling together resources to defend Jupiter from zikzaw rings forming close to the solar system. The last thing they would care about was a blow by blow of the mutiny and the losses incurred by the Suhkai. And it certainly wouldn't lift their spirits to know Morgan was down to one ship.

Therefore, Morgan instead focused on describing the strategy he would employ against the rings and urged the two men to do whatever was necessary to enact a similar plan on their end.

Sitting back as he neared finishing the message, Morgan pondered the surreal future ahead. Given the current date and *Renown*'s position, a lightspeed gamma burst from R5 that passed by the ship now, on December 6, 2021, would shoot through Earth's solar system in 578 days, or on July 8, 2023.

Approximately sixty days later for the people on Earth, somewhere in the neighborhood of mid-September 2023, Jupiter would begin its transit through the cone of R5's gamma rays, a short odyssey the Suhkai had projected would last less than two weeks.

While that seemed like a long way into the future, in reality, it meant *Renown* had a ten-week window, beginning now, to disrupt zikzaw rings. After that, nothing they did to foil zikzaws would matter because the gamma rays passing through rings in proximity to *Renown* during the next ten weeks would be the rays that passed through the solar system in September 2023, the danger zone for Jupiter.

And the sad part was that Morgan and his small band of supporters would not learn if their labors paid off until they had nearly returned to the solar system. In a bitter twist, they might end up arriving in time to witness the radiation and debris from Jupiter's explosion ravage the rest of the solar system.

Invoking a silent prayer they would instead return to discover Jupiter, Earth and the rest of the solar system intact, Morgan pressed enter and transmitted his message to Amato and Pritchard. Then, he stood and conferred with Thakur on the progress of the supply recoupment and a new course heading.

During their discussion, Thakur said, "I've been thinking about the deal you cut with Roksana. I don't trust her, Paul. I think we should offload their warheads as soon as possible."

"I don't trust her either, Shyla, but we don't have anywhere to store them. You know that. And besides, Quant and her cytons will keep them in line. Roksana can't stop them from reading their minds."

Thakur stepped closer. In almost a whisper, she said, "Screw keeping them in line. Let them go to Tula. But let's take the nukes before we send them off."

"Again, Shyla, we don't—"

"I'm not suggesting we take the nukes aboard. I have a better idea in mind."

Morgan frowned, unsure of how to respond. But the frown quickly melted as he studied Thakur's determined expression. She was not prone to fancy, nor was she one to grasp at straws. If she had an idea, it was grounded in logic and practicality. But Morgan was damned if he could see it.

"Okay, Shyla. You've got my attention. What's this idea of yours?"

For the next ten minutes, Thakur methodically walked Morgan through her idea. By the time she finished, Morgan was ashamed he hadn't thought of it earlier himself. But he had been thinking in tactical terms, whereas Thakur had obviously been thinking strategically. Like any desperate plan, however, there was a heavy cost involved. Morgan wondered aloud if Quant would bear it.

"I've already discussed it with her," Thakur said. "She's on board if you are."

Thakur's answer didn't surprise Morgan. He had spent enough time in Quant's presence to know the queen was selfless. *Perhaps that's why the Suhkai hold cytons in such high esteem*, thought Morgan. *They care more about the continuation of life than they do their own survival.*

Glancing back at Thakur, he said, "It's a hell of a plan, Shyla. It's bold without being reckless and makes the most of our resources. I say we go for it."

"Roger that," Thakur said, a big smile spreading across her face. "The zikzaws will never know what hit them."

CHAPTER 14

A few hours after arriving on Mars, Anlon Cully was at a small table on the fenced-off patio of the Mexican cantina named the Adobe Grill. In one hand, he held a cold bottle of south-of-the-border beer, while the other held up his phone to take a selfie.

Unsatisfied with the photo, he snapped two more before he put the beer down and began to swipe through the dozens of pictures he had taken earlier at various spots around the Meridiani colony complex. He searched for a suitable one to text Pebbles with the already-typed intro, *"Guess where I am?"*

He had been tempted to send her the text as soon as he deplaned on Mars but decided to wait until a time he knew she would be undistracted by anything else, and that time was now. Per the clock app on his phone, it was now 1:45 a.m. on July 8 in Incline Village. And from his memory of their daily vigils, he recalled Jupiter was set to rise above the eastern mountains astride Lake Tahoe at around 1:54. That meant Pebbles was now likely perched on the edge of the dock, waiting for the twinkling planet to appear.

And according to the tourist information app Anlon had downloaded when he arrived at the colony, the current transmission time for communications between the colony's satellite and Earth was just under nineteen minutes. So, if he sent his message now, it would arrive about ten minutes after

Pebbles' ritual greeting of Jupiter. If her past practice was any guide, she would still be looking up at the starry sky when her phone notified her of his text.

The only unknown was whether she would have her phone with her or not, but Anlon thought she would. She had sent him a few grumpy texts over the last few hours wondering why he had not called to say goodnight from Mayaguana, where it was now an hour from sunrise. Making the whole situation weirder, the area on Mars where the colony was situated was currently experiencing sunset.

He ended up selecting a photo a fellow tourist had kindly taken of him earlier. In it, he stood next to an observation window providing a view of the reddish Meridiani Planum landscape and the waning sun. Gazing at the image of himself in the white-and-silver flight suit, Anlon laughed and sent off the message. *She won't believe it. She'll think it's a scam.*

Still smiling, Anlon put down the phone, reached for his beer and looked beyond the cantina's fence at the main concourse of the colony. To Anlon, it looked like a mini indoor shopping mall with a handful of sit-down restaurants, a food court and a dozen shops lining the perimeter of an oval atrium. Given that it was close to the Martian dinner hour, there were lots of people milling about.

Some were clearly tourists like Anlon, as they gawked and snapped photos of just about everything they saw. Most of them were also clad in the same visitor outfit Anlon had on, but others had ditched the flight suits and were dressed in the kind of casual attire one might see strolling in a park on a summer's day.

Mixed in with the tourists walking about were Gateway employees in their black-and-gold flight suits and a smattering of what appeared to be construction workers clad in blue-and-orange coveralls and hardhats. The rest Anlon could observe were people dressed in other color-combination flight suits, some of whom were clearly restaurant and shop employees.

Earlier, when he toured the publicly accessible areas of the football stadium-sized colony, he had seen *Valor* and *Vanguard* through observation windows overlooking their space docks. He had also walked through a replica of the habitats under construction inside the arks, complete with jungle foliage and a waterfall.

After that, he had checked out his "quarters" in the dormitory on the level above the concourse. It was small and spartan and reminded Anlon of cabins he'd slept in on ocean research vessels in the past. While there, he had briefly considered taking a nap but quickly discovered he was too amped up to sleep. So, instead, he had opted to go in search of a drink.

Hopefully, I won't fall asleep during dinner, Anlon thought. In another hour, he was supposed to meet up with Amato and Gateway's director of the colony, Dennis Pritchard, for dinner. *Perhaps then,* he mused, *I'll finally learn the reason I'm on Mars.*

Forty-five minutes and another beer later, Anlon's eyes were beginning to droop when the ping sound of his phone jarred him to attention. Grabbing the phone, a screen notification informed him he had received a text from Pebbles. He immediately began laughing. While he couldn't see the entire message until he opened the text app, he could see the string of emojis at the beginning of Pebbles' message.

There were three round, yellow faces with bugged-out eyes followed by three similarly round and yellow faces with dropped jaws, then the letters OMG in all caps with several exclamation points. *Apparently,* Anlon mused, *Pebbles didn't think my pic was a scam.* The rest of the message read, *"You… are…shitting me! You're on Mars??? WTF??? When are you coming home?"*

Anlon was in the process of typing a reply when he heard a voice call his name. "Dr. Cully! There you are."

He looked up and saw Mark Myers, Amato's assistant walking toward him apace. Myers sounded a little out of breath as he said, "I've been looking all over for you!"

"Hey there, Mark. What's up?"

Myers motioned for Anlon to get up and said in a curt tone, "Come with me. Hurry."

Anlon frowned as he rose from his seat. "What's the matter? Am I late for dinner? I thought—"

"I'll explain on the way. Please, we need to go. Now."

Moments later, they were racewalking through the main concourse. Ahead, Anlon saw a security checkpoint. Above the checkpoint was a large sign that read "Space dock."

As they neared the checkpoint, Myers waved to the security guards. One of them stepped forward and opened a gate. Myers, still moving at a fast clip, turned to Anlon. "There has been a change in plans. Dinner has been canceled. Mr. Amato wants to see you right away."

In an instant, Anlon thought, *something's happened with R5.*

They stopped at the gate long enough for the guard to scan their ID badges. Once through security, Myers swiftly escorted Anlon through a door marked "Gateway Personnel Only." As soon as the door closed behind them, Myers turned around and said, "Follow this corridor to the stairs at the far end. Go up two flights and exit through the door marked Level C. That'll take you to the space dock terminal. Look for Mr. Amato at Gate 3. He said he'd wait 'til you arrived before he boards."

"Boards? Where's he going?"

Myers started backing toward the door they had just passed through. "He'll explain when you get there."

Anlon frowned as Myers turned to leave. "Come back, Mark. Tell me what's going on."

Without turning around, Myers said, "Hurry, Dr. Cully. There's no time to waste."

Seconds later, Amato's assistant disappeared through the door, leaving Anlon standing in the corridor scratching his head. Just then, his cell phone pinged again. He pulled it from his pocket and saw another text notification from Pebbles. *"Do you have any inside scoop about R5? Is it true it's awoken?"*

She had attached a screenshot of an article from WNN's website. The headline read, *Breaking: Sources at NASA confirm magnetar SGR-RE5 is now active.* The subhead below read, *Gateway officials decline to comment.* Anlon looked at the time-date stamp above the headline. WNN had posted the article within the last hour.

Phone in hand, Anlon began jogging down the corridor. By the time he scaled the stairs and pushed through the Level C door, he was panting heavily. A hundred feet away, Amato stood in a waiting area standing by an open door marked Gate 3. He was engrossed in a conversation with a woman Anlon recognized as Dr. Helen Brock. Both had troubled looks on their faces.

As Anlon slowed to a brisk walk and tried to catch his breath, Amato briefly looked in his direction then turned back to Brock. He said something to her, the two hugged, and Brock rushed away. Anlon followed her with his eyes and saw that she was headed to another open door marked Gate 2.

What the hell is going on? Anlon wondered. *Even if WNN's report is accurate, Jupiter is still two months from crossing into R5's gamma cone. Why is everyone in a panic?*

Ahead of him, Amato sat down on a chair in the empty waiting area and motioned Anlon to the chair on his right. When Anlon was within ten feet, he held up his phone. "Have you heard? NASA's announced R5's awake."

Amato's shoulders slumped as he shook his head and mumbled, "Already?"

Stopping in front of him, Anlon asked, "Is WNN right? Is it legit?"

"Have a seat, Anlon."

Anlon grabbed the back of the chair and pulled it around so he could sit facing Amato. As he lowered onto the seat, he said, "I'll take that as a yes."

Over Amato's shoulder, Anlon saw the door to Gate 2 was now closed. Above the door, a wall monitor displayed the phrase, *Launch Sequence Initiated.* Below the words, a digital clock began a countdown starting at ten minutes. On a line below the clock, the screen announced the shuttle's destination as Dione.

"Anlon, listen to me," Amato said. His voice was soft and sounded grandfatherly. "We need to talk, and, unfortunately, we don't have a great deal of time."

Locking his eyes on Amato, Anlon said, "From the look on your face, Augie, and the way Mark acted, whatever's happened with R5 must be pretty bad."

"Please, Anlon. I need you to focus. I need you to listen."

Anlon edged back in the chair. "Okay, Augie. I'll shut up and listen."

"Thank you." The elderly man paused, smoothed his hand over his bald head and sighed. To Anlon, it seemed as if Amato was trying to formulate the right words to say.

"Just say what's on your mind, Augie. You don't need to sugarcoat anything for me."

Nodding, Amato said, "All right, Anlon. I invited you here to make you and Pebbles an offer. You see, I've held back two dozen passenger berths on our new arks, and I had intended to gauge your interest in accepting two of the berths for the journey to Tula."

"You're kidding," said Anlon.

"No, I'm quite serious. Initially, I had held back the berths for the *Rorschach Explorer* crew and their immediate families, but none of them were interested in relocating to Tula...aside from Ajay Joshi, of course...he's already on his way there aboard *Venture*.

"When the rest said no, I turned to my most valued Gateway colleagues, including people like Dennis Pritchard and Helen Brock, but they declined as well. Too many attachments on Earth. I'm certainly too old to go myself, and I have no family still living, so then I decided to begin making discreet inquiries with people I admire and respect, including you and Pebbles."

Anlon, head spinning, was vaguely aware Amato had paused speaking. Of all the possible explanations he had considered for Amato's invitation to Mayaguana, this was not among them.

"I know it's a lot to absorb," Amato continued, "but unfortunately, I need to know now whether you are interested." He turned and looked at Gate 3's open door. "I'm returning to Mayaguana momentarily, and the shuttle taking me there will be the last one to leave Mars for Earth until after Jupiter has passed through R5's cone...assuming it does.

"If you are remotely interested in accepting my offer, I urge you to stay here in Meridiani while you think it over. It may prove very difficult, if not impossible, for you to make it back to Mars if you return to Earth with me now. I fear one or more of Earth's superpowers will shortly seize control of Mayaguana and Gateway's ships there. If that were to happen, you should also understand that if you stayed here, Pebbles might not be able to join you for the trip to Tula."

Anlon held up a hand to stop Amato from going any further. "I'll save you the suspense, Augie. As flattered and grateful as I am by your offer, I'm going back to Earth with you."

As he spoke, Anlon was distracted by the sight and sound of Mark Myers running toward them with two roller suitcases in tow. One of them Anlon recognized as his. Amato's voice recaptured Anlon's focus.

"Before you make that decision, Anlon, please understand the implications. If the bursts destroy—"

Anlon stood and said, "I got it, Augie. I understand. Been thinking about those implications for four years. So have a lot of other people, I'm sure. Now, let's get the hell out of here and back to Earth."

SPACE DOCK
GATEWAY VENTURES' STATION ON SATURN MOON DIONE

The docking terminal was bustling with people when Helen Brock arrived three hours after departing Mars. Much of the activity appeared connected to the first wave of the evacuation from Callisto, as she noticed many of the luggage-toting people scurrying about were wearing the navy-piped-with-gold flight suits of Gateway's Callisto "residents," researchers invited for year-long rotations on the Jovian moon.

Mixed among them were similarly denoted Dione residents in their purple-gold uniforms and Mars Gateway employees like Brock, clad in black-gold. She also noticed a few white-gold flight suits distributed to tourists.

Most of the gaggle appeared headed for one of three security checkpoints: one for visitors, one for Dione residents and the last for Gateway employees. The rest in the terminal were moving in the opposite direction, presumably on their way to docks for departing shuttles headed to Mars or Earth.

As Brock angled toward the employee checkpoint, she looked around for Hexla. While there were a couple of Suhkai visible in the terminal, none wore tunics with tapestry designs common to Hexla's wardrobe. But Brock did see a familiar face awaiting her on the far side of the checkpoint, Doctor Robyn Martinez.

Brock regarded Martinez as one of Gateway's up-and-coming stars. Currently, she was serving an apprenticeship under Hexla's tutelage, soaking up all she could about Suhkai knowledge of space. Before stepping into the security scan booth, Brock plopped her travel backpack on the luggage conveyor and waved to Martinez.

Once inside the locked booth, Brock placed her right hand on a fingerprint scanner and stared ahead at a facial recognition camera. As soon as the two devices verified her identity and cleared her to enter the Dione station and the luggage scanner had Ok'd her bag, a welcome message sounded from an intercom, and the door on the far side of the security booth opened.

There, Martinez stood beside a waiting transport cart. Martinez smiled and stepped forward, opening her arms for a hug. "Hello, Helen. I'm glad you've come."

For a moment, Brock froze. From the other side of the security area, she had not been in a position to catch more than a glimpse of Martinez' face. But now that she was in full view, Brock was stunned at the change in Martinez' appearance since she had last seen her.

Martinez had always been on the thin side, but not to this extreme. And her skin, normally bronzed, was faded and ashen. Together with her bloodshot eyes, cracked lips and frizzy, unkempt hair, Martinez looked like a withered castaway. Brock's shock must have been apparent to Martinez, who closed in for the hug and said, "I know. I look like shit. Don't judge. And, please, no lectures."

Enclosed in her arms, Brock patted Martinez' back, her hands feeling the ridges of Martinez' ribs and spine. In as reassuring a voice as she could muster, Brock said, "No lectures, I promise. But I am concerned."

"Don't be. I'll be okay." Martinez hugged her more tightly. Brock felt the woman's bony chest pressing against her breasts. Suddenly, she became furious with Hexla. *How could she let this happen to Robyn?* Pulling back from the embrace, Brock asked, "Where's Hexla?"

Martinez moved to the repository of the luggage scanner and collected Brock's cleared backpack. "On a recon mission."

Brock stepped forward and took the pack from Martinez. "What? I was told she was here."

Sliding onto the driver's seat of the cart, Martinez said, "Yeah, sorry about that. If I had known you intended to jump on a shuttle, I would have told

Mary she was gone." The answer confused Brock, and it must have shown because Martinez added, "Hexla didn't want anyone at HQ to know she was gone."

"I don't understand. Why?"

"Hop on," said Martinez, patting the front passenger seat. "I'll fill you in when we get to the lab."

Brock wavered for a moment, then stowed her pack on the back seat of the golf-cart-like transport. As she joined Martinez up front, she said, "What's going on, Robyn? Where did Hexla go?" Eyes forward, Martinez drove the cart away from the docking terminal without a response. Brock pressed for an answer. "Robyn, talk to me."

As Martinez maneuvered the vehicle around people on foot and other carts, she said, "Not yet. Wait until we get to the lab. Too many ears around here."

Reluctantly, Brock sat back while Martinez continued to wind her way through the congested concourse. During the two-mile drive to concourse A, she pondered many things. Among them, she wondered the reason behind Martinez' drastic weight loss and weak appearance.

While Brock considered it possible Martinez had incurred a sickness or developed an eating disorder, she thought it more likely the aerospace engineer had become hooked on neefra.

On Callisto, where Hexla and Martinez primarily resided, each day was equivalent to 16.7 Earth days, meaning daylight and darkness on Callisto each persisted for *over eight Earth days at a time.* So while Dione wasn't as bad, each day there lasted 2.7 Earth days, it was still challenging to adapt to the Saturn moon's longer periods of daylight and darkness.

For someone like Brock, who expected only to stay on Dione for a time equivalent to an Earth/Martian day, it was no big deal. She might experience jet lag-like symptoms at some point, but from experience, she knew the effects would be short-term and mild. But for long-term residents on Callisto and Dione like Martinez, the disruption to human circadian rhythms could be devastating.

To limit biorhythmic disruptions, Gateway had instituted a range of practices to simulate Earth-like days in both facilities. But many people still struggled to adapt. And while common sleep medications used on Earth were of help to some, they were nowhere near as effective as neefra, the potion developed by the Suhkai for deep space travel.

However, tailoring neefra dosages for humans was a tricky proposition. No two people seemed to respond to the potion in the same way, which meant cycles of experimentation to find the sweet spot for each person. And that could lead to addiction.

Turning to Martinez, Brock thought of how hard the young engineer had pushed herself when they were both at NASA. It was easy to imagine Martinez driving herself even harder now, especially since she worked so closely with Hexla. The body clocks of Suhkai deep-space travelers like Hexla were tuned to cycles that required sleep once every nine-to-ten Earth days. And when they did slumber, they were typically out for the equivalent of four to five Earth days.

If they had tried to maximize their working time together, Brock mused, Martinez was the one more susceptible to cycle disruptions, not Hexla. Tired of speculating, Brock broke the silence of their ride to A concourse. They were in B concourse now, and there wasn't a soul within a hundred yards.

"How long have you been on neefra?"

Brock watched Martinez clench her jaw and saw the outline of every muscle, tendon and bone involved in the movement.

"No lectures, remember."

"I'm not lecturing. I'm asking."

"That's what they all say," Martinez said with a laugh. Her voice turned bitter as she briefly looked at Brock. "Then comes the lecture."

"Is it wrong to worry about you?" Brock asked.

Her eyes back on the hallway ahead, Martinez said, "At this point, yes."

Brock frowned. "What's that supposed to mean?"

Martinez swerved the cart and brought it to a screeching halt, inches from crashing into the hallway wall. Turning to face Brock, she said, "Hello? R5? Impending doom? Who gives a shit what neefra's doing to me? You, me and everyone else will fry long before neefra puts me down."

"You don't know that, Robyn. I mean about frying." Brock looked around to make sure no one else was within earshot. Lowering her voice, she said,

"We don't know what will happen. Jupiter could breeze through the gamma cone."

"Bullshit," Martinez said, ejecting spittle along with her retort. "Jupiter's done. Earth too. We'll all be ashes soon!"

Panting heavily, Martinez began to shake from head to toe. Her eyelids fluttered, her pupils rolling up underneath the lids. To Brock, she looked like she was on the cusp of a seizure. Brock took hold of her hand. It was cold and clammy. With her other hand, she reached up and felt Martinez' forehead. It was on fire.

"Take it easy, Robyn," Brock said. "I'm sorry I riled you up. I'll back off, okay?"

Martinez appeared locked in a trance, her face and body still trembling. Brock spoke softly to her. "Take some deep breaths with me. We'll do it together, okay? Breathe in nice and long, just like this." Brock inhaled deeply through her nose. Martinez continued to shiver, staring blindly at the wall. Brock exhaled slowly through her mouth and scooted closer to Martinez, cupping the back of her neck. "Come on, Robyn, give it a try. Breathe in…"

While Brock repeated her breathing prompts, she massaged what little muscle her fingers could detect on Martinez' neck. The young engineer closed her eyes and tipped over. Brock helped guide her down until her head rested on Brock's lap. Martinez began to mimic Brock's deep breathing. Soon, Brock could feel Martinez' trembling begin to subside. She smoothed her hand through Martinez' hair and whispered, "That's it, Robyn…just keep breathing."

A few minutes later, the trembling was gone, and Martinez' breathing returned to normal. Brock continued to stroke her hair and massage her neck and shoulders until it seemed Martinez had fallen asleep. But then, Brock heard her whisper, "You should launch *Vanguard* and *Valor* right now. Before it's too late."

Brock remained silent. She did not want to risk inciting Martinez again. The young woman needed medical attention, not a debate. Martinez, however, would not let it go. She opened her eyes, looked up at Brock and whispered, "I'm serious, Helen. I don't think Hexla will be able to stop them in time. I'm afraid she's making things worse by trying."

Is she hallucinating? Brock wondered. *Stop who? From what?* Against her better judgment, Brock engaged her. "I don't know what you're talking about, Robyn. Who is Hexla trying to stop?"

"Zikzaws." Martinez closed her eyes and turned her head to rest against Brock's lap once again. Returning her voice to a whisper, she said, "There are too many of them. You should launch the arks now."

CHAPTER 15

An hour later, Helen Brock was seated beside Robyn Martinez' hospital bed listening to the rhythmic beeps and chirps of the diagnostic equipment monitoring the sleeping woman's vital signs. They were hypnotic enough to coax Brock's eyes to close. As she drifted toward sleep, she thought, *just a few minutes. Just until the doctor comes back.*

The beeps began to fade, and her mind darkened. Her body seemed to become weightless, and soon she could no longer feel the plastic chair pressed up against her sore back nor her throbbing feet inside her tightly clamped boots. She was vaguely aware of her breathing, feeling the rise and fall of her chest, but otherwise, the rest of her body went numb.

She whispered, "zikzaws," and shapes began to form in her mind. At first, Brock saw a clash of purple, pink and white blobs. They bubbled up here and there at random intervals until they seemed to pop and fade away into clouds of color. In their former places, new blobs arose. Soon, the cloudy, bubbling mixture looked like a simmering sauce amid thick steam.

Then the sauce organized itself into a shape…a writhing snake. The clouds and blobs making up the snake began to randomly flash like heat lightning as the snake oozed and slithered through a starry night sky. Forks of electricity fired out from the snake, spreading out with finger-like tips, reaching, grabbing in the darkness.

Another snake formed, and then a third. As they drew closer and closer, they seemed to display menacing scowls. A silhouette of a small shape passed before them. Against the backdrop of purple, pink and white, it looked like a black dot.

Now, fully immersed in a dream, Brock reached out her arms to try to sweep away the clouds. They hissed and bit at her neck. No matter how fast and hard she tried, she could not push them away. They seemed to disappear and reform elsewhere in an instant. Frantic now, Brock spun around in circles, kicking and flailing as she watched the beasts devour the dot. Teeth dug into her shoulder as if they were trying to tear away meat from her bones. She screamed, "Noooo!"

Her eyes flashed open, and she tugged her shoulder free from the teeth. She spun around as a man in a white coat retracted his hand. Before she knew it, she toppled backward, landing on a cushioned surface. Her ears detected beeps and chirps, and the man speaking to her, "It's okay, Dr. Brock. You fell asleep."

Rapidly becoming aware of her surroundings, Brock looked around and saw she was lying across Martinez' blanket-covered feet. Panting, she pushed off the bed and grabbed hold of the bedrail. Beads of sweat dripped from her face onto the blanket. The doctor's feet came into view next to her.

"I'm so sorry I startled you," he said.

Still breathing hard, Brock nodded and said, "It's okay." Slowly, she raised up into a standing position and wiped her forehead clear of sweat. Then, turning around to face the doctor, she asked, "Is the Sukhai here yet?"

"Yes. His name is Aylor. He brought a cyton translator, as you requested."

"Good. Which way do I go?"

The doctor pointed out the room's doorway. "Into the hall and to your right. The rooms are labeled. You're looking for H14."

"All right, thanks." Brock turned to look down at the still sleeping Martinez. "What about, Robyn? Any update?"

"She's stable right now, but her blood pressure is still lower than I'd like. Also concerned about her circulation." He pointed at her pale face and bluish lips. "Her kidneys aren't in great shape, either, but I think she'll pull through."

A new flash of anger coursed through Brock. *How could Hexla have let this happen to Robyn? How did nobody else notice she was hooked? Why didn't someone intervene?* She looked at the doctor. "You have my number. Call me if her condition worsens or she wakes up."

The doctor agreed and left the room. Brock lingered for a moment, holding Martinez' cold hand. Once again, she felt a spike of anger. Letting go of the hand, she wheeled around and headed out of the room. *Time for some answers.*

When she pushed in the door to room H14, it slammed against the doorstop. Directly ahead of her, seated on the floor, was a Suhkai, presumably Aylor. He looked at her and slightly bowed his head. The golden cyton hovering beside his shoulder floated toward Brock and began to flicker.

"Greetings, Dr. Brock."

She nodded at Aylor and spoke to the cyton. "I'll speak. You translate. Don't transmit my thoughts to him, just what I say out loud. Got it?"

The cyton pulsed in a throbbing motion.

"Thank you," Brock said. She turned and looked up at Aylor. Even seated on the floor, he was taller than the five-foot-five Brock. "I'm mad as hell, and I want some answers."

The cyton flickered, paused, then blinked again. Aylor's telepathic response formed in her mind. *"Yes, I can see that."*

She let go of the door, and it swung shut. Approaching Aylor, she said, "Do you know where Hexla is?"

"Not with precision. The signals from her ship have been sporadic."

"Why did she leave without informing us?"

"I assume she believed time was of the essence."

Brock began to pace. "I don't buy that, Aylor. She could have transmitted a message after she left. Robyn Martinez told me Hexla didn't want us to know she had left. Why?"

"I cannot speak for Hexla. Only she can answer your question."

Brock ceased pacing and approached Aylor. His red and orange tunic seemed to shimmer under the light of the halogen fixture above. Looking into the black orbs of his eyes, Brock said, "Tell me about the zikzaws. Robyn said Hexla had gone to stop them. Stop them from what?"

Brock knew zikzaws were an alien life form that fed on radiation. Cloud-like in appearance, they were scavengers who feasted on the electromagnetic aftermath of cosmic explosions. The crew of the *Rorschach Explorer* had encountered one in the asteroid belt four years ago and had recorded video of the alien.

In the years since then, Brock had learned more from the Suhkai about the beasts, one of the thousands of life forms living in space cataloged by Suhkai in their travels throughout the galaxy. Zikzaws reminded her of sharks or vultures, animals whose keen senses of smell could detect injured or dead prey at a distance. Only, zikzaws didn't rely on smell. Instead, the clouds surrounding their shrouded, snakelike electromagnetic bodies were receptors capable of detecting high-frequency radiation at great distances. But just like sharks and vultures, once they sensed their prey, many of them gathered in a frenzy to consume it.

From the little Martinez had said before passing out, Brock deduced Hexla discovered zikzaws had detected R5's gamma bursts. But she could not fathom why Hexla viewed them as a threat. Still looking into Aylor's eyes, she waited for him to enlighten her.

Finally, the cyton started flickering again. Aylor's answer followed close behind. *"They are uniting to siphon off radiation in R5's bursts."*

Brock frowned. "So what?"

"You are aware of the recent surges in R5's bursts?"

"Yes."

"Zikzaws are causing them. They are manipulating the flow of radiation, condensing the bursts' energy into a more powerful beam."

Confused, Brock backed away from Aylor and sat on a chair she found haphazardly leaning against the wall. Looking around, she realized the Suhkai must have pushed all the small room's furniture aside to make room for his elephant-thick legs. She had been so angered when she entered the room, she had not noticed the tables and chairs were shoved to the walls on both sides of Aylor.

Refocusing her thoughts, Brock replayed Aylor's explanation in her mind. It didn't make sense. She could certainly see how zikzaws might be drawn to R5's bursts, but only for the dribs and drabs of electromagnetic radiation mixed in with R5's gamma rays. As it had been explained to her by the Suhkai before, zikzaws feasted on *magnetized* energy. But the photons in gamma rays were neutral magnetically. They carried no electric charge. Because of this characteristic, photons were not susceptible to manipulation by electromagnetic forces. Yet, Aylor had said they were manipulating the bursts. How? She posed this question to him.

"They have created what you Earthlings call a gravitational lens...or more appropriately, in this case, a gravitational funnel. They have likely formed many of them between R5 and your solar system. They will continue to form more."

Immediately, an image formed in Brock's mind. It was as clear and crisp as if it were hovering right before her eyes. From past interactions, she knew the image was a projection from Aylor through the cyton in the room. The vision showed a circling mass of pink light against a backdrop of stars. Inside of the thickish pink band, there was a thin ring colored blackish gray. To Brock's mind, it appeared the gray mass was rippling back and forth between the open space in the middle of the ring and the encircling pink band. The implications sank in fast. Brock mumbled, "Oh, my God. They're using Suhkonium."

While photons were not influenced by magnetic forces, they were by gravitational forces. Though she did not fully understand how the zikzaws were creating gravity in the image, Brock was pretty sure it had something to do with the interplay between the Suhkonium inside their circle and the centrifugal force of the zikzaw spin. As she watched the vision further, the pink ring enlarged and constricted like the aperture of a camera.

The zikzaws were using gravity to channel photons through the aperture, concentrating them into a more condensed beam. Brock thought of Aylor's analogy of a funnel and imagined the photons as mist spraying from a hose. She saw the zikzaws as hands on the hose nozzle, twisting the nozzle opening smaller, concentrating the harmless droplets of mist into a solitary, powerful jet of water.

With a shake of her head, she said, "But the zikzaws are electromagnetic. How can they exert any kind of force on Suhkon—"

Brock stopped when she realized she was wrong. The gravity system of Suhkai ships relied on electromagnetic sensors to stimulate Suhkonium to spin. She looked at Aylor and said, "That's where your people got the idea for your gravity tech. You copied the mechanics of zikzaw rings."

"Very perceptive. Zikzaws are more than amorphous clouds of electric energy. They are intelligent beings who have learned to use what space provides to aid their survival."

Martinez' earlier plea raced through Brock's mind. *"Launch Vanguard and Valor now. Before it's too late."* She blinked and shook her head to clear her mind of the zikzaw ring image. Glaring at Aylor now, she said, "Why would you hide this from us?" At the same time, she thought, *why would Robyn hide it too?*

Aylor's mannerisms seemed nonchalant to Brock as he answered through the cyton. *"It was Hexla's place to say. She chose not to. As I said earlier, only she can tell you why she remained silent."*

The catty answer infuriated Brock. She rose from the chair and stuck her face within inches of Aylor's snout. "That's the biggest load of Suhkai shit I've ever heard! We had a right to know!"

"You know now," Aylor communicated.

Brock's hand itched to slap him, but she resisted the impulse. Turning away, she closed her eyes and tried to rein in her emotions. Just then, a heavy weight landed on her shoulder. She looked down to see the tips of Aylor's fingers resting there. *"You trouble yourself over something you can do nothing about."*

Brock turned to face him. "What?"

"The rings cannot be stopped. Eventually, one or more will form near your solar system, and zikzaws will detect Jupiter's large magnetic field. They will realize the planet is vulnerable and manipulate R5's bursts to destroy it."

"Surely, there must be something we can do."

"It is possible to disrupt rings, but it is a futile exercise. As soon as one disbands, another forms somewhere else. These are desperate creatures, Dr. Brock. In this sector of the galaxy, there are few sources of concentrated energy for zikzaws to nourish themselves. So when an event of this magnitude occurs — the awakening of a star — they become very determined to ex-

tract every particle of energy they can. And when they detect an opportu-
nity to enhance the yield of their labors, they are relentless."

Brock's anger boiled over. "Damn it, Aylor! We're supposed to work with each other. It's the survival of our species at stake. We had a right to know about a risk like this!"

Brock slid her shoulder away from Aylor's hand and turned to leave. The cyton zoomed in front of her face just as she reached the door. *"Where are you going? There is more to discuss."*

"You bet there is," she said, her gaze riveted to the flickering cyton. "But, first, I need to tell my people about this." Brock turned to face Aylor and poked him in the shoulder. "I'll be back, and you're going to tell me how we can disrupt the rings."

MEDICAL WARD
GATEWAY'S DIONE STATION

After sending her lengthy email to Pritchard on Mars and Amato on Earth, Helen Brock returned to the medical ward to check on Robyn Martinez. Knowing it would be at least three hours before she heard back from either man, she wanted to discuss zikzaw rings with Martinez before reconnecting with Aylor. Brock didn't trust the Suhkai scientist. She also wanted an explanation for Martinez' silence.

At the nurses station, Brock learned Martinez had awoken. Before the head nurse could say anything more, Brock turned and headed toward Martinez' room. The nurse chased after her, telling her the doctor ordered no visitors. Brock ignored her and kept moving. The nurse followed in hot pursuit.

When she reached the closed door to the room, Brock spun around and confronted the nurse. "I'm going in, and you're going to back off. If you've got a problem with that, find the doctor. Tell him to come see me. I must speak to Robyn immediately."

Brock pushed open the door with her rear and backed into the room, her glare locked on the affronted nurse. To her relief, the nurse did not try to prevent her from entering the room. From behind, she heard Martinez' weak, raspy voice say, "I'm sorry."

Turning toward the bed, Brock saw Martinez' bony hand press the bed control to raise the incline. Her skin tone had returned, and she appeared fully alert. But she looked frail enough to break with a strong puff of air. Brock moved to her side and lightly touched her hand. "How are you feeling?"

"Tired. Weak. But better."

Caught between the desire to wrest quick answers from Martinez and the realization she was in no condition for an interrogation, Brock reached up and smoothed errant strands of Martinez' hair and spoke to her gently. "Robyn, I talked with Aylor. I know about the zikzaw rings."

Martinez closed her eyes. "Has he heard from Hexla?"

"No." Brock watched Martinez' head lull as if she were drifting toward sleep. Raising her voice a bit, Brock said, "Robyn, stay awake a little longer, okay?"

The young woman's eyes fluttered open, and she dipped her chin in a slight nod. Brock asked, "Earlier, you said Hexla was trying to stop them. How? Aylor was evasive."

"They can't be stopped," Martinez said, her voice barely above a whisper. "Only delayed."

As Brock tried to make sense of Martinez' answer, the doctor burst into the room. He was accompanied by two Gateway security guards.

"Who in the hell do you think you are?" he snapped.

"Give me five minutes," Brock said. "That's all I need."

"No. This is my patient. Get out, or these gentlemen will escort you out."

Brock turned to look at the security guards. They had already recognized her, which was evident from their hesitance to advance further into the room. She supposed they had noticed the gold comet insignias on her uniform's black collar identifying her as one of the company's top brass. They were bound to obey her orders over his.

The physician turned to the guards and pointed at Brock. "Remove her. Now."

"Sorry, doc, no can do," one of them said. He retreated a step, hands behind his back. "She outranks you."

Throwing up his hands, the doctor turned in a circle, cycling glares at Brock and the guards. "This is insanity. The young lady's barely stable."

Rather than engage the doctor again, Brock leaned over Martinez and asked, "Delay them, how, Robyn?"

"Distract them. Give them something else to eat." In slow motion, Martinez raised her head from the pillow as she gripped Brock's arm. Wild-eyed, she said, "But it's too late, Helen. There are too many of them. And more are coming. They will keep coming for as long as R5 is active. Launch *Vanguard*. Launch *Valor*."

She drew in a sharp breath and began to convulse. The doctor pushed Brock out of the way and angrily ordered her and the guards out. Pressing the call button, he then yelled for nurses while his eyes darted between the now blinking and beeping diagnostic monitors.

Brock felt hands take hold of each arm and pull. Behind her, she heard someone whisper, "We should go." Brock didn't resist as she began to back her way toward the door. Two nurses rushed past, bumping into her as they crossed into Brock's field of vision. All the while, Brock stared helplessly as Martinez' body writhed with spasms.

In a state of shock, Brock sat down on the floor outside the room. Through the still-open door, more nurses raced in. The chatter between the doctor and nurses was urgent and clipped. At some point in the flurry of activity, Brock heard the doctor say, "We're losing her…"

Brock closed her eyes and, for the first time in a very long time, she prayed. But the prayer wasn't answered. A few minutes later, the chatter stopped, as did the beeping of the monitors. One by one, nurses slowly exited the room. With her head bowed, Brock saw only their sneakered feet and a glimpse of their purple scrubs as they passed by. Finally, the doctor emerged, his sneakered feet stopping right in front of her. He sighed and said, "She's gone." As he walked away, Brock heard him mumble, "You should have listened to me."

She wanted to weep for Martinez, but the tears wouldn't come. Nor could she conjure the strength to apologize to her dead colleague or the doctor. Numb to the activity around her, Brock's mind filled with the frantic Martinez' final words, visions of zikzaw rings and thoughts of Jupiter's impending doom.

Brock might have remained in a stupor for longer if not for the sound of pounding feet heading toward her. Hoping it was an indication Martinez had stirred alive, she looked up. It was one of the security guards. He was waving both hands to get her attention. "Dr. Brock! Dr. Brock!"

When he reached her, he bent over and began to pull her up. Breathing hard, he said, "Come with me! Quickly!"

Once on her feet, she asked, "Why? What's wrong?"

A golden cyton appeared from behind him and began to flicker. *"Go to dock. Now! Aylor awaits you."*

Brock felt a pang of urgency flow through her psyche. Together with the guard, she began to run. Ahead of them, the cyton zoomed down the hall. Brock stared at the alien ball of light and projected a thought. *"What now?"*

As the cyton arced out of sight around a corner, it replied, *"Message from Hexla. New ring forming. Very close. Too close."*

DENNIS PRITCHARD'S QUARTERS
MERIDIANI PLANUM COLONY, MARS

The night couldn't have been more restless for Dennis Pritchard. No matter what he did to clear his mind and fall asleep, apprehensions tugged him back awake. Finally, at a little past four in the Martian morning, he gave up and started the new day.

Propped on the edge of his bed, he unhooked his phone from the charging cable and left the bedroom of his small suite to brew coffee. With the Breakfast Blend pod inserted into the coffee machine, Pritchard leaned back against the counter and began to scan the headers of his overnight messages.

The first to demand his attention was a message from Helen Brock accented by a red flag icon beside the header, which read: *URGENT. OPEN IMMEDIATELY.* Pritchard bowed his head and closed his eyes.

In the background, the aroma of coffee filled his nose, and he heard gurgling liquid begin pouring into his mug. Pritchard breathed in deeply and waited for the pour to finish. *Just one sip*, he thought, *one moment of peace. Then I'll read it.*

He opened his eyes and stared at the screen, his thumb hovering over the header of Brock's message. Then he saw another all-caps title in his inbox. It was from Paul Morgan. It, too, was accompanied by a red flag. *IMPORTANT UPDATE. READ ASAP.*

Just below that header, Pritchard saw he had received a message from Jenna Toffy. It did not have a high priority icon attached to it like the others, nor did the subject line scream in capital letters, but it might as well have in Pritchard's mind. *Need to talk with you before the* Valor *tour.* He shook his head as he opened the first of the three messages. So much for a moment of peace.

Two cups of coffee and a hot shower later, Pritchard zipped up his uniform and left his quarters, his mind swimming in caffeine and the content of the three messages.

Aboard the docked *Valor*, Dante Fulton was also awake before the Martian dawn, though as he looked out the window of his home in Habitat A, he saw the simulated purple-blue sunrise of Tula, not the pinkish hue of the Martian daybreak outside the ship.

Seated at the desk in his bedroom, Dante looked down at the laptop in front of him and stared at the message he had composed. *Will Kiera respond this time?* he wondered.

Dante's brief relationship with Kiera had been stormy and ended badly. In the years since their breakup, Dante had come to realize their relationship had never really had a chance from the start. After Kiera returned from the *Rorschach Explorer*'s mission, too much changed too quickly in both of their lives. Though they both had recognized it while it was happening, they naively thought they could navigate the altered dynamics. They couldn't and didn't.

The relationship blew apart in a colossal argument featuring Kiera's accusations of Dante's jealousy and insensitivity, and his equally vitriolic parries about Kiera's selfishness and self-pity. She had not spoken to him since, nor had she communicated with him in any other way over the past three years, six months and nine days. *But who's counting?* thought Dante.

Every now and then during that span, he had written to her. And each time, he had extended an olive branch. But Kiera had never replied. Knowing he would soon pilot *Valor* to Tula, leaving Earth and Kiera behind, possibly forever, Dante resolved to try one more time.

Dearest Kiera, read Dante's message, *it looks as if I may be leaving soon, and I desperately want to see you before I go. Over the past few years, I have apologized more times than I can count, but if another apology will make a difference, I would like to offer it in person. Please allow me a chance to set things right between us before it's too late. I hate the thought I may never see you again. I hate even worse the idea of leaving for Tula on bad terms. You mean a great deal to me. Always have, always will. Love, Dante.*

He didn't know what else to say that he hadn't already said a hundred times before, so he pressed send and prayed this attempt would yield a reply. As soon as the send confirmation appeared on the screen, Dante pushed back from the desk and left to take a stroll through the habitat's commons. He knew it would be his only respite in the long day ahead.

Just as he rose from his seat, though, his planned stroll was nixed by a call from Dennis Pritchard. "I've just received messages from Skywalker and Helen. Meet me in my office in ten minutes and I'll give you the download."

NASA'S JET PROPULSION LABORATORY
PASADENA, CALIFORNIA

When the warning alerts first arrived in EGO's mission control center, Ed Chen was in a JPL break room down the hall, coffee cup in hand, debating which sugary snack to purchase from the two vending machines in front of him.

He had been around NASA long enough to know a sudden burst of commotion and raised voices meant one of two things, either a key mission objective had been achieved, or a catastrophe was in the works. As he listened closer, it quickly became evident the sounds echoing down the hall were of the latter variety.

Instinctively, he knew the sounds came from his EGO team. Although there were other NASA control rooms on the same floor, none managed assets of enough significance to produce the furor of the clamor that had erupted. Chen's intuition was confirmed seconds later when he heard the sound of racing feet and shouts calling out his name.

Chen turned to see Sergei Kolov duck through the break room doorway. The look on his face was as panicked as the sound of his voice. "Come! Quickly!" He disappeared from the room as fast as he had entered. Chen pitched his full coffee cup in a trash can and took off after him.

When he passed into the hallway, Kolov was already twenty yards ahead of him, dodging around curious onlookers drawn out of their offices by the commotion. One of them asked Chen what was going on. As he ran past the woman, Chen said, "Beats the hell out of me, but it ain't anything good."

Closing in on the open entrance to the control room, Chen heard snippets of shouted conversation.

"...LOS, EGO-1 and 2..."

"...Holy shit! Do you see what I'm seeing?..."

"...send a message to Gateway STAT...find out if they know what's happening..."

"...EGO-3 is now LOS too..."

Within five minutes of Chen entering the room, the twelve gamma-ray telescopes making up the EGO array were gone, fried by a massive surge of photons. In truth, EGO had died over an hour beforehand when the last of the satellites' signals began their journey from their positions in the outer solar system toward Earth.

Chen ordered his team to ping the satellites, even though he knew the procedure to reestablish communications was likely a futile effort. He thought of the lost *Juno* probe from five years ago and mumbled, "It's déjà vu all over again."

Only that wasn't entirely true. From the spate of final data transmitted by the satellites, Chen could tell the surge that wiped out EGO wasn't a garden variety gamma burst from R5. This one had *moved*, slashing across the array like the stroke of a sword. He slid onto the nearest chair and thought, *it's not possible.*

CHAPTER 16

D eeply concerned about the gamma burst surges and the implications of enacting Sanctuary, Augustus Amato had ordered the shuttle pilot to return to Mayaguana from Meridiani at maximum velocity. While the order initially seemed to elate the pilot, she quickly informed him she was not yet certified for max-velocity space travel.

"I'm only rated for point five LS," she had said, a reference indicating she was authorized to pilot the Suhkai spacecraft up to half the speed of light, approximately 540 million kilometers per hour.

"Then get us back to Mayaguana at point five LS," Amato replied.

Thus, the shuttle carrying Amato, Anlon Cully and Mark Myers touched down at Mayaguana at 7:15 a.m. local time, after covering the 338 million kilometers between Mars and Earth in a little more than an hour, including the controlled launch into Mars orbit and the landing on Earth.

There, the three men had separated. Myers and Anlon headed off to rooms in the facility's dormitory to sleep. At the same time, Amato stopped in R5's mission control center for status updates on the bursts and the progress of the Sanctuary plan. After the briefings, he, too, then retired to his dormitory quarters for a couple of hours' shut-eye. It was far less sleep than he had needed, but Amato felt he could not afford to be out of action for longer than that.

He was sure the Big-3 superpowers surveilling Mayaguana would quickly learn of the tourist shuttle cancellations and the order to evacuate Callisto and Dione. Presuming they were also keeping tabs on *Valor*'s and *Vanguard*'s training centers in Nicaragua via satellite, they would also notice the Tula colonists marshaling to decamp the facilities.

Amato didn't know how long it would take the Big-3 to respond to these actions, but he was confident they would each react in some fashion during the day. They were already agitated about the gamma surges, believing they were the result of Gateway's interference with their observatories' signals.

So, Amato had to be awake and prepared to deal with them when they responded. He was also anxious to hear what Helen Brock learned from Hexla during her trip to Dione, knowing that Hexla's insights would be valuable in tailoring responses to the Big-3. As it turned out, however, Myers roused Amato from sleep less than an hour after he had nodded off.

"You've just received two high-priority messages," Myers had told him, "One from Col. Morgan and the other from Dr. Brock."

Later, with his mind still grappling with the implications of their independent warnings about zikzaw rings, Amato was urgently summoned to mission control. Unfortunately, by the time he hustled into the center, Gateway's gamma telescope array had already been destroyed by a swordlike slash of photons.

Shortly after, Amato learned the Big-3's telescopes monitoring R5's gamma bursts had also been destroyed, leaving Gateway blind to determine whether the slashing stroke of photons had been an isolated anomaly or an indication of a permanent shift in the magnetar's bursts.

The former possibility was frightening enough, but Amato considered the latter downright paralyzing. If the shift continued toward Jupiter at the rate it had moved through the satellite array, the mission control director told him, the bursts would hit the planet in less than a week versus the two months previously expected.

Now, with that chilling possibility fresh in his mind, Amato turned to Myers. "Send a message to Dennis. Tell him to begin a launch countdown for *Valor* and *Vanguard* immediately."

Myers stared at him for a moment. "But, sir, none of the colonists have left Nicaragua yet."

While that was true, Amato knew that the arks wouldn't be ready to launch for at least forty-eight hours under the best of circumstances, so there would be time to transport at least some of the colonists to Meridiani before the ships blasted off. "Send the message, Mark. Tell Dennis to transmit the expected lift-off time ASAP, and let him know we'll do our best to get the colonists there on time."

As soon as Myers bolted off to send the message, Amato turned to the flight director. "Stall providing NASA and everyone else with any information. Tell them we're still analyzing the latest data. Same answer to any calls and messages from brass further up their food chains. No exceptions."

"Roger that."

As the director began to scurry toward a computer station, Amato said, "And keep me apprised of any further changes with the bursts."

On the short walk back to his office, Amato turned his thoughts to the rest of the Sanctuary plan and wondered if they could fully execute it in less than five days. The original timeline had called for thirty. The biggest bottlenecks would be the number of transport ships available to move people and supplies and the time to load and unload the vessels.

Gateway had a total of twenty-four Suhkai cruisers, and, from what Amato had been told earlier, eight were currently engaged in evacuating Callisto. Another seven were docked on Dione. Technically, there should have been eight on Dione, but Helen Brock's message indicated Hexla had taken one of the ships to investigate a zikzaw ring forming outside the solar system. Of the remaining eight, six were on Mars, and two were parked at Mayaguana.

Somehow, in less than five days, those twenty-four ships would have to evacuate Callisto and Dione and transport the Tula colonists from Mayaguana to Meridiani to launch the arks in two days.

Attempting to accomplish all of that in such a short period would lead to a logistical nightmare on Mars. The Meridiani colony would be overwhelmed with incoming people and material in the midst of trying to load and launch the arks. *It could turn into a fiasco*, thought Amato. *But what choice do we have?*

As he ruminated on that thought, he realized it was sure to turn into a fiasco. The rest of the Callisto and Dione evacuations would have to wait until *Vanguard* and *Valor* were away. So he called Myers in his office and tasked him with communicating the evacuation pause to Pritchard and prodded his assistant to light a fire under the butts of the team marshaling the Tula colonists to expedite the Nicaragua decampment.

Moments after Myers left to follow through on the orders, Amato heard a raised voice through the open door of his office.

"I don't care. I'm going in!"

As he looked up, a fuming Maj. Julia Carillo strode in. She was dressed in her tour shuttle flight suit, and Amato realized she must have just learned of canceled tours. "I want to know what's going on, Augie, and I want to know *right now*! No more stonewalling."

After Carillo finished reading the messages from Morgan and Brock on Amato's computer, she pushed back and looked across the desk at Amato seated in a guest chair on the other side.

"My God," she said. After pausing to stare off, she turned back to Amato and asked, "Have you launched the arks?"

"No, not yet, but I've given the order to start the countdowns."

She immediately followed up with queries about Callisto and Dione. Amato had not briefed Carillo on the details of the Sanctuary Plan, but she was astute enough to anticipate the need to evacuate both moons. It was hard for Amato to lie to her, to tell her the evacuations were underway knowing he had just ordered them paused, but he saw no other choice. There wasn't time to debate the decision.

Once again, Carillo looked away with a vacant stare. This time when she refocused on Amato, she asked, "What about Paul's recommendation to use nukes to distract the zikzaws?"

The question caught Amato off-guard. Carillo had evidently not read the two messages closely enough. He frowned and said, "We have five days, Julia. Recall what Helen said in her message. She indicated Hexla had pegged the closest ring at one-light-month away."

"Where did the five-day number come from?" Carillo asked.

Amato wavered before answering. The five-day figure was a projection based on the gamma bursts' last observed movement before the telescopes were destroyed. Before he could acknowledge the five days was only an estimate, Carillo spoke up again.

"I find it hard to believe a ring of zikzaws feeding on R5's bursts a light-month away could detect Jupiter. That's *800 billion* kilometers away, Augie. And if some did detect Jupiter from that distance, why wouldn't they fly closer? I mean, if they're intelligent enough creatures to know Jupiter exploding would produce a great feast for them, a feast bigger than what they can find in R5's bursts, why wouldn't the zikzaws haul ass to form a new ring closer to Jupiter as soon as they put two and two together?"

She raised another excellent point Amato had not considered. "You think a new ring has formed closer?"

Carillo nodded. "I think it's possible, don't you? Think about the timing, Augie. When did R5's gammas start up? The first bursts passed through the solar system five-to-six weeks ago, right? Which means they would have passed by a point one-light-month away over two months ago."

Amato saw what she was driving at. Helen Brock's earlier message said Hexla had detected the zikzaw ring via a UV scan. UV light is no different than other forms of electromagnetic radiation. It travels at the speed of light. So, the ring Hexla detected a week ago had formed at least a month before her scan, as it would have taken the UV light that much time to reach Hexla's scanner on Dione.

Carillo was suggesting that in the time since Hexla detected the ring, some or all of the zikzaws in the ring had flown closer to form a new one. Then, as Amato thought about this more, he focused on the fact Hexla had left a week ago to try and stop the zikzaw ring. *Why would she have left so urgently, knowing Jupiter was still two months from entering R5's cone?* Amato quickly answered his mental question. *I'll tell you why...because she knew the zikzaws were on the move.*

"Mark," Amato bellowed, "get in here now."

As soon as Myers leaned his head in the doorway, Amato told him to relay an order to the flight director in R5's mission control center. "Tell him to start scanning for UV radiation in the direction of R5's gamma cone. I'll join him shortly to explain why."

"You got it," Myers said before he disappeared from view.

Turning back to Carillo, he said, "Now I know why Paul Morgan valued you so much as a co-pilot, Julia. You don't give up. Thank you for being so ornery."

She stood and said, "Get me a swarm of cytons and some nukes, and I'll go after the bastards myself."

He smiled at her noble statement, a gesture Carillo apparently didn't appreciate.

"I'm not kidding, Augie. I'll take *RE-II* and blow the hell out of them."

He rose from his seat and approached her. Speaking with admiration in his voice, Amato said, "I have no doubt you would, Julia. But remember Paul's message. The rings form *inside* the gamma cone. *RE-II* and missiles wouldn't survive long enough to reach the ring. Not even cytons can survive gamma rays of that magnitude."

Carillo clenched her jaw and shook her head. "Then I'll light up space just outside the cone, just like Paul said he would do. Just get me the nukes and cytons and leave the rest to me."

"Julia, seriously, I appreciate your gallantry, but—"

"*Stop! Listen to me.* What do we have to lose by trying? Huh? It'd be the first God damned productive use of nukes in human history. And who knows? It might work…," She paused to catch her breath then said, "…*we could save eight billion people,* Augie."

DENNIS PRITCHARD'S OFFICE
MERIDIANI PLANUM COLONY, MARS

Dennis Pritchard learned of the telescopes' destructions an hour before Toffy arrived for their 0800 meeting. Unfortunately, due to the communications delay with Earth, there was little he could do to participate in the conversations he suspected were taking place between Amato at Gateway's Mayaguana HQ and the various space agencies.

But he could and did take action on Mars, canceling the *Valor* tour and ordering Dante and Zylun to start countdown clocks for *Valor* and *Vanguard* as Amato instructed. The launches were set for 0900 in two days, the earliest possible time the ships could be loaded with supplies and passengers. He prayed the launches wouldn't be necessary but was well aware they couldn't risk losing the arks.

Now Pritchard faced the most challenging decision of all — who to put on board the ships.

The easy answer was the Tula colonists slated as *Vanguard*'s and *Valor*'s passengers. But Pritchard knew it would be a lengthy process to transport them out of Nicaragua to Meridiani.

One would have thought it was a simple matter to fly the two Suhkai cruisers docked at Mayaguana directly to the training centers and take off for Meridiani from there, but such an option was impossible. The landing thrusters of the Suhkai cruisers would light the surrounding jungle on fire, and taking off would further spread the blaze. Not only could the fires incinerate the wilderness, but they might also kill the colonists before they could board. And a minimum of four sorties would be required to transport all the colonists and their gear, meaning more fires if and when the two shuttles returned to pick up the second batch, presuming the remaining colonists were not consumed by smoke, heat and flames in the meantime.

The next best option was transporting the colonists to the closest airport at Bluefields and executing the landings/liftoffs from there. But this, too, was impossible. Gateway didn't control the airport, and Pritchard was sure the Nicaraguan authorities would deny them permission to land and liftoff. Beyond the disruption the shuttle landings/liftoffs would cause to the airport's normal flight operations, the shuttle's thrusters would destroy the runway's surface, rendering the airport unusable. Standard runways were not built to withstand the forces produced by the thrusters.

So, the 540 colonists and their gear would first have to be airlifted via Gateway's helicopters and flown to the Bluefields airport. There, they would board Gateway jetliners and fly to Mayaguana's airport…all this assuming the Nicaraguan authorities granted permission for the flights in a timely manner. After arriving on Mayaguana, they would need to load on buses and travel to Gateway's spaceport. Finally, the colonists and their gear would have to transfer onto Suhkai shuttles to fly to Mars.

Even under the most aggressive scenario Gateway could mount, Pritchard saw no way all the colonists could make it to Mars in time for the launches.

He loathed the idea of launching the arks with less than their intended capacity, knowing there were hundreds of people on Mars who could supplement any colonist shortfall. But how could he choose who to grant passage and who to leave behind?

Making the decision more difficult, Meridiani Planum had already started receiving evacuees from Callisto and Dione. Though the order to pause the evacuations had been given, there were already over a hundred evacuees who were now part of the colony's population, and there were several shuttles still en route that had left the moons before the pause order.

Pritchard saw the potential for an ugly scene with so many people crammed into the colony. Everyone would discern the reasons for the evacuations and ark launches. There was no way to hide them. It wouldn't matter if Pritchard told them the launches were precautionary, that the arks would return to Mars when Jupiter was no longer in danger. Faced with the possibility of perishing, everyone would clamor for places on the arks. But would there be enough space?

As he wrestled with the vision of a crush of people storming the ark docks, Pritchard heard a commotion outside his office. Though his door was closed, he distinctly made out Jenna Toffy's raised voice. "I will not wait! Now, out of my way."

Pritchard couldn't make out the words uttered in response by his assistant, Hal Barnes, but from his soothing tone, he assumed Barnes was trying to calm Toffy. Seconds later, the door swung open, and Toffy charged in. "What the hell are you pulling?"

An angry Barnes followed close behind her. He was bent over and holding his shin. Looking at Pritchard, he said, "She kicked me! Can you believe it?" Pausing to glare at Toffy, Barnes asked, "Should I send for security?"

Pritchard waved him off. "No, it's okay, Hal. I'll take it from here."

Barnes glared at Toffy a few seconds more before turning to hobble out of the office, but she didn't even seem to notice him. Her eyes were glued on Pritchard. "Answer me! What's going on?"

He found it hard to believe she would barge in like this just because he had canceled the tour, leaving him to conclude word of the ark count-downs had reached her. Either that, or she had received a message from her WNN colleagues on Earth about the telescopes before Pritchard had ordered a colony-wide comms blackout for all but official Gateway transmissions.

As Barnes closed the office door on his way out, Pritchard motioned Toffy to a guest chair. "Have a seat, Jenna." He moved around his desk to sit in the second of his guest chairs. The seething Toffy stood her ground midway into the office. With her fists balled at her sides, she looked as if she might lunge at him.

"If this is a prank, Dennis, it's a pretty God-damned shitty one."

"I'm not a prankster, Jenna." Pritchard lowered down onto the chair, his hand once again pointing toward the empty one beside him. "Come on, sit with me. We've got a lot to talk about, and I don't have much time to spare for you."

The friendly tone of his voice seemed to pierce through her anger. She relaxed her hands and stiff posture. "I'm not sure I like the sound of that."

As she began to walk toward the empty chair, Pritchard asked, "What have you heard?"

"It's more what I haven't heard. Why have you blocked transmissions with Earth? Why did you cancel the tour? Why the extra security at the ark docks? Are you trying to muscle me to keep quiet about the *Venture* sex scandal?"

Pritchard took off his glasses and massaged the bridge of his nose. *If only it were that benign*, he thought. Resting the eyewear on his crossed knee, he said, "I don't care what you do about *Venture*. If you're commit-ted to creating a scandal, I can't stop you. But, you'll have to wait to do it. I don't anticipate lifting the comms blackout anytime soon."

Just as quickly as Toffy's butt touched down on her seat, she pushed back up and starting walking toward the door. "Then my crew and I are out of here on the next shuttle for Earth."

"There won't be any shuttles to Earth. Not for the foreseeable future. I've canceled all non-essential flights."

She spun around. "What? Why?"

"Please. Come back. Sit."

By this point in the conversation, Pritchard realized Toffy was clueless about the destroyed telescopes and apparently unaware of the launch countdowns.

"There have been...developments...with R5, Jenna. I need all the shuttles we have to evacuate Callisto and Dione."

The answer seemed to spark the journalist in Toffy. In the blink of an eye, her indignant expression turned into the steely gaze of an inquisitor as she retraced her steps to the chair. Pritchard could visualize the wheels turning in Toffy's head. Perched on the edge of her seat, her eyes darted left and right. Her mouth parted slightly, and she looked up at him. "Oh, my God. Jupiter. You think it's going to blow."

Folding his hands in his lap, Pritchard said, "Not necessarily, but the gamma bursts from R5 have shown erratic behavior that concerns us. We've decided to evacuate Callisto and Dione as a precaution."

Once again, her eyes began to dart around, only this time, they were scanning him, seemingly vetting the veracity of his response by observing his expression and body language. Still perched on the edge of her seat, she said, "Bullshit. If that were all that was going on, you wouldn't cut off comms with Earth. You wouldn't lock down the arks. You think Jupiter's going to blow."

"I have no way of knowing what Jupiter will do, Jenna. That's God's honest truth. But the nature of the threat went up several notches overnight, and we have to assume the worst."

"Meaning what?"

"Meaning there's a high probability *Vanguard* and *Valor* will launch in the next forty-eight hours."

Toffy slid back on her chair, her cheeks puffing out as she blew out a long gust of air. Blankly staring past Pritchard, she seemed lost in thought.

It was a look Pritchard expected to see on the faces of many in Meridiani Planum as they began to comprehend the possible implications. While she continued to ruminate, he said, "It's not a one hundred percent certainty that we'll launch, but until we have a better handle on the severity of the threat, I don't want word of the launches getting out. It could cause a global panic on Earth for no good reason. If the threat passes, or we judge it to be nominal, we'll abort the launch countdowns. But, until then, no comms or shuttles. I'm sorry."

Her blank stare remained, but Toffy nodded, an indication to Pritchard that she understood the reasons for the restrictions. But he needed more than her understanding. He needed her agreement to forgo any shenanigans to circumvent the strictures. "I would greatly appreciate you and your crew refraining from attempting to bypass the blackout."

Toffy's eyelids fluttered, and she turned to look at Pritchard. "If Jupiter explodes, will Earth definitely be destroyed? I mean, is it an absolute or just a possibility?"

Pritchard leaned forward, resting his elbows on his knees, and clasped both hands together. Looking into her eyes, he said, "It pains me to say it, Jenna, but I don't see any possibility Earth survives if that were to happen. I don't think it will explode like Jupiter, but radiation and debris will assuredly devastate all life on Earth. It won't happen all at once. There will be many who survive the initial shockwaves of radiation. But the shower of debris from the explosion will take care of the rest within a short time afterward."

She nodded again. "The same will happen here too?"

"Eventually, yes, but it will be several months before we cross into Jupiter's path of destruction." Pritchard watched as Toffy's expression turned quizzical. Before she could question why he provided the answer. "Mars, at this moment, is moving behind the sun in relation to Jupiter, meaning the sun should shield us from the aftermath of any explosion until we loop around into the debris field. Earth, unfortunately, won't be so lucky. It's just now emerging from behind the Sun. There won't be anything to shield it from Jupiter."

Toffy's face lost its color, and once again, her eyes began to dart around. To Pritchard, she looked like a frightened animal. It was as if she had never really viewed R5 as a mortal threat until this very moment.

"Can anything be done to stop it from happening?" she asked.

"Honestly, I don't think so." Pritchard's voice trailed off into a near whisper. He bowed his head and thought of the earlier prayer he had muttered to the picture of his wife and daughter. "We just have to hope Jupiter is stronger than the zikzaws think it is."

"Zikzaws?" The sharp tone of Toffy's voice shook Pritchard's wandering mind. He looked up and saw color returning to her face and hands. "What do zikzaws have to do with Jupiter?"

Toffy would, of course, have recalled the *Rorschach Explorer*'s encounter with a zikzaw in the asteroid belt. She had chronicled the crew's journey in her series, *Expedition to Callisto*, and the follow-on series, *A Leap for Mankind*. As Pritchard recalled it, she had devoted an entire episode of the last series to the zikzaw-cyton battle the crew had observed.

He relayed a summary of Brock's and Morgan's description of the zikzaw rings and told Toffy about the telescopes lost to the shift of R5's gamma bursts. "It appears zikzaws have decided to force matters to a head."

"And we can't stop them?"

"I'm sure conversations are going on right now on Earth about every possible option to stop them, but that's not my problem to solve, Jenna." Pritchard paused and held up his index finger. "I've got one responsibility, and only one, at this point. Get *Vanguard* and *Valor* a safe distance from here as fast as possible, and that's what I intend to do."

Toffy went silent again, staring off at the wall behind Pritchard. It was a lot to take in, so this time he just sat back and waited for her to respond. During the impasse, there was a knock on the door. Pritchard looked over as Hal Barnes opened it and said, "You just received a new message from Mr. Amato."

Barnes glanced warily at Toffy then back at Pritchard, a gesture Pritchard took as an indication the contents of Amato's message were sensitive.

"Okay, thanks, Hal. We should be done here shortly."

Barnes nodded, but instead of leaving, he hovered in the doorway. Pritchard had worked with him long enough to know it meant Barnes had something else to convey, something he knew Pritchard would not be pleased to hear. "What is it, Hal?"

The question stirred Toffy's attention. Pritchard watched her twist her torso to look at Barnes. The young man briefly darted his eyes to her before he looked back at Pritchard. "You should read the message as soon as possible."

As Barnes backed out of the doorway and closed it, Pritchard thought, *Oh, God, what now*? Standing, he turned to Toffy. "We'll have to finish our conversation later. Again, I'm sorry to cut you off from Earth, but I hope you now understand why."

She nodded, her helmet of blonde hair waving to-and-fro as she stood. "I do. All things considered, I guess it's better to be here than on Earth."

"I thought you might feel that way after we talked," he said. "You'll keep what we've discussed confidential for the time being? No backdoor messages to Earth? No stirring up troubles here?"

"Yeah, I'll be a good girl. Will you keep me plugged into what's going on?"

"When and if I can, yes, but no more barging into my office or assaulting Hal, please."

The quasi-admonishment caused a smile to emerge on her face. "No more boots to the shin, I promise."

They shook hands and walked side by side toward the door. As they neared it, Toffy stopped and said, "One more question...can you make room for my crew and me? On the arks, I mean? I'm not thrilled with the idea of spending the next eleven years making babies with God knows who, but if it gets me a spot on board, I'll do whatever's asked of me. I'm sure given the alternative, my crew will feel the same."

Pritchard had expected the question. He was surprised it had taken Toffy this long to ask it. And he knew similar questions would soon descend upon him from every angle. "Jenna, I'll tell you the same thing I intend to tell anyone else who asks. I can't say yes, but I won't say no. We'll just have to see how things play out over the next forty-eight hours. There are a lot of moving pieces right now."

Toffy nodded and wiped moisture from the corners of her eyes. "Understood. Just wanted you to know I'm interested if there's room."

He took hold of her hand and gently squeezed it. "I appreciate you letting me know."

Seconds later, she was gone, but the pit left in Pritchard's stomach by the dejected look on her face as she departed lingered far longer.

CHAPTER 17

*V*alor's loading dock was a madhouse when Dante arrived. Forklifts carrying supplies to be loaded on the ark were entangled with habitat construction equipment that had just disembarked. In between the gridlocked vehicles, workers shouted and gestured at each other to move out of the way. In the middle of the mess, Dante saw the hard-hatted Charlie Zimmer nose to nose with *Valor's* flight engineer, Norris Preston. *We don't have time for this*, Dante thought.

He pressed his way through the throng to reach the two men just as Zimmer pushed the lanky Preston back a few steps. Over the clamor around him, Dante heard Zimmer shout, "I'm not moving one piece of equipment, *not one*, until someone tells me what the hell is going on!"

Preston recovered his footing and shouted back, "Gateway orders. That's all you need to know!"

As Zimmer fired back with a suggestion that Gateway could stick its orders "where the sun don't shine," Dante stepped between the jaw-boning men and spoke to Preston. "I've got it from here, Norris. Alert Dr. Pritchard about the delay then continue the pre-checks."

Dante turned to Zimmer and grabbed his arm. "Come with me."

Zimmer was easily a hundred pounds heavier than the rail-thin Dante, most of it muscle, so it was not easy to dislodge him from his stance. But Dante felt Zimmer's bicep relax, and the man began to follow him toward a nearby emergency exit. Once they reached the door, Dante let go of Zimmer and motioned him to pass through. "After you."

With the door closed behind them, the sounds of the conflict brewing on the other side dropped to a low rumble. Dante turned to the sweat-streaked Zimmer and said, "Have you lost your mind, Charlie?"

"You tell me, Captain," Zimmer said. "One minute, my crew's going about their business in Habitat B, then the next minute, I get a message to bug out pronto. No one will tell me why or for how long, but I see Gateway people running around like their asses are on fire."

"So, your solution is to blockade the dock?"

"Not at first, but then I found out the same craziness is going down on *Vanguard*. So then, I hear there's a comms blackout, and the shuttle bays have been sealed off. Then one of your boys let it slip you're prepping to launch in two days, not the sixty-one we thought we were working towards. I may not have fancy degrees like you, but I can smell shit in the wind just fine."

"Good for you," said Dante. "Now, move your equipment out of the way and get the rest of your crew off *Valor*. That's an order."

Zimmer crossed his thick forearms across his chest and shook his head. "Not until you tell me why you've moved up the launch, why everyone's so hyped up."

"Charlie, I don't have time for this. I've given you an order. Carry it out."

"Or else what?" Zimmer said, widening his stance. "You'll fire me? Send for security? Get some of your Suhkai buddies to drag the rest of my crew off *Valor*?"

"All of the above."

Zimmer shook his head again. "Captain, I served two tours in Iraq back in the day. I know a hasty retreat when I see one. You're bugging out…and from the looks of all the supplies you're trying to load, you ain't coming back."

It was safe to say Dante had hoped Pritchard would be the one to break the bad news about the zikzaws to the residents of the colony, so he found himself unprepared to parry with Zimmer. And he also realized scrounging up a security detail to remove the blockade would eat up precious time needed to ready *Valor*. Most of Gateway's security personnel had already been deployed to block unauthorized access to the docks and guard the colony's supply depot while the arks were prepped.

"It's just a precaution, Charlie."

"Save that bullshit for someone else, Captain. I don't buy it." Zimmer's eyes seemed afire as they glared at Dante. "Let me tell you what I think is going down. I've seen the news from Earth over the last couple of weeks. I know the gamma rays have gotten worse. I've also watched the video streams about the debates going back and forth between experts about what it might mean. Hell, my own people have been debating it too. You think those rays are going to nuke Jupiter, and you're getting out of Dodge before it happens."

Dante felt backed into a corner. Zimmer had nailed the truth of the situation, and there was nothing Dante could say to refute him. Lying to him would only make matters worse, but he couldn't bring himself to tell Zimmer about the shift in the gamma bursts. He took a deep breath and said, "Look, Charlie, we're concerned about the rays, for sure. But we don't know what's going to happen to Jupiter, honest to God. All the same, we can't risk losing *Vanguard* and *Valor* if things turn bad. So, we're loading up and taking them out of danger...as a precau—"

Zimmer started to interrupt, but Dante cut him off. "Quiet. Let me finish. If the danger passes, we'll come right back. You know better than anyone else. Neither ship is ready to fly all the way to Tula. But if the worst happens, we'll head for Tula anyway and hope for the best."

The explanation seemed to appease Zimmer. His guarded posture relaxed, and he unfolded his arms. "Now, that wasn't that hard, was it?"

A pique of anger flowed through Dante. Zimmer seemed to think this was some sort of game. He had just wanted Dante to cry uncle and fess up. "Glad you got the answer you were looking for. Now, clear your equipment out of the way and let us load."

"On one condition. Me and my people are coming with you. Day *and* night shift. Same with Tank Grimes' crew over on *Vanguard*."

"That's not possible, Charlie."

"Oh, I think it is. Right now, there are more of my people aboard than yours, and my people know every inch of that ship. Trust me, *Valor* ain't flying unless we're on it. We'll see to that. So will Tank and his crew on *Vanguard*."

"Charlie, you don't understand. The ships can only accommodate a certain number of people. The spots are already spoken for."

"Bull crap. I know the ships' specs. Both are built to carry up to eight hundred people. And I know for a fact they're starting with less than three hundred each. You've got plenty of room for me, Tank and our people. We're talking an extra 180, max. So, I suggest you get on the horn to your boss lickety-split and *make* it possible, or nobody's going anywhere."

Exasperated, Dante began to pace back and forth on the small landing. "That extra space is set aside for children born in flight to Tula, not adults."

Zimmer was ready with a quick answer. "True, but you said you were launching as a precaution. If the ships come right back to Mars after the danger passes, then what's the big deal?"

"The big deal is what happens if the danger doesn't pass, Charlie. You and your people can't go to Tula. It will mess everything up."

Zimmer leaned against the wall of the stairwell and crossed his arms across his chest again. "From where I'm standing, I don't really care what it messes up. If the danger doesn't pass, then we're dead."

Dante came to a stop right in front of Zimmer. "You don't get it. Everything built into these ships, everything put into selecting and training the colonists, was designed to give them the best chance of making it to Tula. Adding you and your crew completely screws up the dynamics. It could cause the whole mission to collapse.

"You guys have no concept of what eleven years of space travel will be like. While I grant you the colonists don't either, they were handpicked based in part on compatibility profiles, and they've been training together, learning to live and work with each other, for a year."

The unimpressed foreman shrugged. "We'll figure it out as we go."

"Just like that, huh?" Dante snapped his fingers close to Zimmer's face. "You'd risk the survival of humanity just to save your ass, betting you can figure it out as you go?"

Zimmer unfolded his arms and nudged Dante back a few steps. "Look, Captain, with all due respect, my people are *well* acquainted with the hardships of space, *far* more acquainted than *any* of your so-called colonists. While they've been playing house in the tropics for the past year, we've been up here building out the guts of the arks.

"In fact, most of my people have been on Mars for damn near three years living and working inside this colony, sleeping in Gateway quarters, eating Gateway grub, following Gateway orders. Yeah, we've all rotated back to Earth for a month's R&R each year and, yeah, we've had some knuckleheads who didn't pan out. But, all in all, I think we've proven we can handle living and working in space. So, you'll forgive me for thinking we can figure the rest out on the fly."

Dante sighed and sat on the steps leading up to the next level. "It's not that simple, Charlie."

"It is to me." Zimmer pushed off the wall and walked toward the stairwell door. "*Valor* and *Vanguard* don't fly without us." He paused with his hand on the door handle and turned back to Dante. "Come find me when you're ready to deal."

As soon as he was gone, Dante bowed his head and rubbed the base of his neck. *How am I going to get through to him? How can I make him understand?* Suddenly, he felt a tingling sensation on his forehead, and a foreign thought entered his mind. *"You cannot make him understand, Dante. I would stop trying."*

Darting his head up, Dante looked around for a cyton but found the stairwell empty. Shortly after, however, he noticed the faint reflection of flickering golden light on the wall above the next landing. Dante called out, "How long has your cyton been listening, Zylun?"

"Long enough for me to learn what is in his mind and yours," came Zylun's reply. *"Zimmer is not bluffing. On the contrary, he is prepared to sabotage* Vanguard *and* Valor *if you do not agree to his demand."*

With his head still tilted up toward the landing above, Dante asked, "Are you suggesting we should agree?"

The cyton finally floated into view and drifted down toward Dante as it communicated Zylun's reply. *"What other alternative do you have? Attempts to negotiate will only waste precious time. He holds all the leverage, and his mind is set. And attempts to force his people off the ships will result in damage that will take time to repair, more time than you have to spare."*

As Dante watched the cyton flicker, an idea popped into his mind. "Couldn't you stop them with cytons?"

Dante knew cytons could cloak themselves and become invisible, making it easy for them to sneak up and zap Zimmer and his co-conspirators into unconsciousness. Dante recalled cytons had used such tactics multiple times on the *Rorschach Explorer* crew four years prior.

"I could, but I will not. Suhkai attacking humans, with or without the assistance of cytons, would be a violation of the treaty agreed to by Haula and Skywalker."

"Even in this circumstance? With all that's at stake?"

"There is a better way. Accede to Zimmer's demand."

Dante was becoming as exasperated interacting with Zylun as he had been talking to Zimmer. "You're not concerned about what might happen if we take on nearly two hundred extra people we know little about?"

Dante's point centered around the criteria Gateway had used to select the Tula colonists, including age, physical condition, reproductive health, genetic background, acuity, mental health, personality traits and so on. Unfortunately, none of this information was known about the construction crews. In Dante's opinion, introducing them into the population of colonists might wreak havoc in multiple ways.

"There are ways we can minimize the jeopardy, Dante," Zylun responded. *"The simplest would be to isolate them in a single habitat until we've assessed their compatibility with the colonists."*

As Dante pondered Zylun's suggestion, he began to nod. Segregating Zimmer and his people might work...assuming the interlopers agreed to the arrangement. That was a big "if" in Dante's mind.

"How can we be sure they'll fall in line?" he asked Zylun. "Given the stunt they're pulling now, how do we know they won't continue to try to assert conditions of their own once we're in flight?"

"We do not know. But I have been inside the mind of Zimmer, Dante. He is not an evil man. He has done this to save the people under his charge, which I consider admirable. And as he told you earlier, his workers have been good citizens on Mars until this incident. In my mind, there is plenty of reason to believe they will continue to be good citizens. However, the decision is yours to make, not mine. But you must make it quickly."

The cyton flew up and out of sight, ending the conversation with Zylun.

Afterward, Dante lingered alone for a few minutes, ruminating over both of his stairwell conversations. He found it hard to suppress his anger at Zimmer but realized anger wouldn't solve the problem at hand. The arks needed to launch as soon as possible, and Dante needed Zimmer's cooperation to make it happen. The problem was as simple as that.

He pulled his cell phone from his pocket and placed a call to Dennis Pritchard. As he waited for the colony director to answer, Dante prayed Pritchard wouldn't balk at Zimmer's demand.

SPACEPORT TERMINAL
GATEWAY'S DIONE STATION

By the time the transport cart bearing Helen Brock neared the spaceport terminal, the order to evacuate Dione was broadcasting over loudspeakers throughout the station. Earlier, she had tried to elicit more information from Aylor's cyton-messenger flying in front of her, but the cyton had ignored her queries and instead urged her to run faster.

She had given it her all for several minutes, but her body eventually ran out of energy, forcing her to slow to a gasping walk. Thankfully, the cyton had noticed her distress and zipped ahead to secure a cart and driver for the rest of the mile-plus trek to the spaceport.

Now, as the cart approached a blocked-off security checkpoint, the fires in Brock's legs and lungs had abated, but her mind was still awash with adrenaline. Caught up by the implications of a new zikzaw ring mixed with the blaring evacuation announcement and lingering thoughts of Robyn Martinez, Brock swooned. She felt like a twig in a fast-moving stream twirling about as the currents swept her along.

In her haze, Brock barely noticed the security guards wave the cart through the checkpoint. Instead, her eyes were transfixed on the pulsing cyton leading the cart driver past bays of Suhkai cruisers prepping for the evacuation. Then, in the distance, Brock's blurry eyes detected a looming figure. Blinking to clear her vision, Brock soon saw the spacesuit-encased Aylor beside another cruiser. The ship stood alone, well past several empty docking bays. Then, the cyton ahead of Brock's cart began to flicker, and a thought from Aylor flowed through her consciousness.

"My apologies for the urgent summons, Dr. Brock, but I needed to see you before I depart."

The cart slowed to a stop, and Brock dismounted. She looked up at Aylor, confused by the sensation of finality that accompanied his telepathic thought. Before she could question him, the cyton relayed more from Aylor.

"A sacrifice is necessary to delay the formation of a new ring."

A vision began to coalesce in Brock's mind just as the cart drove away. A massive swarm of cytons flew toward a thin band of swirling pink light. Inside the swarm was a Suhkai cruiser. As they neared the nascent ring, random ribbons of pink light began to peel away and headed toward them.

The cytons arced away and shot into the blackness of space. The zikzaws that had already peeled from the ring followed the cytons. Soon, other zikzaws joined the chase and the ring dissolved.

Then, as the cyton ball began to throb with light, it also appeared to slow down, allowing the trail of zikzaws to catch up. The swarm turned and started to weave in and around the procession of zikzaws, creating a frenzied churn of the two electromagnetic species. An instant later, there was a blinding flash of light, and the churn was no more. As the vision faded, the cyton resumed transmitting Aylor's thoughts.

"I do not know whether this plan will succeed, but I will attempt it. There is no way to know how many zikzaws will follow me or whether the detonation of my ship's engines will kill all that do. But it must be done."

"I don't understand. I thought you said it was futile to fight the zikzaws?"

"In the long run, yes. But unless I disrupt this ring soon, your people will not have enough time to launch the arks. The zikzaws in the ring have detected Jupiter. They are bending the flow of R5's gamma rays to destroy it."

"Bending? How?"

"By shifting the orientation of the ring to angle the beam they are funneling."

"They can do that?"

"I told you, Dr. Brock. Zikzaws are intelligent and resourceful." Aylor briefly paused before he continued to relay his thoughts through the cyton. *"The explosion of my ship will not prevent another ring from form-ing, but it will provide the remaining zikzaws in the ring a more concen-trated source of radiation than they will find in the magnetar's gamma bursts. Many will flock to feed, weakening what is left of the ring forming now. This should provide enough time to launch your arks and for Dione evacuees to reach the safety of Mars. The rest of Jupiter's defense I leave to you, Dr. Brock."*

Stunned, Brock said, "Me?"

Aylor placed his hand on her shoulder, his long fingers extending down her back to her waist. *"More sacrifice will be needed to save Jupiter. Tell your people. Convince them to act."*

A new vision arose in Brock's mind — missiles headed toward a planet. Brock recognized the planet immediately as Pluto. When the projectiles collided with it, a towering explosion ejected into space. Aylor squeezed hard on Brock's shoulder. *"You must sacrifice this planet to save the rest of your solar system. Your people must attack it again and again until the radiation released by your weapons lures the rest of the zikzaws manipu-lating R5's bursts. If you are successful, you will restore time to help Hexla disrupt rings farther away."*

Aylor lifted his hand from Brock's shoulder and cupped it underneath the glowing cyton hovering between them. *"This one will accompany you to Mars. I have dispatched others to Pluto to assist in the attack. The rest of Dione's colony will go with me."* The Suhkai paused and stared at the cyton. It glowed and swirled around Aylor's head. Aylor smiled and nod-ded. *"Farewell to you too, my friend. And you as well, Dr. Brock."*

Brock felt as if her heart were being ripped from inside her as she pleaded with Aylor. "I don't want you to do this. Please don't. There must be another way."

"In the time left to us, with the resources at hand, there is no other way. But do not be troubled, for I am not. Just ask your fellow humans to honor the forfeit of my life with sacrifices of their own."

He brushed away tears on Brock's face with the tip of his finger then turned away. Frozen in place, she watched him board the cruiser and re-mained there as the shell of the ejection tube closed around the ship.

When the floor beneath her feet began to rumble, and the tube began to shake, Brock backed away. The cyton beside her suddenly zoomed toward the launcher and circled it until it formed a rope of light around it in what Brock interpreted as a final goodbye to Aylor.

Continuing to back away, Brock closed her eyes and wedged her fingers in her ears, knowing what was coming next. Despite the buffer of her fingers, the roar of Aylor's ship launching through the tube was still deafening, and its vibration was strong enough to stagger her until she fell to the floor.

She lay there until the vibrations subsided. Opening her eyes, she saw the cyton bobbing in the air inches from her face. It glowed bright, and Brock's forehead tingled with the sensation of static electricity. The cyton's plea followed shortly after that. *"Rise. We must go. Now."*

A moment later, Brock was on her feet running after the cyton. Ahead, Gateway security guards motioned her to the open door of another cruiser. As soon as she was aboard, the airlock hatch closed behind her. Stewards guided her to the last empty seat in the passenger cabin, strapped her into a safety harness and alerted the flight deck they were ready to launch. Surrounded by a hundred other humans secured in their seats, the cruiser shot through its launching tube and into space.

The g-forces were intense for a short period, but once the gravity system adapted to the ship's acceleration, Brock's discomfort waned, and soon she could move her head freely. Exhausted from stress and the whirlwind of events of the last few hours, she so wanted to close her eyes and fall asleep, but she fought off the urge and looked around for Aylor's cyton.

If it was in the cabin, it had cloaked. But Brock considered it just as likely the alien was flying outside the ship, feeding on ions ejected by the engines. She formed a thought, hoping to connect with the cyton. *"Are you here with me?"*

The skin on the right side of her forehead prickled. Brock reached up and felt a buzzing vibration close to the spot of the prickles. The cyton was beside her, cloaked. Brock relaxed her tensed body and whispered, "Thank God."

She posed a question to the cyton. *"Can you help me communicate with the pilot?"*

"Yes."

"Good. Tell me when you are ready to translate."

A few seconds later, a gruff male voice flowed into her mind. *"Jesus, you trying to give us heart attacks? Your cyton just appeared out of nowhere. Scared the shit out of the whole crew."*

Brock cringed and replied, *"I'm very sorry. Listen, my name is Helen Brock. I'm Gateway's chief science officer. I need access to your comms to transmit several messages to Meridiani Planum and Mayaguana... immediately."*

"Roger that. I'll send a steward to escort you to the flight deck."

A steward appeared from the galley and looked aft. Brock raised her hand and waved. The steward nodded and started walking toward her. Brock unstrapped from her harness and recalled Aylor's parting words, *"Ask your fellow humans to honor the sacrifice of my life with sacrifices of their own."*

DENNIS PRITCHARD'S OFFICE
MERIDIANI PLANUM COLONY, MARS

In his phone call with Dennis Pritchard, Dante Fulton had been surprised by Pritchard's muted reaction to the news of Zimmer's siege. But then he recalled he had directed Norris Preston to alert Pritchard to the situation before leading Zimmer into the stairwell.

Pritchard also told him he had garnered further details from Gateway's security chief and had just finished a telepathic conversation with Zylun. So, by the time Dante reached him, Pritchard already had a full grasp of the situation. He also seemed at peace with giving in to Zimmer. Now seated in Pritchard's office, Dante expressed surprise at his boss' acquiescence.

In reply, Pritchard said, "Dante, if everything weren't so fluid right now, I'd feel differently, but we can't afford to have the arks caught on the ground. Give Zimmer what he wants and load as much as you can as fast as you can. Jupiter's situation continues to deteriorate. You may need to launch well before the countdown we set."

The strain evident in Pritchard's voice and demeanor shook Dante. "Is it that serious?"

"It is. Callisto's spectrometers are still feeding us data, and you would not believe the wild disturbances in Jupiter's magnetic field they've reported within the last hour. Does it mean the zikzaws have zeroed in on Jupiter? I can't say for sure, but whatever's happening to the field isn't a natural phenomenon."

The mention of Callisto caused Dante to wonder out loud if the station had been fully evacuated yet. His stomach turned when Pritchard told him the evacuations of Callisto and Dione had been suspended until *Valor* and *Vanguard* were launched. Head bowed, Dante thought of the people still on Callisto. If Jupiter was under attack, so were all the Jovian moons.

"God, they must be going through hell right now," said Dante. "Trapped. Cut off. Abandoned."

"I'm sure that's exactly how they're feeling, but the faster you get those supplies loaded, the earlier we can launch, and the quicker we can restart the evacuations."

"Got it." Dante pushed up out of his seat. "I'll get Zimmer moving."

As he started for the door, Pritchard stood as well and said, "Dante, one other thing..."

Dante halted and turned around just as Pritchard said, "There's a strong possibility the bulk of the Tula colonists won't make it here in time, so be prepared to launch with whomever I send aboard. I've told Zylun to expect the same."

The news was painful to hear, so much planning had gone into choosing and training the colonists. But under the time crunch they faced, Dante realized the plan was now moot. At this point, they had to save who they could.

"Understood, Dennis. We'll make room for everyone on Meridiani if necessary."

CHAPTER 18

Helen Brock never returned to her seat in the main cabin, opting instead to remain at a vacant station on the flight deck. With the cyton bobbing in the air next to her shoulder, she mulled Aylor's recommendation to bombard Pluto for the better part of two hours.

It was a desperate ploy. Pluto's magnetic field was essentially nil and, while the planet did emit X-rays, its emissions were infinitesimal compared to Jupiter. There was nothing inherent about Pluto that would appeal to zikzaws, and Brock strongly doubted the morsels of radiation released from nuclear explosions on Pluto would distract zikzaws from the feast they could create by annihilating Jupiter.

Maybe I'm giving zikzaws too much credit, she thought. The word *desperate* flowed through her mind again, and she recalled Aylor referring to zikzaws earlier as desperate creatures.

At the edge of her field of vision, the cyton began to blink. *"Yes. Desperate."* As she turned to look at the bobbing ball of golden light, the cyton continued to transmit its thoughts. *"To keep ring alive, they burn much of what they consume."*

Brock paused to reflect on the cyton's analysis — maintaining a ring was almost a zero-sum game for zikzaws. Shaking her head, she mentally replied, *"But surely they realize the benefit of sustaining this particular ring."*

Flickering anew, the cyton answered, *"Some do. Others too hungry."*

Leaning back against the headrest of her seat, Brock imagined a desperately thirsty animal staggering through a desert toward a massive river visible in the distance. With each step, the animal drew closer to the river, but it also expended energy. Would such a creature be lured by a trickling brook closer by? Brock knew she, herself, would want to stop at the brook and replenish before continuing on to the river. It was a basic survival instinct.

"Yes. Survive now. Feast later." This thought from the cyton was followed shortly after by another. *"Not all zikzaws same. Some strong, most weak."*

Nodding, Brock believed she understood what the cyton was communicating. The strongest of the zikzaws were unlikely to be lured away from the ring, not so with the weakest. If they detected another source of nourishment that was closer and easier to consume, their survival instinct would take over, and they would abandon the ring. Brock glanced at the cyton. *"So, the gist of Aylor's plan is to lure the weak ones with a better food-to-labor ratio, which in turn will upset the balance of effort needed to sustain the ring."*

The cyton throbbed with light as it answered. *"Yes. If weak depart, not enough strong left to keep ring alive."*

"Okay, that makes sense, but why Pluto?" Brock queried. *"Why not just keep detonating explosives close to the ring like Aylor plans to do?"*

"Strong ones will attack to protect ring."

The cyton's answer caused Brock to reevaluate her perception of the purpose of Aylor's flyby plan. She had assumed he intended to bait hungry zikzaws away from the ring by tempting them with the electromagnetic radiation from his ship's engines and his accompanying swarm of cytons. *Follow us and get a tasty treat.* And he hoped the detonation of his cruiser would not only kill the zikzaws who had followed him, but that it would create additional bait to draw out more of the hungry zikzaws from the ring.

Now, she realized her assumption was flawed. Aylor's flyby was intended to simulate a threat to the ring. He wanted to lure *strong* zikzaws away and kill as many as he could, thereby robbing the ring of its stoutest members.

With that realization, the rest of Aylor's plan clicked in Brock's mind. Fewer strong zikzaws meant the weaker ones would have to work that much harder to help sustain the ring. That extra effort would stress their low reservoir of energy even more, making them more susceptible to the enticement of radiation from the explosions on Pluto.

And Pluto had been chosen for the site of the explosions because it was close enough to the ring to catch the attention of the hungry-weak zikzaws but far enough away to avoid posing a threat to the strong ones.

Brock asked the cyton to confirm her theory. The alien ball of light did not answer right away. It just bobbed in the air, throbbing brighter intermittently. Finally, it began to flicker, and Brock received its response in the form of a vision.

As explosions appeared in Pluto's atmosphere, a slow procession of zikzaws began to peel away from the ring. Then the ring appeared to shift orientation and, within a short time after, Pluto exploded.

"Must disband ring quickly, or the strong will turn it on Pluto."

The cyton followed its warning with a replay of Aylor's earlier exhortation. *"Your people must attack it again and again…"*

Until now, she had not fully appreciated the urgency Aylor had attached to the words *again and again*. Not only was the cumulative number of explosions significant, so was the frequency at which they should occur. If there were too few explosions, or they were spaced too far apart, the strong zikzaws would have time to react and eliminate Pluto as a threat. Then, the zikzaws would return their attention to Jupiter.

So, the nuclear attack on Pluto had to be intensive and sustained to succeed. But even if it did work, nuking Pluto wasn't a permanent solution, Brock realized. Sooner or later, other rings would form, and there was no guarantee Aylor's strategy would prevail each time.

The only way to eliminate the long-term risk to Jupiter was to disperse R5's gamma rays so much by the time they reached the solar system, the zikzaws would have no readily available weapon they could turn on Jupiter. But there was no point thinking about the long run at the moment. *Focus on Pluto for now, Helen. Worry about the rest later.*

Just then, an interchange between the pilot and comms officer caught Brock's attention. As she sat up straight, the pilot said, "You're shitting me."

"No, sir. Meridiani said their docks are off-limits until further notice. They told us to reduce speed and gave us landing coordinates about a quarter-mile south of the colony. We're supposed to put down there and wait until flight control gives us the go-ahead to dock."

"Unbelievable," said the pilot. "Don't they realize we have to get back to Dione for another load of passengers?"

"The evacuations have been put on hold," the comms officer replied.

"What?"

"That's what the message says."

Brock watched the pilot shake his head as he grumbled, "Unbelievable. Freaking unbelievable. One minute they tell us to scramble. The next, they put everything on ice." He paused to sigh then said, "All right, Ripley. Acknowledge receipt of the order and remind them we have a VIP aboard."

Afterward, the pilot turned to Brock. "Sorry, Doctor, but it looks like our arrival will be delayed. I'm guessing they're overwhelmed with evacuees from Callisto."

"What's our new ETA?" she asked.

"Assuming they clear us to land without any more flight plan modifications, we should touch down in just under two hours from now."

The delay was frustrating, but there was nothing Brock could do about it. Thinking she should clarify her earlier messages to Pritchard and Amato about nuking Pluto to emphasize Aylor's ultimate goal, she turned to the comms officer and said, "I need to send a few more messages."

As she finished speaking, Brock noticed the cyton next to her began to flicker again. An image of Aylor swept into her consciousness, accompanied by a surge of remorse that spread through her body. While the cyton didn't communicate anything else, it was enough for Brock to realize the cyton was telling her Aylor's life had just ended.

Three hours after heading off to Mayaguana's dormitory to catch some sleep, Anlon Cully emerged from an elevator onto the main office floor of Gateway's headquarters complex. Immediately, he could tell the situation with R5 had escalated beyond crisis stage. People scurried past him in both directions, their expressions grim. In the background, he heard raised voices echoing down the hallway.

It was a reflection of the same panic quickly spreading across Earth. This, Anlon knew from a very long phone call he had just finished with an agitated Pebbles. She was sequestered in his Incline Village home with their friend Jennifer Stevens watching events unfold on WNN and over the Internet.

By now, news of the gamma beam shift had been widely reported, as had the lockdown of Meridiani Planum and the aborted evacuations of Callisto and Dione. And from what Pebbles and Jennifer relayed, the media had also learned the Tula colonists were making their way from Nicaragua to Mayaguana.

Then had come the bright flare detected by a host of telescope enthusiasts watching space near Jupiter. Anlon recalled the clash of sounds emanating from his phone as Pebbles dashed outside and down to the lake to see if the flare was visible in the afternoon sky. Of course, it was not, but that didn't stop a stir of panic in Pebbles and many others around the globe.

On television and online, people began to speculate Jupiter had exploded. It didn't matter that within an hour after news of the flare was first reported, professional astronomers on every continent took to the airwaves to adamantly deny the speculation. The flash, they said, came from an unknown explosion beyond the boundary of the solar system.

Jupiter, they assured, was still in one piece and appeared its usual self in telescope images.

But the astronomers' assurances didn't seem to resonate with many people. Anlon observed this for himself as he watched WNN. Their cameras were trained on a mass of people gathered in Times Square as the network broadcasted an interview with a NASA astronomer. The faces in the crowd bore expressions of fear and skepticism. Many were in tears. Others prayed. The mass blocked traffic in every direction. Everyone was out of their cars. Few seemed to buy what the astronomer was saying.

Flipping to other channels, Anlon saw scenes of gridlocked traffic with scores of people abandoning their vehicles in many cities. On one broadcast, the reporter asked a man who ran by where he was going. "Home," the man had shouted as he passed the reporter, "to be with my family."

The following person the reporter encountered said she was on her way to a church a few blocks away. The next two after that were headed to a bar on the corner. One of them, a young man, looked into the camera and told his mother and father he loved them before losing control over his emotions and running off.

Anlon understood the collective disbelief. The timing of the flash, taken together with all the other news, did not strike him as a coincidence. *Jupiter might not have exploded*, he thought, *but something sure as hell did.*

The same leeriness had been evident in Pebbles' voice as she talked to Anlon while watching the same TV scenes twenty-five hundred miles away. "If everything's okay," she had asked, "why hasn't Gateway made a statement yet? They have to know everyone's freaked out."

It was a question being asked in many places, Anlon suspected.

That was when Pebbles pleaded with him to find out what was going on. Well, pleading wasn't the best way to describe her tone, Anlon mused. *Ordered was more like it.*

And so, Anlon had left his Mayaguana dormitory room clad in jeans, golf shirt and loafers to see what he could find out. As he now made his way toward Amato's office suite, he discovered no one he passed in the corridor was in a talking mood. Undeterred, he continued and was within twenty feet of the suite when Amato bellowed, "Find Julia Carillo! She's not answering her phone. Find her quickly!"

Seconds later, Anlon heard the excited voice belonging to Mark Myers, Amato's assistant. The same shrill voice that had beckoned him from the Meridiani cantina. "She's in hangar two with *RE-II*."

Anlon slowed as he reached the open suite doors and peered in just as Amato pointed Myers toward the corridor. "Take the elevator. Get her up here on the double. I'll try to get her attention from the catwalk."

From his brief tour of the facility before the unexpected trip to Mars, Anlon recalled Amato had a door at the back of his office that opened up to a catwalk above the aforementioned hangar where *RE-II* was housed in between flights.

As Myers raced through the suite entrance, he said, "Out of the way, Dr. Cully. Coming through."

The mention of Anlon's name caught Amato's attention as the latter was turning back into his office. He stopped and turned around. When they locked eyes on each other, Anlon nodded briefly to acknowledge Amato and said, "Go. I'll catch up with you later."

Instead of dipping back into his office, however, Amato motioned Anlon to approach. "How loud can you yell?"

"I don't know," said Anlon as he strode forward. "Let's find out."

It turned out Anlon's voice, combined with Amato's, was powerful enough to do the job. On their fourth scream-shout of "Julia," the astronaut came bounding out of the spacecraft airlock onto the boarding ramp. Shortly after, she joined Amato, Anlon and Myers in Amato's office to discuss the message Amato had just received from Helen Brock.

What followed was a conversation that Anlon could never have imagined if given a million chances and one he would never forget. Amato and Carillo discussed nuking Pluto with missiles Carillo would carry aboard *RE-II*. *You're going to do what to what with what?* Anlon thought.

"We have a small window of opportunity," Amato said. "Aylor detonated his ship and weakened the ring."

Who is Aylor? wondered Anlon. *What ring?*

Their rapid-fire conversation flowed back and forth as if both were completely unaware of his presence. Amato told her he would get on the phone right away to secure the necessary weapons. In return, she recommended asking for AGM-86 cruise missiles with W80 warheads. Then Carillo reminded Amato that more than the nukes would be required. She would need a firing and guidance system and weapons specialists experienced with arming and launching the missiles. Until that moment, Anlon had forgotten Carillo had been an Air Force pilot before becoming an astronaut. But the ease with which she discussed her requirements stirred his memory.

"We'll deploy the missiles somewhat like Paul intended to do with his supply of warheads if he had made it to R5," Carillo said. "Release them from the cargo bay into space, have the cytons position them for launch then we'll light 'em off and guide them in once *RE-II*'s clear." She paused then added, "And I'll need a wingman. I won't be able to fly *RE-II* and release the missiles from the cargo bay at the same time."

For a terrifying moment, Anlon thought Amato turned to look his way as Carillo mentioned the need for a wingman, but Amato was apparently looking at Myers standing behind him. "Mark, get Julia the roster of shuttle crew."

"Don't bother," Carillo said, standing up. "I know who I want. How long will it take you to get everything we need?"

Amato shrugged. "I have no idea, but I will stress the urgency of the situation to President Wilcox. If he doesn't oblige, I'll try the Chinese next and the Russians after that."

Carillo gazed at her watch and began verbalizing a timeline. "It's 3:36 p.m. now. Let's say you get hold of Wilcox in the next hour and get his authorization an hour after that. They'll probably source the missiles and crew from Barksdale in Louisiana. At a minimum, it'll take several hours to airlift them to Mayaguana. More if they follow all their safety protocols. So, best case, assuming you don't run into other snags or red tape,

RE-II couldn't lift off until after midnight. That's plenty of time to get Kiera here."

"Kiera?" Amato said, his voice tinged with surprise. "Kiera Walsh?"

"Yep. She knows *RE-II*'s systems and cargo bay like the back of her hand."

"But…she's completely unfamiliar with the Suhkai upgrades, Julia."

"I don't need someone who's up to speed on the Suhkai tech, Augie. I need someone who knows *Rorschach*'s original systems, particularly the cargo bay probe platforms. That's what we'll use to release the nukes into space."

"But, Julia, Kiera hasn't flown in years, and you know of her struggles."

"Yeah. I do. But none of the shuttle crews have any experience launching probes from the cargo bay. Kiera does. Why does that matter? Because I don't want to risk rookies bouncing live nukes around inside the bay. On top of that, Kiera has lots of experience communicating with cytons."

Amato lowered his gaze to the table as he shook his head. "Julia, I understand what you're saying, but I don't think Kiera's fit to fly."

All of a sudden, Anlon felt Carillo grip his shoulder. "We'll get her right, won't we, Dr. Cully?"

Mouth falling open, Anlon darted a look at Amato then up at Carillo. "Excuse me?"

"World's fate in the balance? Eight billion lives at stake?" said Carillo. "You have something better to do?"

Anlon felt the heat of embarrassment rise up his neck and spread over his face. "Well, no. Of course not."

"Good. Let's roll." Carillo turned to Amato and said, "Keep me posted on the missiles. I'll shoot you our ETA back here once we've wrangled Kiera."

Walking in a fog, Anlon trailed Carillo out of Amato's office as she spoke on the phone to make their flight arrangements. When they reached the elevator, Carillo ended the call and turned to him. "Don't worry, Anlon. All I need you to do is help me sober her up. I'll take care of the rest."

Aware his hands were shaking, Anlon slid them in the pockets of his jeans. It had been unnerving enough to be an inside observer to the drama that was about to play out, but now he was a part of it, and that was out-and-out terrifying. "I'll help any way I can, Julia."

"Thanks. I appreciate it." Carillo smiled briefly, then asked, "By the way, have you ridden in a helicopter before?"

"I have," he said. "Several times."

"Good. I won't kid you then, doc. I spoke to the pilot. It's likely to be a rough ride to and from Mayaguana. There's a tropical storm forming between the Bahamas and Miami. He said he'd try to navigate around it, but I told him not to bother. We're kind of pressed for time."

Peachy, thought Anlon. To Carillo, he said, "As long as there are barf bags on board, I'll be all right."

Standing on the catwalk, looking down at flight mechanics prepping *RE-II*, Augustus Amato silently practiced the sales pitch he would make to Grant Wilcox, President of the United States.

Wilcox was not a particularly pleasant man to speak with, even on the most lighthearted of occasions. He was less so when riled up. And he despised Gateway's near-total control over space beyond Earth's orbit. Nor did the president like Gateway's stranglehold on Suhkai technology. In fact, it was widely believed his anti-Gateway rhetoric had helped him defeat his predecessor, Andrew Jennings, in the last election.

As Amato recalled it, the tipping point was Jennings' agreement to sell Gateway the nuclear warheads for Paul Morgan's fleet. Wilcox had pounded his opponent over and over in speeches for becoming a Gateway puppet.

Amato had tried to appease the incoming Wilcox as best he could, spreading around lucrative opportunities to American companies and organizations like NASA to participate in Gateway commercial and scientific endeavors on Earth and in space. But the president was unhappy

Amato had extended similar offers to governments and companies in many other countries.

Gateway was an American company with an American at its helm. As such, Wilcox seemed to believe it was Amato's patriotic duty to keep Suhkai tech out of the hands of the country's chief competitors and potential foes.

But Amato had been wary of exclusively aligning with the US, particularly after what had happened when Amato sought to resolve the *Cetus Prime* mystery. Beyond that, the Suhkai largess belonged to Paul Morgan, not Amato. And Morgan had made it clear before he left to quell R5 that he wanted the world to share in the benefits and opportunities of the new, Suhkai-influenced space age. He also made it clear he was opposed to providing anyone with access to Suhkai tech that could be used for military purposes. It was a stance Amato agreed with and had since enforced…which made his upcoming request to Wilcox all the more ironic.

Hopefully, he'll grasp the gravity of the situation and cooperate, Amato thought. But he feared Wilcox would instead seek to exert control.

Under his feet, the catwalk vibrated and slightly jiggled. Turning around, he saw Mark Myers walking toward him.

"Is it time?" Amato asked.

Myers nodded and told him the president's assistant, Marji Burns, was on hold. As soon as Amato returned to his office and settled in behind his desk, he lifted the phone receiver and said, "Hello, Marji, Augustus Amato here."

On the other end of the line, he heard the pleasant voice of Wilcox's assistant. "Hello, Mr. Amato. One moment, please. I'll connect you with the President."

"It took you long enough to call me, Amato. Do you have any idea of the shit storm you've stirred up?"

Wilcox's opening salvo was standard fare to Amato. In many ways, he was just as hot-headed as his predecessor.

"Good afternoon, Mr. President. I regret to say I don't have time to provide you and your colleagues a full briefing at the moment. I've called to ask for your help."

Amato was well aware there were other people on the line listening in on the conversation electronically and on Wilcox's speakerphone. He imagined they included the national security advisor, NASA's chief administrator and Wilcox's chief of staff. Most likely, someone from the Pentagon was also on the line. In this instance, Amato was happy for the broader audience. It would cut down on the time needed to disseminate his request, and Amato thought some of the cooler heads surrounding Wilcox might help manage his hot temper.

"My help? For years you've done nothing but flip me the middle finger every time I've asked for your help. And now you want my help? Talk about chutzpah!"

Wilcox's characterization of Amato's responsiveness was untrue, but this was not the time to argue about it. "The Earth is in grave danger, Mr. President. Yet, alone, I am powerless to confront the danger. With your help, however, there may be a chance to avert catastrophe. A slim one, mind you, but a slim chance is better than no chance. Wouldn't you agree?"

"So, it's true what I'm hearing from NASA and Space Command? The magnetar's bursts are worse than expected. They say they've already detected disturbances in Jupiter's magnetic field."

"Yes, Mr. President. And it will worsen significantly in the coming days unless we do something about it quickly."

Amato could hear murmurs in the background on Wilcox's end of the line. When the president spoke again, he asked, "What kind of help are you looking for, Amato?"

Amato closed his eyes as he said the words, knowing how the request would be received. "I need nuclear cruise missiles. Six, initially. And I need them airlifted to Mayaguana fast, as in, tonight. I also need equipment and personnel to arm, fire and detonate them."

There was a long pause during which the only sound Amato heard was the creak of a chair. Then, in a long and slow cadence, Wilcox said, "Are you out of your mind?"

"No, sir."

"In case you've forgotten, Amato, I made a promise to the American people. No more weapons sales to Gateway."

"I need them to create a diversion. Hopefully, one that lasts long enough to save Jupiter...and Earth."

"I don't care if you plan to fight Satan himself. The United States is not handing over nuclear weapons to Gateway. End of discussion."

Amato nodded. He had not expected Wilcox to embrace the request. He could only hope his following comment would stir one of the president's underlings to intercede behind the scenes. "I am truly sorry to hear you say that, Mr. President. Sorry for us all. Earth's end will likely begin in less than forty-eight hours. I'd suggest you make precious use of your time. Farewell."

If Wilcox had uttered a retort, Amato didn't hear it. He ended the call immediately after saying farewell. Folding his arms across his prodigious belly, the octogenarian Amato rocked back in his chair and closed his eyes.

He heard a shuffle of feet on the carpet and then Myer's voice. "Is everything okay, Mr. Amato?"

Continuing to rock, Amato shook his head. "I'm not sure, Mark. It depends on what happens next."

One minute turned to five. Five turned to ten. At roughly twelve minutes after hanging up on Wilcox, Myers reappeared at the doorway and cleared his throat. Amato opened his eyes and turned to look at him just as he said, "White House on line one. General Morehouse."

"Very good. Thank you, Mark." Amato leaned his chair forward and reached for the handset while pressing the blinking button for line one. Jerry Morehouse was the national security advisor, a man Amato regarded as pragmatic and fair. *Kudos to Wilcox for listening to Morehouse,* thought Amato. *Either that or kudos to Morehouse for making Wilcox listen to him!*

"General, it's good of you to call."

"That was as good a drop the mic moment as I've ever heard in person, Augie. But it worked. You got the old man's attention. Now, tell me what's going on."

Amato's eyes tilted upward toward the ceiling. *Praise the Lord.* To Morehouse, he said, "As I said to the President, Jerry, there's no time to provide a briefing. You'll just have to trust me."

After a pause, Morehouse said, "Let's talk hypotheticals. Supposing the President was to conditionally authorize the missiles and the support you want, it would take us some time to get everything ready for transport and airlift them to Mayaguana. I'd say the best we could do, hypothetically, is ten to twelve hours. What if we used that time for a full briefing down your way? Wouldn't take us but three hours to get there. That should give you plenty of time to pull together your people for a presentation and Q and A. Then, if the President is satisfied with what he hears, he could give his approval to transfer control of the nukes on the spot. How does that sound to you, hypothetically?"

"It sounds like it's better than nothing, Jerry."

"I was thinking the same. I'll call you back when we're wheels up and give you an ETA."

"Thank you, Jerry. You may have just saved eight billion people."

"Don't count your chickens yet, Augie. The old man will want something in return, even if your briefing is compelling."

"I'd expect nothing less. Godspeed, Jerry."

CHAPTER 19

Sunlight faded on another alcohol numbed day for Kiera. Curled up on the sandy strip of beach on the eastern edge of her private island, she looked up at the faint flicker of Mars. At higher climes along the eastern seaboard, it would appear orange and glow brighter. Here, at sea level, competing for attention among the lights of nearby Miami and Key Largo, Mars was a tiny flickering dot, almost an afterthought. Kiera laid back on her beach blanket and thought of various pithy replies to Dante's latest "I'm sorry, can I see you" message.

You had your chance, dude.

Too little, too late.

Happy trails.

But the one she really wanted to send had a blinking cursor at the end of it, just waiting for Kiera to press Enter on the laptop inside her villa.

You left me. I was pregnant with a child I didn't want, that I didn't willingly conceive, trying to deal with all the craziness after Rorschach...and you left me. You said I wasn't the same, that I had changed, and you didn't recognize me anymore. And then you ran away to Mars. We sleep in the beds we make, Dante. Sleep in yours and leave me alone.

In Kiera's mind, she heard her therapist encouraging her to let go of her anger, but Kiera wasn't very good at that, especially when her ire involved Dante and the Suhkai. Whether it was fair or not, she had lumped them together at the top of her pyramid of hatred.

Rolling onto her side, Kiera rested her woozy head against her arm, closed her eyes and listened to the sounds around her. In the distance, the rumble of military jets taking off from Homestead Air Reserve Base. Closer, there was a succession of echoes from car tires clacking over the road joints on Old Dixie Highway and the lonely churn of a motorboat moving through Card Sound.

Together with the rustling of wind through the trees, the gurgle of rippling water lapping up against the beach and the buzz of birds and insects, the sounds of dusk lulled Kiera to the edge of sleep.

Thoughts of Dante returned, and she pictured him leaving Mars for Tula. Visions of the foreign planet quickly pushed Dante aside. She breezed past the memory of the lavender-colored sky and rainforest in the Tula habitat on the ark now called *Venture*, and the videos of the planet stored in the ark's databank. Instead, her mind came to rest on snippets of the area where Avery Lockett, Christine Baker and Nick Reed had settled.

The snippets had been memories stored in the minds of the trio's children, John and Sarah, who had traveled to Earth on the ark with Nick Reed. Before the teenagers left to return to Tula on *Venture*, they had shared the memories telepathically with the assistance of a cyton.

Kiera had found the memories fascinating because the first-person perspective of visions seemed so real. In one of them, the then five-year-old Sarah walked behind her mother, Christine, along a streambank. Christine carried a fishing pole in one hand and a wooden bucket in the other. She was singing the alphabet song, Sarah was too. The sun of the Tulan solar system was setting in the distance, creating splashes of orange and red on the darkening purple horizon.

As Sarah walked along, she looked everywhere around her, giving Kiera glimpses of glowing fish-like creatures in the flowing water, the dark woods beside the streambank and the reddish clay on which Sarah walked. Kiera could smell the aroma of burning wood and feel the squish of Sarah's feet on the soil.

Revisiting Sarah's and John's memories like this now made Kiera regret passing up on the opportunity to see Tula in person, to experience the simplicity of the new world and to start fresh on a new life. But back when Mr. Amato extended the offer, Kiera had no interest in the long journey to get there, nor in turning her body into a baby oven for decades to come. She still had no interest in either, but felt a pang of jealousy for Ajay Joshi aboard *Venture* and now Dante. Unlike Kiera, they would get to walk on Sarah's streambank and explore new frontiers.

Kiera opened her eyes and drew designs in the sand around the empty wine bottle by her blanket. *Maybe when* Venture *returns for another shipload, I'll go. Mr. Amato said I had a standing invitation. Jasmine will be over twenty-one by then. Maybe she'll want to go with me.*

As she thought more about the possibility, Kiera realized the motorboat she heard earlier was much closer now, too close to be passing by her tiny island. She stood and wiped the sand off her hands and snatched up her blanket. *Probably another perv photographer,* she thought.

She disappeared into the thicket of trees covering most of the island and headed in the direction of the motor sound. If it was a paparazzi photographer, Kiera considered him pretty ballsy. The ones who snuck onto her island usually came by canoe in the wee hours of the morning, beaching quietly on the sand before slinking up to Kiera's villa compound. Not this clown. He made no effort to silence his boat engine nor turn off the lights illuminating the bow and stern. To boot, he appeared to be headed directly for her dock!

Oh, sure, just tie up and come ashore, Kiera thought as she staggered from tree to tree. *I'll drop my shorts and fling off my shirt, and you can get your snaps while we have a drink or two and chat about how fat I've become.*

She briefly considered going inside for her phone to call 911 but instead ducked down behind some bushes and crept closer. Kiera knew the security lights lining the dock would soon detect the boat's movement and illuminate, hopefully scaring the intruders away.

But when the lights came on, the boat kept on course, cut its engine and bumped up against the pier opposite of Kiera's yacht. With the area now awash with light, Kiera could see two people in the boat. A man and a woman. The woman hopped up on the dock, and the man threw her mooring lines.

In her drunken haze, she couldn't make out their facial features from her place behind the bushes. The woman had her back to Kiera, and the man was bent over, tying up the boat. But she could tell they were both Caucasians and on the older side. Her black hair was peppered with gray, and the man had sandy-gray hair. Instead of the camouflage typically worn by snooping paparazzi, they each wore jeans. He had on a golf shirt, and she wore a T-shirt.

They aren't paparazzi, Kiera thought. *They're freaking* Rorschach *groupies.* One of the reasons Kiera had purchased the island was to escape the constant badgering from people wanting autographs and pictures with her and Jasmine. The strategy had largely worked, but now and then, uninvited visitors showed up. They ignored the "Private Property, No Trespassing" signs posted on the dock and various spots around the island perimeter and strolled right up to her front door with phone cameras and pens at the ready.

Kiera emerged from the bushes and slurred, "You're trespassing. This is a private island. Get the hell out of here, or I'm calling the cops."

Both of the boaters looked in her direction, but neither seemed fazed by her threat. Finally, Kiera stomped to the start of the dock and said, "I'm not kidding. Get back in your—" Kiera staggered back a step when the woman started walking toward her. "What the hell are *you* doing here?"

Julia Carillo smiled and opened her arms. "Kiera, it's good to see you."

Confused, the tipsy Kiera lost her balance and fell backward. Her head hit a paving stone, and she blacked out.

CONFERENCE ROOM
GATEWAY HEADQUARTERS
MAYAGUANA ISLAND, THE BAHAMAS

Soon after Amato's call with Gen. Morehouse ended, Amato ordered shuttle crews of the two Suhkai cruisers at Mayaguana to lift off into

Earth's orbit. He knew Air Force One's flight to Mayaguana would quickly be noticed and feared it would lead the Russians and Chinese to conclude Amato had cut a deal to evacuate the president. Moving the ships ahead of Wilcox's arrival would hopefully dampen their suspicions.

Additionally, given elements of all three countries' navies were patrolling the waters around the island, Amato expected the president's plane to arrive with an accompanying force of fighter jet escorts and likely a host of soldiers. Add to that the arrival of a military cargo plane sometime later loaded with nuclear missiles, and the spaceport faced all the makings of a highly volatile situation.

To keep the situation from escalating out of control, Amato planned to use the orbiting Suhkai cruisers for leverage with the leaders of all three countries. If push came to shove, he would tell the leaders he would reserve them passage on the arks if they refrained from interfering with *RE-II*'s mission.

No such bartering proved necessary, however, thanks to Gen. Morehouse. Shortly after Wilcox and his entourage of advisors and military leaders arrived at the spaceport complex, Amato learned Morehouse had telephoned his counterparts in both countries before departing Washington. He alerted them to the president's itinerary and the purpose of their visit to Mayaguana. Morehouse did so, he told Amato, to avoid Mayaguana becoming ground zero for the onset of World War III. To temper the potential for a conflict with the Chinese and Russians, Morehouse had said, he had offered to provide them teleconference access to the meeting and further agreed to the in-person participation of the D.C. stationed ambassadors of each country.

When Morehouse finished relaying all of this to Amato, he had said, "I didn't think you'd mind. I know you've got a lot of irons in the fire now, and I know diplomacy isn't a Gateway strength to begin with."

Amato took the jab in stride. Then, shaking Morehouse's hand vigorously, he said, "Thank you, Jerry. I feel like kissing you."

Morehouse had held up his free hand and replied, "Steady now, Augie. Don't want to give our guests the wrong impression."

In the briefing Amato provided after that, tensions flared on several occasions, mainly in the form of animosity aimed at Gateway. Wilcox had captured the reigning sentiments of the three nations' leaders when he said, "You've toyed with us, Amato, like we were nothings, nobodies. You've made us look like impotent fools to all of our peoples. You've hidden things from us. You've lied to us. And, now, in what seems to be the last minute of the last hour of hope, you come hat in hand asking us to trust you, asking us to aid you. Your balls must be made of titanium."

Amato struggled to patch together a response. So much of what he had shared with the leaders he had learned himself in the last twenty-four hours. It wasn't as if Amato had kept them in the dark for years. But, on the other hand, Amato could not deny he had flexed Gateway's muscles often. He also could not deny he had burned more bridges than he had built.

"You are right, Mr. President, and I regret—"

"Stow it, Amato," barked Wilcox. "There will be a reckoning someday, and there will be a price to be paid, but we didn't race down here for blood. We came here to help you stop these alien bastards."

Wilcox turned to Morehouse. "I've heard enough, Jerry. Give them the nukes." He looked toward the Chinese and Russian ambassadors. "Any objections?" The man and woman said nothing and darted looks at the teleconference camera. Wilcox turned to the camera too and said, "Boris? Li? If you've got a problem with my decision, speak up now."

President Li Zhen spoke first. In unaccented English, he said, "Mr. Amato, you must be held to account for the terror you have caused our peoples. Let us hope there is a day for such a tribunal. Until then, China stands ready to assist Gateway to defeat the zikzaws without reservation."

"Russia, too, offers its unqualified assistance," said President Boris Lenkov in a thick Russian accent, "and I echo President Zhen's and President Wilcox's demand for a full accounting after victory is achieved."

Wilcox trained an icy stare at Amato and said, "Well, you've got your nukes, Amato. Don't fucking miss with them."

KIERA WALSH'S RESIDENCE
PUMPKIN KEY, FLORIDA

When Kiera awoke, she found herself lying on the wicker sofa in the sunroom of her villa. Julia Carillo was sitting beside her, looking down on her with a concerned expression. Kiera felt something cold on the side of her throbbing head. As Kiera reached up to touch the coldness, Julia said, "It's a bag of ice. You fell and hit your head."

Kiera pulled the bag from her head to look at it.

"It's my fault," said Julia. "I startled you."

As Kiera's brain reassembled fragments of memory, she replaced the bag on her head and closed her eyes. There was still a slur in her voice as she said, "You can say *that* again."

"I'm sorry. We tried calling. I sent you texts, but you didn't answer."

We? Kiera then recalled the sandy-haired man. She opened her eyes again and looked around. "Where's the man from the boat?"

"He's...uh...tidying up a bit in the kitchen."

A visage of empty bottles and dirty dishes flashed through Kiera's mind. "How lovely. You'll have to let me drop in on you unexpectedly sometime."

Carillo's hand landed atop hers and squeezed. "I'm sorry, Kiera. I wouldn't have intruded if it weren't important. I know how much you value your privacy."

Kiera found Julia's sentiment laughable. Kiera didn't value her privacy. She'd earned it by pushing away everyone in her life. "Who is he? The man tidying up the pity party in my kitchen?"

"You didn't recognize him?" Julia sounded surprised as she clarified the identity of her companion. "It's Anlon Cully. You remember him, don't you? He's the one who met us on Late Island when we returned to Earth."

"Ah, yes. The dude with the big boat." Kiera remembered the yacht well. She and Dante had fallen over the side in their excitement to reunite. "To what do I owe the honor of your and Anlon's intrusion?"

Julia didn't answer right away. Instead, her eyes drifted in the direction of the kitchen and she said, "She's okay."

Kiera tried to crane her neck to follow Julia's gaze but her pounding head suggested she reconsider. Instead, she called out, "Hello, Anlon. Sorry you got stuck with the dishes."

"It's all good," she heard Anlon reply. He came into view and smiled down at her. "I've seen worse."

Kiera laughed, but that too was quickly discouraged by sharper throbs. She winced and gently rubbed her head under the ice bag. The bag slid off and landed on her shoulder. Anlon knelt next to her and picked up the bag. "Sorry, I'm not very good at comic relief. Here, let me have a look at your noggin."

As Anlon's hand gently pushed away her wet, matted hair, she noticed the pleasant scent of the dish detergent and thought, *great, I haven't showered in, what, two days? Or has it been three? I must smell like pickled garbage.* Her thoughts turned to the state of her bedroom. "Please tell me you haven't tidied up in my bedroom."

"Nope, just the kitchen and patio," said Anlon. He patted her on the shoulder. "Feel up to sipping some water? You seem a little… dehydrated."

"I'm not dehydrated. I'm drunk off my ass."

"Really?" Anlon smiled and replaced the ice bag on her head. "Hadn't noticed. I'll go get the water. Meanwhile, you two should talk."

He disappeared from Kiera's field of vision, leaving only Julia within sight. Kiera nudged her knee and said, "So, you gonna tell me why you're here or am I supposed to guess?"

"I need your help."

"*My* help? For what?"

"You really have unplugged from the world, haven't you?"

Julia's comment seemed laced with admonishment. Kiera stared up at her freckled face and graying curls. "Geez, Julia, there's no need to get all judgy. Why should I care what's going on in the world?"

Anlon returned with an uncapped bottle of water. Kneeling beside Kiera, he coaxed her to take a sip while Julia said, "R5 awoke. Unfortunately, Paul and Haula didn't make it in time to prevent it from erupting."

While the information was new to Kiera, it didn't surprise her. She had never thought it possible Skywalker, and his Suhkai buddy could stabilize the magnetar. She also never thought it would be that big a deal, even if it did erupt. Kiera had been swayed by the physicists who viewed the magnetar as harmless to anything but space probes caught in its cone of gamma bursts.

In between sips of water, Kiera said, "Yeah, so what?"

As Julia began to answer, Kiera thought of Dante's message. When he had said he might be leaving soon, Kiera had assumed it was just a ploy to get her to reply. Now, listening to Julia, she realized his mention of a near-term departure had been motivated by a different reason.

"The gammas are worse than anyone expected," Julia said, "and Gateway's discovered why. You remember the zikzaw we ran into in the asteroid belt?"

Kiera thought back to the zikzaw-cyton battle she, Julia and their other *Rorschach* shipmates had observed. The bright flashes of the fight had temporarily blinded Kiera, reducing her to a panic-stricken screamer for most of the confrontation.

"Yeah, what about it?"

For the next several minutes, Julia filled Kiera in on the details of the zikzaw rings as passed to her by Augustus Amato earlier in the day. When she finished the recap, she said, "There's a real concern about a new ring that's formed at the edge of the solar system. It appears to be redirecting R5's gammas, meaning Jupiter's likely to enter the cone a lot sooner than anyone anticipated."

By now, Kiera had ditched the icebag and, with Anlon's help, had inclined to a sitting position in the corner of the sofa. She continued to sip water as she listened to Julia tell her about the paused evacuations of Callisto and Dione and the decision to launch *Vanguard* and *Valor*. When Julia said the beam from the new ring was expected to begin hitting Jupiter in less than twenty-four hours, Kiera felt an urge to ditch the water and crack open a fresh bottle of wine, and she said so to Julia and Anlon.

"You can do that if you want," Julia said. "Or...you can help me try to stop the zikzaws."

Kiera laughed. She couldn't help it. Julia had said the ring was positioned at the edge of the solar system, and she had just said Jupiter was less than a day away from the ring's beam. Setting aside the preposterous notion of stopping God-knows-how-many-zikzaws from doing whatever they wanted to do, there was no time to do anything. Kiera looked at Anlon. "Have you checked to see if *she's* been drinking?"

He nodded. "Yep. She's stone-cold sober...and she could really use your help. We all could. All eight billion of us."

"You're both nuts." Kiera looked back and forth at them. "You just laid it out yourself, Julia. *There's no time.* And even if there was, how can you, me or anyone else stop fricking zikzaws? It took millions of cytons to kill just one of them. Remember?"

"I remember. And you'll remember how easily the cytons lured the zikzaw to its death. They may be intelligent and ruthless, but they can be fooled — especially when they're hungry. And with your help, that's what I intend to try to do."

Kiera gazed at Julia's resolute stare. She looked as serious as her voice sounded. "I'm sorry, Julia. You're crazy."

Anlon interceded. "You know, Kiera, I actually agree with you. Then again, what does Julia, or you, have to lose by trying?"

"By trying what, exactly?" Kiera stood now, her hand crushing the empty water bottle as she glared at her two visitors.

Julia stood too. She was a good six inches taller than Kiera but seemed even taller as she stepped closer. For a moment, Kiera thought she was about to get punched but, instead, Julia reached into the pocket of her jeans, pulled out her phone and tapped on the screen. Handing the phone to Kiera, she said, "If you'd looked at your email today, you'd know already. Read it. It's a message Skywalker sent Augie and Dennis Pritchard. Hurry up, though. Our chopper is refueling, but it will be here soon, and you need a serious scrubbing before we're wheels up."

The message header indicated Amato had received it earlier in the day, but Kiera noted it had been transmitted over a year and a half ago. It read:

"*Dear Augie & Dennis,*

By now, you've probably noticed unusual surges in R5's gamma bursts. Haula's just informed me they're being caused by zikzaws, and he says they will pose a MAJOR problem. Don't ask me why Haula waited until this moment to share this information. You won't like the answer.

*Bottom line: large groups of zikzaws will be attracted to R5's gamma bursts. Strike that, large groups of zikzaws **have already** been drawn to R5's bursts, and Haula says more will follow. They will form rings inside the gamma cone, through which they'll filter radiation to feed on. This is bad news for Jupiter because their filtering process concentrates photons and because multiple rings will form, magnifying their concentrating effect on the bursts.*

Haula says it'll take some time for zikzaws to detect R5's gamma bursts and more time on top of that for enough to gather to form rings, but make no mistake about it, these rings have already started to form out our way. So if (when) one happens to assemble close to the solar system, you'll have to act fast. Eventually, the zikzaws will detect Jupiter's enormous magnetic field, and Haula says they'll stop at nothing to destroy it.

As you might guess, I learned of all this because we've detected zikzaws out our way. But we can't do much to disrupt rings closer to R5. The magnetar's radiation is too rich to distract zikzaws with our warheads. So I've turned the fleet around to work back toward you. We'll attempt to disrupt every ring we encounter with the nukes we brought to deal with R5. We'll detonate them as close as we can to the rings without entering R5's gamma cone. Hopefully, the radiation from the nukes will give them something to feed on besides R5's gammas, but I don't know if the warheads will be enough to lure the zikzaws away. And even if they do the trick, there's a lot of space for these rings to pop up between you, us and R5, and we don't have much time to spare. By my estimate, you'll receive this message about two months before Jupiter enters the cone, so that gives my fleet sixty days to disrupt rings. After that, nothing we do will make a difference for you.

That means you'll have the more daunting task, given how close Jupiter will be to R5's gamma cone when this message reaches you and how little time you'll have to put together a defense. But try anyway! Every ring that's disrupted will help Jupiter survive. And if it does survive, God willing, we'll have twelve years to prepare better defenses for the next pass.

Yes, that's right. Unfortunately, this is a blight we'll face for the next ten thousand years. It's the primary reason Haula remained silent, the primary reason he has been so confident R5 would eventually destroy Jupiter, and the primary reason the Suhkai fled our solar system four thousand years ago. Haula sees little chance of beating the zikzaws in a ten thousand year struggle, but I'm not ready to concede defeat. You shouldn't buckle under either!

With that said, I again advise launching Vanguard *and* Valor *ASAP if you haven't done so already. Also, scan for UV spikes. When zikzaws gather in large numbers, they give off a lot of UV radiation. The spikes will help you pinpoint rings. Consult with Hexla for more details.*

Quant says hope remains alive as long as we do. So don't give up hope! Skywalker out."

When Kiera finished reading, she looked at Julia and blurted, "Fucking Suhkai."

"My thoughts exactly," Julia said. "Now, get your butt in the shower. We need to get to Mayaguana as fast as possible."

Kiera stayed put and frowned. "Mayaguana? Why—"

"I'll explain the rest on the way. Now, move!"

"Look at me, for fuck's sake. I'm in no condition to help anyone."

Julia strode toward Kiera and grabbed her by the arm. "No, you're not. But you will be shortly." She then turned to Anlon. "Go find some soap and some clothes for her. Then, meet us at the pool."

The next thing Kiera knew, Julia was pulling her toward the patio door. Kiera tried to tear away, but Julia held firm and kept moving.

"Let go!" Kiera yelled.

"Not a chance."

Kiera kicked at Julia's legs and dug the fingernails of her free hand into Julia's wrist, but to no avail. She was too drunk, and Julia was too strong. Kiera bent over to bite Julia's forearm as they reached the patio door, but her mouth never made it. Julia had evidently seen it coming and slapped Kiera's face away before she could bite.

The blow was hard and disorienting enough that Kiera was helpless to stop Julia from flinging the door open and tugging her outside. The last few steps to the pool seemed to happen in slow motion, then Kiera felt Julia wrap both arms around her. Seconds later, they tipped over into the water, and Julia let go.

When Kiera surfaced, she spun around to locate Julia. She was a few feet away, slicking her hair back. "You're a bitch, you know that?"

"Been called plenty worse by my daughters, kiddo."

They both turned when the patio door creaked. Anlon stood in the open doorway, a bottle of Kiera's body wash in one hand and a wad of her clothes in the other. Julia raised her hands out of the water. "Toss me the bottle and leave the clothes on the chaise. We'll need some privacy for the rest."

As Anlon lobbed the body wash, Kiera began to swim away toward the far side of the pool. Over her shoulder, she heard Julia say, "Oh, no you don't. Anlon, cut her off."

Kiera kept swimming, but before she reached the side, Anlon came into view. He was crouched down like a linebacker ready to tackle her. Kiera halted her swim and screamed, "Stop! Just stop!" She splashed water at Anlon then spun around to face the approaching Julia. Her voice turning meek, Kiera said, "Leave me alone. Go away. Please."

In the distance, she heard the faint thumps of a helicopter. Julia must have heard it too. She looked past Kiera and spoke to Anlon. "Get the boat ready. We'll join you in a few."

"Roger that."

With her back to Anlon, Kiera only heard his hurried footsteps as he ran away. She once again pleaded with Julia to leave her be. But Julia waded to within inches of her and said, "Stop thinking about what you can and can't do. Think of Jasmine, your parents, your friends. You can help me try to save them like I'm going to try to save my husband, my daughters and my friends."

"But why me?"

Julia wrapped her arms around Kiera and hugged her. "Don't worry about why. Just come with me. Help me. Please." Julia pulled back from the embrace and held out the bottle of body wash. "I'll be at the boat with Anlon. We leave in ten minutes, with or without you."

For the first two minutes after Julia left the pool, grabbed two towels from the chaise and walked off, Kiera floated in the water, the bottle in her hand. It was completely dark outside now, and the sky above was as black as Kiera felt inside.

But she did think of Jasmine...and of her parents...and what was likely to happen to them if the zikzaws were successful. Amid those thoughts, the voice of her therapist refrained in her mind. *"All decisions have unintended consequences, Kiera. Many times they are good."*

Flipping up the cap of the body wash, Kiera said, "Yeah, well, let's hope this one doesn't bite me in the ass."

From the looks on their faces as Kiera strode down the dock, both Julia and Anlon were surprised and relieved to see her. Over the gurgle of the motor boat's idling engines, Anlon called out, "Atta girl!" while Julia stepped up on the dock with a big smile on her face. She was still soaked from head to toe, a towel draped around her neck.

Kiera held out a folded pile of clothes she had rustled from the house. Speaking over the engines, she said, "Here. None of it will probably fit, but they're dry."

Julia took the clothes and hugged her. "Thank you, Kiera. I wasn't sure you'd come."

"Neither was I," Kiera said, hopping down into the boat. "Now, let's go before I change my mind."

CHAPTER 20

The boat ride from Pumpkin Key to North Key Largo was over in minutes, so Julia Carillo only had enough time to swap her soaked top and bra for the sweatshirt Kiera had provided. Later, in the bathroom cabin of the Gateway helicopter, she swapped the rest of her wet clothes for a pair of Kiera's sweatpants and socks. As Kiera had predicted, none of the clothes fit, but Julia was thankful to be warm and dry.

She had intended to thank Kiera again, but when Julia emerged into the main passenger cabin, Kiera was curled up beneath a blanket with her eyes closed. Rather than disturb her, Julia slid into the seat next to Anlon. He removed his headset and leaned close to Julia's ear. "You should try and sleep too. Who knows when you'll get another chance?"

Julia nodded, donned her headset and let the muffled drone of the helicopter engine lull her to sleep. A good while later, she was stirred by the sounds of Kiera's and Anlon's voices. Drifting in a semi-conscious state, she listened to their conversation.

"How did you get mixed up in all this?" Kiera asked.

"I was commandeered into service."

"Ah. Nothing like volunteering, eh?"

"Exactly. Kinda caught me by surprise, but Julia helped me see the light."

"Oh, yeah? Did she throw you into a pool too?"

Anlon laughed before he replied. "No. Nothing like that. She just emphasized what's at stake. That kind of put things in focus for me."

"She's good at that…it's irritating."

There was a lull in their conversation before Kiera spoke again.

"Are you scared? I mean, about what might happen?"

"Are you kidding? I'm petrified."

"Good. I'm glad I'm not the only one."

After another lull, Anlon said, "I understand you turned down a chance to go to Tula. As a matter of fact, Augie told me all of the *Rorschach* crew turned him down except Ajay."

"Yeah, good old goofball Ajay. He couldn't wait to go. Seems like he made the better choice now, doesn't it?"

"Maybe. Maybe not. The game's not over yet."

"Hah. You sound just like Skywalker."

"I'll take that as a compliment."

Anlon's next question stirred Julia's senses fully awake. "So, if you don't mind me asking, I'm curious why you didn't take Augie up on his offer?"

"You don't read the tabloids much, do you?"

Fearing Kiera would explode unless the subject was quickly changed, Julia opened her eyes and loudly yawned. "Oh my gosh. How long was I asleep?"

She turned to look at Kiera. Surprisingly, she didn't look angry despite her sour answer to Anlon's question.

"Let's see." Kiera glanced down at her phone. "I'd say almost an hour and twenty minutes. Feel refreshed?"

Nodding, Julia said, "I do. How are *you* feeling?"

"All things considered, not too bad." Kiera held up a paper coffee cup. "Amazing what a little shut-eye and caffeine can do."

Turning back to Anlon, Julia asked, "What about you? Did you sleep?"

"Nah. I left you two alone and went up front to chat with the pilots. Just came back a little bit ago and saw Kiera was awake. There's more coffee in the galley if you're interested."

"Maybe later."

Julia yawned again just as Kiera said, "You have good timing, Julia. Anlon was just asking me why I didn't accept Mr. Amato's Tula offer. I'll bet he'd like to hear your answer too. I know I was surprised you turned him down."

"Oh, that's ancient history now."

"No, really. I'd like to know. Why didn't you go for it?" Kiera asked.

Julia was leery of stepping on an emotional landmine knowing Tula was a touchy subject to Kiera for several reasons, but Kiera seemed sincerely interested, so she risked an answer.

"We thought long and hard about it. Actually, Sam and the girls were more interested than I thought they'd be. But I couldn't get comfortable with the idea of spending eleven years in space, and I talked them out of it." She turned to Anlon and said, "I'm sure that's a strange thing to hear from an astronaut, but I've logged a lot of hours in space, both before the *Rorschach Explorer* and since and, let me tell you, it's best experienced in small doses.

"Anyway, it turned out they all had reservations about going, but none of them said anything until I said I didn't want to go. Once that was out on the table, Sam and the girls bailed pretty quickly on the idea."

"I get it," Kiera said. "I thought about it, too, but just like you guys, I talked myself out of it. Kinda regret that decision now, but, hey, live and learn. Right?"

Kiera smiled when she finished speaking, reinforcing the gallows humor quality of her quip. Julia thought of offering a reassuring comment but refrained, knowing Kiera would only swat it down. Anlon, however, rose to the bait. "There will be other arks. You can always catch a ride on the next one Augie builds."

Julia bit her lip, expecting the defeatist in Kiera to fire back a "fat chance of that happening" type of comment, but Kiera's response was almost optimistic. "Let's hope we live to have the choice, Anlon."

A moment later, Kiera turned to Julia. "While we're on the subject of living, are you going to tell me how we fit into the stop-the-zikzaw-ring plan, or am I supposed to figure it out on my own?"

Hoo, boy, she's not going to like the answer, thought Julia. They weren't part of the plan. They were *all* of the plan, at least in the near term. "We have a solitary goal. Give the zikzaws a reason to break up their ring."

Skepticism crept into Kiera's expression. "And how, might I ask, are we to accomplish that goal?"

It didn't feel right to just blurt it all out, so Julia eased into the plan with a partial answer. "Zikzaws feed on radiation. We're going to use *RE-II* to give them an alternative to R5's gamma bursts."

"In other words, we're supposed to be bait again?"

Kiera's reference to bait harkened back to the *Rorschach Explorer*'s zikzaw encounter four years prior when cytons in control of *Rorschach* had lured a zikzaw into a trap with the aid of the radioactive output of the ship's engines.

"No," Julia said. "This time, we're supposed to *create* the bait, not *be* the bait."

The scowling Kiera leaned forward. "The more you tiptoe, Julia, the more suspicious I get."

"All right. Fine. We're going to nuke Pluto."

While Kiera stared at her, mouth agape, Julia turned to Anlon. "Can you see if the pilots have any paper and a pen or pencil?" As soon as Anlon departed, Julia returned her attention to Kiera, whose mouth still hung open. "We have to create a lot of radiation between the ring and Jupiter to attract the zikzaws, somewhere where they can easily detect it."

Kiera blinked several times and said, "Did you just say we're going to blow up Pluto?"

"No, we won't have that kind of firepower, but we'll set off enough nukes to create one helluva distraction."

Anlon reappeared with a small notepad and pen. Before he handed them to Julia, he scribbled a note on the top page. The message read, *"Augie just radioed the pilot. Six AGMs en route to Mayaguana with an Air Force weapons team. He said you'll have 40x Hiroshima firepower."*

"Excellent," Julia said. She pulled out her seat tray from the armrest and tore off the note. On the fresh pad, she drew a diagram and held it up for Kiera. The picture showed a crude representation of Jupiter on the far left-hand side about midway down the page. In the upper-right section of the page, she had drawn a small dot that she labeled Pluto. Arcing across the page were two closely placed lines representing R5's gamma cone and labeled as such. Inside the lines depicting R5's cone, she had added an encircling ring at a spot beyond Pluto. Beneath the ring, she had included an arrow pointing toward Jupiter.

Tapping the ring, she said, "I don't know where the ring is now, so this isn't completely accurate, but whether it's close to Pluto or not isn't relevant. The point is, the zikzaws in this ring are teaming up to divert R5's gamma rays at Jupiter. But from what we've learned, maintaining these rings is hard work for zikzaws, and they don't get much nourishment from what they siphon from the gammas. That's why this ring will be so hard to bust up. It's so close to Jupiter, the zikzaws can sense there is a much bigger reward for sticking with it than there would be, say, to zikzaws in a ring a trillion kilometers away."

Julia paused to add squiggly lines around the ring. "Our job is to give the zikzaws a reason to give up on the ring." She pointed the pen at the dot representing Pluto. "Of the planets in the outer system, Pluto's the closest to R5's gamma cone right now, so it's our best shot to give the zikzaws something else to concentrate on.

"So, we attack the side of Pluto facing the ring, creating a cloud of radiation that will hopefully draw a bunch of the zikzaws from the ring. If it works, the ring will collapse."

Julia turned to see Kiera nodding and pointing at the ring. "I get it. If the ring collapses, then all of a sudden Jupiter gains back sixtyish days before it transits through R5's gammas."

"That's right."

For a moment, Kiera quietly stared at the pad, then looked back at Julia. "Not a bad plan. Kinda reminds me of Koi ponds at resorts. The Koi start to gather when they see someone walk up to the pond. They know that means there's a good chance they'll be fed. They go nuts when the feeding starts, but if someone else shows up at a different spot and starts tossing in pellets, some of the Koi in the frenzy break off and head toward the new food. As more and more of them notice the other feeder, the first frenzy fizzles and reforms at the second spot. On and on it goes as more people show up and throw in pellets. Before you know, the whole damn pond is hopping with fish going this way and that."

Julia gave a vigorous nod. Kiera didn't realize it yet, but the tail end of her Koi analogy was particularly apropos. They would only be the first to nuke Pluto. If the plan worked, other sorties would follow until Jupiter had cleared through R5's cone. Meanwhile, other ships would go to help Hexla draw zikzaws farther away from the solar system.

"There's one part I don't get," Kiera said. "Why us? Why not get someone already on Dione to do it? They're much closer to Pluto than we are."

"Simple. We're bringing the bang."

"Excuse me?"

"There are no nuclear missiles on Dione. Yeah, the Suhkai have a stockpile of liquid metallic helium and hydrogen fuel cells, but they don't have a way to detonate them unless they crash their ships into Pluto. The cruisers aren't outfitted with a weapons system."

Kiera's enthusiasm seemed to drain from her demeanor. "So, where are these missiles coming from? I mean, I'm pretty sure Mr. Amato doesn't have nukes just lying around on Mayaguana." As Julia started to answer, Kiera interrupted. "And how are we supposed to fire them? *RE-II* doesn't have a weapons system, either."

Julia briefly looked over at Anlon before returning her eyes to Kiera. "No, but it does have a cargo bay large enough to fit the missiles."

Once again, Kiera's mouth was agape. "Are you saying we're going to ram Pluto with *RE-II* like some kind of space kamikazes?"

"No, of course not," Julia said. "We're going to deploy the missiles into space like we deployed CubeSat probes on *Rorschach*, only we'll use cytons to position the missiles instead of maneuvering thrusters. Once the nukes are in position, we'll fire them at Pluto. Well, you and I won't be the ones doing the shooting. We'll have weapons specialists on board who'll do the actual deed. Our job will be to maneuver into orbit, release our payload, make sure the cytons line 'em up like we want and get out fast."

Kiera didn't respond. She just stared out the helicopter window at the night sky over the Caribbean while Julia exchanged glances with Anlon. Over the intercom, the pilot informed them they would be landing in twenty minutes. Julia felt her heart begin to race, knowing *RE-II*'s launch countdown clock would start as soon as they touched down.

DENNIS PRITCHARD'S OFFICE
MERIDIANI PLANUM COLONY, MARS
JULY 9, 2023

Dennis Pritchard hustled down the corridor linking Gateway's executive offices with the colony's main concourse. Ahead at the elevator was the head of security, Yasiel Romero and three of his officers. Two of the men had bloodied faces, and all of them had disheveled hair and clothes, the results of a revolt underway in the main concourse. Meridiani residents, visitors and Callisto refugees had reached their limit waiting for someone at Gateway to tell them why the facility was essentially locked down.

As Pritchard approached them, he said, "Gentlemen, I'm sorry it's come to this. I should have made an announcement earlier." He turned to Romero and asked, "Has anyone been seriously injured?"

"No, sir, so far as I know, it's been mostly pushing and shoving," said the chief. "But if we don't settle things down quickly, I'm afraid there will be serious injuries."

During Romero's answer, Pritchard heard his wireless phone begin to ring. He retrieved the device from his flight suit pocket and nodded toward the elevator door. "Understood, Yasiel. Lead the way."

Once inside, Pritchard glanced down at the phone. It was a call from the operations center. He was just about to answer it when Romero said, "There appears to be a ringleader. She seems to be the one who's fired everyone up."

Pritchard closed his eyes and swore under his breath. He knew precisely who the ringleader was…Jenna Toffy.

Earlier, she had tried to push into his office again, but Hal Barnes had successfully fended her off. She had returned an hour later with a handful of what Barnes had described as "thugs" who tried to smash through the locked doors to Pritchard's office suite. Just before they were about to break through, Gateway security had arrived and chased them off.

Not to be thwarted, Toffy had then resorted to fomenting a revolt among the colony residents, visitors and evacuees from Callisto and Dione who had disembarked their shuttles before Pritchard shut down the docking terminal.

"How big is the crowd now?" Pritchard asked Romero as he diverted his gaze to his phone again.

"At least two hundred. Most of them are pretty chippy too. The ringleader's been egging them on, giving several of them a chance to air their grievances, and it's just riling everyone else up. They've not only tried to break into the office tower. They've also been trying to bust through to the docking terminal."

Pritchard was now doubly regretting his decision to delay a colony-wide announcement and triple-ruing his decision to take Toffy into his confidence.

As the elevator came to a stop, Pritchard heard muffled chants and shouts through the doors. The chief pressed and held the close-doors button while he turned to him and said, "We'll try to give you as much of a physical buffer as possible, but if shit gets out of hand and we can't hold the line, get your ass back in the elevator."

Pritchard nodded, slid his phone back in his pocket and took a deep breath. The call would have to wait. "Okay. Let's go."

The scene that greeted his eyes when the doors opened was beyond frightening. Directly ahead of the elevator was a six-or seven-foot semicircle of clear space defended by a dozen security personnel. The four in the elevator with Pritchard quickly joined them as the angry mob on the other side pushed forward.

Some had raised fists. Others shouted obscenities or screamed hateful statements. Pritchard saw a few grasping tools, metal objects and other makeshift weapons. Their faces were twisted with expressions of disgust and animus. Sprinkled among them, Pritchard also saw people in tears, including children.

Looking past the revolt's front line, Pritchard saw Toffy standing on a table about fifty feet beyond the checkpoint. She was waving more people to join the mob.

"You have no right!" one woman shouted at him.

Another man railed, "You can't hold us prisoner!"

Several pleaded with him to tell them what was going on. A chant went up that soon encompassed everyone. "*Valor, Vanguard...Valor, Vanguard...Valor, Vanguard...*"

Pritchard raised his hand above his head in a gesture to communicate his desire to speak, but the crowd didn't seem interested in hearing anything he had to say. They just kept chanting. Pritchard looked up at the smirking Toffy, who appeared to be enjoying the fruits of her power play. Pritchard started to speak in a calm, measured voice, "If you would let me speak, I've come to make a statement and take your questions."

But the crowd was chanting so loud, he doubted only a few actually heard him. At a loss for what to do, Pritchard considered pressing his way through the throng to reach Toffy, but as he edged forward, the security chief grabbed him and pulled him back, shouting, "Are you out of your fricking mind?"

"They won't listen to me."

"And you think getting closer's going to work?" the chief said. "Get back in the elevator. We'll go to the security office and use the intercom."

Pritchard was just about to follow the chief's suggestion-slash-order when a small golden light arced through the air above the crowd. Several others noticed the cyton, too, as Pritchard saw multiple arms shoot up and point at the alien.

Then Pritchard felt a vibration from the floor that felt like a drum beat. He looked down for a moment, trying to make sense of the sensation, just as a chorus of gasps arose from the crowd. As the clamor started to subside, Pritchard heard a man shout out, "Holy shit. Look, it's a Suhkai!"

Casting his gaze toward the direction of the man's pointing hand, Pritchard saw Zylun striding through the concourse at an aggressive pace.

Suddenly, the cyton flared bright white, and a thought from Zylun penetrated his mind. "*Greetings, Earthlings. I am Zylun.*"

Another chorus of gasps riffled through the now silent crowd. Finally, one woman said, "Oh my God, I can hear him in my head."

Pritchard noticed the front line of protestors starting to back away from the security guards as Zylun closed within ten feet of the gawking, table-top Toffy.

"*You are angry. I know. You are also scared. That, too, I perceive,*" Zylun communicated to the crowd. "*Many things have happened which have not been explained to you. Some information has been withheld for good reasons. Other information has been withheld out of fear. There will be a time to explain all, but it is not now.*"

Glancing around, Pritchard could see the people around him were as confused by the tail-end of Zylun's mini-speech as he was. The Suhkai looked directly at him, and Pritchard received another relayed message. This one seemed directed at him alone. "*It is time, Dennis. We must evacuate Mars as soon as possible. There have been new developments.*"

"*Oh no. What's happened?*" Pritchard mentally asked in return.

But Zylun did not answer. Instead, he turned his attention back to the rapt throng. "*Return to your quarters. Gather your belongings. Return to this hall in one Earth hour and await boarding instructions.*"

"Boarding instructions?" a man asked. "Where are we going?"

"*That is undetermined. But we cannot stay here.*"

"Why?" asked another.

"*All will be explained later. Now, please, do as I ask.*"

Pritchard tried again to get an answer from Zylun without stirring up the crowd again. Closing his eyes, he concentrated on a new thought. "*Zylun, tell me what's happened.*"

"*After we are finished here.*"

It took a few more prods from Zylun before the crowd began to break up, but when they did disassemble, Pritchard was amazed at how calmly they dispersed. Whether they were mesmerized by the experience of directly interacting with Zylun and his cyton or were simply relieved to have their grievances acknowledged and a plan communicated, Pritchard could not say. But they headed away without debate or hostility, seemingly content to follow Zylun's instructions.

All except Jenna Toffy. She remained behind in the concourse and was now anchored in front of Zylun with a defiant glare on her face. Floating in the air between them, the golden cyton flickered in short, rapid bursts, a sign the two were engaged in a rather frothy telepathic conversation.

Finally, Zylun snorted through his crest tubes and motioned his arm for her to leave. She seemed ready to comply, but before Toffy departed, she turned to Pritchard and said, "You suck as a leader, Dennis. I know things are happening fast, but you just can't leave people twisting in the wind. You're damned lucky Zylun showed up to save your ass."

She didn't wait for a response, and he didn't have a rebuttal to offer. But, after watching how easily Zylun quelled the uprising, it was hard to disagree with Toffy's assessment.

"Do not despair, Dennis," Zylun communicated. *"Though her words bite, she admires you. She will not say it, but she is afraid of dying, and that fear rules her actions and tongue."*

Pritchard watched her stomp away and turned to Zylun. "Thank you for settling things down."

Zylun bowed in return. *"Come with me to the dock. We will converse on the way."*

To keep pace with the determined strides of the ten-foot-tall Suhkai, Pritchard jogged with Zylun's cyton gliding through the air next to his shoulder.

"You know of Aylor's attempt to disrupt the new ring?" Zylun asked.

Pritchard had received Helen Brock's messages detailing Aylor's valiant plan. "I have. I am sorry for your loss, Zylun, and humbled by Aylor's sacrifice."

"The attempt weakened the ring, but it still survives. And now the zikzaws have acted to protect the ring from further attack."

"Protect it how?"

"Cytons from the Dione colony who traveled with Aylor have communicated with me. They say a number of zikzaws followed them back to Dione and attacked the facility."

The news shocked Pritchard. He had received no report of trouble on Dione from the Meridiani communications center. But then he recalled the earlier phone call from the center he had declined to answer. "Dear God, are they capable of destroying it?"

"Not entirely, but they can inflict heavy damage. Undoubtedly, some inside the facility have died. So, you see, we must leave quickly."

Pritchard was now out of breath and stopped just outside of the perimeter of the security guards protecting the docking terminal entrance. In between gulps of air, he said, "No...I...don't see."

Zylun continued walking and the guards stepped aside. He ducked slightly to clear through the eight-foot-tall security doors just as he replied, *"Zikzaws are intelligent, perceptive beings, Dennis, and they have been threatened."*

Following closely behind, Pritchard angled around Zylun's legs and sped up to come alongside him on the crowded dock. The loading of supplies was still in process. "I understand that, Zylun, but if Aylor weakened the ring, why do we need to push up the launch schedule?"

The Suhkai behemoth halted. In lieu of another exchange of thoughts, Pritchard received a vision from Zylun's flickering cyton. It showed a Suhkai cruiser flying through space with an artistic depiction of a shimmering trail in the ship's wake. Following behind was a zikzaw.

Pritchard quickly grasped the implication of the vision. Zikzaws had not only detected the cytons traveling with Aylor, but they had also noticed the trail of ions from the engines of Aylor's ship. And that trail had led them to Dione. Once there, they would have detected other, similar trails...trails of the cruisers in the first wave of Dione's evacuation...tracks that led to Mars.

"Holy shit. They're on their way here?"

"Yes. And when they arrive, they will destroy the colony, the arks and every ship they detect."

At that moment, Pritchard recalled Helen Brock's synopsis of her conversations with the now-deceased Robyn Martinez. Martinez had told Brock she feared Hexla's attempts to disrupt zikzaw rings would make things worse. Now he knew why.

And he thought of the dozen Suhkai cruisers now parked on Meridiani's southern plain, including the one with Brock aboard. Darting a look up at Zylun, Pritchard said, "What can we do?"

Zylun swept his thick hand through the air. *"Flee. Flee as fast and as far as you can from here and hope they do not follow."*

Given the urgency in Zylun's reply, Pritchard was puzzled the alien had directed the concourse crowd to fetch their belongings instead of heading straight for the docking terminal. Before he could pose this question to Zylun, the Suhkai replied, *"The zikzaws move cautiously. They suspect a trap. There are multiple trails to follow. Recall some of the early Callisto evacuees were sent to Dione, not Mars."*

Pritchard winced, realizing that meant Callisto would come under attack as well. Looking back at Zylun, Pritchard asked, "How much time do we have?"

"In your measure of time, four to five hours. But the sooner the arks depart, the better."

"Then we should tell everyone to forget their belongings and get aboard the arks right now."

"No. There is time. Before the arks leave, we must first dock and unload the passengers on the cruisers outside."

"Why? They can dock and board the arks once they're in flight."

"No. The cruisers will be needed to create two diversions. One to cover the escape of the arks. The other to aid in the attack on Pluto."

Pritchard staggered back a step. He had been so consumed by the risk to Mars, he hadn't considered the threat the incoming zikzaws posed to the plan to nuke Pluto. Removing his glasses, Pritchard massaged the bridge of his nose and shook his head. "Jesus, Zylun. How did we end up here?"

CHAPTER 21

I n the sanctity of the small conference room, Julia Carillo was on the phone with her husband, Sam, and her young adult daughters, Dena and Anne.

Bent over with one hand clutching her abdomen and the other holding her cell phone against her ear, Julia had just finished telling her family what she, Kiera and the two Air Force officers were about to attempt, leaving out the part about the zikzaw-hunters she had just learned about upon arriving at Mayaguana.

She had tried to sound confident when she described the mission, but Julia faltered during the long silence that followed afterward. There was more to say, but it contradicted every ounce of optimism she had just tried to convey.

No longer speaking with the self-assured voice of a veteran combat pilot and astronaut, Julia talked to her family as a wife and mother.

"I have to go now, but I want you to do something for me," she said. "I want you to take care of each other. I want you to be strong. And I want you to know I love you."

The children had been born long after Julia's fighter pilot days and her first flight into space aboard the space shuttle *Horizon*, so only Sam had known the kinds of risks Julia had faced back then. And even when Julia returned to space aboard the *Rorschach Explorer*, she had portrayed the mission as more of an adventure than a dangerous pursuit to her then-teenaged girls. In the time since, Julia had acted like her piloting job for Gateway was a breeze when talking about it with them. She had never spoken words like this before to the girls. Their reactions showed it.

Twenty-one-year-old Anne, the younger of the two, broke into tears. "Don't talk like that, Mom. I love you too, but you're scaring me."

Dena held herself together better, but Julia could hear wavering in her voice as she tried to reflect Julia's earlier confidence. "We love you, Mom. And we know you can do this. So, don't worry about us. Okay? You just do what you have to do and come home. All right?"

Sam was the last to speak, and his soothing voice washed through Julia like a gentle stream. "I don't know many things, my sweet, but I do know this. You are the bravest, toughest person I've ever known, and I am so proud of you. We all are. Go with our love and come home to it too. We'll be waiting for you."

A few more exchanges of affection and support flowed back and forth between all of them before Julia said goodbye. For a few minutes afterward, she remained in the conference room and bathed in memories of her family before thoughts of Pluto and zikzaws drowned them out.

Anger built inside. Soon, her fury was so intense, Julia slammed her fist against the table, threw her chair aside and spewed a stream of obscenities. On her way out of the room, she directed a mental warning to the zikzaws. *If it's hell you want, it's hell you'll get.*

Down the hall, Kiera Walsh, now changed into a Gateway flight suit, sat at an unoccupied station in R5's mission control room. She, too, had been reflecting on family in the short span between arriving at Mayaguana and now, and she, too, was full of anger.

But her ire wasn't directed at the zikzaws. It was aimed at herself. *I've wasted so much time wallowing, she thought. And I've pushed so many people away. If I get through this, no more of that shit. No more hiding on my little island. No more booze. No more ignoring my child…and no more ignoring Dante.*

She spent the next fifteen minutes composing short messages to her parents, to Jasmine and to Dante, expressing remorse for her behavior, vowing to do better and affirming her love for them. There was no time to say anything more. When the last was sent, she pushed back from the station console and started walking toward the exit.

Suddenly, she became aware all the people in the room were standing, watching her as she walked past. They began to applaud and shout well wishes. One of those cheering was Anlon Cully.

"Give 'em hell, Kiera!" he said.

"You da wo-man!" another person cried out.

More shouts followed.

"Good luck! Kick some ass!"

"We're with you, Kiera!"

And so the cheerleading went on…out the mission control door, down the corridor, at the elevator vestibules at both ends, through the hangar and out onto the tarmac. It seemed every person on Mayaguana had lined up to send them off.

On the one hand, Kiera found the rah-rah spirit exhilarating. On the other, with each well-wish that met her ears, the burden of her task weighed heavier.

Ahead in the inky darkness, floodlights shined on *RE-II*. Attached to it was a boarding ramp where Kiera saw a small group gathered at the entrance. Although they were shaking hands and talking with one another, all of them appeared stern.

Three of the people Kiera recognized right away: Julia Carillo, Mr. Amato…and the freaking president of the United States. Next to them were two bad-ass looking dudes in Air Force flight suits, a general with so much bling on his uniform he sparkled in the floodlights and a be-suited man and woman.

When she reached the group, Mr. Amato stepped forward and hugged her. "It's good to see you, Kiera. Thank you for coming to help us."

Her mouth was so dry, Kiera found it hard to say anything more than, "You're welcome."

He next introduced Pres. Wilcox, whose grip was so firm it hurt Kiera's hand. "All of our hopes ride with you, with your shipmates." He turned to include Carillo and the two Air Force men in his gaze. "I wish I had something profound to say to you, but words escape me right now. Hard for you to believe, I'm sure." He paused and said, "May God bless you and bring you home safe and sound."

Kiera half-consciously uttered, "Amen."

Next up were the two "suits" whom the president introduced to Kiera as the ambassadors of Russia and China. They briefly addressed the group as well. Then Wilcox introduced Gen. Morehouse, whom Kiera learned would be riding along in *RE-II* to authorize the missile launches.

Finally, Kiera met her two Air Force shipmates. Combat Systems Officers Dwayne Collins and Emmet Lowrie. Kiera couldn't tell if their stern expressions and clipped responses were a sign they were locked in or freaked out. She hoped it was the former, but she had a feeling it was the latter.

Shortly after Kiera met Collins and Lowrie, the impromptu ceremony broke up. With no other fanfare, *RE-II*'s slapped together crew began their way up the boarding ramp. As she walked, Kiera breathed in the thick, salty air and felt the Caribbean Sea breeze on her face. She couldn't help but wonder if they were the last breaths she would take on Earth.

SPACEPORT - MERIDIANI PLANUM COLONY, MARS

Helen Brock was in the third of the shuttles parked on Meridiani's southern plain to dock at the spaceport. As soon as she appeared through the airlock hatch linking the docking bay's jetway-like bridge with the shuttle's airlock, Dennis Pritchard motioned her to join him off to the side.

Accompanied by a golden cyton that glided through the air above her shoulder, Brock sidestepped around other disembarking passengers and headed in his direction. After a brief hug and kiss, Pritchard stepped back and said, "Are you sure you want to do this, Helen? It's a hell of a risk."

"My mind's made up, Dennis. Now, where is Zylun?"

Over the previous hour, Pritchard and Brock had exchanged several wireless calls to discuss the colony's situation and the plan to bombard

Pluto. Part of that discussion had focused on their respective roles in the evacuation of Meridiani.

Pritchard had told her he intended to stay in the colony with a small group of volunteers who would ensure the facility was secured, and he urged Brock to board one of the arks. She had declined, indicating she had already communicated with Zylun through her cyton and intended to ride with him in one of the shuttles that would escort *RE-II* to Pluto.

"Aylor gave up his life for us," she had said. "I want to make sure his sacrifice counts."

Zylun had earlier expressed similar sentiments when he informed Pritchard and Dante that he would not pilot *Vanguard* as initially planned. With Aylor gone and Hexla far from the solar system, he was the last Suhkai officer left who could aid *RE-II*'s plan. He told Pritchard he could not in good conscience leave. *"My knowledge and experience with zikzaws are needed to defend Jupiter. Dante can find a suitable replacement to pilot Vanguard."*

Pritchard had tried to dissuade Zylun, too, telling him his experience and knowledge would be more valuable to *Valor* and *Vanguard* in the long run. But the Suhkai had rebuffed the appeal. *"If all goes well, I can join up with Vanguard after it returns to Mars."*

"I'm more concerned about what happens if all doesn't go well," Pritchard argued back.

But just like Brock, Zylun was unmoved. And so Pritchard led Brock to another Suhkai cruiser which had already been cleared of passengers. As they walked, he briefly glanced at Brock's cyton companion and said, "Zylun's already aboard. He's apparently dispatched his cyton to rendezvous with *RE-II*. He said he wants to have a direct line of communication with Julia Carillo."

Brock nodded but didn't say anything in return. She was frowning and appeared deep in thought. Pritchard assumed she was girding herself for dangers ahead, so he kept quiet as they continued to walk.

As they neared the shuttle docking bridge, Brock halted and grabbed his arm hard, causing Pritchard to stop walking as well. Turning to look at her, he noticed her troubled expression. "What's the matter, Helen?"

She squeezed his arm and said, "Dennis, listen. I have an idea how we might get rid of the zikzaws. Not temporarily, but for good. It's not something we could pull off on our own. We'd need help from the Suhkai. And it would take years to create and deploy, so it won't help our immediate problem. But I think it's worth investigating if the Pluto plan works."

Pritchard was taken aback by the timing of her inspiration as well as by the content. Before he could respond, Brock continued. "I suspect the Suhkai have already thought of the idea, and it wouldn't surprise me if they have tried it, so I intend to run the idea by Zylun. But in case we don't make it back, I want to share what I was thinking with you."

He thought about pointing out that if she didn't make it back, it would likely mean the Pluto plan had failed, and there was little chance he or anyone else would survive long enough to do anything with her idea. Instead, he said, "Okay, Helen. Go ahead. Tell me about it."

She looked around at the other people moving through the terminal and motioned him to a nearby spot away from the traffic flow. Once there, she said, "While I was on the shuttle, I was thinking of Aylor and a comment he made before he left. He told me there was nothing else we could do with the resources and time we have at hand other than trying to distract the zikzaws. As that comment bounced around in my mind, I started to wonder what he might have said if I had thought to ask what could be done if we *did* have the resources and time."

Brock paused and stared deeper into Pritchard's eyes. "I think he had a specific alternative in mind, Dennis. And I don't think it was just sending out more ships to help Hexla disrupt rings farther away.

"So, as I started to contemplate what that idea might be, the image of a zikzaw ring popped into my head. And it reminded me of another exchange I had with Aylor. The Suhkai designed their gravity system based on the mechanics of zikzaw rings, Dennis. Zikzaws combine their spinning action with Suhkonium to create gravity, which in turn helps them funnel photons through their rings."

She paused again, seemingly expecting Pritchard to grasp the implication of this revelation, but when he told her he was not following her line of thought, she said, "The zikzaws near Pluto are *bending* R5's gamma rays. They're capable of using their rings to *redirect* R5's bursts."

Brock jabbed him in the chest with a finger. "If they can do it, why can't we? Why can't the Suhkai? They know how to collect Suhkonium *and* how to manipulate it to create gravity. Why can't we use that knowledge to build our own ring and redirect R5's bursts?"

Pacing back and forth now, Brock continued to talk as if she were thinking through the idea out loud. "Ideally, we'd want to create the ring damned close to R5. And we'd have to be mindful of where we redirected the bursts. But zikzaws wouldn't care. We wouldn't be competing for the radiation in the bursts. We'd just be channeling it in a different direction. So long as they could still feed, they wouldn't care which way the bursts were aimed."

Conceptually, Pritchard thought Brock's idea had merit. *But is it feasible?* he wondered. *If it is, then why the hell didn't the Suhkai ever propose it?* As soon as he formed the latter question in his mind, he was distracted by the flickering light of the cyton aside Brock. He looked up just as he received a thought from Zylun.

"It is a massive undertaking. One that requires expertise, equipment, ships and technology not available to us here. We did not believe there was enough time to acquire and transport all that was needed. Haula deemed it a better use of time and resources to attempt to prevent R5 from awaking...and to build more arks."

Pritchard and Brock exchanged glances. She had evidently received Zylun's thought as well. She looked directly at the cyton and said, "But it is possible?"

"Not exactly as you have conceived, but yes."

With her eyes still on the cyton, Brock said, "Then we have a lot to talk about on the way to Pluto, Zylun." Turning, she embraced Pritchard. "I wish we had more time to say goodbye, Dennis, but we don't. Share the ring idea with Augie, Kiera Walsh, NASA and anyone else who'll listen. Find a way to get in contact with Hexla or Haula. Talk to them about it too."

He held her tight and said, "You can talk to them yourself when you get back."

Brock nodded as if agreeing with Pritchard, but she wouldn't look him in the eye as she pecked him on the cheek. "Take care, Dennis."

"You too, Helen. Good luck."

With a heavy heart, Pritchard lingered until Brock disappeared through the jetway airlock. Then he sighed and turned to walk away. It pained him to push thoughts of Brock from his mind, but his undivided attention was needed to finish evacuating Meridiani.

Standing at the head of the queue, Dante Fulton watched Gateway security personnel scan IDs and direct people to board either *Valor* or *Vanguard*. The assignments to one ship or the other were, for the most part, random, a far cry from the diligent process used to select the Tula colonists. But it was more important to load passengers quickly than to divide them up intelligently at this point. They would sort out the long-term assignments later if Tula became their only destination option.

The people in line didn't seem to mind the A-B-A-B boarding approach, although there were many requests to board with friends, co-workers or family on one ship or the other. When the requests began, Dante quickly approved the first few then delegated his authority to the security team.

"So long as we end up with balanced counts between the two ships," Dante had said, "I don't care how you pair them up. Just keep the line moving."

He had too many other things on his mind to arbitrate special boarding requests. The loss of Zylun as *Vanguard*'s pilot was foremost in his thoughts, especially after learning the arks might be pursued by zikzaws. From what Dante knew about the cloud-shrouded aliens, they were dogged adversaries and challenging to evade. As the only being with experience contending with zikzaws, Zylun's experience would have been invaluable.

As it was, Dante would have to rely on a man he had just met to play the role of combat tactician in the event the arks ran into zikzaws — Capt. Garrett Jones. He was the pilot of one of the shuttles now docked at the colony, and, according to his Gateway personnel file, he had flown fighter jets for the US Navy in his previous life.

Jones had seemed to relish the role when Dante approached him about it shortly after Zylun bowed out, expressing confidence he could keep the "SOBs off our ass." However, while Dante appreciated Jones' brash answer, he doubted Jones had any idea what was in store for them if a zikzaw got on their tail.

Thinking again of Jones caused Dante's mind to shift to another distraction clouding his focus — Kiera Walsh. When Pritchard told him Kiera was aboard *RE-II* and would deploy the ship's Pluto-bound missiles, his jaw had almost come unhinged.

He could not believe Kiera had been tapped for the mission, nor could he come to grips with the fact she had agreed to it. The last he knew of Kiera's situation, she had shut herself off from the world and was struggling with addiction.

But when he questioned the virtue of vesting such a vital role to Kiera, Pritchard had said, "I don't know, Dante. From what I remember of Kiera, she's pretty tenacious when she's motivated and, from what Augie said, she was pretty fired up."

Then Dante had received the email Kiera had sent just before lifting off from Mayaguana. When he read of her desire to make peace, he suddenly rued her role on *RE-II* for another reason. Their reconciliation would likely never happen. She would be flying directly toward the pissed-off zikzaws at the same time Dante flew away from them. While he thought it possible one of them might survive, he doubted they both would.

CHAPTER 22

Bracketed by Air Force officers Collins and Lowrie on one side and Gen. Morehouse on the other, Kiera Walsh gazed at the business ends of the six cruise missiles and listened to Lowrie comment on the plan to nuke Pluto.

"It's batshit crazy, sir."

The comment was directed to Morehouse, who had granted Lowrie permission to speak his mind. Kiera turned toward Morehouse just as the general replied, "No truer words have been spoken, Lowrie, but batshit crazy is our only option."

Lowrie then rephrased his objection in more professional terms, pointing out that the missile guidance system relied on pre-loaded terrain maps and strike coordinates. The weapons specialist also noted it was impossible to accurately set the fuzing parameters without precise altitude measurements.

"We don't have any of that data, General, and we don't know how far out the cytons will position the missiles or how strong of a push they'll give them into Pluto's atmo."

"I fully understand the challenges," Morehouse said. "We'll have to make best guesstimates for the first launch and fine-tune our settings as we go along."

As the Air Force men continued to discuss the attack plan, Kiera began to feel queasy. The way Julia Carillo had envisioned and described the attack, they would deploy all six missiles at one time and then fire them in quick succession. But Morehouse, Lowrie and Collins seemed to have much more deliberate tactics in mind.

They wanted to deploy and launch one missile at a time, pausing in between to assess the effectiveness of each strike and evaluate the data returned by the missiles' guidance systems to recalibrate the launch of the next nuke in the queue.

While she considered their approach more prudent and likely to yield more effective results, it struck her as significantly slower. In a situation where time was not a factor, Kiera would have been entirely on board with prudence, but time was a factor...a significant factor.

"Uh, not to add to the batshit level," she said, "but I don't think we'll have the time to refine settings all that much. After the first one detonates, zikzaws will start showing up."

Morehouse nodded. "Understood. But the first one might not detonate if we don't get the settings right. We risk the same outcome for all six if we don't pause to recalibrate."

Kiera realized the gist of the issue was Pluto's thin atmosphere and low surface gravity. The missiles were designed to launch in a free fall, igniting their rocket engines at a pre-determined altitude to strike and detonate a target on or above a precise area on the ground. But the dynamics of a free fall on Pluto would not be the same as on Earth, necessitating a push from the cytons into Pluto's atmosphere and rocket ignition immediately after that.

The problem was that the altitude of rocket ignition was set during the arming process, as were the strike coordinates. In other words, whatever data was loaded when a missile was armed was the data that would rule the missile's behavior, understanding that no one knew how differently a rocket would perform in Pluto's atmosphere. *Luckily, we have one thing in our favor*, thought Kiera, *a big ass target to aim at.*

As fate would have it, *Sputnik Planitia*, the most prominent topographical feature on Pluto, would face the zikzaw ring by the time *RE-II* arrived at Pluto. And it would remain within line-of-sight of the zikzaws for nearly forty-eight hours given the planet's slow rotation.

Looking back at Morehouse, Kiera said, "Well, we better hope the zikzaws are too hungry to detect us cuz we'll be sitting ducks if they do." Then, with a smile, she addressed the two weapons specialists. "By the way, which of you lucky gentlemen will be joining me to release the missiles?"

Lowrie pointed at Collins. The latter seemed cotton-mouthed as he answered, "That would be me, ma'am."

"All right. Follow me, Dwayne. We need to suit up and start decompressing ASAP."

As Collins cast determined looks at Lowrie and Morehouse, Kiera turned back to the general. "Once we turn our life support modules on, we'll have eight hours of oxygen, so don't drag your feet recalibrating."

Shortly after Kiera and Collins began their abbreviated decompression regimen, Julia Carillo received a hail from Zylun aboard one of the three Suhkai cruisers en route to escort *RE-II* to Pluto. Zylun's transmission was delivered by a golden cyton who had rendezvoused with *RE-II* an hour earlier and now hovered on the flight deck next to Carillo.

"Your engine trail has been detected by two zikzaws. Alter course immediately. We will attempt to entice the zikzaws."

As Zylun's thoughts flowed through Carillo's mind, so did a vision relayed by the cyton. It showed two Suhkai cruisers firing their engines and arcing away from a third ship. Then the cyton communicated a new heading.

"I will follow you," Zylun continued. *"Do not resume course for Pluto until instructed. Use thrusters sparingly."*

Before adjusting course, Carillo darted a quick look at a computer monitor displaying UV radiation data captured by *RE-II*'s UV spectrometer. She saw no spikes indicating the presence of zikzaws but, given the instrument's field of vision was limited, that was not necessarily surprising. She asked the cyton, "Did Zylun provide coordinates for the zikzaws?"

"No."

Carillo was inclined to believe the zikzaws were approaching on *RE-II*'s port side, given Dione was directionally on the ship's port side bow and Mars was on the starboard side of the stern. Therefore, zikzaws following the ion trails of evacuation shuttles from Dione to Mars would eventually cut across *RE-II*'s ion trail.

But Zylun's new course instructions directed Carillo to veer to port, which seemed ill-advised. If she were right about the direction from which the zikzaws were approaching, the new heading from Zylun would lead *RE-II* toward the zikzaws instead of away from them.

"Send a message to Zylun," she said. "Ask him to provide coordinates for the zikzaws. I want to know where they are relative to us before I change course. Also, if he has a bead on their intercept course, I want to know that too."

The cyton flickered briefly, too briefly to have transmitted a message to Zylun. Then, it provided an explanation of its own to Carillo. *"New course leads you to cone."*

Ah, thought Carillo. I see. *Zylun hopes our trail will be obscured by R5's gamma radiation.* The ploy made sense. Carillo had powered off the ship's engines after achieving targeted velocity more than an hour prior so, even though ions continued to radiate from the now-idle engines, they had dissipated substantially over time. Thus, flying upstream close to the radiation from R5's cone would help hide *RE-II*'s now-faint trail.

Carillo fired thrusters to alter course per Zylun's instructions then focused her attention back on the cyton. "Ask Zylun for the zikzaw coordinates and heading anyway. I want to know where they are in case his cone plan doesn't work."

OBSERVATION PLATFORM
MERIDIANI PLANUM COLONY, MARS

The sight, sound and vibrations of *Valor*'s liftoff from Meridiani Planum were beyond awe-inspiring to Dennis Pritchard. He had seen many NASA rocket launches over the years, but they paled in comparison to the ark's ascension from the surface of Mars.

Pritchard supposed his perception of the launch's grandeur was due to his close proximity to *Valor* during liftoff. Rather than viewing the launch from a distant grandstand or on a monitor in mission control, Pritchard had observed the event from an observation window on the colony's highest level, which overlooked the space dock.

Even up that high, the rumble of the ark's Suhkai engines pushing the ship off the ground rattled every bone in his body. Then, there was the thick cloud of swirling Martian dust that quickly enveloped the aircraft carrier-sized ship and the bolts of lightning that randomly pierced through the cloud.

Holding onto a railing below the window, Pritchard found himself cheering *Valor* to reappear from the devilish concoction obscuring it from view, but his voice was drowned out by the roar of the engines.

Then, like a blossoming flower, the cloud spread out at its apex and *Valor*'s gleaming fuselage began to rise from inside. From Pritchard's vantage point, he could only see the bulged, blimp-like bow of the windowless ship emerging from the cloud. It looked so much like a menacing, giant monster as it rose, Pritchard half-consciously took a step back as if expecting *Valor* to bare jagged teeth and take a bite of the colony.

Moments later, the cloud gushed away from the ship, coating the window and blocking Pritchard's view. He could still hear and feel the ark flexing its engines as the rest of the spacecraft climbed above the colony.

When the roar and vibrations abated, Pritchard closed his eyes and said a prayer for a safe flight for all those aboard. After the prayer's conclusion, he turned from the window and headed for the colony's command and control center. There, he would monitor *Valor*'s journey, watch *Vanguard*'s liftoff and scan the heavens beyond Mars for signs of incoming zikzaws.

On the elevator ride down, Pritchard thought of his wife and daughter and wondered if he would ever see them again. He had desperately wanted to send a message to them expressing his love, but he feared it would only add to their angst.

By now, everyone on Earth knew the solar system was teetering on the brink of destruction, and Pritchard was sure his wife and daughter were deep in prayer like everyone else, seeking comfort, begging for salvation and making peace with God.

As the elevator came to a stop, Pritchard was roused from his thoughts by the sound of his wireless phone ringing. At the same time as he reached into his pocket to retrieve the phone, the elevator doors slid open, and he heard raised voices emanating from the C&C center.

Fearing something had happened to *Valor*, he answered the call and began running toward the center. "Pritchard here."

The voice on the other end belonged to the center's director of operations, Jaylen Bowers. "Hold on, Dennis…"

Through the phone, Pritchard heard Bowers rattling off commands. "…abort *Vanguard*'s launch…radio *Valor* and tell them to forget waiting for *Vanguard*. Tell Dante to haul ass…alert Zylun and *RE-II* pronto…and someone contact Mayaguana, see if they can help us triangulate the spikes."

Upon hearing the urgent instructions, Pritchard hung up and sprinted the last twenty feet to the center entrance. He whipped inside and made for Bowers' command station. The black, middle-aged former astronaut looked like he was at the helm of a ship in a raging storm as he pressed the people around him with tasks.

While issuing another command, Bowers made brief eye contact with Pritchard then turned to finish delivering instructions to the station operator in front of him. As soon as he finished speaking, he removed his headset and began walking toward Pritchard.

When the two men met, Bowers shook his head and said, "I'm not sure what to lead with. So much has happened in the last fifteen minutes." He paused to take a deep breath before continuing. "Everybody was so focused on *Valor*'s launch, we didn't notice the other stuff going down."

"What other stuff? What's happened? Why did you abort *Vanguard*'s launch?"

"Gamma levels near Jupiter have dropped like a rock." Bowers snapped his fingers. "Just like that."

Pritchard frowned. "Are you certain?"

"Yes, and I'm pretty sure I know why."

Bowers motioned Pritchard to follow him back to his station. He leaned over his keyboard, typed a command and up popped a graph with an accompanying data chart. "We've been scanning for UV spikes to spot zikzaw rings. You see this spike right here?" Bowers pointed at a sharp peak near the center of the graph. "That's the ring *RE-II*'s hoping to break up."

After Bowers entered a few more keystrokes, the monitor displayed a split-screen with two graphs. "Look at what's happened to the ring in the last hour."

Pritchard leaned closer and examined the two graphs. The spike on the righthand-side graph looked like a wide, shallow mound rather than the thin, sharp peak evident on the other chart.

"I'm not an expert on the radiation profile of zikzaw rings," Bowers said as he pointed at the second graph, "but that sure looks to me like something bad happened to the ring."

For a moment, Pritchard wondered if *RE-II* had achieved its mission, but then he recalled the ship was still hours from reaching Pluto. Something else had disrupted the ring. *But what?* Pritchard wondered.

The only idea that came to mind was a delayed reaction to Aylor detonating his ship. If too many of the weak zikzaws had left the ring to feed on the radiation and too many strong ones had departed to defend against further threat, the stress on the remaining zikzaws in the ring might have reached a tipping point.

Pritchard shared this hypothesis with Bowers, finishing his synopsis by saying, "It cost them too much energy to sustain the ring, and they said *to hell with it.*"

Bowers looked Pritchard in the eye. "You're right they said *to hell with it*, but I think you're wrong about *why* they said it."

He bent forward and rattled off a new set of keystrokes, and the two previous graphs were replaced by a new one. "This is a depiction of X-ray data of the same sector of space. Again, captured within the last hour. Look at the spikes." Bowers used his finger to tap the screen in three different places. "The smaller one on the left is the remains of the radiation from the explosion of Aylor's ship."

The other two spikes were more prominent and clumped close together toward the center of the graph. Pritchard looked at Bowers. "You think the zikzaws were distracted by these other X-rays?"

"More than distracted, Dennis. I think whatever caused these spikes cut off the gammas the zikzaws were funneling through their ring. Well, cut off is too strong a description. Diluted is more like it." Bowers once again tapped his finger on the screen. "We don't have the exact locations of these spikes triangulated yet, but, directionally, they're awfully close to R5's cone."

Pritchard's eyebrows arched. "Hexla! She detonated her ship just like Aylor."

Bowers shook his head. "If she did, she was a magician."

Frowning, Pritchard said, "What do you mean?"

"There were *two* explosions, Dennis. And there's enough of a gap between the spikes to suspect they're a good distance apart. But that's neither here nor there at the moment. We've got a more immediate issue on our hands."

The tenor of Bowers' *immediate issue* comment caught Pritchard by surprise. The collapse of the ring near Pluto was good news — the pressing threat to Jupiter had been eliminated. And yet, Bowers seemed unnerved by the development.

"What issue, Jaylen?" Pritchard asked.

"If you were a zikzaw and you just had your pipeline of food taken away, you'd be kind of pissed, don't you think? After all, a portion of them attacked Dione and Callisto because they sensed a threat *close* to their pipeline. So what do you think they'll do now that the pipeline has been turned off?"

Bowers toggled to another graph on his computer that Pritchard quickly realized was an overlay of the two UV graphs they had viewed side-by-side earlier. "Given everything we've heard about zikzaws' detecting radiation at great distances, they had to have noticed the same X-ray spikes we've picked up. Right? Then, why haven't they all taken off for the X-rays?"

Pritchard eyed the UV graph as he listened to Bowers and quickly realized his point. The previous spike now looked like a plateau, somewhat evenly distributed on both sides of the pre-collapse peak. But that made no sense if the zikzaws had detected the appearance of the new X-rays. There should have been a noticeable skew of the spike indicating movement of the zikzaws toward the X-rays. Whether to feed on the new X-rays or investigate the drop in gamma radiation, the zikzaws should have headed toward the magnetar. But, instead, they appeared to be spreading out within the vicinity of their collapsed ring.

"Maybe they sense the dilution of gammas is temporary," Pritchard said. "Either that or they're finding it hard to give up on Jupiter. I don't know. Maybe they're just in limbo, confused as to what to do."

"Whatever the reason," said Bowers, "we now have a bunch of zikzaws hanging around…probably hungry zikzaws…probably pissed too…which is bad news for *RE-II* and her escorts. They're heading right at 'em."

We have to warn them, Pritchard thought. But then he realized they must already know. They were much closer to the ring. Their instruments would have detected the collapse before Meridiani. He clasped his hands atop his thinning pate. "Jesus, their ion trails will stick out like flares."

"Exactly," said Bowers. "Now you know why I aborted *Vanguard*'s countdown. Launching her would have just added one more flare for zikzaws to follow. As it is, we have to pray they don't go after *Valor*."

Pacing now, Pritchard concentrated his thoughts on *Valor*. Before launch, when the ring was still active, there had been hope the ship would escape the solar system without notice, especially after learning the zikzaws headed for Meridiani had picked up *RE-II*'s ion trail and had turned to follow her.

The collapse of the ring dashed that hope. Pritchard was sure the radiation spewed from the ark's massive engines as it zoomed from Mars would attract the attention of the now-ringless zikzaws milling about in R5's cone. He was equally sure some of the aliens would pursue *Valor*. The need to feed would be too great for some.

As Pritchard pondered whether *Valor* was capable of outrunning and outmaneuvering the relentless creatures, he was jolted from his thoughts by an excited voice.

"Oh…my…God…"

Pritchard stopped pacing and looked up to see one of the control center personnel standing with a frozen expression on her face. She darted her eyes between Bowers and Pritchard and said, "You are *not* going to believe this!"

"What is it, Padilla?" said Bowers.

"Mayaguana just sent us their best estimates for the locations of the two X-ray spikes. They say the closest occurred approximately 260 billion kilometers from Earth. That's consistent with Hexla's last reported position…essentially ten light-days away. But the second one occurred over 2.8 trillion kilometers farther from Hexla, more like 117 light-days away."

Pritchard and Bowers exchanged puzzled glances as the smiling Maria Padilla began to hop up and down. "Don't you get it? It's freaking Skywalker!"

Amid a burst of excited chatter from the other controllers, Pritchard lowered his head. *Was it possible?* he wondered. In the last message he had received from Morgan, the fleet had turned to work their way back to Earth. That message had been sent roughly a year-and-a-half prior — on December 6, 2021, as Pritchard recalled it — from a position close to 15 trillion kilometers from the solar system.

Looking up, Pritchard raised his voice above the chatter. "Someone do the math. At max velocity, could the fleet have flown 12 trillion kilometers in time to detonate a warhead 117 days ago?"

The beaming Padilla said, "I've already done the calculation. It's possible!"

"Are you sure about that?" Bowers asked. "How much time did you allot for resupply diversions?"

"None," said Padilla. "Resupply stops weren't necessary."

Pritchard frowned. The fleet had resupplied six times on the way to R5. Further, Morgan had indicated he intended to break up zikzaw rings on his return journey. While Pritchard didn't know how much time was needed to disrupt any given ring, he doubted it was a quick process. "It can't be the fleet. They would have absolutely had to resupply multiple times."

"I agree," Bowers said. "Even if they put all their eggs in one basket, loaded all of their provisions onto one of the ships and cut the crew complement down to just a couple of people, they couldn't fly 12 trillion kilometers without resupplying at least once."

Padilla shook her head. "You don't understand."

"Look, Maria, I'd love to believe it was possible," Pritchard said. "I just don't see how it could have been. There just wasn't enough wiggle room, timewise, to make it feasible."

He also wanted to point out that no one had heard from Morgan since his December 6, 2021, message arrived a day and a half ago. If he was traveling back toward the solar system at near lightspeed and transmitting messages and data as the fleet flew along, Mayaguana or Meridiani should have received slews of updates over the last day and a half. But, so far as he knew, none had been received.

"Then what caused the second explosion?" Padilla shot back.

"I have no idea. But does it really matter?"

"With all due respect, sir, I think it does," said Padilla. "It may mean more help from Skywalker is on the way."

Padilla's insistence was starting to irk Pritchard. As was her apparent hero-worship of Paul Morgan. But before he could shut down further discussion, Padilla blurted out, "Cytons, Dr. Pritchard. Skywalker sent cytons."

Dumbfounded, Pritchard stared at her for several seconds. Then it hit him. Cytons wouldn't have needed to stop when the fleet resupplied. They could have continued uninterrupted, feeding on the stream of ions at the periphery of R5's cone as they flew at near lightspeed.

A possible scenario began to coalesce in Pritchard's mind. At some point during the journey back to the solar system, Morgan had dispatched part of Quant's colony as an advance force. Provided with a warhead, the electromagnetic aliens had proceeded along R5's cone until they selected a target of opportunity close to the solar system while the rest of the fleet concentrated on rings farther away. *It was the ultimate "Go Long" strategy*, thought Pritchard, *a strategy that may have saved our butts.*

He looked at Padilla. "By God, I think you may be right, Maria. Paul knew he couldn't get back here in time to stop rings from forming, but he knew a swarm of cytons could."

Padilla nodded vigorously. "Swarm or *swarms*, Dr. Pritchard. What if Skywalker sent more than one? What if there are more of them still out there? That explosion happened 117 days ago, and we've just received its light…"

She didn't need to finish the rest of her sentence. Pritchard understood her point. A swarm traveling at near lightspeed over the last 117 days would be damn near the solar system by now. He wheeled toward Bowers. "Send a message to Zylun. Tell him what's happened. Tell him to try and make contact with Quant's cytons."

CHAPTER 23

H elen Brock knelt on the seat of the cube-like chair in Zylun's cruiser, feeling like a small child. Like everything else in the flight deck compartment, the chair was proportioned to accommodate the ten-foot-tall, elephant-wide Suhkai, not humans.

As such, the chair's seat was as wide as a typical sofa but twice as deep. And to reach it, Brock had needed the assistance of a stepladder. Zylun had offered to lift her onto the seat, but she had declined. She also refused the "booster" slab the Suhkai had offered to layer upon the chair so she could see over the edge of the oval table that served as Zylun's flight-control console.

Instead, she opted to kneel with her hands propped on the table's edge. And there she had remained for the past three hours as they chased behind *RE-II* on the way to Pluto, standing or sitting on the seat occasionally to relieve knee soreness. All the while, Aylor's golden cyton hovered beside her.

Meanwhile, Zylun had predominately remained standing while he peered at a collection of spheres displaying holographic-like images hovering above the table. The spheres were the Suhkai equivalent of human computer monitors, but the images they displayed were far more sophisticated than human-created holographs.

Of the six spheres currently above the table, Brock could only make sense of three of them. One showed a "live" 3D image of the zikzaw ring *RE-II* would attempt to disrupt. The ring was in motion. Brock could see the rippling Suhkonium and flashes of white as the zikzaws whirled around at a speed that blurred the cloud-like pink plasma that shrouded their bodies.

Another of the spheres showed a "live" view of Pluto with the prominent Sputnik Planitia formation bathed in the sun's light.

The last of the ones Brock could interpret was a holographic representation of a radarscope showing the position of their cruiser in relation to *RE-II*. Also depicted in the scope was a symbol denoting a zikzaw who had not been fooled by Zylun's previous diversion attempt. The zikzaw was still tracking toward *RE-II*, though it had slowed, seemingly wary of more trickery.

The other three spheres were the Suhkai-equivalent of data screens, but Brock could not interpret the symbols on two of them, and the last was dominated by randomly appearing blips of light. Earlier, Zylun had informed her the latter sphere was essentially a radio to communicate with cytons near Pluto, the zikzaw ring and one aboard *RE-II*. The symbol-laden spheres, she learned, were dashboard-like data screens feeding Zylun information about the ship's performance and radiation levels outside the vessel.

Brock had a difficult time fathoming how Zylun managed to process all of the spheres' images and data. She had never seen a Suhkai multi-tasking to such a degree. Leery of disrupting his concentration, Brock queried her cyton for status updates rather than probing Zylun for information.

This alternative proved helpful for a second reason. Communicating with the cyton provided Brock with an interface to the cyton traveling with *RE-II*, allowing her to interact with Julia Carillo.

Those interactions had been sporadic early in their flight due to the communications time lag resulting from the physical distance between Zylun's ship and *RE-II*. But as Zylun's cruiser closed the gap with the slower-flying *RE-II*, the comms lag had shrunk. Now, the delay was less than a minute.

While the narrower gap made her dialogues with Carillo feel closer to live conversations, there was a cost. Every kilometer closer they drew toward *RE-II* lengthened the comms delay with Mayaguana and Meridiani. According to the last update Brock had received from Carillo, that delay had stretched to over seventy-five minutes for transmissions with Mayaguana and ninety minutes for Meridiani.

Consequently, Brock had no idea whether *Valor* and *Vanguard* had launched yet, nor whether zikzaws had descended upon Meridiani. Amid that reflection, Brock caught a glimpse of Zylun backing away from the table. His massive hands dropped to his sides as his eyes rapidly darted between the spheres. Snorting sharply through his crest tubes, his gaze seemed to come to rest on the "cyton-radio" sphere. Suddenly, the blips of light inside the holograph multiplied exponentially. If Zylun had been human, Brock would have interpreted the look on his face as an "oh, shit" moment.

She pushed up from her kneeling position. "What's wrong, Zylun?"

Pointing toward the sphere with the zikzaw ring, Zylun relayed a terse reply through the flickering cyton. *"See for yourself."*

To her astonishment, the ring seemed to be faltering. Tendrils of pink sheared off in ribbons while the shape of the ring began to wobble and twist amid bright pops of white light. Inside the ring, the gray-black band of Suhkonium seemed to fly away as if blown on by a giant wind.

As she stared at the unlikely scene, her cyton flickered with another message from Zylun. As it passed through her mind, she realized he was broadcasting the message to *RE-II*.

"Hard to starboard. Engage your engines. Full power. The ring is collapsing." Zylun paused and took three thundering strides toward Brock. Reaching out his hand, he roughly grabbed hold of her torso and pulled her down from the chair. A couple of feet from the floor, he dropped her like a rag doll. Brock landed on her rear with a painful thud. *"Secure yourself in the passenger compartment. Notify me as soon as you are harnessed."*

A sensation of urgency...and panic...flowed through Brock's whole body. As she tried to stand, she glanced up at the image of the ring again. It was now a swirling, tangled mess. Lightning bolts shot in every direction. Though she couldn't be sure, it looked as if the zikzaws were attacking each other. She looked back at Zylun, her mouth hanging open.

He stomped his foot on the floor, shaking the entire compartment. Then, loud and long, he blasted out a sound through his crest tubes. Brock heard the word clearly. "Move!"

Waiting no longer, she turned and hobbled from the flight deck. Mind racing, she was only vaguely aware of the flickering cyton floating beside her as she stumbled onto a human-sized jump seat and fumbled with the safety harness. It took three tries before she could steady her hands enough to secure the chest buckle. With the cyton now hovering directly before her eyes, she panted, "Tell Zylun to go!"

ABOARD *RE-II* EN ROUTE TO PLUTO

Inside *RE-II*'s cargo bay airlock, the space-suited Kiera Walsh and Dwayne Collins sat on jump-seat benches on opposing walls of the chamber.

With his eyes closed, Collins looked serene, but his tapping foot and frequent oxygen mask adjustments told Kiera he was very nervous. She, on the other hand, felt strangely calm. For a moment, she wondered if the pure oxygen she was inhaling was making her high but then realized she hadn't been nervous before they began the decompression protocol either.

It's so weird, she thought. *I should be in full-freak-out mode. It's been half a day since I've had a drink. I've barely slept. There are six nuclear warheads a door away. I haven't been in space in four years. We're being chased by zikzaws. And if we fuck up with the missiles, we die, and so does everyone on Earth.* Kiera inhaled deeply. *So why do I feel so chill?*

After pondering the question for a few minutes, Kiera gave up thinking about it. She couldn't come up with an answer. Turning her attention to the leg-jiggling Collins, she pulled down her oxygen mask and said, "So, I gotta know. What did you do wrong to pull this duty?"

Collins' eyes snapped open as if he had been startled from sleep. *Huh, maybe he's not that nervous after all*, Kiera thought.

The airman lowered his mask as well and said, "Come again?"

"Did you piss off your CO? Drop a missile on the wrong target? I mean, you must have done something pretty bad to get picked for this. What was it?"

Cracking a smile, Collins said, "I've been wondering that myself. What about you?"

After inhaling deeply from her mask, Kiera said, "I wasn't picked. I was kidnapped."

Collins laughed. "Nothing like volunteering, eh?"

"Ain't that the truth."

In the brief lull that followed, Kiera noticed Collins' leg had stopped moving. She also saw him studying her face closely.

"You look different in person," he said.

Ah, she thought. *He's seen pics of me.*

"Do I? It's probably because I have clothes on."

His face twitched as he smiled, and his light-brown skin blushed ever so slightly, responses Kiera took as confirmation he had seen her paparazzi nudes.

"I didn't mean it like that," he said.

She nudged his boot with hers and smiled. "I know. I was just being the sarcastic bitch I am. So, how do I look different? Fatter, older or shorter than you thought, or all three?"

Collins shook his head and drew in some more oxygen before answering, "Nah, nothing like that. You just look real. Know what I mean? Like a normal person, not someone who's famous."

Kiera felt herself blushing. It was honestly the nicest thing anyone had said to her in a long time. "That's pretty cool of you to say, Dwayne. A lot of the time, I don't feel like a normal person. Most people don't treat me that way either."

"Yeah, I'll bet a lot of other celebrities feel that way too. Folks view them in a certain way and forget they're just regular people."

She nudged his boot again. "Let's change the subject before I start getting all weepy."

Sliding the mask back on her face, Kiera wiped at the corners of her eyes and thought of her therapist's favorite line. *"All decisions have unintended consequences. Many times, they're good."*

A moment later, she noticed Collins looking toward the cargo bay. Then he looked back at her and asked, "You think this will work?"

Kiera shrugged and removed her mask. "I dunno…it sounds good in theory, but—"

She stopped in midsentence as Julia Carillo's voice blared from the intercom. "Buckle up immediately. We're changing course. The G's are going to be rough."

Collins shot a panicked look at Kiera then down at his bulky spacesuit. "Immediately? Is she serious? In these?"

Kiera looked toward their life support packs clamped onto the walls next to them. "Get up. I'll help you lock into your pack."

"Roger that."

Collins tossed aside his oxygen mask and pushed himself up. Sidestepping toward the pack, he said, "How do we do this?"

Kiera let go of her oxygen line and raised off her jump seat. "Just back up until you hit the pack. I'll take care of the rest." Turning, she walked a few steps to the intercom panel and hailed the flight deck. "Julia, we need time to lock into our life packs."

"No time, kiddo. Secure your suits to the pack tethers as best you can."

"Shit." Kiera turned from the panel and shuffled toward Collins. Pointing at the metal loops on the waist of her suit, she said, "There are tether lines on your pack's utility belt. Attach the carabiners through these loops on your suit. Don't pull the lines out too far. You'll become a yoyo. We're going to bounce around enough as it is."

Nudging past him, she reached for her pack's belt and pulled on one of the carabiners. As she clamped it to her suit, Carillo called again over the intercom. "Engine start in ten, nine…"

As the harried countdown continued, Kiera clamped on another carabineer and shouted to Collins over Carillo's voice. "You tethered?"

"Copy that."

Kiera said, "Good. Cover your head," just as Carillo declared main engine start and announced a long burn of the portside thrusters.

Closing her eyes, Kiera cupped her arms around her head and prayed the sudden change in velocity wouldn't snap her neck.

As soon as Julia Carillo finished the thruster burn, the g-forces began to moderate, allowing her to turn her head to study the radarscope at her station. The zikzaw that had been angling toward *RE-II* was no longer visible. Unfortunately, neither was Zylun's cruiser.

Looking up at the cyton bobbing in the air above her right shoulder, she said, "Contact Zylun. Find out what's going on."

The golden alien glowed brightly and began to flicker. Meanwhile, Carillo typed a command to view the ship's internal camera feeds, starting with the cargo bay. The missile restraints had held. Cycling next to the airlock, Kiera and Airman Collins appeared conscious, though she could see splatters of red on their white spacesuits. Speaking through the microphone attached to her headset, Carillo said, "Kiera? What's your status?"

While she waited for Kiera's answer, she toggled to the camera feed from the lab compartment where Gen. Morehouse and Airman Lowrie were stationed. Both men were firmly strapped to seats, and from what she could tell, both were conscious. Activating her microphone again, she said, "General? Lowrie? Are you okay?"

Lowrie nodded and gave a thumbs up to the camera while Morehouse donned a headset.

"We're okay, Major," Morehouse said. "What happened?"

"Zylun ordered us to take evasive action. Apparently, the ring is collapsing."

Carillo watched the two men look at each other, then Morehouse said, "I don't understand. If the ring is failing, why was evasive action necessary?"

Until she connected with Zylun, Carillo couldn't definitively answer the general's question, but she could guess. "To protect the ship. We've had a zikzaw stalking us for the last couple of hours."

On the video screen, the men exchanged glances again. Morehouse looked angry. Carillo couldn't blame him. She would have been mad too to find out she'd been kept in the dark about a lurking enemy. But she had not wanted to distract Morehouse and the others from their roles in the mission.

Flipping back to the airlock camera, Carillo saw that Collins had untethered from his life support pack and was walking toward the intercom panel. Kiera had untethered too and was sitting on the airlock floor with her hand pressed to her forehead. Carillo saw streaks of blood between her fingers.

"Collins, there's a med kit in the cabinet below the intercom," said Carillo.

He flashed an okay sign with his hand as he neared the panel, just as Morehouse responded from the lab.

"Jesus, you Gateway people are all the same. Always hiding something."

Seconds later, Collins replied from the airlock. "Roger that, Major. Dr. Walsh wants to know whether we should abort the decompress."

Great question, thought Carillo. If the ring had collapsed, the zikzaws were no longer redirecting R5's beam at Jupiter, which also meant there was no need to distract them by nuking Pluto. But Zylun had said the ring *was* collapsing. For all she knew, the zikzaws might have recovered from whatever had disturbed the ring and quickly reformed it.

"How bad is Kiera hurt?" she asked.

"She's bleeding pretty good, but other than that, she seems okay."

"What about you?"

"I'm all right," said Collins. "Guess my noggin's a little thicker than hers."

"Roger that. Try to stop the bleeding, then bandage her up and continue the decompression for now. I still have to sort out our situation."

As Collins acknowledged her order, Carillo heard the clank of footsteps behind her. Swiveling her seat, she saw Morehouse marching into the flight deck.

"Major, we need to talk," he said, his voice deep with authority.

Carillo unbuckled from her seat and darted a look at the cyton. "Go to the airlock. Help Collins with Kiera's injury and let me know as soon as you've heard back from Zylun."

The cyton blinked twice and shot past Morehouse on its way from the flight deck. Carillo stood and addressed the approaching general. "I should have let you know about the zikzaw. I'm sorry."

"You're damned right you should have. This is a joint endeavor, Major. Any information that affects the success of our mission will be shared...immediately...without reservation. Is that clear?"

"Yes. It is."

Her quick acquiescence seemed to irritate Morehouse further. He pounded the ledge of the comms station. "Damn it, Carillo. We're not hauling pixie sticks, for Christ's sake. You can't just vector off like that with *nuclear warheads* aboard! The stress of the Gs could easily have damaged components."

Raising her voice to match the level of his, Carillo said, "So could an attack by a zikzaw, General. I had a split second to make the call, and I made it. We're still here, so I'd say it worked out okay."

With a vigorous shake of his head, Morehouse said, "You don't know that. If the missiles are damaged, and we try to use them, it could be goodnight Irene for all of us. There's only so much we can do to inspect them with the equipment and personnel we have."

Over Morehouse's shoulder, Carillo saw the cyton glide back into view. "Then let's hope we don't have to use them. Now, if you'll excuse me, General, I need to find out what's going on with the ring. If you want to keep in the loop, stick around."

As the cyton neared Carillo, she said, "How is Kiera?"

"Her wound has been tended."

"Good. Have you heard from Zylun?"

"Yes."

"All right. What's the message?"

"Zikzaw has headed for collapsed ring. Resume course for Pluto. Arm missile one and stand by for further instructions."

Carillo darted a look at Morehouse, who now stood a few feet away. From the expectant look on his face, she knew he was waiting for her to share Zylun's message. Before clueing him in, she formed a mental reply to the cyton. *"But we're nowhere near Pluto. Why arm a missile now?"*

"Unknown."

"That's not good enough. Tell Zylun I need to know why."

As the cyton began to flicker, Carillo turned to the now glaring general. "Zylun wants us to resume our previous heading and prep one of the missiles...as in, arm it."

His reaction was the same as hers. He pressed her to know why, although he expressed it in more colorful terms.

"I don't know." Carillo nodded toward the flickering cyton as she returned to the pilot's station. "I've asked for clarification. Hopefully, we'll get a quick response. In the meantime, take a seat and buckle in, General."

Morehouse remained where he stood. "I will not authorize arming a missile, Carillo. Not without a defined target."

Carillo layered her safety harness over her head. "Copy that, General. We're on the same page. Now, please, man the copilot station and monitor the radar while I start maneuvering us back on course."

"You're not going to shoot off like a sidewinder again, I hope," Morehouse said, sliding onto the copilot seat.

"Not if I can help it," she said, "but if a zikzaw pops up on radar, we may have no choice."

CHAPTER 24

O n the advice of her cyton companion, Helen Brock had remained in the passenger compartment for a solid twenty minutes after Zylun steadied the ship. During that interval, she had prodded the golden ball of light several times to help her understand what was going on.

"Are zikzaws still trailing us and *RE-II*?" Brock had asked.

"*No,*" the cyton had answered.

"What caused the ring to collapse?"

"*Hexla destroyed next ring.*"

"So, the gamma beam they were redirecting at Jupiter is gone?"

"*Yes. The star's bursts have returned to their previous state.*"

"What happened to the zikzaws in the collapsed ring? Where are they now?"

"*They remain. Some are disarranged. Others attempting to restart ring.*"

"What does that mean for *RE-II*'s mission?"

"*Must prevent zikzaws from reforming ring.*"

"How?"

The cyton didn't answer. Instead, it flared brightly and immediately zoomed through the flight deck door. Sensing another development had occurred, Brock unbuckled from her seat and dashed for the flight deck.

When she entered the room, the cyton was inches from Zylun's face and was flickering with intense speed. So rapt were they in their telepathic conversation, neither appeared to notice Brock approaching them.

She climbed back onto her "high chair" and scanned the holographic displays hovering above Zylun's console table. In one of the spheres, a ribbon of pink-white clouds moved away from what appeared to be a swirling melee of other zikzaws.

Zylun turned toward her as a thought from him passed through her mind, *"It is not a melee. They are reassimilating Suhkonium."*

Of course, Brock thought. As the ring collapsed, the forces applied by the zikzaws on the Suhkonium gravity funnel would have faltered, disrupting the surface tension holding the funnel together. As a result, Suhkonium would have spewed asunder.

"So, the Suhkonium has dispersed?" she asked.

"Not entirely. But unless they quickly reassemble what remains of the Suhkonium, it will disperse into too many particles for them to manipulate. It will be impossible to reform the ring in the near term. The zikzaws will be forced to seek out new pools of Suhkonium. That is why you see them working so furiously."

"Can we do anything to prevent the reassimilation?"

"Someone is already trying. You see the trail of zikzaws leaving? They have been drawn by a new threat."

A twinge of fear flowed through Brock as she looked at the number of zikzaws flying away from the jumbled mass. "Oh, my God. They've detected *RE-II.*"

"No. The zikzaws you see leaving are moving away *from the solar system, not toward it. "*

"Hexla, then?"

Zylun shook his head. *"Hexla, like Aylor, is no more."*

The cyton next to Zylun began to throb with golden light, attracting Brock's attention. Then, a vision formed in her mind. It was a large swarm of blue cytons. She jerked her head to look up at Zylun and said, "It can't be."

"But it is."

"Is the rest of the fleet with them?"

"No. *The swarm has traveled back alone, but the cytons bear one of Skywalker's weapons. They will lure as many of the zikzaws as possible from the remains of the ring and destroy them with the weapon. I have pledged our assistance and proposed a secondary objective — deprive the zikzaws of their Suhkonium.*"

"Deprive, how?" Brock asked.

The cyton shared a new vision. In it, a shimmering pool of gray liquid rippled outward from the center in rhythmic concentric waves. Then, the pool began to roil, the liquid pitching and rolling as if a sudden storm had broken out. A blinding flash followed and, when it cleared, the Suhkonium was gone.

The word *dyne* arose in Brock's mind, an antiquated term that had once been used to quantify the amount of force needed to accelerate a mass a defined distance. Nowadays, the word dyne was more commonly used as a measurement of surface tension.

"I see," said Brock. "If we can disrupt the surface tension of the pool with a concentrated force, we disorganize the Suhkonium molecules. We weaken the bonds holding them together, making them much easier to disperse. In this case, a powerful wave of energy from a nuclear explosion is our concentrated force, our *dynewave*."

Zylun nodded.

"But how can we get close enough to the Suhkonium to pull it off? The pool is inside R5's cone. We can't penetrate it with weapons. The gammas will fry any nuke before it can be detonated."

"*Simple. We will incent the zikzaws to bring the pool to us.*"

ABOARD *RE-II*
ORBITING THE DARK SIDE OF PLUTO

It was frustrating to have such a pivotal discussion through the airlock intercom, but Kiera understood there wasn't another option. If she and Collins exited the chamber, they would have to start the decompression protocol all over again. And there was no time for that.

But at least Carillo, Morehouse and Helen Brock had opted to come to the airlock, so that Kiera and Collins could see them through the door's window as they talked.

At present, *RE-II* was docked with Zylun's cruiser and Brock was outlining the latest plan to foil the zikzaws. Kiera found it comforting to see Brock, she had lost touch with her over the last four years. But Kiera was not as enthused about the plan Brock described, which she made clear when Brock finished speaking.

"Sounds like a suicide mission to me."

Through the window, Kiera noticed a slight twitch on Brock's face as she replied, "I hope not, but I understand where you're coming from. It is dangerous."

Clad in the bulky spacesuit, Kiera turned to Collins. "Dangerous, she says. More like insane."

With a shrug, he said, "I don't know, Kiera. Doesn't sound any crazier than nuking Pluto."

"Oh, it's a lot crazier than that." Kiera glanced back at the trio on the other side of the glass. "Around Pluto, we might have encountered a handful of zikzaws, but they would have been more interested in the radiation from the nukes than they were in us. *This* plan is a whole different animal. It'll be like shoving your hand inside a beehive. We'll be surrounded by zikzaws and they won't exactly be happy to see us."

"It's the best plan we've got, Kiera," said Carillo.

"Uh-huh." Kiera glared at Brock. "And whose brainchild was it? Your Suhkai buddy Zylun?"

"For the most part," said Brock. She turned and nodded toward Morehouse. "The General here added the flanking maneuver."

Kiera looked at Morehouse. "*RE-II*'s not like a cyton, you know. It can't maneuver with the same kind of agility. One direct hit by a zikzaw in the wrong place, we go boom and the plan is wrecked. Ditto if we fly too fast or too slow and get caught in a nuke blast zone. Same outcome if we run into R5's gamma rays."

Unlike Brock, Morehouse didn't flinch at Kiera's challenge. In fact, he seemed incredibly composed. *Cool as a cucumber*, thought Kiera. He placed his hand on Carillo's shoulder and said, "I have faith in the Major's piloting skills."

"Um, not to be a bitch," Kiera said, "but Julia ain't gonna be the one piloting."

Part of the plan Brock had described included allowing one of the blue cytons from Quant's colony to penetrate her head and essentially take over Carillo's mind and body. The cyton would be the one flying *RE-II*, not Carillo. Brock had said it was necessary to ensure synchronization with the other cytons involved in the assault.

"We'll get it done, Kiera," said Carillo. "You just worry about your part."

She paused then addressed both Kiera and Collins. "Now, time's a wasting. Every minute we delay is another minute the zikzaws have to reform their ring. So, lock on your helmets, activate life support and let's get those missiles positioned."

Later, Carillo watched the cargo bay camera feed as Kiera and Collins readied the last of the nukes from their station on the flight deck. Over the previous hour, the two had released the other five, one by one, to the waiting cytons Zylun had dispatched from Dione to Pluto.

Once each missile was free of the cargo bay, the golden Dione cytons had split up into mini-swarms and enveloped the missiles. At present, the quintet of nukes was lined up below *RE-II* in a V formation.

Gazing back at her radarscope, Carillo studied the disorganized mass of electromagnetic clouds at the periphery of the screen. Quant's cytons were clearly having success stirring the zikzaws into a frenzy, allowing *RE-II*, Zylun and the cytons from Dione to prep for their attack unnoticed.

Carillo doubted their luck would hold out much longer, though. As soon as they began their run and appeared on the sunlit side of Pluto, she was sure one or more of the zikzaws would detect them.

Success would then hinge on the zikzaws' reactions. Would they bond together and fight as a coherent unit or would the attack group face a chaotic jumble of individual, ravenous predators? If the latter, Zylun's plan had a chance. *Otherwise, we're screwed*, Carillo thought.

FLIGHT DECK, ZYLUN'S CRUISER

Many thoughts and emotions flowed through Brock as she prepared to say goodbye to Zylun and reboard *RE-II*. She wanted to believe they would all make it through, but she saw little chance of it happening. There were too many zikzaws to evade who had too much to fight for.

Whether they zapped *RE-II* and Zylun's ship before, during or after the attack, Brock expected the zikzaws to exact their fury on the vessels. Even with one of Quant's cytons at *RE-II*'s helm and Zylun at the controls of his cruiser, neither ship was capable of the stop-on-a-dime, non-ballistic maneuvers of cytons. Eventually, zikzaws would fire bolts of lightning the ships could not escape. She could only hope they lived long enough to see the Suhkonium pool destroyed.

As she looked up at Zylun, Aylor's cyton glided in between them. She glanced at it and formed a mental message. *"Allow Zylun to read my thoughts."*

Almost immediately, Brock's mind filled with a rush of sensations and she received a message back from the cyton. *"Zylun shares his mind too."*

She could feel apprehension in the Suhkai's consciousness, but it was overshadowed by a palpable vibe of confidence. Zylun seemed almost euphoric.

"You're happy?" Brock asked aloud.

The cyton flickered with Zylun's response. *"I embrace what is to come."*

"You're not afraid?"

"Fear is in me, but it does not control me."

"It doesn't control me, either, but it weighs on me, knowing what lies ahead."

Zylun knelt, bringing his face closer to Brock's. He smiled, exposing his alligator-like teeth, and cupped his hand around her back. *"There is more than danger that lies ahead. And do not doubt the skill of cytons, especially the one who will manage the attack."*

His gestures and thoughts did inspire a small rise in her spirit, but her apprehension still reigned. "I can't thank you enough for what you've done, Zylun. For what you, Aylor, Hexla and the rest of your kind risked for us. I only wish the Suhkai had been more open with us four years ago. We could have prepared for the zikzaws had we known."

Zylun nodded. *"Perhaps we underestimated your willingness to fight. But understand, Dr. Brock, even if we are victorious today, this battle will go on for ten thousand of your Earth years. You and your people must maintain the will to fight for a very long time."*

As Brock thought about a conflict stretching ten millennia, she thought about the gravitational lens idea she had discussed with Dennis Pritchard and hoped he would not forget it. The best long-term strategy to end the battle was to redirect R5's rays elsewhere.

"It is an idea worth pursuing," Zylun responded. *"But it will be extremely challenging to build and maintain. And it will take many Earth years to gather the necessary resources, transport them to the optimum location and deploy the lens. In the meantime, zikzaws will continue to form rings."*

"I understand," Brock said. "We have to win here first to even have a chance at thinking about the long-term, and we'll have to keep winning until the lens is in place."

"Well said." Zylun unbent his knee and stood. *"Farewell, Dr. Brock. Let us hope the seeders lead us to victory."*

Moments later, Brock crossed through the airlocks linking the two ships and made her way to *RE-II*'s flight deck. She arrived just in time to witness the appearance of the cyton who would control the destiny of Zylun's plan and the survival of Earth. As she watched it drift toward Julia Carillo, she thought, *"They're not just the seeders of life. For us, they may be the savers of life."*

Gen. Morehouse was the first to see the blue cyton on the flight deck. "Major, blue cyton on your six."

Carillo looked up from the radarscope and turned toward the rear of the flight deck. About midway into the compartment hovered a small blue light. Beyond it, Carillo saw Brock in the hatchway. Smiling, she said to Brock, "Good timing."

Looking back at the approaching cyton, Carillo said, "Hello, there."

The alien ball of light turned from blue to white as Carillo received its telepathic reply. *"Greetings. We meet again."*

For a moment, Carillo frowned, unsure of what the cyton meant. A vision filled her head. She was seated on the floor of the *Rorschach Explorer*'s central corridor with her legs crisscrossed. Paul Morgan was kneeling beside her. They were both looking at a cyton who had just uncloaked a few feet from them.

"Oh, my God," Carillo mumbled. "It's the alpha."

"The what?" Morehouse asked.

Before answering him, Carillo nodded toward the cyton. "It's good to see you again." Then she turned toward Morehouse. "I've met this cyton before. Four years ago, it led the attack against the zikzaw chasing *Rorschach.*" Brock entered the conversation and told Morehouse that each cyton swarm had a "pack alpha" who dictated the actions of the other cytons in the swarm. Meanwhile, the cyton exchanged further thoughts with Carillo.

"The time has come to join minds. Are you ready?"

A wave of anxiety flowed through Carillo. The notion of allowing an alien inside her brain had seemed a lot less scary an hour ago. Now, however, it felt like a supremely bad idea. But there was no other way to ensure the precise coordination necessary for their plan to work.

"As ready as I'll ever be," she replied mentally. After a short pause, Carillo asked, *"How exactly do we join? Please don't say through my nose."*

The cyton glided close to her forehead. Carillo felt a tingling buzz. As the sensation intensified, she backed her head away. *"Wait. A couple of questions. Will I be conscious? Will I be able to communicate with my crew?"*

"To a limited extent."

"Okay. I understand. Before we start, let me talk to my people." Carillo turned to her station and pressed the intercom button. While she looked at Brock and Morehouse, she spoke to the full crew, including Kiera and Collins in the cargo bay, as well as Airman Lowrie in the lab compartment. "All right, folks. This is it. In a minute, I'm turning control of *RE-II* over to Quant's cyton. Whatever I say, or rather, whatever the cyton says through me, you do. No exceptions. Acknowledge."

After a chorus of "roger that," Carillo strapped into the pilot seat and donned her headset. Seconds later, she heard Kiera ask Morehouse, "Got any great battle cries for the occasion, General?"

Morehouse chuckled as he resumed his place at the co-pilot station. After donning his headset, he replied, "None suitable for mixed company I'm afraid."

"Oh, come on, General," said Kiera. "This moment screams for testosterone. Let it rip."

Carillo watched Morehouse look past her to Brock at the science console before he returned his gaze to her. Carillo nodded and said, "Go for it."

Morehouse smiled and raised the microphone bar closer to his lips. "All right, rocket jockeys, let's grab 'em by the throat and cut their balls off."

A lusty round of profane retorts sounded from everyone, followed by Kiera asking, "Do zikzaws have balls?"

Carillo couldn't help but laugh as she answered, "Guess we're about to find out." Then, growing serious, she activated the flight deck window shield and hit the button to close the cargo bay doors. Turning toward the cyton, Carillo closed her eyes and said, "Okay, I'm all yours. Don't break anything inside my head, please."

CHAPTER 25

The first few moments after the alpha passed through her forehead and into her brain seemed no different to Carillo, but then she began to feel a prickling sensation throughout her body and brain. They were not painful at first, but the intensity of the prickles escalated quickly.

Carillo tensed her limbs and winced in response. The cyton urged her to relax, telling her the pain would subside as soon as it had made all the connections necessary to link its mind with hers and their collective mind with the rest of the swarm.

But the pain was too intense for Carillo. She grimaced, arched her back off her seat and loudly groaned. In the background, Morehouse said, "Hang in there, Major. You can do it."

Seconds later, Carillo's body began to convulse and thousands of images began to cycle through her mind so fast they seemed to blur into a single blob. Soon, the sizzling prickles began to subside and the flow of images slowed down enough for Carillo to delineate one from another. She saw zikzaws, other cytons, Zylun, the missiles and *RE-II*. She received a glimpse of the space-suited Kiera and Collins in the cargo bay, as well as the faces of the other crew. There was even a brief look at the pool of Suhkonium, their ultimate target. It seemed as if the alpha was connected to every cyton inside and outside of *RE-II*.

The next thing Carillo knew, her hand reached for the engine controls and she heard a monotone voice spill from her lips, "Brace for acceleration."

Carillo tried to lift her arms to tighten her safety harness but they did not respond. Instead, while one hand began to manipulate the engine power, the other took hold of the thruster controls.

Instinctively, Carillo opened her eyes to examine the radarscope, but just as quickly, her view of the scope was overwhelmed by more images racing through her mind. Her head felt hot as if spiking with a fever and she was aware of sweat beginning to coat her face.

Feeling helpless, Carillo shut her eyes again and fully surrendered her mind to the cyton. Almost immediately after, the flurry of visions began to blend into a coherent view of the battlefield ahead.

Against a black backdrop, there was a tornado-like churn of pink and white whipping around at incredible speed. Above the tornado, there was a widely spaced horizon of snaking zikzaws shooting out lightning bolts this way and that. They looked as if they were chasing each other's tails, but then Carillo noticed small blue dots zooming between the clouds.

The scene in Carillo's mind shifted suddenly to the five mini-swarms of Dione cytons directly beneath the conjoined *RE-II* and Zylun's cruiser. The swarms seemed to bump up against the ships' hulls, a tactic to obscure their presence amid the ion output of the ships' engines.

As they raced on, a new vision swept through Carillo's consciousness. It was a view of the two zikzaw masses from the opposing side. Judging from the haze of blue shading the vista, Carillo realized the alpha-cyton was interacting with the portion of its swarm not engaged in harassing the zikzaws. Instead, they were carrying the warhead from Morgan's fleet, lining up to make their flanking run when commanded.

Abruptly, the vision shifted again, and Carillo saw a couple of zikzaws separating from the melee with the blue cytons. They appeared to be headed toward *RE-II*'s small armada. As Carillo watched them snake through space, Carillo was surprised it had taken the zikzaws so long to act and how few had noticed the oncoming force. However, Carillo considered both developments as good signs. It suggested the zikzaws did not yet view them as threats or were too preoccupied.

Now seemed as good a time as any to arm the missiles. The alpha apparently agreed with her assessment and it spoke through Carillo again. "Arm missiles."

Carillo heard Morehouse acknowledge the command and relay it to Lowrie manning the Air Force's weapons control system. Shortly after Lowrie confirmed the missiles were hot, Carillo sensed the alpha passing a mental command to Zylun. *"Undock. Take the lead."*

Moments later, Brock's voice penetrated through the alpha's visions. "Julia...we've been detected. Multiple zikzaws are coming at us fast!"

If the alpha felt any apprehension, Carillo couldn't sense it. The mental commands it issued to the cyton swarms below the ships and Zylun were as steady and measured as its manipulation of Carillo's hands on the engine and thruster controls.

It first directed two of the missile-carrying swarms to accelerate ahead of Zylun's ship. Then, it used Carillo's hand to fire the forward thrusters, slowing *RE-II* down enough for a gap to emerge between the stern of Zylun's cruiser and *RE-II*'s bow. Into that gap, the alpha ordered two more of the swarms to take positions. The last of the swarms it kept beneath *RE-II*'s hull.

The armada was now strung out in a line, with two swarms at the leading edge, followed by Zylun's cruiser, two more swarms and *RE-II* and the last swarm at the rear.

Carillo felt her heart pounding as she watched the alpha's view of the slithering zikzaws converging on the ragtag fleet. They raked space all around them with tendrils of electric bolts, the most intense of them shooting forward.

She felt her hand on the thruster controls again and, in unison with the leading members of the fleet, *RE-II* began to snake to the left and right between the bolts. It seemed now that the alpha was no longer issuing commands to the others in the fleet, it was directly controlling their actions.

In a flash, the armada zipped past the first of the zikzaws and arced away from the second. In the vision Carillo was observing, she could see others of the beasts now beginning to flow in their direction. The blue cytons who had been harassing the zikzaws outside of R5's cone suddenly disappeared behind the wall of pink and white clouds shooting toward the fleet.

At the righthand periphery of the vision, Carillo could see the tornado-like funnel of zikzaws still inside R5's cone. While she could not be sure, the funnel appeared to have widened since the alpha's last view of it.

Just as it seemed the crisscrossing network of lightning bolts was within striking distance, the alpha projected a fleetwide command. *"Disperse!"*

The two swarms at the point arced in opposite directions, one to the right and the other to the left. Zylun's ship continued straight into the zikzaws, almost as if trying to pierce the clouds like a knife. Behind his cruiser, the next two swarms broke left and right, respectively, following somewhat behind the swarms that had dispersed moments before. The last of the swarms, the one beneath *RE-II*, shot forward and followed Zylun's ship into the cloud wall of zikzaws.

"Detonate now!" the alpha said through Carillo.

"Roger that," Morehouse said. "Lowrie, you heard the lady. Nuke the bastards!"

The first blinding flash caused Carillo to clamp her eyes tight, even though there was no escaping the mental vision. At the same time, she felt the crush of g-forces as the alpha manipulated her hands to acceler-ate *RE-II* and thrust the ship hard to starboard.

Carillo opened her eyes and blinked in a futile attempt to shake the flashes erupting in the vision. However, the alpha must have sensed her discomfort and the vision quickly faded. In fact, her head cleared of all the alpha's projected images. Meanwhile, the ship was buffeted with blows. Thinking they were either jolts of electricity from the zikzaws or aftereffects of the exploded nukes, Carillo gritted her teeth, expecting *RE-II* to disintegrate at any moment. But the ship held together.

Then, as the Suhkai gravity system began to adapt to the ship's change in velocity and the g-forces began to fall off, Carillo turned her head and looked at Morehouse.

He was intently glaring at the computer screens on his station console. "It's working!" he exclaimed. "Hot damn, it's working!"

Carillo spun her seat around to face the console occupied by Brock. "What's the radar show?"

"The blasts wiped out a lot of them. The rest are flocking to the nukes' radiation!"

"What about the funnel?" Carillo asked.

"Zikzaws are fleeing it," Brock said. "They're headed for the radiation too."

Zylun's plan was working. The armada had sliced in between the morass of zikzaws battling blue cytons and the zikzaws in the swirling funnel. The detonations had then created a wedge between the two zikzaw groups, killing those closest to the blasts and providing the rest with an instant X-ray feast.

"Is the funnel moving?" Carillo asked.

They needed the rest of the zikzaws left in the funnel to draw the Suhkonium pool closer to the edge of R5's gamma cone. They didn't need them to fully exit the cone, but they did have to move close enough for their remaining nukes to finish the job.

"It's hard to tell," Brock said. "So many are leaving, the radar's just a mass of blobs."

If Zylun's suspicion was right, the zikzaws fleeing the funnel would create a panic in those who remained cultivating the Suhkonium. They would be stuck in a no-win situation. If they stayed with the Suhkonium pool, they would miss out on the feast. If they abandoned the pool, there would be no chance to reform the ring without harvesting more Suhkonium from elsewhere in the galaxy.

One of two things was bound to happen as a result. Either the funnel would entirely disband, leaving the Suhkonium pool unguarded, or the zikzaws maintaining the funnel would move it closer to the nuke radiation so they, too, could partake of the feast without sacrificing the Suhkonium.

Whichever they chose didn't matter. One way or another, the pool was now in jeopardy and it was time for Morehouse's addition to the plan, a double envelopment of the funnel. On the far side of the radiation spheres created by the nukes, the swarm of blue cytons carrying the warhead from

Morgan's fleet would swoop toward the edge of R5's gamma cone. *RE-II* would attack along the same line from the near side.

Still in control of her voice and actions, Carillo spoke into the microphone of her headset. "Kiera, I'm opening the cargo bay doors. Get ready to release missile six."

"Roger that," replied Kiera.

"General," Carillo said, "prepare to arm the missile on my command."

Concentrating, Carillo then posed a question to the alpha still inside her mind. *"Is Zylun still out there? Is he in position?"* The Suhkai was their Plan C if all else failed.

Zylun, himself, replied through the alpha. *"I am here. I am ready."*

Taking a deep breath, Carillo spun her seat back around, knowing the alpha would soon need her hands on the ship's controls for the final assault.

In Morehouse's piece of the plan, the blue cyton swarm would attack first, detonating their warhead as they neared the funnel. If the blast occurred close enough to the zikzaws, Zylun had indicated a number of the beasts would die, hopefully enough to cause the survivors to give up on the pool in lieu of the warhead's radiation.

Then, it would be down to *RE-II* to blast the pool with the final nuke, whether zikzaws remained around it or not. If they failed, then Zylun would be the only one left to strike a fatal blow. He would fly head-on into the pool, entering R5's cone if necessary, and detonate his ship before R5's gamma rays disintegrated the cruiser.

As Carillo watched her hands reach for *RE-II*'s controls, she prayed they would get a clear shot at the pool.

In Carillo's mind, there was a solitary vision of a blue swarm spiraling like a corkscrew at the disorganized mob of cytons around the funnel, or what was left of it. The tornado-like spin of the zikzaws had ceased. Amid flashes of light and darting movements, some zikzaws appeared dazed, randomly twisting their miles-long bodies as if searching for something. Meanwhile, other zikzaws seemed enraged. They shot bolts indiscriminately around them, hitting the fleeing contingent of the electromagnetic beasts.

Carillo called out to Brock. "Helen, are the zikzaws clear of R5's cone?"

"No, they're still inside."

"What about our gamma readings? How close are we to the cone?"

"Too close. Gammas are spiking all around us."

Come on, Carillo thought, urging the blue cytons to detonate their warhead. *Do it. Do it now!*

But before she finished the thought, a gigantic bolt of lightning pierced through the ball of cytons. A millisecond later, the swarm vanished in a tremendous flare of energy. The explosion was so unexpected, Carillo's whole body twitched with a frightened spasm.

Recovering quickly, she prodded the alpha to launch *RE-II*'s attack. The cyton responded immediately and a new spate of mental images overwhelmed Carillo's consciousness. The alpha inside her head flooded her mind with rapidly changing visions of the swirling zikzaw gauntlet in front of *RE-II*.

One moment flashes and bolts of lightning arced through her mind's eye like tracers. The next moment, she was in the middle of a cyton swarm shooting through a gap between two zikzaws. Milliseconds later, she was looking at an image of Zylun's cruiser navigating a gauntlet of its own. Then, more licks of lightning shot forth from pink-white clouds. Each seemed directly aimed at Carillo, and she couldn't help but flinch.

Meanwhile, as thousands of other images cycled through her consciousness, Carillo's hands involuntarily operated the ship's thruster and engine controls. Feeling like a marionette, Carillo closed her eyes and marveled at how effortlessly the alpha slipped *RE-II* between the zikzaws' sizzling fingers of electricity. It seemed impervious to danger or risk.

How can it manage so many different activities at once and still fly with such precision? Carillo wondered. *How can it make sense out of so much feedback?*

The alpha was networked with thousands of other cytons flying outside the ship. It sensed what they sensed and, from what Carillo could tell, it appeared to be controlling their actions just as it was controlling hers. It also appeared to be linked to Zylun's brain and Kiera's too. Carillo knew this because their thoughts and sensations were mixed among the visions riffling through her mind.

Her eyes opened and darted between the computer screens in yet another involuntary action. The cyton seemed mainly focused on the radarscope, freezing Carillo's eye movements to study a small gap at the center of the blob-like clouds otherwise dominating the screen.

Then, suddenly, Carillo felt her hands working the engine controls and, in an instant, *RE-II* accelerated violently. The abrupt rise in Gs rippled her face and battered her body while Gen. Morehouse next to her groaned in pain.

Through her headset, Carillo heard the echo of Kiera's groans, too, and her mind filled with the view through the sun-visor of Kiera's helmet. The cargo bay was open, the doors appearing black against the horizon of pink and white clouds outside. Kiera looked down, giving Carillo a glimpse of the cruise missile on the docking platform and a sphere of golden cytons swarming around it. She also saw the glimmer of other cytons circling Kiera's spacesuit and the tether lines anchoring Kiera to the platform.

Just as the g-forces began to abate, *RE-II* was struck by something. The spacecraft shuddered, and Carillo felt the sensation of the ship yawing. A surge of panic and adrenaline seemed to squeeze Carillo's heart. She gasped for breath and tensed her body, fearing *RE-II* was finally about to break apart.

More visions raced through her mind. In one, she saw Airman Collins. With his helmet's gold visor down, Carillo could not see his face. Instead, the visor reflected the glowing sphere of cytons coating the missile. His hands gripped the safety rail on the platform as his body bucked backward. Through her headset, she heard him growl a stream of obscenities and then Kiera's overlapping voice, "Hold on, Dwayne! We're almost through!"

A new vision appeared. Amid the hurricane of zikzaw fury around the ship, Carillo saw a rippling, stretching pool of gray. Kiera must have seen the image, too, because she shouted, "There it is! Go, boys! Go!"

The cytons began to spin, lifting the cruise missile off the platform. Her skin seemed to prickle with static created by the cyton cocoon sheltering the missile as they propelled the nuke out of the bay. Airman Collins announced, "Missile away."

Stirred by Collins' voice, Carillo said, "Roger that."

The alpha allowed her to press the button to close the cargo bay doors before it returned her hands to the engine and thruster controls. Then, sensing the cyton was about to change course again, Carillo spoke aloud to the alien. "Wait!"

With the shred of autonomy she still possessed, Carillo turned her head to Morehouse. "Arm the warhead!"

He nodded and spoke into his headset. Carillo heard his order to Lowrie and the Airman's acknowledgment back. Seconds later, Lowrie said, "Missile is hot and ready in all respects."

Carillo watched Morehouse turn his head to her. As he spoke, his eyes were aflame with intensity. "As the President said to Augie, don't fucking miss!"

"Copy that." Carillo moved the microphone bar of her headset close to her lips. "Brace for Gs."

Closing her eyes, she flexed her hands and mentally prodded the alpha. *"Go! Get us out of here."*

While the ship lurched to port, the stream of the alpha's visions dominating her consciousness began to fade. Soon, only one remained — the cyton-shielded missile zooming toward the rippling pool of gray. Struck by the cyton's graceful movements, Carillo couldn't help but imagine the rocket as a bird gliding above the peaceful eddies of a lake.

Just then, *RE-II* was rocked by another blow, and a third, but Carillo barely noticed them. Locked in on the vision, she inhaled deeply and watched the cytons glide closer and closer to the pool, waiting for them to slice an electromagnetic wake across the surface.

When the knife-like slice began to appear, Carillo leaned forward, her heart racing. Beneath her closed eyelids, she darted her eyes left and right, examining the vision of the pool. As the wake met rippling Suhkonium, small clashing waves began to appear.

It was now or never. With the Suhkonium's surface tension in flux, Carillo gave the command, "Detonate!" and prayed the explosion would generate enough dynes to break the bonds holding the molecules of Suhkonium together.

The vision evaporated in a blinding flash of light. Instinctively, Carillo winced and turned her head. Then, she heard Kiera say, "All decisions have consequences, bitches."

CHAPTER 26

GATEWAY HEADQUARTERS
MAYAGUANA ISLAND, THE BAHAMAS
JULY 10, 2023

Augustus Amato had never felt so helpless. He imagined those gathered with him in Gateway's mission control center shared his angst. So much was riding on *RE-II* and her crew, and yet so little was known about their status.

The ship was 5.5 billion kilometers from Earth, or so it had been when Mayaguana received a message from Julia Carillo outlining Zylun's plan to destroy the zikzaws' Suhkonium pool. At that distance, there was a five-and-a-half-hour communications delay, meaning that the fate of the solar system had likely already been determined by now, but Amato and the others in the center wouldn't learn of it for hours to come.

As he paced back and forth behind the telescope analysts watching their data screens for signs of gamma and X-ray spikes, Amato was accosted by Pres. Wilcox. The American leader and the delegation who had accompanied him to Mayaguana had elected to remain at Gateway's HQ pending the outcome of *RE-II*'s mission. Amato had kept them apprised of developments as they emerged, but there had been little to share over the past couple of hours.

"I'd like a word with you in private," said Wilcox, now blocking his path.

"Now isn't a good time, Mr. President."

"It won't take but a minute." Wilcox pointed to a conference room at the back of the center and began walking. "Follow me."

Amato reluctantly complied. Once behind the closed door, Wilcox said, "I want to talk to you about those two Suhkai ships you've got in orbit."

Wilcox paused for a moment and stared at him with a knowing look. Though Amato had not told the president about the cruisers, it did not surprise him Wilcox knew about them. Amato was sure the launches had been observed by military satellites and the ships subsequently tracked. Suddenly he had a sinking feeling Wilcox was about to demand their surrender.

"What about them?" Amato asked.

"We ought to put them to use."

"*We*?"

Wilcox glared at him. "Yes. *We*." After pausing, he said, "I've been talking to my advisors and they think we should load 'em up with more nukes and launch them as a backup force...just in case something goes wrong with *RE-II*."

Amato's jaw dropped. "You would do that?"

"Considering the alternative...hell, yes." Wilcox paused again before continuing. "But if we're going to do it, let's not waste time bringing the missiles here. Instead, tell your pilots to land at Barksdale."

For a moment, Amato wondered if the offer was genuine or a ruse to confiscate the ships. Wilcox must have sensed his skepticism. He turned redfaced and said, "Damn it, Amato, I'm not trying to pull a fast one. I'm trying to make sure we all get to see another sunrise."

As Amato mulled the offer and Wilcox's earnest words, he quickly realized he had no choice but to trust the man. Even if Zylun's plan succeeded, the respite from zikzaws would be brief. Whether new rings formed in days, weeks, or months, zikzaws would eventually return.

"Very well. I'll contact the pilots and direct them to Barksdale."

"Good." Wilcox extended his hand. "We've got a long fight ahead of us, Amato. We'll have a better chance of succeeding if we start trusting one another."

Amato grasped and shook Wilcox's hand. "I suppose you're right, Mr. President."

Wilcox squeezed hard and said, "Damned straight I'm right. Now, let's get to it."

A short while after relaying the Barksdale instructions to the shuttle pilots, Amato received a message from Dennis Pritchard on Mars. In part, the note said, "Vanguard *and escorts launched. So far, no sign of zikzaws in pursuit.* Valor *reports same. Will apprise you immediately if circumstances change.*"

Amato would have liked to breathe a sigh of relief, knowing that both arks were now safely off Mars, but he knew it was too early to relax. While the vessels were safe at present, it did not mean they would remain so. R5's gamma cone didn't terminate in Earth's solar system. Instead, it *passed through it*, meaning zikzaws might be flocking toward the cone from any direction. Until the ships were well beyond the solar system, the risk of detection loomed.

He turned from the computer screen displaying Pritchard's message and refocused his attention on the monitors of the telescope analysts next to him. Staring at their data screens, Amato mumbled, "Come on, Julia. Come on, Zylun. Bring us good news."

Seated on a chair pulled from a nearby conference room, Anlon Cully leaned his head against the back wall of the mission control center and closed his eyes. He was desperate for sleep but couldn't bring himself to leave the center until the outcome of Zylun's bold plan was known.

And Anlon was not alone in his weary wait, as he learned from his ongoing text exchange with Pebbles back in Incline Village. Some time ago, the White House press corps had caught wind of the president's unscheduled trip to Mayaguana and immediately spread the news.

At first, the reigning gossip Anlon read on social media sites suggested Wilcox had flown to Mayaguana to save his own tail, leaving the rest of America and the world to fry. This speculation was further flamed by news videos of Gateway vehicles moving *RE-II* from its hangar onto the launch apron. From what Anlon gathered from further surfing on his phone, for hours after that, the White House press secretary denied the rumors but refused to provide an alternative explanation for Wilcox's trip.

Then an insider at Barksdale Air Force base tipped off a local reporter that crews were loading cruise missiles armed with nuclear warheads on a B52. According to a reporter's social media posts Pebbles had shared with Anlon, the insider said the scuttlebutt around the base indicated the B52 was destined for Mayaguana.

So, by the time the helicopter carrying Anlon, Julia Carillo and Kiera Walsh had landed at Mayaguana later that night, conspiracy theories were circulating around the Internet like wildfire. The craziest one Anlon had seen suggested Wilcox and Amato intended to protect their getaway by threatening to launch the nukes at any force that tried to stop their departure.

Meanwhile, unbeknownst to Anlon at the time, the news media contingent based on Mayaguana had positioned numerous cameras around the perimeter of Gateway's spaceport complex, including several airborne drones.

Thus, television viewers and Internet users worldwide watched live as the missiles were loaded onto *RE-II*, and later witnessed the pre-boarding sendoff of the ship's crew. Apparently, Anlon discovered, the appearance of the uniformed Julia Carillo and Kiera Walsh on the tarmac kneecapped the Wilcox-Amato-cowardly-escape narrative.

And the narrative was fully shattered when viewers saw Wilcox and Amato bidding farewell to not only Carillo and Walsh, but to three Air Force officers, one of whom was easily identified by the press as Gen. Morehouse.

In the resulting whirlwind of new speculation, a White House correspondent lobbed fuel onto the fire. Anlon still couldn't believe his eyes when he read the post Pebbles had shared. *"BREAKING:* RE-II *to nuke Pluto in desperate attempt to save Jupiter. Developing...stay tuned."*

While the posting drew ridicule in the early moments after it was published, as Anlon could attest after reading the thread of comments, the mocking quickly abated with the correspondent's next few posts.

"*Authorities say species of electromagnetic aliens called zikzaws are concentrating/redirecting R5's gamma rays to destroy Jupiter.*"

"*Same authorities indicate zikzaws intend to feed on radiation from Jupiter's explosion.* RE-II *has been launched to stop them...*"

"*...by detonating nuclear missiles on Pluto. Officials hope fallout from nukes attracts zikzaws away from R5's gamma rays.*"

The well-informed correspondent quickly became the go-to source for the world at large. He was later the first to report the zikzaw attacks on Dione and Callisto and also broke the news about the pending evacuation of Meridiani Planum aboard *Valor* and *Vanguard*.

Anlon had been amazed at the global reaction to the developments. For four years, R5 had been an enigma. While some people surely harbored opinions about whether the magnetar was a threat or not, most didn't know what to make of the distant star.

But many people recalled the *Rorschach Explorer*'s previous encounter with a zikzaw. Whether from stories published about the event, Jenna Toffy's episode chronicling the encounter or from programs on Gateway's streaming service, people knew what a zikzaw was. And those who didn't quickly educated themselves from the same sources.

As a result, people now had a tangible, hostile enemy they could visualize. And once it became clear that the enemy had attacked human settlements and was trying to destroy the solar system, the world's populations galvanized in support of *RE-II*'s valiant mission.

Across the globe, everything came to a standstill as people either honed their attention on the Internet, television and radio or gathered in large groups to pray and demonstrate solidarity. Some enterprising astronomers even created telescope live streams of outer space surrounding Pluto so people could see the detonations "live."

A misnomer, of course, thought Anlon. Any "live" action detected near Pluto would be five hours old by the time it reached Earth. Still, many people viewed the streamed video feeds as an unfiltered front-row seat to whatever drama unfolded. Pebbles was one of them. So were billions of others.

However, as the hours ticked by with no flashes on the live streams, and still no official statement from Gateway, the US government or any other government, fear and frustration bubbled over. Some of the large groups who had gathered began to turn contentious as some despaired the likelihood of *RE-II*'s failure while others argued to remain steadfast. The same kind of tensions exploded online.

It was well known the Suhkai-enhanced *RE-II* was capable of near lightspeed travel, so everyone had expected something to happen ten to twelve hours after the ship's launch from Mayaguana...five-to-six hours for *RE-II* to reach Pluto and detonate the nukes, five-to-six hours for the light from those explosions to travel through space back to the observing telescopes.

But as thirteen hours passed with no new developments, rumors claiming zikzaws had destroyed *RE-II* began to make the rounds. Unfortunately, civilization outside of Gateway's mission control center didn't know the real reason for the delay. Unlike Anlon, they were unaware the zikzaw ring had collapsed and that *RE-II* had teamed with Zylun and cytons for a different, more dangerous mission.

It was into this void, with the world teetering on panic, that Amato and Wilcox had finally addressed the media in person. Anlon recalled standing at the back of the briefing room as the two men made opening statements, revealing all they knew. Then, under withering questioning from reporters, they had provided brutally candid answers.

Understandably, there were mixed reactions to the briefing but from what Anlon could tell from further scrolling through the Internet on his phone, it went a long way to stemming the rising tensions. People refocused on *RE-II* and its revised mission. Telescopes were aimed at new coordinates. Private and public vigils began anew.

So had gone the roller coaster ride of the last fourteen hours, a stretch that for Anlon sat atop a crazy preceding thirty hours. He was as exhausted as he ever recalled, but he couldn't, wouldn't, fall asleep until he knew the outcome of *RE-II*'s quest.

Opening his eyes, he glanced at the large center screen in the mission control center where the video feed from a Gateway telescope displayed a view of outer space near the coordinates of the collapsed ring. There was nothing but the black background and a dotting of stars. He closed his eyes again and thought of Julia Carillo, Kiera Walsh and the others 5.5 billion kilometers away. Before long, he nodded off.

The moment the first flashes appeared on the telescope live streams, a raised voice echoed over the mission control center intercom, rousing Anlon from his sleep. "Flight, we have multiple X-ray spikes!"

"Jesus, look at that," cried out a man's voice nearby him. It was Pres. Wilcox. "There goes one, two…"

By the time Wilcox recounted the third explosion, Anlon was wide awake, sitting up straight and looking at the live stream feed. Though his vision was blurred for the fourth detonation, he was able to blink his watery eyes clear in time to witness the fifth and sixth flashes.

He would forever remember the short span of stunned silence in the room, as he would the absolute pandemonium of excitement that erupted directly afterward. Nor would he ever forget jumping up and down with Wilcox as they danced in a circle around one another, whooping and hollering.

But later, in a quiet moment when he was able to reflect on the scene, the most poignant memory Anlon recalled was the worried face of Augustus Amato rushing toward the flight director just as a seventh explosion, far brighter than any of the others, illuminated the screen.

Anlon stopped dancing and, with mouth agape, watched the ball of light continue to shine instead of fading away like the preceding flashes. He didn't need to know the data associated with the seventh blast to realize it had been significantly more powerful than the others. Returning his attention to Amato, he saw tears running down the man's face. At a distance, Anlon couldn't tell if the tears were born of sorrow or joy.

That question was answered less than ten minutes later in a short message transmitted by Julia Carillo aboard *RE-II*. A beaming Amato read the note aloud for everyone in the center to hear. "*CC* RE-II *to MAYA and MERIDIANI: Mission accomplished. Suhkonium destroyed. Many zikzaws too. Rest feeding on nuke radiation or dispersing. CC* RE-II *out.*"

Amid the raucous celebration that ensued, Augustus Amato was tapped on the shoulder by the flight director. The somber look on the director's face instantly squelched Amato's joy.

"Just got another message from *RE-II*," said the director. "You should read it."

He guided Amato to his control station where Amato sat and read the on-screen message.

"*CC RE-II to MAYA and MERIDIANI: Cytons from Skywalker fleet report* Renown *is mayday (ship damaged, supplies nearly gone), approximately three light weeks from RE-II current position. RE-II en route to provide succor. Link up ETA T+12 days at estimated velocities of* Renown *and RE-II. Cytons report Skywalker and seven crew on* Renown *are all that remain from fleet. Zylun en route to Dione to restart evac. He has more info on* Renown *status. Request additional cruisers to assist Zylun with Dione and Callisto evacs. CC RE-II out.*"

A wave of nausea passed through Amato as he admonished himself for reveling in the moment. There was still much work to do. The time for celebration would have to wait. Looking around, he searched the throng of happy faces for Pres. Wilcox. As soon as he spied him, Amato headed in Wilcox's direction and pulled him aside.

"Do you have medical personnel at Barksdale?" Amato asked.

"I don't know. I assume so. Why?"

"We have a new mission for the shuttles. A rescue mission."

SPACEPORT TERMINAL
MERIDIANI PLANUM COLONY, MARS

When Zylun arrived on Meridiani with the first load of injured evacuees from Dione, the skeleton crew of Gateway staff in the colony were there to greet them. At their head was Dennis Pritchard.

He hadn't been sure what to expect when the evacuees came through the boarding bridge and into the space dock terminal. They had been through hell. Stranded and attacked by zikzaws, Pritchard imagined they had felt abandoned and petrified. He also anticipated many of them were angry — angry at the zikzaws, Gateway, and Pritchard specifically. The message aborting the initial evacuation had come from him.

But the faces of those who came through the bridge door exhibited no expressions of animus. Some appeared in shock, others seemed relieved, but most just looked exhausted. He supposed their anger would come out later, after they had time to absorb and reflect. In the meantime, Pritchard helped where he could, carrying gurneys, offering water and food, and lending comfort.

At one point, as Pritchard helped a badly burned woman sip water from a straw, Zylun came into view with a blue cyton floating beside him. Pritchard caught Zylun's attention. "You are a credit to all Suhkai, thank you."

Focusing on the cyton, Pritchard realized it was one from Skywalker's fleet. Pritchard bowed briefly as he formed a thought in his mind. *"Cytons are not only seeders of life. You are savers of life too. Thank you for saving ours."*

The cyton glowed brightly and began to flicker as it transmitted a reply from Zylun. *"The battle for your planet's survival is far from over, Dr. Pritchard, but we thank you for your words of gratitude. Now, come. Accompany us to Earth. There is much we must discuss with your leaders."*

ABOARD THE GATEWAY ARK *VALOR*
FLYING AWAY FROM EARTH'S SOLAR SYSTEM

Valor had flown more than 9 billion kilometers from Mars in the opposite direction of the zikzaw ring when Dante Fulton received a relay of Julia Carillo's message from Dennis Pritchard.

Seated at *Valor*'s helm as he read the message, emotion overwhelmed Dante, but he was not naïve. He knew this was only the opening salvo in the ten thousand-year war to come. But it still felt good to know Kiera and Zylun and their fleet mates had won the first battle. His fingers trembled as he typed a message of congratulations to *RE-II*, paraphrasing Corinthians 13:13:

"CC *Valor to* CC RE-II: *In the end, three things survive. Hope, faith and love. Thank you for showing us the meaning of all three virtues. CC* Valor *out.*"

Before pressing enter, Dante had contemplated including a special message to Kiera in his transmission, but he resolved to send her a personal message later. So instead, he composed and sent a separate message to Zylun. "*Thank you for everything, brother. It feels weird to type it, but...I love you, man.*"

A few hours later, *Valor* and her escort cruisers slowed to allow *Vanguard* and her sister ships to catch up. Once the link-up was completed, Dante had been confronted with another dilemma. Should he turn the vagabond fleet in the direction of Tula or return to Mars? A subsequent transmission he received from Augustus Arturo Amato put the decision in his lap.

"A3 MAYA to CC *Valor*: *Imminent threat has passed, but danger remains for Earth and for you/the arks. As such, I leave the decision re:* Valor *and* Vanguard *flight plans in your hands. Above all other considerations, weigh the survival of humanity, Dante. No one here will ever question your choice, one way or the other. If you decide to return to Mars, we will be ready and waiting for you. If you opt for Tula, know you go with our love, blessing and prayers. A3 MAYA out.*"

Amato's message echoed in Dante's mind as he approached the house at the center of *Valor*'s Habitat B cul-de-sac. He didn't even bother knocking as he entered the home. Walking like a zombie, he made his way to the common area at the back of the house and found a drunk Jenna Toffy and Charlie Zimmer arguing with each other over opposite sides of a coffee table. On the table between them was a bottle of tequila, which Dante promptly grabbed and hoisted to his mouth.

After a few slugs, he pulled the bottle back and discovered Toffy and Zimmer were staring at him. He collapsed on a couch beside Toffy and announced, "It's done. The ring is gone."

Initially, both were ecstatic about returning to Earth, but their euphoria abated quickly. Dante, half-paying attention, noticed the lull in their celebration and looked up to see them staring at him.

"What's with the long face, Dante?" Zimmer asked. "This is good news, right?"

Dante nodded. "It's excellent news."

"You sure don't seem happy about it."

Shrugging at Zimmer's comment, Dante said, "I'm happy, Charlie. But this isn't the end. More zikzaws will come. And each time they form a new ring to destroy Jupiter, we'll have to fight them off. It'll go on for thousands of years like that."

"Yeah, but we know how to deal with them, right?" Toffy said. "So, we'll just have to get better and better at fighting them off."

Dante stared at the half-empty tequila bottle and mumbled, "I guess. But it'll be like a perpetual dark cloud hovering over our heads." Raising his gaze, he looked at Toffy. "And if we mess up just once, it's bye-bye solar system."

The comment seemed to put a damper on Toffy's and Zimmer's spirits. For a minute or so, no one spoke. In the silence, a flurry of thoughts raced through Dante's mind. He thought of the people on Earth, the people aboard the arks and Kiera. Interspersed with these mental images were visual snippets of Tula and visages of snaking zikzaws and their spinning pink rings.

"You're thinking of heading for Tula instead of turning back for Mars, aren't you?" Toffy said.

With a shake of his head, Dante said, "I don't know yet. Gateway's left that decision to us. Well, to me. But I'm not making that kind of decision for a bunch of people who didn't make the choice to leave Earth for good. All these folks know is we had to evacuate Meridiani. They have no idea Tula's on the table."

He paused and looked back and forth between Toffy and Zimmer. "I'm sure most, if not all of them, are expecting us to return to Mars and eventually to Earth. And that's okay. We'll go back, unload everyone and reload with the colonists who volunteered to settle on Tula in the first place. But I wonder if the people who get off will regret that decision every time a new ring forms. This is probably the only chance any of them will ever have to go to Tula."

"I see what you mean," Zimmer said. "Staying on Earth could end up feeling like a lifetime game of Russian roulette. Keep playing the game and, sooner or later, you're bound to lose."

Toffy reached for the tequila bottle and took a swig. When she finished, she handed the bottle to Zimmer. "God, you're such a killjoy."

Zimmer smiled as he took the bottle. "Hey, just telling it straight."

"Yeah, well, there are already a million ways to die on Earth," said Toffy. "Zikzaw rings are just one more to add to the list. I think people will get used to the risk. Especially if we defeat a few more of the rings."

"Maybe," said Zimmer after a drink from the bottle. "But I doubt life on Earth will ever be the same as it was before. There will be a lot of people who won't get used to the risk. Could create a lot of tension that affects everyone for a long time to come."

Zimmer passed the bottle to Dante as Toffy responded. "You're right about that. Life will never be the same. But that might not end up being such a bad thing. It might bring us closer together. You know, fighting a common enemy instead of fighting each other."

Another stretch of silence followed Toffy's musing. During the lull, Dante sipped from the bottle and pondered a point he was reluctant to raise. Going back to Mars bore risks. They might be intercepted by zikzaws. Or, if they made it back to Meridiani and a new ring formed before the arks could relaunch, *Valor* and *Vanguard* might never make it to Tula.

As it stood now, the arks were safe. Yes, there remained a risk of encountering zikzaws but the farther they flew away from the solar system, and away from R5's gamma cone, that risk plummeted. In truth, he was reluctant to risk the arks by returning to Mars.

With that consideration looming in his mind, Dante thought of a line from Amato's earlier message, *"Above all other considerations, weigh the survival of humanity."* It was good advice, but Dante was not prepared to play God with several hundred lives.

So, he resolved to meet with the passengers on both vessels. He'd lay out the facts as well as the pros and cons and the expectations, and let each person make their own decision. Those who wanted to return to Mars, he'd send back on the escort shuttles. The shuttles could then bring back some or all of the colonists initially slated for the journey. Those aboard the arks now who opted for Tula, he'd accommodate. When he presented his plan to Zimmer and Toffy, both agreed it was the fairest solution available. However, Zimmer said, "If you're gonna play it that way, we better finish the build-outs before you go zooming off for Tula. So, you probably want to hold in place at some point and use the shuttles to ferry our equipment and materials til the job is done."

"It's a good suggestion, Charlie," said Dante. "But the more we send shuttles back and forth, the more likely the shuttles will attract zikzaws. So we'll have to be damned careful and limit the number of flights."

Zimmer stood and said, "Roger that. I better get started on an inventory of what we need then. The sooner we get back to work, the sooner *Valor* and *Vanguard* can be on their way."

After he departed, Toffy turned to Dante. "You know something? I was really pissed when Dennis Pritchard locked down Meridiani. I felt like a caged animal, a prisoner. I really thought you all were going to take off in the arks and maroon us there to die. But now it feels like it's the best thing that's ever happened to me."

"Why is that?"

"Chronicling the trip to Tula is going to make for one hell of a story."

EPILOGUE

I n the days leading up to *RE-II*'s rendezvous with *Renown*, many messages were exchanged between the two ships. So, by the time the linkup occurred, Paul Morgan and his beleaguered crew had shared much of the tale about their journey home. Conversely, Morgan and his team also learned much of what had transpired over the several weeks since R5's first gamma rays passed through the solar system.

Morgan had been charitable in describing Baronova's and Douglas' mutiny, indicating they had departed on good terms after surrendering their warheads to Quant's cytons. As it turned out, Shyla Thakur's suggestion to send the armed cytons ahead of *Renown* had played a pivotal role in weakening the zikzaws' influence on R5's bursts. Had the mutiny not occurred, the fleet would have likely stayed together and the zikzaws' ring near Pluto would have destroyed Jupiter before *RE-II* and Zylun could prevent it.

The cytons' disruption of the ring upstream had been the catalyst that precipitated the collapse of the ring near Pluto. And another group of cytons from Quant's colony had harassed the zikzaws from the collapsed ring long enough to delay the reforming.

It was a good thing, too. *Renown*'s own efforts to disrupt rings had been far less successful. A solitary warhead was not enough of an enticement to lure a critical mass of zikzaws from their rings. So *Renown* had depleted its supply of warheads very quickly after parting ways with *Ranger* and *Resolute*.

But Morgan, Thakur and Mey Wan had learned a tremendous amount about zikzaws over the year-and-a-half journey home, and they had cataloged the location of every ring they encountered on the way back. Morgan was confident their accumulated knowledge and experience would prove helpful in future confrontations with the electromagnetic beasts.

Some of that information had already been relayed to Amato and Pritchard to assist in preparing measures for the next ring that formed too close to home.

Morgan was sad to learn that Zylun was the sole surviving Suhkai left in the solar system. The losses of Haula and his crew weighed heavily on Morgan. While Haula had rejected the idea of combating zikzaw rings, he had valorously charged his flagship *Flash* and its sister ship *Fortune* into a pack of the beasts to save Morgan's ships. Earlier in the skirmish with the first zikzaw, Haula's other ship, *Fortitude*, had also succumbed.

The further passing of Hexla, Aylor and other Suhkai who had defended Callisto and Dione also troubled Morgan. Though these Suhkai had also frustratingly kept quiet about the zikzaws and their rings until it was nearly too late to combat them, the arks *Valor* and *Vanguard* would never have been constructed without their help. And if not for Aylor's and Hexla's selfless sacrifices to buy Earth time to mount a defense, the solar system would have become a glowing debris field by now.

Similar praise was due to Quant and her colony, Morgan realized. Not only had they proved valiant zikzaw fighters, but they had also kept hope alive aboard *Renown*. As supplies dwindled and the churn of time ate away at Morgan's resolve and the resolve of his crew, Quant had used her energy, wisdom and keen senses to bolster the crew's spirits. Morgan was sure they would not have survived without her.

As it was, the crew of *Renown* had all become emaciated, filthy and weak — physically, mentally and emotionally — over the final few months of their return trek. There was many a moment during that stretch when Morgan thought he wouldn't make it through another day, and he had observed similar expressions of despair among his team.

When those moments came on, Quant filled their minds with encouragement, visions of Earth, wonderous stories of cytons' travels throughout the galaxy and heartwarming sensations that penetrated their bodies.

But her ministrations were no longer needed now. As soon as *Renown* received Julia Carillo's message indicating *RE-II* was on its way to meet them, Morgan hadn't experienced a single incidence of gloom, nor had he witnessed one among the crew.

Earth had been saved…at least for a while. And they were now just days away from the warmth of the sun on their faces, the tickle of grass beneath their feet, the sounds of birds, ocean waves and the joy of reuniting with loved ones.

Their four-year foray into black, empty space to save Earth was nearly over, and that was a damned good feeling. So thought Morgan as he stood on *Renown*'s flight deck, bracketed by Thakur, Wan, Duncan Kassa, Bobby MacDowell, Lucas Bekker and Janie Gillespie.

Together, they watched co-pilot Jun Ikeda's computer monitor as *RE-II*'s illuminated hull grew from a small approaching light into a shining spaceship. Then, arm in arm, they cheered with teary eyes as Julia Carillo's voice sounded over the intercom.

"*Renown*, this is CC *RE-II*, requesting permission to dock."

Voice cracking as he replied, Ikeda said, "Roger that, *Renown*. You are go for docking…and might I say, you're a beautiful sight for sore eyes."

Morgan heard Kiera Walsh's wavering voice next as she replied to Ikeda. "Back atcha, *Renown*. We've missed you more than you'll ever know."

Later, when the airlock door opened and the two crews met, Morgan shared some of the longest, deepest hugs of his life. At one point, while clutching Julia Carillo in his arms, Morgan spied Quant hovering close by. Too emotional to speak, Morgan closed his eyes and formed a thought to share with the cyton queen. *"Thank you for everything, Quant. Especially for believing in us. And for giving us hope."*

The alien glowed bright blue. *"Hope was always in you, Skywalker. I just reminded you of it. Now you must remind all humans. The fight will be long and hard, but so long as hope remains alive among you, the sun will continue to shine on Earth."*

GLOSSARY OF CHARACTERS

Dr. Anlon Cully: retired animal biomechanics expert who also appeared in *Skywave* and *Magwave*. Anlon is also the main character in my archaeology-based mystery series, the Anlon Cully Chronicles. In *Skywave* and *Magwave*, Anlon helped Augustus Amato interpret the behavior of the electromagnetic aliens known as cytons (also known as UMOs).

Eleanor "Pebbles" McCarver: Anlon Cully's companion/sidekick. She also appeared in *Skywave* and *Magwave* and participated in most of the scenes between Anlon and Augustus Amato.

Jennifer Stevens: friend of Anlon Cully and Pebbles McCarver. She appeared in *Magwave* and participated in most of the scenes between Anlon, Pebbles and Augustus Amato.

Colonel Paul "Skywalker" Morgan: legendary retired NASA astronaut who spearheads a six-ship fleet in *Dynewave* to stabilize the magnetar known as R5. Morgan was also a major character in the series prequel, *UMO*, as well as books 1 and 2 of the Rorschach Explorer Missions series, *Skywave* and *Magwave*. In *UMO*, Morgan was CAPCOM for the crew of *Cetus Prime*, the primary liaison between mission control and the spaceship. In *Skywave*, he was part of Augustus Amato's team that searches for the long-lost *Cetus Prime*. In *Magwave*, Morgan was the commander of the *Rorschach Explorer*, the spaceship launched to investigate the *Cetus Prime* wreckage on the Jupiter moon Callisto.

Captain Nick Reed: one of the three *Cetus Prime* astronauts from the series prequel, *UMO*. He returned to Earth in *Magwave* in a space ark built by the humanoid aliens known as the Suhkai to collect humans to help colonize Tula, a planet eleven light-years from Earth.

Dr. Christine Baker: one of the three *Cetus Prime* astronauts from the series prequel, *UMO*. Baker now lives on a planet called Tula, eleven light-years from Earth.

Lieutenant Colonel Avery Lockett: one of the three *Cetus Prime* astronauts from the series prequel, *UMO*. Lockett now lives on a planet called Tula, eleven light-years from Earth.

Augustus "Augie" Amato: billionaire and aerospace industry titan. He conceived/built the *Rorschach Explorer*, the spacecraft featured in *Skywave* and *Magwave* and funded the search for the long-lost *Cetus Prime*. In *Dynewave*, Amato leads a company called Gateway Ventures, an enterprise formed to hold/manage the assets bestowed on Col. Morgan by the humanoid aliens known as the Suhkai at the end of *Magwave*.

Dr. Kiera Walsh: aerospace engineer. In *Skywave*, she was credited with the design of the original propulsion system for the *Rorschach Explorer* and was part of Augustus Amato's team that searched for the long-lost *Cetus Prime*. In *Magwave*, Kiera was one of the five crewmembers who traveled aboard the *Rorschach Explorer* to investigate the *Cetus Prime* wreckage on the Jupiter moon Callisto.

Jasmine Walsh: the toddler daughter of Kiera Walsh and Ajay Joshi.

Ajay Joshi: amateur astronomer. In *Skywave*, Ajay discovered radio signals that led to the discovery of the long-lost *Cetus Prime* on the Jupiter moon Callisto. In *Magwave*, Ajay was one of the five *Rorschach Explorer* crewmembers who launched to investigate the *Cetus Prime* wreckage on the Jupiter moon Callisto. In *Dynewave*, Ajay is en route to the planet Tula aboard the Suhkai ark called *Venture* (the ark Nick Reed called *Ethel* in *Magwave*, the ship Nick brought back to Earth to collect colonists to help settle the planet Tula).

Major Julia Carillo: retired NASA astronaut and former Air Force fighter pilot. She was first mentioned in the series prequel, *UMO*, as one of Col. Paul Morgan's crewmembers on a NASA space shuttle mission in the 1980s where she encountered the electromagnetic aliens knowns as UMOs (unidentified magnetic objects – later known as cytons). During the encounter she was rendered unconscious and her spacesuit tether was cut, causing her to drift away into space. Morgan had to use an experimental jetpack to rescue her, hence earning his "Skywalker" nickname. In *Skywave*, the now-retired astronaut Carillo was an aerospace engineering professor who helped Morgan access the Greenbank Observatory radio telescope to communicate with the abandoned *Cetus Prime* on the Jupiter moon Callisto. In *Magwave*, Carillo was one of the five *Rorschach Explorer* crewmembers who launched to investigate the *Cetus Prime* wreckage on Callisto. She was also the first of the *Rorschach* crew to communicate with UMOs/cytons. In *Dynewave*, Carillo is a pilot for the *Rorschach Explorer II*, one of Gateway Ventures' space tourism shuttles.

Dr. Dante Fulton: aerospace engineer. In *Skywave*, Dante was the mission control flight director for Augustus Amato's CubeSat probe fleet launched to investigate the radio signals discovered by Ajay Joshi. Dante was also a close friend (and boss) of Kiera Walsh, and he designed many of the *Rorschach Explorer*'s systems, including its gravity environment. In *Magwave*, Dante was the flight director for the *Rorschach Explorer* mission to investigate the *Cetus Prime* wreckage on Callisto. In *Dynewave*, Dante is stationed at Gateway Ventures' Meridiani Planum colony on Mars and is slated to captain a new space ark called *Valor* for its journey to Tula.

Jenna Toffy: television journalist for World Network News. Toffy appeared in *Magwave* as the host of a television series called *Expedition to Callisto* that chronicled the *Rorschach Explorer*'s flight to investigate the *Cetus Prime* wreckage on Callisto. She was also briefly mentioned in *Skywave*.

Sam Carillo: Julia Carillo's husband.

Haula: one of the humanoid aliens known as the Suhkai and commander of the three Suhkai-crewed ships in Col. Paul Morgan's six-ship fleet launched in *Dynewave* to stabilize the magnetar known as R5. Haula appeared in *Magwave* as the co-commander of the Suhkai ark that returned to Earth with Nick Reed to collect human colonists to help settle the planet Tula.

Mark Myers: Augustus Amato's executive assistant. He appeared in *Skywave* and *Magwave* in the same capacity.

Dr. Dennis Pritchard: aerospace engineer. He first appeared in the series prequel, *UMO*, as the flight director for the *Cetus Prime* mission. In *Skywave*, Pritchard was the chief administrator of NASA. In that capacity, Pritchard attempted to discover what Augustus Amato was searching for on Callisto. In *Magwave*, Pritchard joined Amato's company and assisted Dante Fulton in managing the *Rorschach Explorer*'s mission to investigate the *Cetus Prime* wreckage on Callisto. In *Dynewave*, Pritchard is now part of Amato's new company, Gateway Ventures, and is the administrator/governor of Gateway's Meridiani Planum colony on Mars.

Dr. Albert Lyman: sociologist, member of the colonist selection committee for the space arks *Venture*, *Valor* and *Vanguard*.

Hal Barnes: executive assistant to Dr. Dennis Pritchard. Stationed at Meridiani Planum, Gateway Ventures' colony on Mars.

Zylun: one of the humanoid aliens known as the Suhkai. Stationed at Meridiani Planum, Gateway Ventures' colony on Mars, Zylun is slated to captain a new space ark called *Vanguard* for its journey to Tula.

Charlie Zimmer: construction foreman responsible for the build-out of the space ark *Valor*. Stationed at Gateway's Meridiani Planum colony.

Ed Chen: NASA project manager. In *Magwave*, Chen was the project manager for NASA's *Juno* space probe orbiting Jupiter, and later *Juno*'s role managing telemetry transmitted by the Callisto-marooned *Cetus Prime*. In *Dynewave*, Chen is the project manager for a NASA telescope array named the Einstein Gamma Observatory. The satellite telescopes are positioned in space near Jupiter to monitor the magnetar known as R5.

Sergei Kolov: a member of NASA's Einstein Gamma Observatory team. He appeared in *Magwave* as part of NASA's *Juno* probe team.

Dr. Helen Brock: astrophysicist. In *Skywave*, Brock was NASA's chief science officer and Dr. Dennis Pritchard's right-hand executive. In this role, she helped Pritchard unravel Augustus Amato's purpose in sending CubeSat probes to Callisto. In *Magwave*, Brock had ascended to become NASA's chief administrator. In this capacity, she played a consultative role to Dante Fulton and Dennis Pritchard as they contended with the *Rorschach Explorer*'s multiple crises. In *Dynewave*, Brock has joined Gateway Ventures as the company's chief science officer and is stationed on Mars at the company's Meridiani Planum colony.

Mary Evans: executive assistant to Dr. Helen Brock. Stationed with Brock at Gateway Ventures' Meridiani Planum colony on Mars. Evans appeared in *Magwave* as Brock's executive assistant at NASA.

Hexla: one of the humanoid aliens known as the Suhkai. In *Dynewave*, she serves as the chief scientific liaison between the Suhkai and Dr. Helen Brock.

Dr. Reshma Desai: astrophysicist. In *Dynewave*, Desai is one of Col. Paul Morgan's crewmembers aboard the Gateway Coalition spacecraft *Resolute*. She appeared in *Magwave* as the project manager for NASA's reconstituted *Cetus Prime* project team.

Dr. Mey Wan: astrophysicist. Wan is the chief science officer for Col. Paul Morgan's fleet. She is stationed aboard the Gateway Coalition spacecraft *Resolute*, Morgan's flagship and one of the three human-crewed Suhkai vessels in the six-ship fleet launched to stabilize the magnetar known as R5.

Lieutenant Lucas Bekker: communications officer aboard the Gateway Coalition spacecraft *Resolute*, Morgan's flagship and one of the three human-crewed Suhkai vessels in the six-ship fleet launched to stabilize the magnetar known as R5.

Major Eamon Douglas: astronaut, commander of the Gateway Coaliition spacecraft *Ranger*, one of the three human-crewed Suhkai vessels in the six-ship fleet launched to stabilize the magnetar known as R5.

Captain Jaime Silva: astronaut, co-pilot to Maj. Eamon Douglas aboard the Gateway Coalition spacecraft *Ranger*, one of the three human-crewed Suhkai vessels in the six-ship fleet launched to stabilize the magnetar known as R5.

Dr. Roksana Baronova: physician, chief medical officer for Col. Paul Morgan's Gateway Coalition fleet. Baronova is stationed aboard *Ranger*, one of the three human-crewed Suhkai vessels in the six-ship fleet launched to stabilize the magnetar known as R5.

Quant: In *Dynewave*, Quant is the alien queen of the cyton colony traveling with Col. Paul Morgan's Gateway Coalition fleet. Quant and her colony are expected to play a pivotal role in stabilizing the magnetar known as R5. The blue ball of electromagnetic energy also appeared in

Magwave as the BLUMO queen. In *Dynewave*, she is also referred to as "seeder" by the Suhkai commander Haula.

Zoor: one of the humanoid aliens known as the Suhkai. Zoor is only mentioned in *Dynewave* but was a major character in *Magwave*. She was the co-commander (along with Haula) of the space ark that brought Nick Reed back to Earth to collect human colonists to settle/populate the planet Tula.

Major Shyla Thakur: astronaut, commander of the Gateway Coalition spacecraft *Renown*, one of the three human-crewed Suhkai vessels in the six-ship fleet launched to stabilize the magnetar known as R5.

Captain Jun Ikeda: astronaut, co-pilot to Col. Paul Morgan aboard the Gateway Coalition spacecraft *Resolute*, one of the three human-crewed Suhkai vessels in the six-ship fleet launched to stabilize the magnetar known as R5.

Captain Duncan Kassa: astronaut, co-pilot to Maj. Shyla Thakur aboard the Gateway Coalition spacecraft *Renown*, one of the three human-crewed Suhkai vessels in the six-ship fleet launched to stabilize the magnetar known as R5.

Dr. Bobby MacDowell: physician. Stationed aboard the Gateway Coalition spacecraft *Resolute*, Col. Paul Morgan's flagship in the six-ship fleet launched to stabilize the magnetar known as R5.

Dr. Adam Hazan: astronomer. Stationed aboard the Gateway Coalition spacecraft *Ranger*, one of the three human-crewed Suhkai vessels in the six-ship fleet launched to stabilize the magnetar known as R5.

Lieutenant John Grimes: logistics officer. Stationed aboard the Gateway Coalition spacecraft *Ranger*, one of three human-crewed Suhkai vessels in the six-ship fleet launched to stabilize the magnetar known as R5.

Lieutenant Paula Epps: flight engineer. Stationed aboard the Gateway Coalition spacecraft *Renown*, one of the three human-crewed Suhkai vessels in the six-ship fleet launched to stabilize the magnetar known as R5.

Dr. Kyle Thurmont: physician. Stationed aboard the Gateway Coalition spacecraft *Renown*, one of the three human-crewed Suhkai vessels in the six-ship fleet launched to stabilize the magnetar known as R5.

Lieutenant Janie Gillespie: flight engineer. Stationed aboard the Gateway Coalition spacecraft *Renown*, one of the three human-crewed Suhkai vessels in the six-ship fleet launched to stabilize the magnetar known as R5.

Dr. Robyn Martinez: scientist. Stationed normally at Gateway Ventures' facility on the Jupiter moon Callisto, Martinez appears in *Dynewave* as a visitor to the Gateway facility on the Saturn moon Dione.

Aylor: one of the humanoid aliens known as the Suhkai. Stationed at Gateway Ventures' facility on the Saturn moon Dione (formerly a Suhkai refinery/spaceport). Aylor is an underling to Hexla.

Norris Preston: engineer. Stationed at Gateway Ventures' Meridiani Planum colony on Mars. Aide to Dante Fulton aboard the *Valor* space ark.

Tank Harris: construction foreman responsible for build-out of space ark *Vanguard*. Stationed at Gateway's Meridiani Planum colony on Mars.

President Grant Wilcox: current president of the United States in *Dynewave*.

President Andrew Jennings: former president of the United States in *Dynewave*. Jennings was the U.S. president in *Skywave* and *Magwave*.

Marji Burns: executive assistant to President Grant Wilcox.

General Jerry Morehouse: national security advisor to President Grant Wilcox.

President Li Zhen: president of the People's Republic of China.

President Boris Lenkov: president of the Russia Federation.

Yasiel Romero: chief of security at Gateway Ventures' Meridiani Planum colony on Mars.

Dena Carillo: daughter of Maj. Julia Carillo.

Anne Carillo: daughter of Maj. Julia Carillo.

Combat Systems Officer Dwayne Collins: Air Force nuclear weapons specialist.

Combat Systems Officer Emmett Lowrie: Air Force nuclear weapons specialist.

Captain Garrett Jones: pilot for one of Gateway Ventures' Suhkai spacecraft used to shuttle people and supplies between Earth and their facilities on Mars, Callisto and Dione.

Jaylen Bowers: director of operations, Gateway's Meridiani Planum colony spaceport command and control center on Mars.

Maria Padilla: flight control operations specialist, Gateway's Meridiani Planum colony spaceport on Mars.

ABOUT THE AUTHOR

Kevin Patrick Donoghue is the author of three series: the Anlon Cully Chronicles archaeology-based mystery series, the Rorschach Explorer Missions science fiction series and the Unity of Four futuristic medical thriller series. His books include:

THE ANLON CULLY CHRONICLES SERIES:

Book 1: *Shadows of the Stone Benders*
Book 2: *Race for the Flash Stone*
Book 3: *Curse of the Painted Lady*
Book 4: *Priestess of Paracas*

THE RORSCHACH EXPLORER MISSIONS SERIES:

Prequel: *UMO* (novella)
Book 1: *Skywave*
Book 2: *Magwave*
Book 3: *Dynewave*

THE UNITY OF FOUR SERIES:

Book 1: *The GODD Chip*

Ways to stay in touch with the author: follow <u>K. Patrick Donoghue — Novelist</u> on Facebook or join the author's email subscriber list by visiting <u>kpatrickdonoghue.com</u> and clicking on the "Join Email List" link on the main menu.

Manufactured by Amazon.ca
Bolton, ON

34293988R00192